By Danielle Steel

*published outside the UK under the title PASSION'S PROMISE

DANIELLE STEEL

Changes

sphere

SPHERE

Published in the United States of America by Delacorte Press 1983
First published in Great Britain by Sphere Books Ltd 1984
Reprinted 1984 (three times), 1985 (three times), 1986 (twice),
1987 (twice), 1988, 1989, 1990, 1991
Reprinted by Warner Books 1993
Reprinted 1993, 1994, 1995 (twice), 1996, 1999
Reprinted by Time Warner Paperbacks 2002
Reprinted 2004
Reissued by Sphere in 2009

5 7 9 11 12 10 8 6

ISBN 978-0-7515-4244-8

Printed and bound in Great Britain by
Clays Ltd, St Ives plc

Papers used by Sphere are from well-managed forests
and other responsible sources.

MIX
Paper from
responsible sources
FSC® C104740

Sphere
An imprint of
Little, Brown Book Group
100 Victoria Embankment
London EC4Y 0DY

An Hachette UK Company
www.hachette.co.uk

www.littlebrown.co.uk

To Beatrix, Trevor, Todd,
Nicky, and especially John,
for all that you are, and
all that you have given me.

With all my love,
                    d.s.

And with special thanks to Dr Phillip Oyer

CHAPTER 1

'Dr Hallam . . . Dr Peter Hallam . . . Dr Hallam . . . Cardiac Intensive, Dr Hallam . . .' The voice droned on mechanically as Peter Hallam sped through the lobby of Center City Hospital, never stopping to answer the page since the team already knew he was on his way. He furrowed his brow as he pressed six, his mind already totally engaged with the data he had been given twenty minutes before on the phone. They had waited weeks for this donor, and it was almost too late. Almost. His mind raced as the lift doors ground open, and he walked quickly to the nurses' station marked Cardiac Intensive Care.

'Have they sent Sally Block upstairs yet?' A nurse looked up, seeming to snap to attention as her eyes met his. Something inside her always leapt a little when she saw him. There was something infinitely impressive about the man, who was tall, slender, grey-haired, blue-eyed, soft-spoken. He had the looks of the doctors one read about in women's novels. There was something so basically kind and gentle about him, and yet something powerful as well. The aura of a highly trained racehorse always straining at the reins, aching to go faster, farther . . . to do more . . . to fight time . . . to conquer odds beyond hope . . . to steal back just one life . . . one man . . . one woman . . . one child . . . one more. And often he won. Often. But not always. And that irked him. More than that, it pained him. It was the cause for the lines beside his eyes, the sorrow one saw deep within him. It wasn't enough that he wrought miracles almost daily. He wanted more than that, better odds, he wanted to save them all, and there was no way he could.

'Yes, Doctor.' The nurse nodded quickly. 'She just went up.'

7

'Was she ready?' That was the other thing about him and the nurse marvelled at the question. She knew instantly what he meant by 'ready'; not the I.V. in the patient's arm, or the mild sedative administered before she left her room to be wheeled to surgery. He was questioning what she was thinking, feeling, who had spoken to her, who went with her. He wanted each of them to know what they were facing, how hard the team would work, how much they cared, how desperately they would all try to save each life. He wanted each patient to be ready to enter the battle with him. 'If they don't believe they have a fighting chance when they go in there, we've lost them right from the beginning,' the nurse had heard him tell his students, and he meant it. He fought with every fibre of his being, and it cost him, but it was worth it. The results he'd got in the past five years were amazing, with few exceptions. Exceptions which mattered deeply to Peter Hallam. Everything did. He was remarkable and intense and brilliant . . . and so handsome, the nurse reminded herself with a smile as he hurried past her to a small lift in the corridor behind her. It sped up one floor and deposited him outside the operating rooms where he and his team performed bypasses and transplants and occasionally more ordinary cardiac surgery, though not often. Most of the time, Peter Hallam and his team did the big stuff, as they would tonight.

Sally Block was a twenty-two-year-old girl who had lived most of her adult life as an invalid, crippled by rheumatic fever as a child, and she had suffered through multiple valve replacements and a decade of medication. He and his associates had agreed weeks before when she'd been admitted to Center City that a transplant was the only answer for her. But thus far, there had been no donor. Until tonight, at two thirty in the morning, when a group of juvenile delinquents had engaged in their own private drag races in the San Fernando Valley; three of them had died on impact, and after a series of businesslike phone calls from the splendidly run organisation for the location

8

and procurement of donors Peter Hallam knew he had a good one. He had had calls out to every hospital in Southern California for a donor for Sally, and now they had one – if Sally could just survive the surgery, and her body didn't sabotage them by rejecting the new heart they gave her.

He peeled off his street clothes without ceremony, donned the limp green cotton surgery pyjamas, scrubbed intensely, and was gowned and masked by surgical assistants. Three other doctors, two residents and a fleet of nurses did likewise. But Peter Hallam seemed not even to see them as he walked into the operating room. His eyes immediately sought Sally, lying silent and still on the operating-room table, her own eyes seemingly mesmerised by the bright lights above her. Even lying there in the sterile garb with her long blonde hair tucked into a green cotton cap she looked pretty. She was not only a beautiful young woman but a clever human being as well. She wanted desperately to be an artist . . . to go to college . . . to go to a prom . . . to be kissed . . . to have babies . . . She recognised him even with the cap and mask and she smiled sleepily through a haze of medication.

'Hi.' She looked frail, her eyes enormous in the fragile face, like a broken china doll, waiting for him to repair her.

'Hello, Sally. How're you feeling?'

'Funny.' Her eyes fluttered for a moment and she smiled at the familiar eyes. She had come to know him in the last few weeks, better than she had known anyone in years. He had opened doors of hope to her, of tenderness, and of caring, and the loneliness and isolation she had felt for years had finally seemed less acute to her.

'We're going to be pretty busy for the next few hours. All you have to do is lie there and snooze.' He watched her and glanced at the monitors nearby before looking at her again. 'Scared?'

'Sort of.' But he knew she was well prepared. He had spent weeks explaining the surgery to her, the intricate process, and the dangers and medications afterwards. She knew what to expect now, and their big moment had come. It was almost like giving birth. And he would be giving birth to her, almost as though she would spring from his very soul, from his fingertips as they fought to save her.

The anaesthetist moved closer to her head and searched Peter Hallam's eyes. He nodded slowly and then smiled at Sally again. 'See you in a little while.' Except it wouldn't be a little while. It would be more like five or six hours before she was conscious again, and then only barely, as they watched her in the recovery room, before moving her to intensive care.

'Will you be there when I wake up?' A frown of fear creased her brows and he was quick to nod.

'I sure will. I'll be right there with you when you wake up. Just like I'm here with you now.' He nodded to the anaesthetist then, and her eyes fluttered closed briefly from the sedative they had administered before. The sodium pentathol was administered through the intravenous tube already implanted in her arm; a moment later, Sally Block was asleep, and within minutes, the delicate surgery began.

For the next few hours, Peter Hallam worked relentlessly to hook up the new heart, and there was a wondrous look of victory on his face as it began to pump. For just a fraction of a second, his eyes met those of the nurse standing across from him, and beneath the mask he smiled. 'There she goes.' But they had only won the first round, he knew only too well. It remained to be seen if Sally's body would accept or reject the new heart. And as with all transplant patients, the odds weren't great. But they were better than they would have been if she hadn't had the surgery at all. In her case, as with the other people he operated on, it was her only hope.

At nine fifteen that morning, Sally Block was wheeled into the recovery room, and Peter Hallam took his first break since four thirty a.m. It would be a while before the anaesthetic wore off, and he had time for a cup of coffee and a few moments of his own thoughts. Transplants like Sally's drained everything from him.

'That was spectacular, Doctor.' A young resident stood next to him, still in awe, as Peter poured himself a cup of black coffee and turned to the young man.

'Thank you.' Peter smiled, thinking how much the young resident looked like his own son. It would have pleased him no end if Mark had had ambitions in medicine, but there were other plans: business school, or law. He wanted to be part of a broader world than this, and he had seen over the years how much his father had given of himself and what it had cost him emotionally each time one of his transplant patients died. That wasn't for him. Peter narrowed his eyes as he took a sip of the inky brew, thinking that maybe it was just as well. And then he turned to the young resident again.

'Is this the first transplant you've seen?'

'The second. You performed the other one too.' And performed somehow seemed the appropriate word. Both transplants had been the most theatrical kind of surgery the young man had witnessed. There was more tension and drama in the operating room than he had ever experienced in his life, and watching Peter Hallam operate was like watching Nijinsky dance. He was the best there was. 'How do you think this one will do?'

'It's too soon to tell. Hopefully, she'll do fine.' And he prayed that what he said was true, as he covered his operating-room garb with another sterile gown and headed towards the recovery room. He left his coffee outside, and went to sit quietly in one of the chairs near where Sally lay. A recovery-room nurse and a battery of monitors were watching Sally's every breath, and so far all was well. The trouble, if it arose, was likely to come later than this, unless of course everything went wrong from the beginning. And that had happened before too. But not this time . . . not this time . . . please God . . . not now . . . not to her . . . she's so young . . . not that

11

he would have felt any differently if she had been fifty-five instead of twenty-two.

It hadn't made any difference when he lost his wife. He sat looking at Sally now, trying not to see a different face . . . a different time . . . and yet he always did . . . saw her as she had been in those last hours, beyond fighting, beyond hope . . . beyond him. She hadn't even let him try. No matter what he said, or how hard he had tried to convince her. They had had a donor. But she had refused it. He had pounded the wall in her room that night, and driven home on the motorway at a hundred and fifteen. And when they picked him up for speeding, he didn't give a damn. He didn't care about anything then . . . except her . . . and what she wouldn't let him do. He had been so vague when the police stopped him that they made him get out of the car and walk in a straight line. But he wasn't drunk, he was numb with pain. They had let him go with a stiff warning, and he had gone home to wander through the house, thinking of her, aching for her, needing all that she'd had to give, and would give no more. He wondered if he could bear living without her. Even the children seemed remote to him then . . . all he could think of was Anne. She had been so strong for so long, and because of her he had grown over the years. She filled him with a kind of strength he drew on constantly, as well as his own skill. And suddenly that wasn't there. He had sat terrified that night, alone and frightened, like a small child, and then suddenly at dawn, he had felt an irresistible pull. He had to go back to her . . . had to hold her once more . . . had to tell her the things he had never said before .__. He had raced back to the hospital and quietly slipped into her room, where he dismissed the nurse and watched her himself, gently holding her hand, and smoothing the fair hair back from her pale brow. She looked like a fragile porcelain doll, and once, just before morning burst into the room, she opened her eyes . . .

' . . . Peter . . .' Her voice was less than a whisper in the stillness.

'I love you, Anne . . .' His eyes had filled with tears and he had wanted to shout, 'Don't go.' She smiled the magical smile that always filled his heart, and then with the ease of a sigh she was gone, as he stood in bereft horror and stared. Why wouldn't she fight? Why wouldn't she let him try? Why couldn't she accept what other people accepted from him every day? He stood and he stared at her, sobbing softly, until one of his colleagues led him away. They had taken him home and put him to bed, and somehow in the next days and weeks he had gone through all the motions that were expected of him. But it was like an ugly underwater dream, and he only surfaced now and then, until at last he realised how desperately his children needed him. And slowly, he had come back, and three weeks later he returned to work, but there was something missing now. Something that meant everything to him. And that something was Anne. She never left his mind for very long. She was there a thousand times a day – as he left for work, as he walked in and out of patients' rooms, as he walked into surgery, or back out to his car in the late afternoon. And when he reached his front door, it was like a knife in his heart again every time he went home, knowing that she wouldn't be there.

That was over a year ago now, and the pain was dimmer, but not yet gone. And he somehow suspected that it never would be. All he could do was continue with his work, give everything he could to the people who turned to him for help . . . and then of course there were Matthew, Mark, and Pam. Thank God, he had them. Without them he would never have survived. But he had. He had come this far, and he would live on . . . but so differently . . . without Anne . . .

He sat in the stillness of the recovery room, his long legs stretched out before him, his face tense, watching Sally breathe, and at last her eyes opened for an instant and fuzzily swept the room.

'Sally . . . Sally, it's Peter Hallam . . . I'm here, and you're fine . . .' For now. But he didn't say that to her, nor did he even let himself think that. She was alive. She had done well. She was going to live. He was going to do everything in his power to see to it.

He sat at her bedside for another hour, watching her, and speaking to her whenever she came round, and he even won a small, weak smile from her before he left her shortly after one in the afternoon. He stopped in the cafeteria for a sandwich, and went back to his office briefly, before coming back to the hospital to see patients at four o'clock, and at five thirty he was on the motorway on his way home, his mind once again filled with Anne. It was still difficult to believe that she wouldn't be there when he got home. When does one stop expecting to see her again? he had asked a friend six months before. When will I finally understand it? The pain he had come to know in the past year and a half had etched a certain vulnerability into his face. A visible hurt of loss and sorrow and pain. There had only been strength before, and confidence, the certainty that nothing could ever go wrong. He had three perfect children, the perfect wife, a career he had mastered as few men do. He had climbed to the top, not brutally but beautifully, and he loved it there. And now what? Where was there left to go, and with whom?

CHAPTER 2

As Sally Block lay in her room in intensive care at Center City in L.A., the lights in a television studio in New York shone with a special kind of glare. There was a bright whiteness to them, reminiscent of interrogation rooms in B films. Outside their intense beam, the studio was draught and chill, but directly beneath their intense gaze, one could almost feel one's skin grow taut from the heat and glare. It was as though everything in the room focused on the object of the spotlight's beam, all points came together as one, intensifying moment by moment, as even the people in the room seemed drawn to its centre, a narrow ledge, a shallow stage, an unimpressive desk, and a bright blue backdrop with a single logo on it. But it wasn't the logo that caught the eye, it was the empty chair, thronelike, waiting for its king or queen. Hovering about were technicians, cameramen, a makeup man, a hairdresser, two assistant producers, a stage manager, the curious, the important, the necessary, and the hangers-on, all of them standing ever nearer to the empty stage, the barren desk, on which shone the all-revealing spotlight beam.

'Five minutes!' It was a familiar call, an ordinary scene, yet in its own remote way, the evening news had an element of 'show biz' to it. There was that faint aura of circus and magic and stardom beneath the white lights. A mist of power and mystery enveloping them all, the heart beating just a shade faster at the sound of the words, 'Five minutes!', then 'Three!', then 'Two!'. The same words that would have rung out in a backstage corridor on Broadway, or in London, as some grande dame of the stage emerged. Nothing here was quite so glamorous, the crew standing by in running shoes and jeans, and yet, always that magic, the whispers, the waiting, and Melanie

Adams sensed it herself as she stepped briskly onto the stage. As always, her entrance was timed to perfection. She had exactly one hundred seconds to go before they went on the air. One hundred seconds to glance at her notes again, watch the director's face to see if there was any last-minute thing she should know, and count quietly to herself just to calm down.

As usual, it had been a long day. She had done the final interview on a special on abused kids. It wasn't a pretty subject, but she had handled it well. Still, by six o'clock, the day had taken its toll.

Five . . . the assistant director's fingers went up in the final count . . . four . . . three . . . two . . . one . . .

'Good evening.' The practised smile never looked canned, and the cognac colour of her hair gleamed. 'This is Melanie Adams, with the evening news.' The President had given a speech, there was a military crisis in Brazil, the stock market had taken a sharp dip, and a local politician had been mugged that morning, in broad daylight, leaving his house. There were other news stories to relate as well, and the show moved along at a good clip, as it always did. She had a look of believable competence about her, which made the ratings soar and seemed to account for her enormous appeal. She was nationally known, and had been for well over five years, not that it was what she had originally planned. She had been a political science major when she dropped out of school to give birth to twins at nineteen. But that seemed a lifetime ago. Television had been her life for years. That, and the twins. There were other pastimes, but her work and her children came first.

She collected the notes on her desk as they went off the air, and as always the director looked pleased. 'Nice show, Mel.'

'Thanks.' There was a cool distance about her, which covered what had once been shyness, and was now simply reserve. Too many people were curious about her, wanted to gawk, or ask embarrassing questions, or pry. She was Melanie Adams now, a name that rang a certain magic bell

. . . I know you . . . I've seen you on the news! . . . It was strange buying groceries now, or going shopping for a dress, or just walking down the street with her girls. Suddenly people stared, and although outwardly Melanie Adams always seemed in control deep within it still felt strange to her.

Mel headed towards her office to take off some of the excess makeup and pick up her handbag before she left, when the story editor stopped her with a sharp wave. 'Can you stop here for a sec, Mel?' He looked harried and distracted as he always did, and inwardly Mel groaned. 'Stopping for a sec' could mean a story that would keep her away from home all night. Normally aside from being the anchor on the evening news she only did the major stories, the big newsbreaks, or the specials. But God only knew what they had in store for her now, and she really wasn't in the mood. She was enough of a pro now that the fatigue rarely showed, but the special on abused kids had left her feeling drained, no matter how alert and alive she still looked, thanks to her makeup.

'Yeah? What's up?'

'I've got something I want you to see.' The story editor pulled out a reel of tape and flicked it into a video machine. 'We did this on the one o'clock. I didn't think it was big enough for the evening news, but it could make an interesting follow-up for you.' Mel stared at the video machine as the tape began to roll, and what she saw was an interview with a nine-year-old girl, desperately in need of a heart transplant, but thus far her parents had been unable to get her one. Neighbours had started a special fund for Pattie Lou Jones, an endearing little black girl. And as the interview came to an end, Mel was almost sorry she had seen the film. It was just one more person to hurt for, to care about, and for whom one could do nothing at all. The children in her child abuse special had made her feel that way too. Why couldn't they give her a good political scandal on the heels of the other piece? She didn't need this heartache again.

'Yes.' She turned tired eyes to the man removing the reel. 'So?'

'I just thought it might make an interesting special for you, Mel. Follow her for a while, see what you can set up. What doctors here would be willing to see Pattie Lou.'

'Oh, for chrissake, Jack . . . Why does that have to fall to me? What am I, some kind of new welfare bureau for kids?' Suddenly she looked tired and annoyed, and the tiny lines near her eyes were beginning to show. It had been a hell of a long day, and she had left her house at six o'clock that morning.

'Listen,' he looked every bit as tired as she, 'this could be a hot piece. We get the station to help Pattie Lou's parents find a doctor for her, we follow her through the transplant. Hell, Mel, this is news.'

She nodded slowly. It was news. But it was ghoulish too. 'Have you talked to the family about it?'

'No, but I'm sure they'd be thrilled.'

'You never know. Sometimes people like taking care of their own problems. They might not be so crazy about serving Pattie Lou up to the evening news.'

'Why not? They talked to us today.' Mel nodded again. 'Why don't you check out some of the big-wheel heart surgeons tomorrow and see what they say? Some of them like being in the public eye, and then you could call the parents of that kid.'

'I'll see what I can do, Jack. I have to tie up my child abuse piece.'

'I thought you finished that today.' He scowled instantly.

'I did. But I want to watch them edit some of it at least.'

'Bullshit. That's not your job. Just get to work on this. It'll be an even tougher piece than the child abuse thing.' Tougher than burning a two-year-old child with matches? Cutting off a four-year-old's ear? There were still times when the business of news made her sick. 'See what you can do, Mel.'

'Okay, Jack. Okay. I'll see what I can do.' . . . Hello,

18

Doctor, my name is Melanie Adams and I was wondering if you'd like to perform a heart transplant on a nine-year-old girl . . . possibly for free . . . and then we could come and watch you do it, and blast you and the little girl all over the news . . . She walked hurriedly back to her office, with her head down, her mind full, and collided almost instantly with a tall dark-haired man.

'My, don't you look happy today. Being on the news must be fun.' The deep voice, trained long ago as a radio announcer, brought her eyes up from the floor and she smiled when she saw her old friend.

'Hi, Grant. What are you doing here at this hour?' Grant Buckley had a talk show that went on every night after the late news, and he was one of the most controversial personalities on the air, but he was deeply fond of Mel, and she considered him one of her closest friends, and had for years.

'I had to come in and check out some tapes I want to use on the show. What about you? It's a little late for you, isn't it, kid?' She was usually gone by then, but the story of Pattie Lou Jones had kept her around for an extra half hour.

'They saved an extra treat for me today. They want me to set up a heart transplant for some kid. The usual, no big deal.' Some of the clouds lifted from her face as she looked into his eyes. He was incredibly bright, a good friend, an attractive man, and women all over the network envied the obvious friendship they shared. They had never been more than just friends, although there were rumours from time to time. They only amused Grant and Mel.

'So what else is new? How'd the special on child abuse go?'

Her eyes were serious as they met his. 'It was a killer to do, but it was a good piece.'

'You have a way of picking the heavy ones, kid.'

'Either that, or they pick me, like this heart transplant I'm supposed to arrange.'

'Are you serious?' He had thought she was kidding at first.

'I'm not, but apparently Jack Owens is. You got any bright ideas?'

He frowned for a minute as he thought. 'I did a show on that last year, there were some interesting people on. I'll look at my files and check the names. Two of them instantly come to mind, but there were two more. I'll see, Mel. How soon do you need the stuff?'

She smiled. 'Yesterday.'

He ruffled her hair, knowing she wasn't going back on the air. 'Want to go out for a hamburger before you go home?'

'I'd better not. I should be getting home to the girls.'

'Those two.' He rolled his eyes, knowing them well. He had three daughters of his own, from three different wives, but none of them twins, or quite as adventurous as Mel's two girls. 'What are they up to these days?'

'The usual. Val has been in love four times this week, and Jess is working on straight A's. Their combined efforts are defying all my efforts to remain a redhead, and giving me grey hair.' She had just turned thirty-five, but looked nowhere near her age, despite the responsibilities she bore, the job which weighed heavily on her at times, but which she loved, and the assorted crises that had come through her life over the years. Grant knew most of them, and she had cried on his shoulder more than once, about a disappointment at work, or a shattered love affair. There hadn't been too many of those, she was cautious about whom she saw, and careful too about keeping her private life out of the public eye, but more than that she was gun-shy about getting involved after being abandoned by the twins' father before they were born. He had told her he hadn't wanted kids, and he had meant every word he said. They had married immediately after school and gone to Columbia at the same time, but when she told him she was pregnant, he didn't want to hear.

'Get rid of it.' His face had been rock hard, and Mel still remembered his tone.

'I won't. It's our child . . . that's wrong . . .'

20

'It's a lot more wrong to screw up our lives.' So instead he had tried to screw up hers. He had gone to Mexico on holiday with another girl, and when he came back he announced that they were divorced. He had forged her signature on the forms, and she was so shocked that she didn't know what to say. Her parents wanted her to fight back, but she didn't think that she could. She was too hurt by what he'd done, and too overwhelmed at the prospect of being alone for the birth of her child . . . which then turned out to be two. Her parents had helped her for a while, and then she had gone out on her own, struggled to find a job, and done everything she could from secretarial work to door-to-door sales for a vitamin firm. At last she had wound up as a receptionist for a television network, and eventually in a pool of secretaries typing up pieces for the news.

The twins had thrived through it all, though Mel's climb hadn't been easy or quick, but day after day, typing other people's words made her realise what she wanted to do. The political pieces were the ones that interested her most, reminiscent of her college days before her whole life had changed. And what she wanted was to become a writer for the news. She applied countless times for the job, and eventually understood that it wouldn't happen for her in New York. She went first to Buffalo, then Chicago, and at last back to New York, finally succeeding. Until a major strike, when suddenly management looked at her and someone jerked a thumb towards the set. She was horrified, but she had no choice. It was either do what they said, or lose her job, and she couldn't afford that. She had two little girls to support, their father had never contributed ten pence and had gone on his merry way, leaving Mel to cope alone. And she had. But all she wanted was enough for them, she had no dreams of glory, no aching desire to deliver the stories she wrote herself, and yet suddenly there she was, on TV, and the funny thing was, it felt good.

They farmed her out to Philadelphia after that, and

back to Chicago again for a while, Washington DC, and at last home. In their estimation, she had been properly groomed, and they weren't far wrong. She was damn good. Powerful and interesting, strong, and beautiful to watch on the air. She seemed to combine honesty with compassion and brains to such an extent that at times one actually forgot her striking looks. And at twenty-eight she was near the top, co-presenting the evening news. At thirty, she broke her contract and moved to another show, and suddenly there she was. Sole presenter, delivering the evening news. The ratings soared and they hadn't stopped since.

She had worked like a dog after that, and her reputation as a top newswoman was well deserved. What's more, she was well liked. She was secure now. The hungry days were long gone, the juggling, the struggling – her parents would have been desperately proud, had they still been alive, and she wondered now and then what the twins' father thought, if he regretted what he'd done, if he even cared. She had never heard from him again. But he had left his mark on her, a mark that had dulled, but never quite been erased over the years. A mark of caution, if not pain, a fear of getting too close, of believing too much, of holding anyone too dear . . . except the twins. It had led her into some unfortunate affairs, with men who were taken with who she was, or used her cool distance to play around, and the last time around with a married man. At first, to Mel, he had seemed ideal, he didn't want anything more than she did. She never wanted to marry again. She had everything she wanted on her own: success, security, her kids, a house she loved. 'What do I need marriage for?' she had said to Grant, and he had maintained a sceptical view.

'Maybe you don't but at least get yourself someone who's free.' He had been insistent and firm.

'Why? What difference does it make?'

'The difference it will make, my friend, is that you'll wind up spending Christmas and holidays and birthdays and weekends alone, while he sits around happily with his wife and kids.'

'Maybe so. But I'm special to him. I'm the caviar, not the sour cream.'

'You're dead wrong, Mel. You'll get hurt.' And he had been right. She had. Eventually it all began to cause her pain for just the reasons he had feared and there had been a terrible parting in the end, with Melanie looking gaunt and drawn for weeks. 'Next time, listen to Uncle Grant. I know.' He knew a great deal, mostly about how carefully she had built walls around herself. He had known her for almost ten years, meeting while she was on the way up, and he had known then that he was watching a bright new star rise in the heavens of television news, but more than that, he cared about her, as a human being and a friend. He cared enough not to want to spoil what they had. They had both been careful never to get involved with each other. He had been married three times, had a stable of 'temporaries' he enjoyed spending his nights with, but Mel was much more than that to him. She was his friend, and he was hers, and with Mel it was important not to betray that trust. She had been betrayed before, and he didn't want to be the second one to hurt her. 'The truth is, love, most men are shits,' he had confessed to her late one night after interviewing her on his show, which had been fun. And afterwards they had gone out for a drink, and sat around at Elaine's until three a.m.

'What makes you say that?' There had suddenly been something distant and cautious in her eyes. She knew one who had been, but it was grim to think that they all were.

'Because damn few want to give as good as they get. They want a woman to love them with her whole heart and soul, but they keep an important piece to themselves. What you need is a man who'll give you as much love as you have to give.'

'What makes you think I have that much love left?' She tried to look amused, but he wasn't convinced. The old hurt was still there, distant, but not gone. He wondered if it ever would be.

'I know you too well, Mel. Better than you know yourself.'

'And you think I'm pining to find the right man?' This time she laughed and he smiled.

'No. I think you're scared to death you will.'

'Touché.'

'It might do you good.'

'Why? I'm happy by myself.'

'Horseshit. No one is. Not really.'

'I have the twins.'

'That is *not* the same thing.'

She shrugged. 'You're happy alone.' She searched his eyes, not sure what she'd find, and was surprised to see a trace of loneliness there. It came out at night, like a werewolf he hid by day. Even the illustrious Grant was human too.

'If I were so happy alone, I wouldn't have married three times.' They both laughed at that, the evening wore on, and eventually he dropped her at her front door with a fatherly peck on the cheek. Once in a while she wondered what it would be like to get involved with him, but she knew that it would spoil what they had, and they both wanted to avoid that. It was too good like this.

And in the corridor outside her office, she looked up at him now, tired, but relieved to see his face at the end of a long day. He gave her something no one else did. The twins were still young enough to take from her, they had a constant need for attention, for love, for discipline, limits, new ice skates, designer jeans. But he put something back in her soul, and there was really no one else who did.

'I'll take a rain check on that hamburger tomorrow night.'

'Can't.' He shook his head with regret. 'I've got a hot date with a sensational pair of boobs.'

She rolled her eyes and he grinned. 'You are without a doubt the most sexist man I know.'

'Yup.'

'And proud of it too.'

24

'You're damn right.'

She smiled and looked at her watch. 'I'd better get home, or Raquel will lock me out, tyrant that she is.' She had had the same housekeeper for the last seven years. Raquel was a godsend with the girls, but she ran a tight ship. She was inordinately fond of Grant, and had tried to press Mel into a relationship with him for years.

'Give Raquel my love.'

'I'll tell her it was your fault I'm late.'

'Fine, and I'll give you that list of cardiac surgeons tomorrow. Will you be around?'

'I'll be here.'

'I'll call.'

'Thanks.' She blew him a kiss, and he went his way. She stepped into her office and picked up her bag with a quick look at her watch. It was seven thirty and Raquel was going to have a fit. She hurried downstairs and hailed a cab and in fifteen minutes the driver turned into Seventy-ninth Street.

'I'm home!' She called out into the silence, passing through the front hall. It was done in delicate flowered wallpaper and there was a white marble floor. From the moment one walked in, one sensed the friendly, elegant mood of the place, and from the bright colours, big bouquets of flowers, and touches of yellow and pastel everywhere, one had an instant feeling of good cheer. The house always amused Grant Buckley. It was so obviously a woman's house. One would have had to begin decorating from scratch were a man to make his home there. There was a big antique hat rack in the front hall, covered with Mel's hats and the favourites left there by the two girls.

The living room was done in a soft peach, with silky deep couches that invited one to be swallowed up, and delicate moiré curtains that hung in lush folds with French tiebacks, and the walls were painted the same delicate peach shade, with creamy trim on the mouldings and delicate pastel paintings everywhere. As Melanie sank

25

down now into the couch with a contented sigh, it was the perfect setting for her with her creamy skin and her flaming red hair. Her bedroom was done in soft blues, in watered silks, the dining room was white, the kitchen orange and yellow and blue. Melanie's home had a happy feeling that made one want to wander around and hang out. It was elegant, but not too chic and not so much so that one was afraid to sit down.

It was a small house, but perfect for them, with the living room, dining room, and kitchen on the main floor, Mel's bedroom, study, and dressing room were one flight up, and above that were two big sunny bedrooms for the two girls. There wasn't an inch of unused space, and even one extra body in the house would have seemed like too much. But just for them, it was exactly the right size, as Melanie had known it would be when she'd first seen it and fallen in love with it the same day.

She walked hurriedly up the stairs to the girls' rooms, faintly aware of an ache in her back. It had been a hell of a long day. She didn't stop in her own room, knowing already what would be there, a stack of mail she didn't want to see, mostly bills relating to the girls, and an assortment of other things. But that didn't interest her now. She wanted to see the twins.

On the third floor, she found both their doors closed, but the music was so loud, she could already feel her heart pound halfway up the stairs.

'Good God, Jess!' Melanie shouted above the din. 'Turn that thing down!'

'What?' The tall, skinny redheaded girl turned towards the door from where she lay on her bed. There were school books spread all around, and she had the telephone pressed to her ear. She waved to her mother, and went on talking on the phone.

'Don't you have exams?' A silent nod, and Melanie's face began to look grim. Jessica was always the most serious of the twins, but lately she had been losing ground in school. She was bored, and the romance she'd had all year had just gone down the tubes, but that was no excuse, and she still had to study for her exams. 'Come on, hang up, Jess.' She stood leaning against the desk, arms crossed, and Jessica looked vaguely annoyed, said something unintelligible into the phone, and hung up, looking at her mother as though she were not only overly demanding but rude. 'Now turn that thing down.'

She unwound the long coltlike legs from the bed, and walked to the stereo, flinging her long coppery mane over her shoulders. 'I was just taking a break.'

'For how long?'

'Oh, for chrissake. What do I have to do now? Punch a time clock for you?'

'That's not fair, Jess. You can have all the leeway you need. But the fact is, your last grades . . .'

'I know, I know. How long do I have to hear about that?'

'Until they improve.' Melanie looked unimpressed by her daughter's speech. Jessica had been testy since the end of the romance with a young man named John. It was probably what had affected her grades, and for Jessica that was a first. But Melanie already sensed that things were on their way back up. She just didn't want to let Jessica off the hook yet, not till she was sure. 'How was your day?' She slipped an arm around her daughter's shoulders and stroked her hair. The music had been turned off, and the room seemed strangely still.

'It was okay. How was yours?'

'Not bad.'

Jessie smiled, and when she did, she looked very much as Melanie had when she was a little girl. She was more angular than her mother was, and already two inches taller than Mel in her bare feet, but there was a lot of her mother in her, which accounted for the rare bond the two women shared; there were times when it didn't even require words. And other times when their friendship exploded because of the similarities that made them almost too close. 'I saw the piece you did about the legislation for the handicapped on the evening news.'

'What did you think?' She always liked to hear what they said, especially Jess. She had a fine mind, and was very direct with her words, unlike her twin, who was kinder, less critical, and softer in a myriad ways.

'I thought it was good, but not tough enough.'

'You're mighty hard to please.' But her sponsors were too. Jessica met her eyes with a shrug and a smile. 'You taught me to question what I hear and be demanding of the news.'

'Did I do that?' The two women exchanged a warm smile. She was proud of Jess, and in turn Jessica was proud of her. Both twins were. She was a terrific mother to them. The three of them had shared some damn tough years. It had brought them closer, in respect, and attitudes.

Mother and daughter exchanged another long look. In a way, Melanie was just a shade gentler than her oldest child. But she was of another generation, another lifetime, a different world. And for her time, Melanie had already come far. But Jessica would go farther, move ahead with even more determination than Mel had. 'Where's Val?'

'In her room.'

Melanie nodded. 'How are things in school?'

'Okay.' But she thought Jessica sagged a little as she asked, and then sensing her mother's thoughts, she once again sought Melanie's eyes. 'I saw John today.'

'How was that?'

'It hurt.'

Melanie nodded and sat down on the bed, grateful for the openness that they always shared. 'What did he say?'

'Just "hi." I don't know, I hear he's going out with some other girl.'

'That's rough.' It had been almost a month now, and Melanie knew that it was the first real blow Jessica had suffered since she had started school. Always near the top of her class, surrounded by friends, and chased by all the best boys in school since she'd turned thirteen. Just shy of her sixteenth birthday, she had experienced her first

..eartbreak, and it hurt Melanie to watch it, almost as much as it hurt Jess. 'But you know, what you've forgotten by now is that there were times when he really got on your nerves.'

'He did?' Jessica looked surprised.

'Yes, ma'am. Remember when he showed up an hour late to take you to that dance? When he went skiing with his friends instead of taking you to the football game? The time he . . .' Melanie seemed to remember them all, she knew her girls' lives well, and Jessica grinned.

'Okay, okay, so he's a creep . . . I like him anyway . . .'

'Him, or just having someone around?' There was a moment's silence in the room, and Jessica looked at her with surprised eyes.

'You know, Mom . . . I'm not sure.' She was stunned. The uncertainty was a revelation to her.

Melanie smiled. 'Don't feel alone. Half the relationships in the world go on because of that.'

Jessica looked at her then, her head turned to one side; she knew how difficult her mother's standards were, how badly she'd been hurt, how careful she was not to get involved. Sometimes it made Jess sorry for her. Her mother needed someone. Long ago, she had hoped it would be Grant, but she knew long since that was not destined to be. And before she could say anything more, the door opened and Valerie walked in.

'Hi, Mom.' And then she saw their serious looks. 'Should I go?'

'No.' Melanie was quick to shake her head. 'Hello, love.' Valerie bent to give her a kiss and a smile. She looked so different from Melanie and Jess that one almost wondered if she were related to the other two. She was smaller than both Melanie and her twin, but with a voluptuous body that made men drool as she walked by, large, full breasts, a tiny waist, small, rounded hips, shapely legs, and a curtain of blonde hair that fell almost to her waist. There were times when Melanie saw men's reactions to her child and almost visibly cringed. Even

29

Grant had been taken aback when he'd seen her recently. 'For God's sake, Mel, put a bag over the child's head until she turns twenty-five, or you'll drive the neighbourhood mad.' But Melanie had responded with a rueful smile, 'I don't think putting it over just her head would do the trick.' She watched Valerie with a careful eye, more so than Jess, because one sensed instantly that Valerie was almost too open and very naïve. She was bright, but not as sharp as her twin and part of her charm was that she was almost totally unaware of herself. She breezed in and out of a room with the happy-go-lucky ease of a child of three, leaving men panting in her wake, as she unconcernedly went on her way. It was Jessica who had always watched over her in school, and even more so now. Jessica was well aware of how Valerie looked, so Valerie had two mothers watching over her.

'We watched you tonight on the news. You were good.' But unlike Jessica, she didn't say why, didn't analyse, didn't criticise, and in a funny way, what went on in Jessica's head made her almost more beautiful than her dazzling twin. And together, they were quite a pair, the one redheaded and long and lean, the other so voluptuous and soft and blonde. 'Are you having dinner with us tonight?'

'I sure am. I turned down dinner with Grant to have dinner with you two.'

'Why didn't you bring him home?' Val looked instantly chagrined.

'Because I enjoy being alone with you sometimes. I can see him some other time.' Val shrugged, and Jessica nodded, and that instant Raquel buzzed them from downstairs on the intercom. Val picked it up first, said 'Okay,' then hung up, and turned to her mother and twin.

'Dinner's on, and Raquel sounds pissed.'

'Val!' Melanie didn't look pleased. 'Don't talk like that.'

'Why not? Everyone else does.'

'That's no reason for you to.' And with that, the threesome went downstairs, bantering about their day,

Mel told them about the special on child abuse, she even told them about Pattie Lou Jones, desperate for a heart transplant which Mel had been assigned to find.

'How are you supposed to do that, Mom?' Jess looked intrigued. She loved stories like that, and thought that her mother did them exceedingly well.

'Grant said he'd give me some names, he did a show on four big heart-transplant specialists last year, and the network research people will give me some leads.'

'It should be a good piece.'

'Sounds disgusting to me.' Val made a face as they walked into the dining room and Raquel glared.

'You think I gonna wait all night?' She grunted loudly and whisked through the swinging door as the threesome exchanged a smile.

'She'd go crazy if she couldn't complain,' Jessica whispered to them both, and they laughed, sobering their faces for her benefit as she returned with a platter of roast beef.

'It looks great, Raquel!' Val was quick to offer praise as she helped herself first.

'Hrmph.' She whisked out again, returning with baked potatoes and steamed broccoli, and the three of them settled down to a quiet evening at home. It was the only place in Mel's life where she could totally, completely free herself of the news.

CHAPTER 3

'Sally? . . . Sally? . . .' She had been drifting in and out of consciousness all day, and Peter Hallam had been to see her five or six times. It was only her second postoperative day, and it was still difficult to tell how she would do, but he had to admit to himself that he wasn't entirely pleased. She opened her eyes at last, realised who he was, and greeted him with a warm smile, as he pulled up a chair, sat down, and took her hand. 'How're you feeling today?'

She spoke to him in a whisper. 'Not so good.'

He nodded. 'It's still pretty soon. Every day you'll feel stronger.' He seemed to will his strength into her through his words and his voice, but slowly she shook her head. 'Have I ever lied to you?'

She shook her head again, spoke again, despite the uncomfortable naso-gastric tube scratching the back of her throat. 'It won't work.'

'If you want it to, it will.' Everything inside him went tense. She couldn't afford to think like that. Not now.

'I'm going to reject.' She whispered again. But he doggedly shook his head, a muscle tensing in his jaw. Dammit, why was she giving up? . . . and how did she know? . . . It was what he had feared all day. But she couldn't give up the fight . . . couldn't . . . dammit, it was like Anne . . . why did they suddenly lose their grasp? It was the worst battle he fought. Worse than the drugs, the rejections, the infections. They could deal with them all, at least to a point, but only if the patient still had the will to live . . . the belief that they would live. Without that, all was lost.

'Sally, you're doing fine.' The words were determined and firm, and he sat by her bedside for over an hour, holding her hand. And then he went to make rounds, in each room, turning his full attention to the patient he saw, spending as much time as was needed to explain either surgical procedures that were going to be conducted soon, or what had already happened, what they felt, why they felt it, what the medications and steroids had done. And then at last, he went back to Sally's room. But she was asleep once again, and he stood for a long time watching her. He didn't like what he saw. She was right; he sensed it in his gut. Her body was rejecting the donor's heart, and there was no reason why it should. It had been a good match. But he instinctively sensed that it came too late for her, and as he left the room, he had a sense of impending loss which weighed on him like a lead balloon.

He went to the small cubicle he used as an surgery when he was there, and called his office to see if they needed him there.

'Everything's fine, Doctor,' the efficient voice said. 'You just had a call from New York.'

'From whom?' He didn't sound overly interested in the call, it was probably from another surgeon wanting to consult on a difficult case, but his mind was filled with Sally Block, and he hoped it could wait.

'From Melanie Adams, on Channel Four news.' Even Peter knew who she was, as isolated as he sometimes was from the world. He couldn't figure out why she had called him.

'Do you know why?'

'She wouldn't say, or at least not in detail. She only said that it was urgent, something about a little girl.' He raised an eyebrow at that. Even television newswomen had kids and maybe this had to do with her own child. He jotted down the number she had left, glanced at his watch, and dialled.

They put him through at once, and Melanie ran halfway across the newsroom to pick up a phone.

'Dr Hallam?' She sounded breathless.

'Yes. I had a message that you called.'

'I did. I didn't expect to hear from you so soon. Our

research department gave me your name.' She had heard it often too, but as he was on the West Coast it hadn't occurred to her to call, and the four names she'd got from Grant had done no good at all. Not one of them would do the surgery for the little black child – the publicity frightened them too much and the surgery had to be performed. Melanie had also called a surgeon of some note in Chicago, but he was in England and Scotland doing a lecture tour. She explained to Hallam quickly about the little girl, and he asked her a number of pertinent questions. She had learned a lot in one day, talking to the other four.

'It sounds like an interesting case.' And then he spoke bluntly. 'What's in it for you?'

She took a quick breath, it was hard to say. 'On the surface, Doctor, a story for my network, about a compassionate doctor, a desperately sick little girl, and how transplants work.'

'That makes sense. I'm not sure I like the publicity angle though. And it's damn hard to find a donor for a child. Most likely we'd try something a little more unusual with her.'

'Like what?' Mel was intrigued.

'It depends on how severe she is. I'd like to see her first. We might first repair her old heart and put it back in.' Mel knit her brows. 'Does that work?'

'Sometimes. Do her doctors think she'd survive the trip?'

'I don't know. I'd have to check. Would you actually do it?'

'Maybe. For her sake, not yours.' He sounded blunt again, but Mel couldn't fault it. He was offering to do the surgery for the child, not make a spectacle of himself on the news. She respected him for that.

'Would you give us an interview?'

'Yes.' He spoke up without qualm. 'I just want to make it clear why I'd do it at all. I'm a physician, and a surgeon, committed to what I do. I'm not looking to turn this into a circus, for any of us.'

'I wouldn't do that to you.' He had seen her stories on television before, and suspected that that was true. 'But I would like to interview you. And if you do the transplant on Pattie Lou, it would provide an opening for a very interesting piece.'

'On what? On me?' He sounded shocked, as though he'd never thought of that before, and at her end Mel smiled. Was it possible that he didn't realise how well known he was? Maybe he was so involved in his work that he really didn't know. Or care. The possibility of that intrigued her.

'Heart surgery and on transplants in general if you prefer.'

'I would.' She heard a smile in his voice, and went on.

'That could be arranged. Now what about Pattie Lou?'

'Give me her physician's name. I'll call and see what I can find out from here. If she's operable, send her out, and we'll see.' And then he had another thought. 'Will her parents agree to this?'

'I think so. But I'd have to speak to them too. I'm kind of the matchmaker in all this.'

'Apparently. Well, at least it's all for a good cause. I hope we can help the child.'

'So do I.' There was an instant's silence between them, and Mel felt as though miraculously she had fallen into the right hands, and so had Pattie Lou. 'Shall I call you back, or will you call me?'

'I've got a critical case here. I'll get back to you.' And suddenly he sounded desperately serious again, as though he were distracted. Mel thanked him again, and a moment later he was gone.

That afternoon she went to see the Jones', and their desperately ill child, but Pattie Lou was a game little thing, and her parents were thrilled at even the faint shred of hope Mel offered them. There was enough in their meagre fund to pay for the plane fare to LA, for one of the parents at least, and the child's father was quick to urge his wife to go. There were four other children at home, all older than Pattie Lou and Mr Jones felt sure that they could all manage on their own. Mrs Jones cried, and her husband's eyes were damp when they said goodbye to Mel, and two hours after she returned to her office, Hallam called again. He had spoken to Pattie Lou's physicians and in their estimation it was worth taking the risk of the trip. It was the only hope she had. And Peter Hallam was willing to take the case.

Having seen Pattie Lou that afternoon, tears instantly filled Mel's eyes, and her voice was husky when she spoke again. 'You're a hell of a nice man.'

'Thank you.' He smiled. 'How soon do you suppose you could arrange to have her on the plane?'

'I'm not sure. I'll have the network work out the details. When do you want her there?'

'From what her doctors said, I don't think tomorrow would be too soon.'

'I'll see what I can do.' She checked her watch, it was almost time to do the evening news. 'We'll call you in a few hours . . . and Dr Hallam . . . thank you . . .'

'Don't. It's part of what I do. And I hope we understand each other about all this. I will do it gratis for the child, but there will be no cameras in surgery with us. And what you get is an interview after it's all done. Agreed?'

'Agreed.' And then she couldn't resist stretching it a bit. She had an obligation to the network and her sponsors too. 'Could we interview you about some other cases too?'

'In what regard?' He sounded faintly suspicious of her now.

'I'd like very much to do a story on heart transplants as long as I'll be out there with you, Doctor. Is that all right?' Maybe he had some preconceived prejudice about her. She hoped not, but one never knew. Maybe he hated the way she did the evening news. It was broadcast to California after all, so she couldn't be totally unknown to him, and of course she was not. But her fears were ill founded, as he nodded at his end.

'Of course. That's fine.'

There was a momemt of silence between them, and then he spoke up, his voice thoughtful. 'It's odd to think of a human life in terms of a story.' He was thinking of Sally, hovering on the verge of a massive rejection. She wasn't a 'story', she was a twenty-two-year-old girl, a human life, as was this child in New York.

'Believe it or not, after all these years, it's hard for me to think of it that way too.' She took a deep breath, wondering if she seemed callous to him. But the news business was that way sometimes. 'I'll get in touch with you later, and let you know when we're coming out.'

'I'll make arrangements here to receive her.'

'Thank you, Doctor.'

'This is what I do, no thanks necessary, Miss Adams.'

To Mel it seemed a far more noble task in life than reporting news 'stories', and as she hung up, she thought of what he had said as she went about making arrangements to get Pattie Lou Jones and her mother to California. In less than an hour she had taken care of everything from the ambulance from their home to the airport, special service on the flight, a nurse to travel with them, to be paid for by the network, a camera crew to join them from point of departure all the way to California, a similar crew to continue with them in LA, and hotel accommodation for herself, the crew, and Pattie Lou's mother. All that remained was to let Peter Hallam know, and she left a message with his service. He was not available when she called him several hours later, and that night she told the twins that she was going to California for a few days.

'What for?' She explained the story to both girls.

'Boy, Mom, you're turning into a regular paramedic.' Val looked amused, and Mel turned to her with a tired sigh.

'I feel like it tonight. It ought to be a good story though.' That word again, a 'story', as weighed against a human life. What if it were Valerie or Jessie? How would she feel then? How much of a 'story' would it be to her? She cringed inwardly at the thought, and understood again Peter Hallam's reaction to the term. She wondered too what it would be like to meet him, if he would be pleasant, easy to work with, or terribly egocentric. He didn't sound it on the phone, but she knew that most surgeons had that reputation. Yet he had sounded different. She had liked him, sight unseen, and she had deeply respected his willingness to help Pattie Lou Jones.

'You look tired, Mom.' She noticed that Jessica had been staring at her.

'I am.'

'What time do you leave tomorrow?' They were used to her comings and goings, and were comfortable with Raquel in her absence.

'I should leave the house by six thirty. Our flight's at nine, and I'm meeting the camera crew outside the Jones house. I'll be up by five, I guess.'

'Urghk.' Both girls made a face, and Mel smiled at them.

'Exactly. Not always as glamorous as it seems, eh girls?'

'You can say that again,' Val was quick to answer. The girls knew what hard work Mel's career was, how often she had stood outside the White House, freezing in snow storms, covering hideous events in distant jungles, political assassinations and other horrendous moments. Both of them respected her more for it, but neither of them envied what she did, or longed for the same career. Val thought she'd just like to get married, and Jess had her heart set on becoming a doctor.

Mel went upstairs with them after dinner, packed her bag for the trip to the West Coast, and went to bed early. Grant called her just after she turned the light out, and asked her how his lists of doctors had worked out that morning.

'None of them would help, but research gave me Peter Hallam's number. I called him in LA and we're all flying out tomorrow.'

'You and the kid?' He sounded surprised.

'And her mother and a nurse, and a camera crew.'

'The whole circus.'

'I think that's what Hallam felt about it.' In fact he had even used the same word.

'I'm surprised he agreed to do it.'

'He sounds like a nice man.'

'So they say. He certainly doesn't need the publicity, although he keeps a lower profile than the others. But I think that's by choice. Will he let you film the surgery on the kid?'

'Nope. But he promised me an interview afterwards, and you never know, he may change his mind once we get there.'

'Maybe so. Call me when you get back, kiddo, and try to stay out of trouble.' It was his usual warning and she smiled as she turned off the light again a few minutes later.

At the opposite end of the country, Peter Hallam wasn't smiling. Sally Block had gone into massive rejection, and within an hour, she had slipped into a coma. He stayed with her until almost midnight, emerging from her room only to speak to her mother, and at last, he allowed the sorrowing woman to join him at Sally's side. There was no reason not to. The fear of infection no longer mattered, and at one o'clock that morning, LA time, Sally Block died without ever regaining consciousness to see her mother or the doctor she had so greatly trusted. Her mother left the room in bereft silence, with tears pouring down her cheeks. Sally's war was over. Peter Hallam signed the death certificate, and went home to sit in his study in total darkness, staring out into the night, thinking of Sally, and Anne, and others like them. He was still sitting there two hours later when Mel left her apartment to go to the Jones apartment in New York. Peter Hallam wasn't even thinking of Pattie Lou Jones at that moment, or Mel Adams . . . only of Sally . . . the pretty twenty-two-year-old blonde girl . . . gone now . . . gone . . . like Anne . . . like so many others. And then, slowly, slowly, feeling the weight of the world on his shoulders, he walked up to his bedroom, closed the door, and sat on his bed in the silence.

'I'm sorry . . .' the words were whispered, and he wasn't even sure to whom he spoke them . . . to his wife

. . . his children . . . to Sally . . . to her parents . . . to himself . . . and then the tears came, falling softly as he lay down in the darkness, sorrowing in his soul for what he hadn't been able to do this time . . . not this time . . . but next time . . . next time . . . maybe next time . . . And then at last, Pattie Lou Jones came to mind. There was nothing to do but try again. And something deep within him stirred at the prospect.

CHAPTER 4

The plane left Kennedy airport with Mel, the camera crew, Pattie Lou, the nurse, and Pattie's mother all safely ensconced in a segregated first-class section. Pattie had an IV, and the nurse seemed highly skilled in the care of cardiac patients. She had been recommended by Pattie's own physician, and Mel found herself praying that nothing untoward would happen before they reached Los Angeles. Once there she knew that they would be in the competent hands of Dr Peter Hallam, but before that, Mel's idea of a nightmare was having to land in Kansas with a dying child, suffering from cardiac arrest before they could reach the doctor in California. She just prayed that that wouldn't happen, and as it turned out, they had a peaceful flight all the way to Los Angeles, where Hallam had two members of his team and an ambulance waiting, and Pattie Lou was whisked off to Center City with her mother. By previous agreement with Dr Hallam, Melanie was not to join them. He wanted to give the child time to settle in without disruption, and he had agreed to meet Mel in the cafeteria at seven o'clock the following morning. He would brief her then on Pattie Lou's condition, and how they planned to treat her. She was welcome to bring a notepad and a tape recorder, but there was to be no camera crew at that meeting. The official interview would come later. But Mel found that she was grateful for the reprieve from the medical tension, and she went to her hotel and called the twins in New York, showered, changed, and walked around her hotel area in the balmy spring air, her mind constantly returning to Peter Hallam. She was desperately curious to meet him, and at six the next morning, she rose swiftly and drove her rented car to Center City.

Melanie's heels clicked rhythmically on the tiled floor as she turned left down an endless hall, and passed two maintenance men dragging wet mops behind them. They watched her back recede into the distance with an appreciative glance, until she stopped outside the cafeteria, read the sign, and pushed open the double doors. Her nostrils were assailed with the rich aroma of fresh coffee. And as she looked around the brightly lit room, she was surprised at how many people were there at that hour of the morning.

There were tables of nurses having coffee and breakfast between shifts, residents taking a break, interns finishing a long night with a hot meal or a sandwich, and one or two civilians sitting bleakly at tables on the sidelines, undoubtedly people who had been up all night waiting for news of critically ill relatives or friends. There was one woman crying softly and dabbing at her eyes with a hankie as a younger woman dried her own tears and tried to console her. It was an odd scene of contrasts, the silent fatigue of the young doctors, the mirth and chatter of the nurses, the sorrow and tension of people visiting patients, and behind it all the clatter of trays and steaming water being splashed on dirty dishes in efficient machines. It looked like the operations centre of a strange modern city, the command post of a spaceship floating through space, totally divorced from the rest of the world.

As Melanie looked around, she wondered which white-coated figure was Peter Hallam. There were a few middle-aged men in starched white coats, conferring solemnly at one table over doughnuts and coffee, but somehow none of them looked the way she expected him to, and none of them approached her. At least he would know what she looked like.

'Miss Adams?' She was startled by the voice directly behind her, and she wheeled on one heel to face it.

'Yes?'

He extended a powerful, cool hand. 'I'm Peter Hallam.' As she shook his hand, she found herself looking up into

42

the sharply etched, handsome, well-lined face of a man with blue eyes and grey hair and a smile that hovered in his eyes but didn't quite reach his lips. Despite their conversation on the phone, he wasn't at all what she had expected. He was much taller, and powerfully built, his shoulders were pressed into the starched white coat he wore over a blue shirt, dark tie, and grey trousers, and one instantly guessed he had played football in college. 'Have you been waiting long?'

'Not at all.' She followed him to a table, feeling less in control than she would have liked. She was used to having a certain impact on her subjects, and here she had the impression of simply being dragged along in his wake. There was something incredibly magnetic about him.

'Coffee?'

'Please.' Their eyes met and locked, each one wondering what they would discover in the other, friend of foe, supporter or opponent. But for the moment they had one thing in common. Pattie Lou Jones, and Mel was anxious to ask him about her.

'Cream and sugar?'

'No, thanks.' She made a move as though to join him on the food line, but he waved a hand towards an empty chair.

'Don't bother. I'll be right back. You keep an eye on the table.' He smiled then and she felt something gentle wash over her. He looked like a kind man, and a moment later he returned with a tray bearing two steaming cups, two glasses of orange juice, and some toast. 'I wasn't sure if you'd had breakfast.' There was something so basically decent and thoughtful about him, she found herself instantly liking him.

'Thank you.' She smiled at him and then couldn't hold back any longer. 'How's Pattie Lou?'

'She settled in nicely last night. She's a courageous little kid. She didn't even need her mother to stay with her.' But Mel somehow suspected that had to do with the comforting welcome she got from Peter Hallam and his team, and she was right on that score. His patient's mental well-being was of major importance to him, which was extremely rare for a surgeon. He had spent several hours with Pattie Lou after she arrived, getting to know her, as a person, not just an accumulation of data. With Sally gone, Peter had no other major crisis to attend to and now he wasn't thinking of Sally, only Pattie.

'How do her chances look, Doctor?' Mel was anxious to hear what he thought, and hopeful that the prognosis would be good.

'I'd like to say good, but they aren't. I think fair is a more accurate assessment of the situation.' Mel nodded sombrely and took a sip of coffee.

'Will you do a transplant on her?'

'If we get a donor, which isn't very likely. Donors for children are very rare, Miss Adams. I think my first thought was the right one – repairing her own heart as best we can.'

'When?'

He sighed and narrowed his eyes, thinking about it as she watched him. 'We'll run a battery of tests on her today, and we might do the surgery tomorrow.'

'Is she strong enough to survive it?'

'I think so.' Their eyes met and held for a long moment. There were no guarantees in this business. There were never sure wins, only sure losses. It was a tough thing to live with, day by day, and she admired what he was doing. She felt a strong urge to tell him that, but somehow it seemed too personal a statement to make, so she didn't, and kept the conversation to Pattie Lou and the story. After a while, he looked searchingly at Mel. She was so interested, so human. She was more than just a reporter. 'What's your interest in all this, Miss Adams? Just another story or something more?'

'She's a special little girl, Doctor. It's difficult not to care about her.'

'Do you always care that much about your subjects? It must be exhausting.'

'Isn't that true of you? Do you care about them all, Doctor?'

'Almost always.' He was being very honest with her and it was easy to believe him. The patient he didn't care deeply about would be a very, very rare exception. She had already sensed that about him. And then he looked at her with a curious smile: her hands were folded in her lap as she watched him. 'You didn't bring a notebook. Does that mean you're taping this?'

'No.' She quietly shook her head and smiled. 'I'm not. I'd rather we get to know each other.'

That possibility intrigued him, and he couldn't resist asking another question. 'Why?'

'Because I can do a better job of reporting what you do here if I learn something about you. Not on paper, or on tape, but by watching, listening, getting to know you.' She was good at what she did, and he sensed that. It was just that she was well known in the business, a star actually, she was in truth a real pro, and an unusually good one. Peter Hallam liked that. It was like being perfectly matched to your opponent in a competitive sport, and it gave him a feeling of excitement, which suddenly led to an offer he hadn't planned to make her.

'Would you like to follow me on rounds this morning? Just for your own interest.'

Her eyes lit up. She was flattered by the unexpected offer, and hoped that it meant that he liked her, or better yet, was already beginning to trust her. That was important for the smooth flow of any story.

'I'd like that very much, Doctor.' She let her eyes convey to him how touched she was by the offer.

'You could call me Peter.'

'If you call me Mel.' They exchanged a smile.

'Agreed.' He touched her shoulder as he stood, and she leapt up, excited by the prospect of following him on rounds. It was a rare opportunity and she was grateful for it. He turned to her again, this time with a smile, as they left the cafeteria. 'My patients will be very impressed to

see you here, Mel. I'm sure they've all seen you on TV.'
For some reason, the remark surprised her and she smiled.

'I doubt that.' There was a modesty about her that those
who knew her well always teased her for, especially Grant
and her daughters.

But this time he laughed at her. 'You're hardly an
anonymous figure, you know. And heart patients watch
the news on TV too.'

'I just always assume that people won't recognise me off
camera.'

'But I'll bet they do.' He smiled again and Melanie
nodded in answer. It was intriguing to him that she hadn't
let her success go to her head over the years. He had
expected someone very different.

'In any case, Doctor Hallam,' she went on, 'you're the
star here, and rightly so.' Her eyes shone with frank
admiration, but this time a similarly humble side turned
up in him.

'I'm hardly a star, Mel.' He was serious as he said it. 'I
just work here, as part of a remarkably good team. Believe
me, my patients will be a lot more excited to see you than
me, and rightly so. It'll do them good to see a new face.'
He pressed the button for the lift, and when it came, he
pressed six, and they entered amidst a group of white-
coated doctors and fresh-faced nurses. The shifts were just
changing.

'You know, I've always liked your views, and the way
you handle a story.' He spoke softly as the lift stopped at
each floor, and Mel noticed two nurses staring discreetly at
her. 'There's something very direct and honest about your
approach. I suppose it's why I agreed to do this.'

'Whatever your reason, I'm glad you did. Pattie Lou
needed you desperately.' He nodded, he couldn't disagree
with her on that score. But now there was more to it. He
had opened himself up to an interview on network news,
and as they sat in his cubicle on the sixth floor, a few
minutes later, he looked with honesty at Mel and tried to
explain to her the risks and dangers of transplants. He

warned her that she might even come away from the story with negative feelings about them. It was a possibility he'd thought of before agreeing to the interview, but he was willing to take that risk. There was more to be gained by telling all than by hiding from the press, and if she handled it right, she could warm up public opinion considerably, but she seemed startled by the risks he described and the odds he gave.

'Do you mean I could possibly decide that heart transplants aren't a good idea? Is that what you're saying, Peter?'

'You might, although that would be a very foolish view. The fact is that transplant patients are going to die anyway, and quite soon. What we give them is a chance, and sometimes not a very good one at that. The risk is high, most of the time the odds are poor, but there *is* that chance, and the patient makes up his own mind. Some people just don't want to go through what they'd have to, and they opt not to take the chance. I respect that. But if they let me, I try. It's all anyone can do. I'm not advocating transplant for all patients, that would be mad. But the fact is that for some it's ideal, and right now we still need to open new doors. We can't just operate with human heart donors, we need more than there are, so we're groping for new paths, and it's that process that the public resists. They think we're trying to play God, and we're not, we're trying to save lives, and doing our best, it's as simple as that.' He stood up, as she followed suit, and he looked down at her from his considerable height. 'You tell me what you think at the end of today, and tell me if you disagree with the means we pursue. In fact' – he narrowed his eyes as he looked at her – 'I'd be particularly interested in what you think. You're an intelligent woman, yet relatively uneducated in this field. You come to it with fresh eyes. You tell me if you're shocked, if you're appalled, or if you approve.' And as they left his cubicle, he had another thought. 'Tell me something, Mel, have you formed any kind of preconceived opinion at all?' He watched her face intently as they walked and she furrowed her brow.

'Honestly, I'm not entirely sure. Basically, I think that everything you're doing makes sense, of course. But I must admit, the odds you're talking about frighten me. The chances of survival, for any reasonable length of time, are so slim.'

He looked long and hard at her. 'What may seem unreasonable to you may be the last straw of hope to a dying woman or man or child. Maybe to them, even two months . . . two days . . . two hours longer sounds good. Admittedly, the odds frighten me too. But what choice do we have? Right now, that's the best we've got.' She nodded and followed him into the hall, thinking of Pattie Lou, and she watched him as he began to read through his patients' charts, face intent, brows knit, asking questions, looking at the results of tests. Again and again, Melanie heard the names of the drugs given to heart-transplant patients to allay rejection of the new heart. And she began to make a few notes herself, of questions she wanted to ask him when he had time, about the risks of these drugs, their effects on the patients' personalities and minds.

Suddenly she saw Peter Hallam get up, and walk quickly down the hall. She followed him a few steps, and then stopped, unsure of whether or not he wanted her with him, and as though sensing her indecision, he suddenly turned to her with a wave.

'Come on.' He waved to a stack of white coats on a narrow stainless steel cart and indicated to her to grab one, which she did on the run, and caught up with him as she struggled to put it on. He had his arms full of charts, two residents and a nurse were following respectfully behind. Peter Hallam's day had begun. He smiled once at Mel and pushed open the first door, which revealed an elderly man. He had had a quadruple bypass two weeks before and said that he felt like a boy again. He didn't look much like a boy, he still looked tired and pale and a little wan, but after they left his room, Peter assured her that he was

48

going to be fine. They moved on to the next room, where suddenly Melanie felt a tug at her heart. She found herself staring down into the face of a little boy. He had a congenital heart and lung disease, and nothing surgical had been done for him yet. He wheezed horribly and was the size of a five- or six-year-old child, but a glance at his chart told Mel that he was ten. They had been contemplating a heart-lung transplant on him, but thus far, there had been so few done that they felt it was too soon to attempt it on such a young child, and intermediary measures were being taken to keep him alive. Melanie watched as Peter sat down in a chair next to his bed and talked at great length to him. More than once, Melanie had to fight back tears, and she turned so the boy wouldn't see her damp eyes. Peter touched her shoulder again as they left the room, this time in comfort.

They moved on to a man who had been given a plastic heart, which Melanie learned was powered by air. The patient was suffering from a massive infection, which apparently was often a problem. And then there was another patient, comatose, and after speaking briefly to the nurse, Peter didn't linger in the room. There were two moon-faced men who had undergone heart transplants within the year, and Melanie already knew from the material she'd read that often the steroids they took had that side effect, but eventually it would be controlled. Suddenly these people came alive to her. And what was even more real to her now was how poor the odds were. Peter answered some of her questions now, as they sat in his cubicle again. And as she looked at her watch, she was amazed to discover that it was almost noon. They had been doing rounds for four hours, had probably been to twenty rooms.

'The odds?' He looked at her over his coffee cup. 'Heart-transplant patients have a sixty-five per cent chance of living for one year after the surgery is performed. That's roughly two chances in three that they'll make it for a year.'

'And longer than that?'

He sighed. He hated these statistics. They were what he fought every day. 'Well, the longest we can give anyone is about a fifty-fifty chance for five years.'

'And after that?' She was making notes now, appalled by the statistics, and sympathetic to the defiance in his voice.

'That's about it right now. We just can't do better than that.' He said it with regret, and simultaneously they both thought of Pattie Lou, willing her better odds than that. She had a right to so much more. They all did. One almost wanted to ask what was the point except that if it were one's own life, or one's child, wouldn't one take any chance at all, for a day, or a week, or even a year?

'Why do they die so soon?' Mel looked grim.

'Rejection mostly, in whatever form. Either a straight across-the-board rejection, or they get hardening of the arteries, which will lead to a heart attack. A transplant will kind of steps things up. And then the other big problem we face is infection, they're more prone to that.'

'And there's nothing you can do?' As though it all depended on him. She was casting him in the role of God, just as some of his patients did. And they both knew it wasn't fair, but it all seemed to be in his hands, even if it was not. In a way, she wanted it to be. It would have been simpler like that. He was a decent man, he'd make things all right . . . if he could.

'There's nothing we can do right now. Although some of the new drugs may change that. We've been using some new ones lately that may help. The thing you have to remember,' he spoke gently to her, almost as though she were a child, 'is that these people would have no chance at all without a new heart. So whatever they get is a gift. They understand that. They'll try anything, if they want to live.'

'What does that mean?'

'Some don't. They just don't want to go through all this.' He waved at the charts and leaned back in his chair, holding his coffee cup. 'It takes a lot of guts, you know.' But she realised something else now. It took a lot of guts for him too. He was a matador of sorts, going into the ring with a bull named Death, trying to steal men and women and children from him. She wondered how often he'd been gored by dashed hopes, by patients who had died whom he cared about. Somehow one sensed about him that he was a man who really cared. As though he heard her thoughts, his voice suddenly grew soft. 'My wife decided not to take the chance.' He lowered his eyes as Mel watched, feeling suddenly rooted to her chair. What had he said? His wife? And then he looked up, sensing her shock, and his eyes looked straight into Mel's. They weren't damp, but she saw a grief there that explained something to her about him. 'She had primary pulmonary hypertension, I don't know if that means anything to you or not. It damages the lungs, and eventually the heart, and it requires a heart-lung transplant, but at the time there had only been two done anywhere in the world, and neither of them here. I wouldn't have done it myself of course' – he sighed and leaned forward again in his chair – 'she would have been operated on by one of my colleagues and the rest of the team, or we could have taken her to any of the great men around the world and she very quietly said no. She wanted to die as she was, and not put herself, or me, or the children through the agonies she knew my patients go through, only to die anyway in six months, or a year, or two years. She faced it all with terrifying calm' – and now Mel saw that his eyes were damp, – 'I've never known anyone like her. She was perfectly calm about it, right up until the end.' His voice cracked and then he went on, 'It was a year and a half ago. She was forty-two.'

He looked deep into Mel's eyes then, unafraid of what he felt, and the silence was deafening in the tiny room. 'Maybe we could have changed all that. But not for long.' He sounded more professional now. 'I've done two heart-lungs myself in the last year. For obvious reasons, I have particularly strong feelings about that. There's no reason

51

why it can't work, and it will.' It was too late for his wife. But in his heart he would never give up the fight, as though he could still convince her to let him try. Mel watched him with a pain in her soul for what he'd been through, and the helplessness he felt which still showed in his eyes.

Her voice was very soft when she spoke. 'How many children do you have?'

'Three. Mark is seventeen, Pam will be fourteen in June, and Matthew is six.' Peter Hallam smiled then as he thought of his children and looked at Mel. 'They're all great kids, but Matthew is the funniest little kid.' And then he sighed and stood up. 'It's been hardest on him, but it's hard on all of them. Pam is at an age when she really needs Anne, and I can only give her so much. I try to get home early every day, but some crisis or other always comes up. It's damn hard to give them everything they need when you're alone.'

'I know.' She spoke softly. 'I have that problem too.'

He turned and looked at Mel, seeming not to have heard what she said. 'She could at least have given us a chance.'

Mel's voice was soft. 'And she'd most likely still be gone now. It must be very hard to accept.'

He nodded slowly, looking sorrowfully at Mel. 'It is,' and then as though suddenly shocked at all he had said he picked the charts up in his arms, as though to put something between them again. 'I'm sorry. I don't know why I told you all that.' But Melanie wasn't surprised, people often opened their hearts to her, it had just happened a little more quickly this time. He tried to brush it off with a smile. 'Why don't we go down the hall and visit Pattie now.' Mel nodded, still deeply moved by all he'd said. It was difficult to find the right words to say to him now, and it was almost a relief to see the child she'd brought out from New York. Pattie Lou was obviously thrilled to see both of them, and it reminded Mel of why she was there. They spent a comfortable half hour chatting with the child and as Peter read the results of her tests, he seemed pleased. He turned to her at last with a fatherly look in his eyes.

'Tomorrow is our big day, you know.'

'Is it?' Her eyes grew wide, she seemed at the same time both excited and unsure.

'We're going to work on your old heart, Pattie, and make it as good as new.'

'Can I play baseball then?' Mel and Peter both smiled at the request.

'Is that what you want to do?'

'Yes, sir!' She beamed.

'We'll see.' He explained the procedures of the following day to her, carefully, in terms she could understand, and although she seemed apprehensive, she was obviously not desperately afraid. It was easy to see that she already liked Peter Hallam, and she was sorry when they both left her room. Peter glanced at his watch, as they left. It was after one thirty.

'How about some lunch? You must be starved.'

'Getting there,' she smiled. 'But I've been too engrossed to think of food.'

He looked pleased. 'Me too.' And then he led her outside and it was suddenly a relief to be out in the fresh air. Peter suggested a quick lunch, and Mel agreed, as they strode in the direction of his car.

'Do you always work this hard?' she asked him and he looked amused.

'Most of the time. You don't get much time off from something like this. You can't afford to turn your back on it even for a day.'

'What about your team? Can't you share the responsibility of all this?' Otherwise the burden would be too much to bear.

'Of course we do.' But something about the way he said it made her doubt his words. One had the feeling that he took most of the responsibility on himself, and that he liked it like that.

'How do your children feel about your work?'

He seemed to think for a moment before he spoke. 'You know, I'm not really sure. Mark wants to go into law, and Pam changes her thoughts on the subject every day, especially now, and of course Matthew is too little to have any idea what he wants to be when he grows up, other than being a plumber, which he decided last year.' And then Peter Hallam laughed. 'I suppose that's what I am, isn't it?' He grinned at Mel. 'A plumber.' They both laughed in the warm spring air. The sun shone down on them both, and Melanie noticed that he looked younger here. Suddenly, she could almost imagine him with his children.

'Where shall we go to lunch?' He smiled down at her from his great height, obviously comfortable in his kingdom, but it wasn't just that. There was something more. There was a new bond of friendship between them now. He had bared his soul to her, and told her about Anne. And as a result, he felt suddenly freer than he had in a long time. He almost wanted to celebrate the lightness he felt in his heart, and Mel sensed his mood as she smiled at him. It was remarkable to think that he dealt in life and death, and she had come to Los Angeles to deliver a desperately sick child to him. And yet, in the midst of it all, they were still alive, still young, and slowly coming to be friends. And not so slowly at that. Something about him reminded her of the instant openness she had felt when she met Grant, and yet she realised that she felt something more for this man. He was potentially enormously attractive to her, his strength, his gentleness, his vulnerability, his openness, his modesty coupled with his enormous success. He was an unusual man, and as he watched her, Peter Hallam was thinking many of the same things about her. He was glad he had asked her out to lunch. They had earned the break. They were both people who worked hard and paid their dues, and it didn't seem out of place to take a little time together now. Mel told herself that it would help the interview.

'Do you know LA well?' he asked.

'Not very. I always come here to work and dash from

one place to the next until I leave. I never have much time for relaxed meals.' He smiled, neither did he, but today it felt right. He also felt as though he had made a new friend. And she smiled up at him now. 'I suspect you don't usually go out to lunch, do you?'

He grinned. 'Once in a while. Usually, I eat here.' He waved at the hospital behind them, and stopped at his car. It was a large, roomy silver-grey Mercedes sedan, which surprised her. The car didn't really look like him, and he read her thoughts.

'I gave this to Anne two years ago.' He said it quietly, but there was less pain in his voice this time. 'Most of the time I drive my own car, a little BMW, but it's in the garage. And I leave the station wagon at home for my housekeeper and Mark to drive.'

'Do you have someone good with your kids?' They were just two people now as they drove in the direction of Wilshire Boulevard.

'Terrific.' He looked over at Mel briefly with a smile as he drove. 'I'd really be lost without her. She's a German woman we've had since Pam was born. Anne took care of Mark herself, but when Pam was born she was already having cardiac problems and we hired this woman to take care of the baby. She was to stay for six months' – he smiled at Mel again – 'and that was fourteen years ago. She's a godsend for us now' – he hesitated only slightly – 'with Anne gone.' He was getting used to words like that now.

And Mel was quick to pick up the conversational ball and keep it rolling. 'I have a wonderful Central American woman to help me with my girls.'

'How old are they?'

'Almost sixteen. In July.'

'Both of them?' He looked surprised and this time Mel laughed.

'Yes. They're twins.'

'Identical?' He smiled at the idea.

'No, fraternal. One is a svelte redhead, whom people say looks like me, but I'm not sure she does. And the other

55

one I know doesn't look like me at all, she's a voluptuous blonde who gives me heart failure every time she goes out.' She smiled and Peter laughed.

'I've come to the conclusion, in the last two years, that it's easier to have sons.' His smile faded as he thought of Pam. 'My daughter was twelve and a half when Anne died. I think that the loss compounded with the onset of puberty has been almost too much for her.' He sighed. 'I don't suppose adolescence is easy for any child, but Mark was so easy at her age. Of course he had us both.'

'That makes a difference, I guess.' There was a long pause as he searched her eyes.

'You're alone with the twins?' She had said something about that, hadn't she?

Mel nodded now. 'I've been alone with them since they were born.'

'Their father died?' He looked as though he hurt for her. He was that kind of man.

'No.' Mel's voice was calm. 'He walked out on me. He said he never wanted kids, and that's exactly what he meant. As soon as I told him I was pregnant, that was it. He never even saw the twins.'

Peter Hallam looked shocked. He couldn't imagine anyone doing a thing like that. 'How awful for you, Mel. And you must have been very young.'

She nodded with a small smile. It didn't really hurt any more. It was all a dim memory now. A simple fact of her life. 'I was nineteen.'

'My God, how did you manage alone? Did your parents help you out?'

'For a while. I dropped out of Barnard when the girls were born, and eventually I got a job, a whole bunch of jobs' – she smiled – 'and eventually I wound up as a receptionist for a television network in New York, and a typist in the newsroom after that, and the rest is history, I guess.' She looked back on it now with ease, but he sensed what a gruelling climb it had been, and the beauty of it was that it hadn't burned her out. She wasn't bitter or hard, she was quietly realistic about the past, and she had made it in the end. She was at the top of the heap, and she didn't resent the climb.

'You make it sound awfully simple now, but it must have been a nightmare at times.'

'I guess it was.' She sighed, and watched the city slide by. 'It's actually hard to remember it now. It's funny, when you're going through it, there are times when you think you won't survive, but somehow you do, and looking back it never seems quite so hard.' He wondered, as he listened, if one day he would feel that way about losing Anne, but he doubted that now.

'You know, one of the hardest things for me, Mel, is knowing that I'll never be both a mother and a father to my kids. And they need both, especially Pam.'

'You can't expect that much of yourself. You're only you, and you give the best you have to give. More than that you can't do.'

'I guess not.' But he didn't sound convinced. And he glanced over at her again. 'You've never thought of remarrying for the sake of the girls?' It was different for her, he told himself, she didn't have the memory of someone she had loved to overcome, or perhaps she had loved him but there was anger she could hang on to and in that way she was far freer than he, and for her, also, it had been a much longer time.

'I don't think marriage is for me. And I think the girls understand that now. They used to bug me about it a lot, when they were younger. And yeah, there were times when I felt guilty too. But we were better off alone than with the wrong man, and the funny thing is' – she smiled sheepishly at him – 'sometimes I even think I like it better like this. I'm not sure how I'd adjust to someone sharing the girls with me now. Maybe that's an awful thing to admit, but sometimes that's what I feel. I've got very possessive about them I guess.'

'That's understandable if you've been alone with them for all this time.'

He sat back against his seat and looked at her.

'Maybe. Jessica and Val are the best things in my life. They're a couple of terrific kids.' She was all mother hen as they exchanged a smile and he got out of the car to open her door. She slid off the seat and looked up at him with a smile. They were in posh Beverly Hills, only two blocks from the illustrious Rodeo Drive. And Melanie looked around. The Bistro Gardens was a beautiful restaurant that seemed to combine art deco and a riot of plants leading to the patio outside, and everywhere she looked were the chic and the rich and the fashionably dressed. Lunch was still in full swing. She saw faces she knew at several tables, movie stars, an ageing television queen, a literary giant who made the bestseller lists every time, and then suddenly as she looked around, she noticed that people were looking at her, she saw two women whisper something to a third, and when the headwaiter approached Peter with a smile, his eyes took in Melanie too.

'Hello, Doctor. Hello, Miss Adams, it's nice to see you again.' She couldn't remember ever seeing him before, but it was obvious that he knew who she was and wanted her to know. She was amused as she followed him to a table beneath an umbrella outside and Peter looked at her with a questioning glance.

'Do people recognise you all the time?'

'Not always. It depends on where I am. I suppose that in a place like this they do. It's their stock in trade.' She glanced at the well-filled tables all around, the Bistro Gardens catered to the moneyed, the chic, the celebrated, the successful, a host of important names. And then she smiled at Peter again. 'It's like being around Dr Hallam at the hospital where everyone was staring at you. It depends on where you are.'

'I suppose.' But he had never noticed people staring at him. He could see a number of people watching Melanie now, and she handled it very well. She didn't seem aware of the curious stares at all.

'This is a wonderful place.' She breathed a sigh in the

balmy air, and turned so that she would get the sunshine on her face. It really felt like summer here, and one didn't have the feeling of being trapped in a city, which could happen in New York. She closed her eyes, enjoying the sun. 'This is just right.' And then she opened them again. 'Thank you for bringing me here.'

He sat back in his seat with a smile. 'I didn't think the cafeteria was quite your style.'

'It could be, you know. Most of the time, it is. But that's what makes something like this such a treat. When I'm working I don't have much time to eat, or to bother with the niceties of a delightful place like this.'

'Neither do I.'

They exchanged a grin, and Melanie raised an eyebrow with a smile. 'Do you suppose we both work too hard, Doctor?'

'I suspect we do. But I also suspect we both love what we do. That helps.'

'It sure does.' She looked peaceful as she looked at him, and he felt more comfortable than he had in almost two years.

As she watched him, she realised again that she admired his style. 'Will you go back to the hospital again today?'

'Of course. I want to do some more tests on Pattie Lou.' Mel frowned at his words, thinking of the child.

'Is it going to be very rough for her?'

'We'll make it as easy as we can. Surgery is really her only chance.'

'And you're still going to take her old heart out, repair it and put it back?'

'I think so. We haven't had any suitable donors for her in weeks, we may not in months. There are few enough donors for the adults, for whom it's easier to find matches. On the average we do twenty-five to thirty transplants a year. As you saw from our rounds today, most of what we do is bypass surgery. The rest is very special work and we don't do very much of it, although of course that's all you hear about in the press.'

Mel looked puzzled and took a sip of the white wine the waiter had brought. She found that she was growing fascinated by his work, and regardless of the story she was here to do, she wanted to learn more. 'Why are you using a pig valve?'

'We don't need blood thinners with animal valves. And in her case, that's a real plus. We use animal valves all the time and they don't reject.'

'Could you use the whole animal heart?' He was quick to shake his head.

'Not a chance. It would reject instantly. The human body is a strange and beautiful thing.'

She nodded, thinking of the little black girl. 'I hope you can fix her up.'

'So do I. We've got three others waiting for donors right now too.'

'How do you determine which one gets the first chance?'

'Whoever is the best match. We try to come within thirty pounds from donor to recipient. You can't put the heart of a ninety-pound girl in a two-hundred-pound man, or vice versa. In the first case, it wouldn't support the man's weight, and in the second, it wouldn't fit.'

She shook her head, more than a little in awe at what he did. 'It's an amazing thing you do, my friend.'

'It still amazes me too. Not so much my part in it, but the miracle and mechanics of it all. I love my work, I guess that helps.' She looked carefully at him for a moment, and then glanced around the glamorous crowd at the restaurant and back at him. He was wearing a navy blue linen blazer over his light blue shirt, and she decided he had a casual but distinguished air.

'It feels good to like what you do, doesn't it?' He smiled at her words. Obviously her own work made her feel that way. And then Melanie suddenly found herself thinking about Anne.

'Did your wife work?'

'No.' He shook his head, remembering back to the

constant support she'd given him. She was a very different breed of woman from Mel, but he had needed her to be that way at the time.

'No, she didn't. She stayed home and took care of the kids. It made it even harder on them when she died.' But he was curious about Mel now.

'Do you think your daughters resent your work, Mel?'

'I hope not.' She tried to be honest with him. 'Maybe once in a while, but I think they like what I do.' She grinned and looked like a young girl. 'It probably impresses their friends, and they like that.' He smiled too. It even impressed him.

'Wait till my kids hear I had lunch with you.' They both laughed and he paid for their lunch when the bill came. They stood up regretfully, sorry to leave, and to end the comfortable exchange. She stretched as they got in the car.

'I feel so lazy.' She smiled happily at him. 'It feels like summer here.' It was only May, but she would have enjoyed lounging at the pool.

And as he started the car, his own mind drifted ahead. 'We're going to Aspen, as usual this year. What do you do in the summer, Mel?'

'We go to Martha's Vineyard every year.'

'What's that like?'

She squinted her eyes, with her chin in her hand. 'It's a little bit like being a little kid, or playing Huckleberry Finn. You run around in shorts and bare feet all day, the kids hang out at the beach, and the houses look like the kind of place where you'd visit your grandmother, or a great-aunt. I love it because I don't have to impress anyone if I don't want to, I can just lie around and hang out. We go there for two months every year.'

'Can you leave your work for that long?' He seemed surprised.

'It's in my contract now. It used to be one month, but for the last three years it's been two.'

'Not bad. Maybe that's what I need.'

'Two months at the Vineyard?' She looked enchanted at

the idea. 'You would adore it, Peter! It's an absolutely wonderful, magical place.'

He smiled at the look on her face, and suddenly noticed the texture of her hair. It shone like satin in the sun and he suddenly wondered to himself how it felt to the touch. 'I meant a contract for my work.' He tried to pull his mind and his eyes away from her shimmering copper hair. And her eyes were of a green he had never seen before, almost emerald with gold flecks. She was a beautiful woman, and he felt something deep within him stir. He drove her back to the hospital then, and tried to keep the conversation centred on Pattie Lou. They had come close enough in the past few hours, almost too close, and it worried him. He was beginning to feel as though he had betrayed Anne by what he felt for Mel. And as they walked back into the hospital, Mel wondered why he was suddenly cool.

CHAPTER 5

The next morning, Mel left her hotel at exactly six thirty, and drove to Center City, where she found Pattie Lou's mother seated in a vinyl chair in the corridor outside her daughter's room. She was tense and silent, as Mel slipped quietly into the seat beside her. The surgery was scheduled for seven thirty.

'Can I get you a cup of coffee, Pearl?'

'No, thanks.' The soft-spoken woman smiled at Mel, and she looked as though she had the weight of the world on her frail shoulders. 'I want to thank you for everything you've done for us, Mel. We wouldn't even be here if it weren't for you.'

'That's not my doing, that's the network.'

'I'm not so sure of that.' Her eyes met Mel's. 'From what I know, you called Peter Hallam for us, and you got us out here.'

'I just hope he can help her, Pearl.'

'So do I.' The black woman's eyes filled with tears, and she turned away, as Mel gently touched her shoulder.

'Is there anything I can do?' Pearl Jones only shook her head in answer, and dried her eyes. She had already seen Pattie Lou that morning, and now they were prepping her for surgery. It was only ten minutes later when Peter Hallam came down the hall, looking businesslike and wide awake despite the early hour.

'Good morning, Mrs Jones, Mel.' He said nothing more, but disappeared inside Pattie Lou's room. A moment later they heard a soft wail from within and Pearl Jones stiffened visibly in her chair, and spoke almost to herself.

'They said I couldn't go in there while they prep her.' Her hands were shaking and she began to twist a hankie, as Mel firmly took one of her hands in hers.

'She's going to be fine, Pearl. Just hang in there.' Just as she said the words, the nurses wheeled the child out on a stretcher, with Peter Hallam walking beside her. They had already begun the intravenous, and inserted the ominous-looking nose and gastric tube. Pearl steeled herself as she walked quickly to her daughter's side and bent to kiss her. Her eyes were bright with tears, but she spoke in a strong, calm voice to her daughter.

'I love you, baby. I'll see you in a little while.' Peter Hallam smiled at them both and patted Pearl's shoulder, glancing quickly at Mel. For an instant, something rapid and electric passed between them, and then he turned his full attention back to Pattie. She was faintly groggy from the shot they had just given her, and she looked wanly at Peter, Mel, and her mother. Hallam signalled to the nurses, and the stretcher began to roll slowly down the hall, with Peter holding Pattie's hand, and Mel and Pearl walking just behind him. A moment later she was wheeled into the lift to the surgery on the floor above, and Pearl stood staring blankly at the doors, and then turned to Mel, her shoulders shaking. 'Oh, my God.' And then the two women clung to each other for a long moment, and returned to their seats to wait for the news of Pattie.

It was a seemingly endless morning, with silence, spurts of conversation, countless cardboard cups of black coffee, long walks down the corridor, and waiting, waiting . . . endless waiting . . . until finally Peter Hallam reappeared, and as Mel held her breath, she searched his eyes, as the woman beside her froze in her seat, waiting for the news. But he was smiling as he came towards them, and as he reached Pattie Lou's mother, he beamed.

'The operation went beautifully, Mrs Jones. And Pattie Lou is doing just fine.' She began to tremble again, and suddenly slipped into his arms as she burst into tears.

'Oh my God . . . my baby . . . my God . . .'

'It really went very well.'

'You don't think she'll reject the valve you put in?' She looked worriedly up at him.

Peter Hallam smiled. 'Valves don't reject, Mrs Jones, and the repair work went very well indeed. It's too soon to be absolutely sure of course, but right now everything looks very good.' Mel's knees felt weak as she watched them both, and she fell limply into a chair. They had waited for four and a half hours – the longest in her life. She had really come to care about the little girl. She smiled up at Peter then, and he met her eyes. He seemed ebullient and jubilant as he took a seat beside her.

'I wish you could have watched.'

'So do I.' But he had forbidden her to, and he had been adamant about not wanting a camera crew there.

'Maybe another time, Mel.' He was slowly opening all his private doors to her. 'What about doing our interview this afternoon?' He had promised to do it after the surgery on Pattie Lou, but he hadn't said how soon.

'I'll line up the crew.' And then she looked suddenly concerned. 'But are you sure that's not too much for you?'

He grinned. 'Hell, no.' He looked like a boy who had just won a football game. It made up for all the other times. And Mel just hoped that Pattie Lou didn't begin to fade and dash all their hopes again. Her mother had just gone to call her husband in New York, and Mel and Peter were left alone. 'Mel, it really went very well.'

'I'm so glad.'

'So am I.' He glanced at his watch then. 'I'd better do rounds, then I'll call my office, but I could be free for you by three. How would that be for the interview?'

'I'll see how fast the camera crew can be here.' They had been waiting in the wings for two days, and she was pretty sure it could all be arranged. 'I don't think it'll be a problem though. Where do you want to do it?'

He thought for a minute. 'My office?'

'That sounds fine. They'll probably come at two and start to set up.'

'How long do you think it'll take?'

'As long as you can spare. Does two hours sound like too much?'

'That's fine.'

She thought of something else then. 'What about Pattie Lou? Any chance we can get a few minutes on her today?'

He frowned and then shook his head. 'I don't think so, Mel. Maybe a couple of minutes tomorrow though, if she does as well as I think she will. The crew will have to wear sterile gowns, and it'll have to be short.'

'That's fine.' Mel jotted down a few quick notes on a pad she always kept in her bag. She would get an interview with Pearl Jones that afternoon, then Peter, then Pattie Lou the following morning, and the camera crew could shoot some more general footage the following day, and that would wrap it up. She could catch the 'red-eye' flight to New York the following night. End of story. And maybe in a month or so, they could do a more lengthy interview with Pattie Lou, as a follow-up, about how she had felt, how she was doing by then. It was premature to think of that. The crux of the story could be done now, and it was going to be powerful stuff to show on the evening news. She looked up at Peter then. 'I'd like to do a special on you one day.'

He smiled benevolently, still basking in their success with the child. 'Maybe one day that could be arranged. I've never gone in for that kind of thing much.'

'I think it's important for people to know what transplants and heart surgery are all about.'

'So do I. But it has to be done in the right way, at the right time.' She nodded in agreement and he patted her hand as he stood up. 'See you in my office around two, Mel.'

'We won't bother you until three. Just tell your secretary where you want us to set up, and we will.'

'Fine.' He hurried to the nurses' station then, picked up some charts, and a moment later he disappeared. Mel sat alone in the hall, thinking back on the long wait they'd all been through and feeling relief sweep over her. She made her way to a bank of pay phones then, and waved at Pearl, crying and laughing in an adjoining phone booth.

She got the camera crew set up for an interview with Pearl at one o'clock. They could do it in a corner of the hospital lobby, so she wouldn't have to be far from Pattie Lou. Mel looked at her watch, and mentally worked it all out. At two o'clock they would go over to the complex where Peter's offices were, and set up for the interview with him. She didn't expect any problem with the interviews, and she began to think about going home to the twins the following night. It had been a good story, and she would have only been gone for three days, though it felt more like three weeks.

She went downstairs to wait for the crew. They arrived promptly and interviewed a deeply grateful and highly emotional Pearl Jones. The interview went very well, sketched out beforehand by Mel as she gobbled a sandwich and gulped a cup of tea. And at two o'clock they moved on, and were ready for Peter promptly at three. The office where he sat for the interview was lined with medical books on two walls, and panelled in a warm rose-coloured wood. He sat behind a massive desk, and spoke earnestly to Mel about the pitfalls of what he did, the dangers, the realistic fears, and the hope they were offering people as well. He was candid about both the risks and the odds, but since the people they did transplants on had no other hope anyway, the risks almost always seemed worthwhile, and the odds were better than none at all.

'And what about the people who choose not to take that chance?' She spoke in a soft voice, hoping that the question wasn't too personal and wouldn't cause him too much pain.

He spoke softly too. 'They die.' There was a moment's pause and he went back to talking specifically about Pattie Lou. He drew diagrams to explain what had to be done, and he seemed very much in command as he described the surgery to both the camera and Mel.

It was five o'clock when they finally stopped, and Peter seemed relieved. It had been a long day for him, and he was tired by the two-hour interview.

'You do that very well, my friend.' She liked the term he used, and smiled as the cameramen turned off the lights. They were pleased with what they'd got too. He presented well, and Mel instinctively knew that they had got exactly what she needed for the extended piece for the news. It was to be done as a fifteen-minute special report, and she was excited now about seeing what they had on tape. Peter Hallam had been both eloquent and remarkably at ease.

'I'd say you're pretty good at that stuff too. You handled it very well.'

'I was afraid I'd get too technical or too involved.' He knit his brows and she shook her head.

'It was just right.' As had been, in its own way, the interview with Pearl. She had cried and laughed, and then soberly explained what the child's life had been like for the past nine years. But if the surgery was as successful as he thought it would be, Peter's prognosis for her was very good. And viewers' hearts would undeniably go out to her as Mel's had, and Peter's too. Sick children were impossible to resist anyway, and Pattie Lou had a magical kind of light to her, perhaps because she had been so sick for so long, or maybe that was just the way she was. And over the past nine years, a great deal of love had been lavished on her.

Peter watched Mel as she instructed the crew, and there was frank admiration in his eyes, much as there had been in hers whenever she watched him. But his train of thought was interrupted as one of his nurses came in. She spoke to him in a low voice, and he immediately frowned, just as Mel turned, and she felt her heart sink. She couldn't stop herself from walking toward them and asking if something had happened to Pattie Lou.

But Peter was quick to shake his head. 'No, she's fine. One of my associates saw her an hour ago, this is something else. Another transplant case just came in. A red hot. She needs a donor now, and we don't have anything for her.' He was instantly enveloped by the new

68

problem to solve. He glanced quickly at Mel. 'I have to go.' And then, on impulse he turned to Mel. 'Do you want to come?'

'To see the patient with you?' She was pleased that he would ask, and he was quick to nod.

'Sure. Just don't explain who you are. I can always explain you as visiting medical personnel from a hospital in the East.' He smiled briefly. 'Unless they recognise you. I just don't want the family to get upset, or think that I'm exploiting the case.' It was one of the reasons why he had always been gun-shy about publicity.

'Sure. That's fine.' She grabbed her handbag, said a few words to the crew, and hurried out to his car with him. And moments later, they were back at Center City, on the sixth floor, hurrying down the hall to the new patient's room.

As Peter opened the door for Mel, she was startled at what she saw. A remarkably beautiful twenty-nine-year-old girl.

She had pale, pale blonde hair and huge sad eyes, the most delicate milky blue-white skin that Melanie had ever seen, and she seemed to take in each one of them as they were introduced, as though she had to remember each face, each pair of eyes. And then she smiled, and suddenly she seemed younger than she was, and Melanie's heart went out to her. What was this lovely girl doing in this terrifying place? She already had a thick bandage on one arm, covering where they had had to cut down to reach her veins to take extensive amounts of blood, and the other arm was black and blue from an intravenous she had received only a few days before. And yet somehow one forgot about all that as one listened to her speak. She had a soft lilting voice, and it was obviously hard to breathe, yet she seemed happy to see them all, said something funny to Mel when they were introduced, and she bantered easily with Peter as they all stood around. Melanie suddenly found herself praying for a heart for her. How could all these people be in such desperate need, and what was wrong with the world to strike all these people down, dying slowly with their weak hearts, while others dug ditches, climbed mountains, went dancing, skied? Why had they been so cheated, and while still so young. It didn't seem fair. And yet there was no resentment in the girl's face. Her name was Marie Dupret, and she explained that her parents had been French.

Peter smiled. 'It's a beautiful name.' But more than that, she was a beautiful girl.

'Thank you, Dr Hallam.'

And on those words, Mel noticed that she had a slight Southern drawl, and a moment later Marie mentioned that she had grown up in New Orleans, but she had been in LA now for almost five years. 'I'd like to go back to N'Orleans someday' – the way she said the words delighted the ear as she smiled up at Peter again – 'after the good doctor here patches me up.' And then she looked searchingly at him as her smile faded and one began to glimpse her worry and pain. 'How long do you think that will be?' It was a question no one had an answer to, save God, as they all knew, including Marie.

'We hope soon.' Just the tone of his voice was reassuring, and he went on to reassure her about other things, and to explain to her about what they would be doing to her that day. She didn't seem frightened about the endless tests, but she kept wanting to come back to the big questions again, her enormous blue eyes turned up to him in a pleading way, like a prisoner on death row, seeking a pardon for a crime she did not commit. 'You're going to be very busy for the next few days, Marie.' He smiled again and patted her arm. 'I'll stop in again to see you tomorrow morning, Marie, and if there's anything else that comes to mind, you can ask me then.' She thanked him, and he and Mel left the room, but once again Melanie was struck with the enormity of each circumstance, the terrors that each one faced, alone, in the end. She wondered who Marie would have to hold her hand, and she somehow sensed that the young woman was alone in life. If not, wouldn't

70

her husband or her family have been there? In other rooms there was evidence of spouses or at least friends, but not here, which was why she seemed so much more dependent on Peter than the others had, or perhaps it was because she was new. But as they walked slowly down the hall, somehow Melanie felt as though they were abandoning her. And Mel looked sadly up at Peter as they went downstairs.

'What'll happen to her.?'

'We have to find a donor. And soon.' He seemed preoccupied as well as concerned, and then he remembered Mel. 'I'm glad you came along.'

'So am I. She seems like a nice girl.' He nodded, to him they all were, the men, the women, the children. And they were all so desperately dependent on him. It would have frightened him if he had dwelled on it too much. But he seldom did. He just did what he could for them. Although sometimes there was damn little he could do. Mel had wondered for days how he bore the burden of it. With so many lives with so little hope in his hands, and yet there was nothing dismal about the man. He seemed almost a vehicle of hope himself, and once again Melanie was aware of how much she admired him.

'It's been quite a day, hasn't it, Mel?' He smiled at her as they walked outside, still side by side.

'I don't know how you do this every day. I'd be dead in two years. No' – she smiled up at him – 'make that two weeks. My God, Peter, the responsibility, the strain. You go from operating room to sickbed to office and back again, and these aren't just people with bunions, each one is a matter of life and death . . .' She thought of Marie Dupret again. '. . . like that girl.'

'That's what makes it worthwhile. When you win.' They both thought simultaneously of Pattie Lou, the last report of the day had still been good.

'Yeah, but it's incredibly rough on you. And on top of everything else, you gave me a two-hour interview.'

'I enjoyed that.' He smiled, but his mind was still half

71

engaged with Marie. He had checked the charts, and his colleagues had her well in hand. The main issue was whether or not they would find a donor in time, and there was nothing he could do about that, except pray. Mel found herself thinking of that too.

'Do you think you'll find a donor for Marie?'

'I don't know the answer to that. I hope we do. She doesn't have much time to spare.' None of them did. And that was the worst of it. They sat waiting for someone else to die and give them the gift of life, without which they were doomed.

'I hope so too.' She took a deep breath of the spring air and glanced over at her rented car. 'Well' – she stuck out her hand – 'I guess that's it for today. For me anyway. I hope you get some rest after a day like this.'

'I always do when I go home to my kids.'

She laughed openly at that. 'I don't know how you can say that, if they're anything like mine. Invariably, after an absolutely bitching eighteen-hour day, I crawl home, and Val is torn between two boys she absolutely *has* to discuss with me, and Jess has a fifty-page science project I have to read that night. They both talk to me at once, and I explode and feel like a total bitch. That's the hard part of being alone, there's no one else to share the load, no matter how tired you are when you get home.'

He smiled. It had a familiar ring. 'There's some truth to what you say, Mel. At my house, it's mostly Matt and Pam. Mark is pretty independent by now.'

'How old is he?'

'Almost eighteen.' And then he suddenly had an idea. He looked at Melanie with a small smile as they stood in the parking lot. It was six fifteen. 'How about coming home with me now? You could have a quick swim, and eat dinner with us.'

'I couldn't do that.' But she was touched by the thought.

'Why not? It's no fun going back to a hotel room, Mel. Why not come home? We don't eat dinner late, and you could be home by nine o'clock.'

72

She wasn't sure why, but she was tempted by the idea. 'Don't you think your kids would rather have you to themselves?'

'No. I think they'd be very excited to meet you.'

'Don't overestimate that.' But suddenly, the idea really appealed to her. 'You're really not too tired?'

'Not at all. Come on, Mel, it would be fun.'

'It would for me.' She smiled. 'Shall I follow you in my car?'

'Why not just leave it here?'

'Then you'll have to drive me back. Or I could take a cab.'

'I'll drive you. Then I can have another look at Pattie Lou.'

'Don't you ever stop?' She smiled as she slid into his car, pleased to be going home with him.

'Nope. And neither do you.' He looked as pleased as she as they pulled out of the parking lot and headed for Bel-Air.

Melanie leaned back against the seat with a sigh as they drove through the huge black wrought-iron gates leading into Bel-Air.

'It's so pleasant here.' It was like driving around in the country as the road swooped and turned, giving glimpses of secluded but palatial homes.

'That's why I like it here. I don't know how you can stand New York.'

'The excitement makes it all worthwhile.' She grinned.

'Do you really like it, Mel?'

'I love it. I love my house, my job, the city, my friends. I'm sold on the place, and I really don't think I could live anyplace else.' And as she said the words, she suddenly realised that it wouldn't be so bad after all to go home the next day. New York was where she belonged, however much she liked LA and admired him. And when he glanced at her again, he saw that she looked more relaxed, and with that he made one final left turn, into a well-manicured drive, which led to a large, beautiful, French-style house, surrounded by neatly trimmed trees and flower beds. It looked like something on a French post-card and Melanie looked around in surprise. It wasn't at all what she'd expected of him. Somehow she had thought he would live in something more rustic, or a ranch house. But this was actually very elegant, she noticed as he stopped the car.

'It's beautiful, Peter.' She looked up at the mansard roof, and waited to see children but there were none in sight.

'You look surprised.' He laughed.

'No.' She blushed. 'It just doesn't look like you.'

And then he smiled again. 'It wasn't at first. The design was Anne's. We built it just before Matthew was born.'

'It's really a magnificent house, Peter.' It was, and now she was seeing a whole other side of him.

'Well, come on.' He opened his door and looked over his shoulder for one last instant. 'Let's go in, I'll introduce you to the kids. They're probably all around the pool with fourteen friends. Brace yourself.' And with that they both stepped out of the car, and Melanie looked around. It was so totally different from her town house in New York, but it was fun to see how he lived. She followed him inside, with only a slight feeling of trepidation about meeting his children, wondering if they would be terribly different from her twins.

CHAPTER 6

Peter unlocked the front door and stepped into a front hall whose floor was inlaid with black and white marble in a formal French diamond pattern, with crystal sconces on the wall. There was a black marble console table with gold Louis XVI legs and on it was set a magnificent crystal bowl filled with freshly cut flowers that sent a spring fragrance into the air as Melanie looked around. It was somehow so totally different from what she had expected. He seemed so relaxed and so unassuming in his ways, that she had never imagined him in a home furnished in elaborate French antiques. But indeed this was. Not in a vulgar, opulent way, but in an obviously expensive way, and as she glimpsed the living room, she saw that there, too, was more of the same, the fabrics on the delicate fauteuils were mostly cream-coloured brocades. The walls were beautifully done in several shades of cream, with the mouldings in lighter shades and the detailing on the ceiling intricately highlighted in beige and white and a soft creamy grey. There was still a look of surprise on her face as she looked around and Peter led her into his study and invited her to sit down. Here, everything was in deep rich reds, with antique English chairs, a long leather couch, and hunting scenes on the walls, all handsomely framed.

'You look so surprised, Mel.' He was amused and she laughed and shook her head.

'No, I just saw you in something very different from this. But it's a magnificent home.'

'Anne went to the Sorbonne for two years, and then stayed on in France for two years after that. I think it made a permanent impression on her taste.' He looked around, as though seeing her again. 'But I can't complain. The house is less formal upstairs. I'll give you a tour in a

75

little while.' He sat down at his desk, checked the messages on the pad, spun around to face her, and then clapped a hand to his head. 'Damn. I forgot to have you stop at your hotel and pick up a bathing suit.' And then he squinted as he looked at her. 'Maybe Pam can help out. Would you like to swim?' It was amazing. They had spent the whole day at the hospital and in the interview, he had operated on Pattie Lou, and suddenly they were talking about taking a swim, as though they'd done nothing else all day. It was mind boggling, and yet somehow everything seemed normal here. Maybe that was the way he survived it all, she thought.

Peter stood up and led the way outside to an enormous stone patio surrounding a large oval pool, and here Mel felt more at home. There were at least a dozen teenagers and one little boy running around, dripping wet, shrieking at the top of his lungs. Remarkably, she hadn't been aware of the noise before but she was now, and she began to laugh as she watched their antics and the boys showed off, pushing each other in, playing water polo at one end, riding on each other's shoulders and falling in. Several well-endowed young girls watched. Peter stood to one side, getting splashed as he clapped his hands, but no one heard, and suddenly the little boy ran up and threw his arms around Peter's legs, leaving his wet imprint where his arms had been, as Peter looked down at him with a grin.

'Hi, Dad. Come on in.'

'Hi, Matt. Can I change first?'

'Sure.' The two exchanged a warm look that passed only between them. He was an adorable impish-looking child, with fair hair bleached by the sun.

'I'd like to introduce you to a friend of mine.' He turned to Mel, and she approached. The little boy looked just like him, and when he smiled, she saw that he had lost both front teeth. He was the cutest child she had ever seen. 'Matthew, this is my friend, Melanie Adams. Mel, this is Matt.' The child frowned and Peter grinned. 'Excuse me, Matthew Hallam.'

'How do you do.' He proffered a wet hand, and she formally shook his, remembering briefly when the twins were that age. It had been ten years before, but there were times when it seemed only a moment ago.

'Where's your sister, Matt?' Peter looked around. There seemed to be only Mark's friends around the pool, but he had been unable to catch the attention of his eldest son, who was throwing two girls in at once, and then dunking another friend. They were having a grand time as Mel watched.

'She's in her room.' A look of disgust crossed Matthew's face. 'Probably on the phone.'

'On a day like this?' Peter looked surprised. 'Has she been inside all day?'

'Pretty much.' He rolled his eyes then, and looked at both his father and Mel. 'She's so dumb.' He had a rough time with Pam, as Peter knew. At times they all did, but she was going through a difficult stage, particularly in a male family.

'I'll go inside and see what she's up to.' Peter looked down at him. 'You be careful out here, please.'

'I'm okay.'

'Where's Mrs Hahn?'

'She just went inside, but I'm okay, Dad. Honest.' And as though to illustrate the point, he took a running leap into the pool, splashing them both from head to foot. Melanie jumped back with a burst of laughter, and Peter looked at her apologetically as Matthew surfaced again.

'Matthew, will you please not . . .' But the little head disappeared beneath the surface of the pool and he swam like a little fish underwater to where the others were, just as Mark caught sight of them and gave a shout and a wave. He had his father's build, his height and grace and long limbs.

'Hi, Dad!' Peter pointed at his youngest son, swimming towards Mark, and the older boy gave an understanding nod, and caught the child in his arms as he surfaced and said something to him, sending him towards the edge of the game, to where he wouldn't get hurt. Peter decided that all was well, and as they walked back into the house, he turned to Mel.

'Are you soaking wet?' She was, but she didn't mind. It was a relief from the seriousness of the earlier part of the day.

'I'll dry off.'

'Sometimes I'm sorry as hell that I put in that pool. Half the neighbourhood spends their weekends here.'

'It must be great for the kids.'

He nodded. 'It is. But I don't very often get a swim, except when they're in school. I come home for lunch once in a while, when I have time.'

'And when's that?' She was teasing him now. It suddenly felt as though everyone was in a lighthearted mood as he laughed.

'About once a year.'

'That's what I thought.' And then she remembered Matt and the toothless smile. 'I think I'm in love with your little boy.'

'He's a good kid.' Peter looked pleased, and then thought of his older boy. 'So is Mark. He's so responsible, it's frightening sometimes.'

'I have one like that too. Jessica, the oldest twin.'

'Which one's that?' Peter looked intrigued. 'The one that looks like you?'

'How did you remember that?' Mel was surprised.

'I remember everything, Mel. It's important in my field. A little forgotten detail, a hint, a clue. It helps when you're constantly balancing life against death. I can't afford to forget anything.' It was his first open admission to his extraordinary skill, and Mel watched him with interest again as she followed him into the house, into a large sunny room filled with large white wicker chairs, wicker couches, a stereo, an enormous TV, and ten-foot palms that swept the ceiling with their fronds. It looked like a nice room to be in on a sunny day. And here suddenly, Melanie saw half a dozen pictures of Anne scattered around in silver frames, playing tennis, with Peter in a photograph in front of the Louvre, with a tiny baby, and one with all the children in front of the Christmas tree. It was as though all at once everything stopped, and Melanie found herself mesmerised by her face, her blonde hair, her big blue eyes. She was an attractive woman, with a long, lanky athletic frame. And in some ways she and Peter looked alike. In the photographs, she seemed like the perfect mate for him. And Melanie realised suddenly that Peter was standing at her side, looking down at one of the photographs too.

'It's hard to believe she's gone.' His voice was soft.

'It must be.' Melanie wasn't sure what to say. 'But in some ways, she lives on. In your heart, in your mind, through the children she left.' They both knew that wasn't the same thing, but it was all that was left of her. That and this house, which was so much to her taste. Melanie looked around the room again. It was an interesting contrast to the formal living room and study that she had seen when she came in. 'What do you use this room for, Peter?' Melanie was curious. It was so much a woman's room.

'The kids use it to hang around in. Even though it's mostly white, there isn't too much damage they can do in here.' Melanie noticed a wicker desk then, looking out at the pool. 'She used to use this a lot. I spend most of my time at home in my den, or upstairs.' And then he gestured towards the hall. 'Come on, I'll show you around. We'll see if we can find Pam.'

Upstairs everything was formal and French again. The hall floors were done in a pale beige travertine, with matching console tables at either end, and a beautiful French brass chandelier. And here there was another smaller but equally formal sitting room done in soft blues. There were velvets and silks, and a marble fire-place, and wall sconces and a crystal chandelier, pale blue silk curtains with pale yellow and blue trim, tied back with narrow brass arms that allowed one a view of the pool.

Beyond it was a little office done in dusty pinks, but Peter frowned as they passed that room and Melanie instantly sensed that it was unused. Not only that, but that it had been Anne's.

And beyond that was a handsome library done in dark greens. There were walls and walls of books, a small mountain of chaos on the desk, and on one wall an oil portrait of Anne, and double French doors leading into their bedroom, which Peter now slept in alone. It was all done in beige silk, with French commodes, a beautiful chaise longue, and the same rich curtains and sconces and another beautiful chandelier. But there was something about the place that made one want to take off one's clothes and dance around, and defy the formality of it all. It was almost too much, no matter how beautiful it was, and the more Melanie saw, the more she felt that it just didn't look like him.

They took another staircase upstairs then, and on this floor everything was brightly coloured and fun, and the open doors showed three large, sunny children's rooms. The floor of Matt's was littered with toys, Mark's half-closed door showed total chaos within, and the third door was ajar and all Mel could see was a huge white canopied bed, and a girl's back as she lay on her side on the floor near the bed. At the sound of their footsteps in the hall, she turned and stood up, whispering something into the phone and then hung up. Melanie was astonished at how tall and grown up she looked. If this was his middle child, it was difficult to believe that she was just fourteen. She was long and lanky and blonde, with a shaft of wheat-coloured hair like Val's, and big wistful blue eyes. But most of all she looked like the photographs of Anne that Mel had just seen.

'What are you doing inside?' Peter searched her eyes and Mel felt them both grow tense.

'I wanted to call a friend.'

'You could have used the phone at the pool.'

She didn't answer him at first and then she shrugged. 'So?'

He ignored the remark and turned to Mel. 'I'd like you to meet my daughter, Pam. Pam, this is Melanie Adams, the newswoman from New York I told you about.'

'I know who she is.' Pamela didn't extend a hand at first, but Mel did, and she shook it at last. Her father had begun to seethe. He never wanted it to be like this between them, but she always did something to upset him, to be rude to his friends, to make a point of not cooperating when there was no reason for her not to. Why, dammit, *why?* They were all unhappy that Anne had died, but why did she have to take it out on him? She had for the last year and a half, and was even worse now. He told himself that it was the age, a passing phase, but sometimes he wasn't so sure.

'I was wondering if you could lend Mel a bathing suit, Pam. She left hers at the hotel.'

There was a fraction of a moment of hesitation again. 'Sure. I guess I could. She's' – she hesitated on the word, Mel was by no means large, but she wasn't as rail thin as Pam – 'she's bigger than me though.' And there was something else too, a look that had passed between them that Pam didn't like. Or more exactly the way her father looked at Mel.

And Mel quickly understood. She smiled gently at the girl. 'It's all right if you'd rather not.'

'No, that's okay.' Her eyes searched Melanie's face. 'You don't look the same as on TV.' There was no smile in the girl.

'Don't I?' She smiled at the slightly uncomfortable but very attractive young girl. She looked nothing like Peter, and there was still an undefined childishness about her face, despite the long legs and full bust, and body that had already outstripped her chronological age. 'My daughters always say I look more "grown up" on TV.'

'Yeah. Sort of. More serious.'

'I think that's what they mean.'

The three of them stood in the pretty white room, as Pam continued to stare at Melanie, as though looking for

81

an answer to something in her face. 'How old are your daughters?'

'They'll be sixteen in July.'

'Both of them?' Pam was confused.

'They're twins.' Melanie smiled.

'They are? That's neat! Do they look alike?'

'Not at all. They're fraternal twins.'

'I thought that just meant they were boys.'

Mel smiled again and Pam blushed. 'That means they're not identical twins, but it is a confusing term.'

'What are they like?' She was fascinated by Mel's twins.

'Like sixteen-year-old girls.' Mel laughed. 'They keep me on my toes. One's a redhead like me, and the other one is a blonde. Their names are Jessica and Valerie, and they love to go out to dances and they have lots of friends.'

'Where do you live?' Peter was watching the exchange intently but he said nothing at all.

'In New York. In a little town house.' She smiled at Peter then. 'It's very different from this.' And then she turned back to Pam. 'You have a beautiful house, and it must be nice to have a pool.'

'It's okay.' She looked unenthused as she shrugged. 'It's either full of my brother's obnoxious friends, or Matthew's peeing in it.' She sounded annoyed and Mel laughed but Peter was not amused.

'Pam! That's not something to say, and it's not true.'

'It is so. The little brat did it an hour ago, as soon as Mrs Hahn went inside. Right from the edge of the pool too. At least he could do it while he's swimming around.' Mel had to suppress the laughter she felt and Peter blushed.

'I'll say something to Matt.'

'Mark's friends probably do it too.' It was obvious that she didn't enjoy either of the boys. She went to hunt for a suit for Mel, and came back with a white one-piece bathing suit she thought might fit. Mel thanked her and looked around again.

'You really have a lovely room, Pam.'

'My mom did it for me just before . . .' Her words

82

trailed off and there was something desperately sad in her eyes and then she looked at Peter defiantly. 'It's the only room in this house that's all mine.' It seemed an odd thing to say and Mel felt for her. She seemed so unhappy and so much at odds with them all. It was as though she couldn't show them her pain, only the anger she felt instead, as though they were all responsible for taking Anne from her.

'It must be a nice room to share with your friends.' Mel found herself thinking of her own girls, and their friends who sat around on the floor of their rooms, listening to records, talking about boys, laughing and giggling and sharing secrets with each other, which they eventually always shared with Mel. They seemed very different from this awkward, hostile girl, with the body of a woman and the mind of a child. It was obviously a very difficult time for her, and Mel could see that Peter had a lot on his hands. No wonder he tried to come home early every day. With a six-year-old child hungering for love, a teenager of the older boy's age to watch over, and an adolescent girl as unhappy as this one was, the household needed more than just a housekeeper's care, it needed a father and a mother too. She understood now why Peter felt such a desperate need to be there for them all, and why he felt at times that he was inadequate to the task. Not that he was, but they all needed a great deal from him, and even something more than that, at least this child did. Melanie found herself wanting to reach out to her, to hold her close, to tell her that eventually everything would be all right. And as though sensing Mel's thoughts, Pam suddenly stepped back from her.

'Well, I'll see you downstairs in a while.' It was her invitation to them to leave. And Peter walked slowly to the door.

'Are you coming downstairs, Pam?'

'Yeah.' But she didn't sound too sure.

'I don't think you ought to spend the afternoon in your room.' He sounded firm but she looked as though she were inclined to argue with him, and Melanie didn't envy him his role with her. She wasn't an easy child to deal with, at least not at the present time. 'Will you be down soon?'

'Yes!' She looked more belligerent still and Mel and Peter left the room. She followed him back downstairs to his room and he opened a door across the hall from him, to reveal a pretty blue and white guest room.

'You can change in here, Mel.' He didn't say anything to her about Pam, and when she came out again ten minutes later, he looked more relaxed. He led the way back downstairs to the big white wicker garden room. There was a refrigerator concealed behind white lacquered doors and he took out two cans of beer and handed one to her, reached for two glasses from a shelf with one hand and then waved for her to sit down. 'We might as well wait a few more minutes for the kids to wear themselves out.' They were already beginning to leave the pool. Melanie noticed then how good-looking Peter was in his dark blue swimming trunks and a French T-shirt and bare feet. He didn't even look like the same man she had interviewed for the past two days, but rather like someone else. Just an ordinary mortal now. She smiled the thought to herself as he watched her eyes, and then his face sobered as he thought of the child upstairs. 'Pam isn't an easy child. She was while her mother was alive. But now she runs the gamut from being intensely possessive of me to hating us all. She thinks nobody understands what she's going through, and most of the time these days she acts as though she's living in an enemy camp.' He sighed with a tired smile as he sipped his beer. 'It's hard on the boys at times too.'

'I think she probably just needs a lot of love from all of you, especially you.'

'I know. But she blames everything on us. And well . . .' He seemed embarrassed to say what was on his mind. 'Sometimes she makes herself difficult to love. I understand it, but the boys don't. At least not all the time.' It was the first time that he had admitted to Mel what a problem he had with her.

'She'll come round. Give her time.'

Peter sighed again. 'It's been almost two years.' But Melanie didn't dare say what she thought to him. It had been almost two years, and yet Anne's photographs were still everywhere in sight, and Mel sensed nothing in the place had been touched since Anne died, and Peter himself acted as though she had only died that week. How could the child be expected to adjust if he himself had not? He was still reproaching himself for what he hadn't been able to convince Anne to do, as though any of it could be changed now. Mel said nothing, but he didn't avert his eyes when she looked at him. 'I know. You're right. I'm still hanging on too.'

'Maybe when you close the door to the past, she will too.' Mel spoke in a gentle voice, and without thinking, Peter's eyes drifted to the nearest photograph of Anne, and Mel suddenly asked something she had promised herself not to say. 'Why don't you move?'

'From here?' He looked shocked. 'Why?'

'To give everyone a fresh start. It might be a relief to all of you.' But he was quick to shake his head.

'I don't think it would. I think it would be more disruptive than helpful, to be in a new house. At least we're all comfortable and happy here.'

'Are you?' Mel didn't look convinced and she knew that he was hanging on, and so was Pam, and she wondered if the others were too. Just as the thought crossed her mind, a stocky woman in a white uniform entered the room, and looked at them both, particularly Mel. She had a face that was well worn by time, and her hands were gnarled from long years of hard work, and yet her eyes were bright and alive and she seemed to take everything in.

'Good afternoon, Doctor.' She seemed to say 'doctor' as though she were saying 'God', and Mel smiled. She knew instantly who she was, and Peter stood to introduce Mel to her. She was the invaluable housekeeper he had spoken of before, the precious Mrs Hahn, who shook Mel's hand with an almost brutal shake, her eyes combing the pretty redhead in the borrowed white bathing suit she instantly recognised as Pam's. She knew everything that happened in the house, who came, who went, where they went, and why. She was particularly careful about Pam. There had already been enough trouble with her the year of her mother's death, with that business of scarcely eating a mouthful of food for six months, and then making herself throw up after every meal for months after that. But now at least that problem was in control, and she was much better than she had been. But Hilda Hahn knew that the girl had had a hard time, and she needed a woman's eye on her, which was why Mrs Hahn was there. She looked Mel over carefully now, and decided that she looked like a nice woman after all. She knew who she was, and that she was doing a story on the doctor's work, but she had expected her to be somewhat arrogant and she didn't seem to be. 'It's nice to meet you, ma'am.' She was both formal and tight-lipped and did not return Melanie's smile, as Mel almost laughed thinking of the contrast to Raquel. In fact, just about everything was different about their two homes, from their maids to their decor, to their kids, and yet she felt as though she had a great deal in common with him. It was funny how differently they lived. 'Would you care for some iced tea?' She looked disapprovingly at their beers, and Mel felt like a wayward child.

'No, thank you very much.' She smiled again, to no avail, and with a curt nod, Hilda Hahn disappeared to her own domain behind the swinging doors that led to the kitchen and breakfast room, pantry, and her small apartment in the rear. She was extremely comfortable here. When Mrs Hallam had built the house she had promised Hilda her own suite of rooms, and that was what she had now. Mrs Hallam had been a fine woman, she always said, and would say so again, many times, and did later on in plain hearing of Mel, before she brought the diinner in. Melanie had noticed Pam's eyes seem to glaze over as Hilda mentioned her mother's name. It was as though they were all still fighting to recuperate. One almost wanted to put away the pictures for them, pack them up, and move them to another house. They were all still so devoted to her, as though they were waiting for her to come home, and it made you want to tell them that she never would. They had to get on with their lives, every one of them. The two boys seemed better adjusted to their mother's death. Matthew had been so young when she died that his memories of her were already dim, and he climbed willingly into Mel's lap after they had a swim, and she told him about the twins. Like Pam, he was fascinated by the idea of twins and wanted to know what they looked like. Mark seemed like a bright easygoing boy of seventeen; there was a look of greater wisdom in his eyes than his years would suggest, and yet he seemed happy as he chatted with both Peter and Mel. He only got annoyed when Pam arrived and complained that his friends were still hanging around the pool. A fight between them seemed imminent until Peter stepped in.

'All right, you two. We have a guest. Several in fact.' He glanced severely at Pam, and then his eyes took in Mark's remaining friends. There were only two boys and one girl left and they were sitting quietly on the cement nearby chatting and drying their hair. But it was as though Pam resented anyone in her home, except Peter and the boys and Mrs Hahn. She had solved the problem of Mel by almost totally ignoring her since she'd arrived at the pool, except for furtive, curious glances from time to time, mainly when Peter was talking to Mel. It was as though she wanted to be sure there was nothing special going on, but some instinct deep within told her that danger lurked there.

'Isn't that right, Pam?' Peter had been talking about her school, but she had been staring intently at Mel and hadn't heard what he said.

'Huh?'

'I said that the athletics programme there is outstanding, and you won two awards for track events last year. And they have access to some fabulous stables too.' Again, it was very different from the school in which she had her girls, which was very much a sophisticated urban school. The life-style in LA was much more geared to the outdoors than what they had back East.

'Do you like your school, Pam?' Mel gently spoke to her.

'It's okay. I like my friends.'

At that, Mark rolled his eyes, quick to show that he disapproved, and Pam took the bait at once. 'What's that supposed to mean?'

'It means that you hang around with a bunch of dumb uptight, anorexic girls.' It was a word that still made her scream.

'I am not anorexic, damn you!' She jumped to her feet, her voice shrill, and Peter began to look tired.

'Stop it, you two!' And then he addressed Mark. 'That was unnecessarily cruel.'

Mark nodded, subdued. 'I'm sorry.' He knew that the very word was now taboo, but he still wasn't convinced that she was totally cured. She looked unnaturally thin to him, no matter what she and her father said. He looked apologetically at Mel and sauntered off to talk to his friends, and Pam went back into the house, followed by Matthew who was in search of something to eat. For a long moment, Peter sat quietly staring into the pool and then he turned his eyes to Mel.

'Not exactly a peaceful home scene, I guess.' He looked hurt by his children's actions and words, as though he held himself responsible for all their turmoil and pain. 'I'm sorry if it was awkward for you, Mel.'

'Not at all. It isn't always smooth sailing with mine either.' Although she couldn't even remember the last time she'd seen the twins have a fight, but this family still seemed in crisis and Pam seemed like a very unhappy girl.

He sighed and laid his head back against the chair, looking out at the pool. 'I suppose eventually they'll all settle down. Mark will be going away to college next year.' But the problem was not Mark, as they both knew, it was

Pam. And she wasn't going anywhere for a long time. Peter glanced at Mel again then. 'Pam took her mother's death the hardest of all.' That much was easy to see, but Peter had taken it harder still, and still was. And what he needed, she sensed, was a woman to replace Anne, and for him to share his burdens with. He needed it as much for him as for the kids. It hurt to think of him so much alone. He was intelligent and attractive, capable and strong, he had a lot to offer anyone. And as she sat there beside him, she smiled to herself, thinking of Raquel and the girls. She could almost hear them ask: 'What about you, Mom? . . . Was he cute? . . . Why didn't you go out with him? . . .' He didn't ask. And suddenly she wondered if she would go out with him on a date, if she had the chance. It was funny to think about as they sat side by side at the pool. He was totally different from the other men she knew. The men she had chosen before were all ineligible in some subtle way. And she had liked it that way. But Peter was different from all of them. He was open and real, and an equal match for her. And more important than that, he appealed to her a great deal. It would actually have frightened her if she weren't leaving the next day.

'What were you thinking just then?' His voice was soft in the late-afternoon sun, and she pulled her thoughts back to him with a smile.

'Nothing much.' There was no reason to tell him about the men in her life, or even what she thought of him. There was nothing personal between them, and yet there was, some intangible presence that she felt when she was near him. It was almost like an illusion that she knew him better than she really did. But there was something very vulnerable about this man, which she liked. Considering who and what he was, he had remained very human, and now that she saw him here at home, she liked him even more.

'You were a million miles away just then.'

'No, not quite that far. I was thinking of some things in New York . . . my work . . . the girls . . .'

89

'It must be rough having to go away for your work.'

'Sometimes. But they understand. They're used to it by now. And Raquel keeps an eye on them while I'm gone.'

'What's she like?' He was constantly curious about her, and Melanie turned to him with a grin.

'Nothing like Mrs Hahn. In fact, before I was thinking how totally different our lives are, externally at least.'

'How?'

'Our houses for instance. Yours is much more formal than mine.' She laughed then. 'I guess mine is a hen house of sorts. It looks like a woman's house.' She glanced at his home. 'Yours is much larger and more formal than mine. And so is Mrs Hahn. Raquel looks like she has never learned to comb her hair, her uniform is always buttoned wrong, and she talks back all the time. But we love her, and she's wonderful with the girls.' He smiled at her description of Raquel.

'What's your house like?'

'Bright and cheery and small, and just right for me and the girls. I bought it a few years ago, and it scared me to death to take it on at the time, but I've always been glad that I did.' He nodded, thinking of the responsibilities she tackled alone. It was one of the things he admired about her. There was a lot about her he liked. And he was intrigued because she was so different from Anne. And then Melanie smiled at him. 'You'll have to come and see me in New York sometime.'

'Someday.' But he instantly found himself wishing that it would be soon, and he wasn't sure why, except that she was the first person in a long time that he had opened up to. And before he could say anything more, Matthew returned with a plate of fresh cakes, and without a second thought, he plonked himself down beside Mel and offered to share them with her. There were crumbs all over his face and his chubby little hands, and he dropped the rest all over himself and her, but she didn't seem to mind. Little boys were a novelty to her. They got into a serious discussion about his school and his best friend while Peter watched, and then left them to go for a swim. When he returned, they were still deeply engrossed in their talk, and Matthew had climbed into her lap and was nestled against her. He seemed totally happy there.

When Peter climbed out of the pool, he stopped at the top of the ladder for a moment and looked at them with a sad smile. The boy needed someone like her, they all did, and for the first time in almost two years he realised how much had been missing from his life. But as the thought crossed his mind, he pushed it from him, and rejoined them with a quick step, grabbing a towel from a table as he approached and drying his hair, as though to chase the new thoughts he'd had from his head. At that moment Mark's friends left, and he joined Melanie and Matthew, and sat down in Peter's empty chair.

'I hope my friends didn't drive you nuts.' He smiled shyly at her. 'They get a little unruly at times.'

She laughed thinking of Val and Jessie's friends, who came near to destroying her house from time to time, and seemed no less unruly than Mark's friends. 'They seemed fine to me.'

'Tell my dad that.' Mark smiled appreciatively at her, and tried not to notice how sexy she looked in his sister's bathing suit.

'What's that? Taking my name in vain again?'

Mark looked victoriously at him. He liked his father's new friend, and the girls had been tremendously impressed that Melanie Adams was just 'hanging out' at their pool.

'Miss Adams thinks my group's not so bad.'

'She's just being polite. Don't believe a word of it.'

'That's not true. You should see Val's and Jessie's friends. They gave a party once, and someone accidentally set fire to a chair.'

'Oh my God.' Peter cringed and Mark smiled. He liked her. She was so easy and open and natural, not like a TV star at all, and if Mel could have heard his thoughts she would have laughed. She never thought of herself that way, nor did the twins. 'What happened after that?'

'I put the girls on restriction for two months, but I let them off the hook after one.'

'They're lucky you didn't send them to reform school.' Mark and Mel exchanged a conspiratorial grin in the face of Peter's tough stance, and Matthew, indifferent to it all, leaned a little closer to her, so she wouldn't forget him. She gently stroked his hair, and he didn't seem to mind having lost her ear. He knew that in her own way she was still paying attention to him. And at exactly that moment she happened to look up at the house, and saw Pam, standing almost hidden at her bedroom window, looking down at them. Their eyes met and held, and then a moment later Pam disappeared. Melanie wondered why she didn't come back to the pool. It was almost as though she wanted to be left out. Or maybe she wanted Peter to herself, and didn't want to share him with her, or the two boys. She wanted to say something about it to Peter, but she didn't want to interfere. Instead the banter between them rambled on, until a slight breeze came up and they all began to feel the chill. It was after six o'clock by then, and Mel looked at her watch, and realised that she'd have to go soon. It was almost dinnertime and Peter had seen her look at her wrist.

'You haven't swum yet, Mel. Why don't you go in for a minute. And then we'll eat. Mrs Hahn will go berserk if we're late.' It all seemed so mechanised, so perfectly run, and without being told, Mel knew it was all the legacy of Anne, who had run her home like a well-oiled machine. It wasn't Mel's style, but it was impressive to see. And it was part of what had kept them all going after she was gone, even though it would probably have done them all good to change now, if they could. But old habits were hard to break, especially for Peter and Mrs Hahn. A moment later, the children left, and Mel dived neatly into the pool as Peter watched. She was so easy to have around and so good to see. He felt an enormous hunger well up within him again as she glided through the water with expert ease, and at last she returned to the side, her hair wet, her eyes bright, with a happy smile on her face, just for him. 'You were right. This was just what I needed.'

'I'm always right. You needed dinner here too.'

She decided to be honest with him. 'I hope the children don't mind too much.' She had already seen a great deal in Pam's eyes. More than Peter would have wanted to see.

'I don't think they quite know what to make of my being here.'

Their eyes met and held and he approached the pool and sat down, unable to stop what he felt, or had to say. 'Neither do I.' He was stunned by his own words, and Mel suddenly looked scared.

'Peter . . .' She suddenly felt that she should tell him something more about herself, her old scars, her fears of getting too deeply involved with men. And yet they both sensed that there was something strange happening to them.

'I'm sorry. That was a crazy thing to say.'

'I'm not sure it was . . . but . . . Peter . . .' And then, as she looked away from him, searching for her words, she glimpsed Pam at the window again, and an instant later she disappeared. 'I don't want to intrude into your life.' She forced her eyes back to his.

'Why not?'

She took a deep breath and pulled herself out of the pool and he almost gasped as he saw the long, lean limbs and the white suit. This time he looked away, but he felt a wave of emotion wash over him. Her voice was almost too gentle as she spoke again. 'Has there been anyone here since Anne?'

He knew what she meant and shook his head. 'No. Not in that sense.'

'Then why upset everyone now?'

'Who's upset?' Peter looked surprised and Mel decided to be blunt.

'Pam.'

And with that Peter sighed. 'That has nothing to do with you, Mel. The last couple of years have been hard on her.'

'I understand that. But the reality is that I live three

thousand miles away and it's not very likely we'll see each other again for a long time. And what we're doing with the interview about you is exciting for both of us. And funny things happen to people when they go through something like that. It's like being cast adrift on a ship, you grow amazingly close. But tomorrow the interview will be complete and I'm going home.' Her eyes were almost sad as she said the words.

'So what harm will one dinner do?'

She sat pensively beside him for a long time. 'I don't know. I just don't want to do anything that doesn't make sense.' She looked into his eyes again and saw that he looked sad too. It was crazy. They liked each other, but what was the point?

'I think you're making too much of all this, Mel.' His voice was deep and almost gruff.

'Am I?' Her eyes never wavered from his and this time he smiled.

'No. Maybe I am. I think I like you a lot, Mel.'

'I like you too. There's no harm in that, as long as we don't get carried away.' But she wished they would. And it was crazy really, sitting there at the side of the pool talking of something that had never been and would never be, and yet there was something there. And Mel couldn't decide if it was illusion created by working so closely side by side for two days or if it was real. There was no way to know, and by the next day she'd be gone. Maybe there was no harm in one dinner after all, and she was expected to stay.

Peter looked down at her again and spoke softly to her. 'I'm glad you're here, Mel.' He sounded like Matt, and she smiled.

'So am I.' For a long moment their eyes met and held and Mel could feel cold chills run up her spine. There was something magical about this man, and he seemed to feel it too. He stood up with a happy smile on his face and held out a hand to her. He looked almost shy, and she smiled and followed him inside, glad that she had decided to stay. She went back to the guest room, and changed her clothes, rinsed out the bathing suit and went upstairs to return it to Pam, her wet hair pulled back into a knot, and her face lightly tanned with only mascara and lipstick on. There weren't many women her age who looked as well with almost no makeup on.

She found Pam sitting in her room, listening to a tape with a dreamy look on her face. She seemed almost startled to see Mel, who knocked on the open door and stepped in.

'Hi, Pam. Thanks for the suit. Shall I put it in your bathroom?'

'Sure . . . okay . . . thanks.' She stood up, feeling awkward with Mel, and Mel suddenly felt the same overwhelming urge to take the young girl in her arms, however tall and grown-up she was. Inside, she was still a lonely, unhappy little girl.

'That's a nice tape. Val has that too.'

'Which one is she?' Pam looked intrigued again.

'The blonde.'

'Is she nice?'

Mel laughed. 'I hope so. Maybe someday if you come east with your dad, you could meet them both.'

Pam sat down on her bed again. 'I'd like to go to New York someday. But we hardly ever get to go away. Dad can't leave his work. There's always someone he has to be around for. Except for a couple of weeks in the summer, when he goes nuts, leaving the hospital, and calls back there every two hours. We go to Aspen.' She looked unimpressed, and Mel watched her eyes. There was something broken there. Everything about her looked as though it needed some pep, some excitement, some joy. But Mel had a feeling that a woman could work wonders for the girl. Someone to love her and take her mother's place. The child was keening for Anne, and no matter how much she would resist someone new, it was what she needed most. That dry stick of a German woman downstairs couldn't give her love. Peter did his best, but she needed something more.

95

'Aspen must be nice.' Mel was fighting to open a closed door between herself and the girl. And once or twice she thought she could see a glimmer of hope, but she wasn't sure.

'Yeah, it's okay. I get bored going there though.'

'Where would you rather go instead?'

'The beach . . . Mexico . . . Europe . . . New York . . . someplace neat.' She smiled hesitantly at Mel. 'Someplace where interesting people go, not just nature lovers and people who hike.' She made a face. 'Yuck.'

Mel smiled. 'We go to Martha's Vineyard every summer. That's the beach. It's not too exciting, but it's nice. Maybe someday you could visit us there.' But at that, Pam looked suspicious again, and before Mel could say anything more, Matthew bounded into the room.

'Get out, squirt!' She leapt quickly to her feet, protecting her domain.

'You're a creep.' Matthew looked more annoyed than hurt, and he looked possessively at Mel. 'Dad says dinner's ready and we should all come downstairs.' He stood waiting to accompany her down, and she had no further time alone with Pam, to reassure her that the invitation was just a friendly thought on her part, and not an omen of things to come between her father and herself.

Mark joined them on the stairs and he and Pam gnawed at each other all the way down, while Matthew kept up a running patter with Mel. Peter was already waiting in the dining room. Mel saw a haunting expression cross his face as they entered the room en masse, but he quickly recovered himself. There must have been a familiar look to it all, something he hadn't seen in a long time.

'Were they holding you hostage upstairs? I was afraid of that.'

'No. I was talking to Pam.'

He looked pleased at that, and everyone took their chairs. Mel hesitated, not quite sure where to sit. Peter quickly pulled out the chair to his right, and Pam looked shocked and half rose from her seat. She sat at the foot of the table, facing Peter, with both boys on one side. 'That's . . .'

'Never mind!' His voice was firm, and Mel knew instantly what he had done. He had put her in his late wife's chair, and she wished that he had not. There was a long, heavy silence in the room, and Mrs Hahn stared as she came in. Mel looked at Peter imploringly. 'It's all right, Mel.' He looked reassuringly at her, and took the others in with one glance. The conversation began again. A moment later the dining room was filled with the usual chatter, as everyone started with Mrs Hahn's cold watercress soup.

As it turned out, it was a pleasant meal, and Peter had been right. There was no need to make a major event of it. He and Mel shared coffee in the den when they were through, and the children went upstairs. Mel didn't see them again until she was ready to leave. Pam rather formally shook her hand, Mel sensed she was relieved to see her go, Mark asked for her autograph, and Matthew threw his arms around her neck and begged her to stay.

'I can't. But I promise I'll send you a postcard from New York.'

Tears filled his eyes. 'That's not the same.' He was right, but it was the best she could do. She held him for a long moment and then gently kissed his cheek and stroked his hair.

'Maybe you'll come to see me in New York one day.' But when he looked into her eyes, they both knew that it wasn't likely to happen for a long time, if at all, and she felt desperately sorry for him. When she finally left, and they drove away from the house, Matthew kept waving as the car pulled down the block. Mel was almost in tears. 'I feel like such a rat leaving him.' She looked at Peter and he was touched by what he saw in her eyes. He reached out and patted her hand. It was the first time he had actually touched her, and he felt a thrill run through his arm. He quickly withdrew his hand and she looked away. 'What a super kid he is . . . they all are . . .' Even Pam. She liked them all, and felt for what they'd been through, and Peter too. She sighed softly then. 'I'm glad I stayed.'

'So am I. You did us all good. We haven't had a happy meal like that in . . . years.' And she knew just how many too. They had been living in a tomb, and again she found herself thinking that he should sell the house, but she didn't dare say that to him. Instead she turned to him, thinking of his children again.

'Thank you for inviting me over this afternoon.'

'I'm glad you came.'

'So am I.'

The hospital parking lot came too soon, and they were standing awkwardly outside her car uncertain of what to say. 'Thank you, Peter. I had a wonderful time.' She made a mental note to send flowers the next day, and maybe something special for the children if she had time to shop before she left. She still had to shop for the twins too.

'Thank you, Mel.' He looked into her eyes for a long time and then held out a hand to shake hers. 'I'll see you tomorrow then.' She would briefly be filming Pattie Lou before she left and it would be her last chance to see him. He walked her to her car, and they stood there for another moment before she slid in.

'Thanks again.'

'Good night, Mel.' He smiled and turned to walk into the hospital for a last look at Pattie Lou.

CHAPTER 7

The filming of Pattie Lou in intensive care went smoothly the next day. Despite the surgery and the tubes, she already looked infinitely healthier than she had before and Melanie was amazed. It was almost as though Peter had wrought a miracle cure, and she didn't let herself dwell on how long it would last. Even if it was only a few years, it was better than a few days. With the living example of Pattie Lou, Peter Hallam had totally won her over.

She saw him in the hall, shortly after she left Pattie Lou. The crew had already left, and she had been about to say goodbye to Pearl. She had to check out of her hotel, and there were a few errands in Beverly Hills she wanted to do, including bringing a little something back for the girls. It was a tradition maintained over the years, so now she was going to steal an hour to do a little shopping on Rodeo Drive.

'Hello there.' He looked handsome and fresh, as though he hadn't worked all day. 'What are you up to today?'

'Winding up.' She smiled. 'I just saw Pattie Lou. She looks great.'

'Yes, she does.' He beamed, a proud rooster. 'I saw her this morning too.' In fact he had seen her twice, but he didn't mention that to Mel, not wanting to make her worry that anything was wrong.

'I was going to call you this afternoon, to thank you for dinner last night. I had a wonderful time.' She carefully sought his eyes, wondering what she would see there.

'The children loved meeting you, Mel.'

'It was nice meeting them.' But she couldn't help wondering if Pam had reacted badly when he returned home again.

She noticed then that he was looking wistfully at her,

and she wondered if something was wrong. He seemed to hesitate, and then he spoke up. 'Are you in a rush?'

'Not really. My flight isn't until ten o'clock tonight.' She didn't mention her shopping on Rodeo Drive for the girls, it seemed far too frivolous here, amidst the battle for human life. 'Why?'

'I wondered if you wanted to stop in and see Marie Dupret again.' She could see that the girl already meant something to him. She was his latest little wounded bird.

'How is she today?' Mel watched his eyes, wondering how any one man could care so much. But he did. It was obvious in everything he did and said.

'About the same. We're getting down to the wire on that donor heart for her.'

'I hope you get one soon.' But again, that seemed a ghoulish thought, as she followed Peter to Marie's room.

The girl seemed paler and weaker than she had the day before, and Peter sat quietly with her and talked, in an almost intimate way, that excluded everyone else in the room save themselves. It was as though there was a special communion between them, and for a fraction of an instant Mel found herself wondering if he was attracted to her. But his style with her had no sexual overtones, it was just that he seemed to care so much, and one had the feeling that they had known each other for years, which Mel knew wasn't the case. It was a striking case of there being an extraordinary kind of rapport between them. After a little while Marie seemed more peaceful than she had been before, and her eyes reached out to Mel.

'Thank you for coming by to see me again, Miss Adams.' She seemed so weak and pale, one sensed that she wouldn't live much longer without the transplant she so desperately needed. She seemed to have worsened since the day before, and Mel felt a tug at her own heart as she walked towards the young woman.

'I'm going back to New York tonight, Marie. But I'll be looking forward to hearing good news about you.'

For a long moment the young woman with the translucent pallor said nothing, and then she smiled almost sadly. 'Thank you.' And then, as Peter watched, she let her fears overwhelm her and two tears slid down her cheeks. 'I don't know if we'll find a donor in time.'

Peter stepped forward again. 'Then you'll just have to hang in there, won't you?' His eyes were so intense in their grasp of the girl that it was almost as though he were willing her to live, and Mel felt as though she could almost touch the magnetic force between them in the room.

'It'll be all right.' Melanie reached out and touched her hand, and was surprised at how cold it was. The girl had practically no circulation, which accounted for the bluish pallor. 'I know it will.'

She turned her eyes to Mel then, and seemed almost too weak to move. 'Do you?' Melanie nodded, fighting back tears. She had the terrifying feeling that the girl was not going to make it, and she found herself silently praying for her as they left the room, and in the safety of the hall, she turned to Peter with worried eyes.

'Can she hold out until you find a donor?' Mel doubted it now, and even Peter looked unsure. He suddenly seemed exhausted by it all, which was rare for him.

'I hope so. It all depends on how soon we find a donor.' Melanie didn't ask the obvious question, 'And if you don't?' because the answer to that was too easily guessed from the condition of the girl. She was the frailest, most delicate girl Melanie had ever seen, and it seemed miraculous that she was still alive at all.

'I hope she makes it.'

Peter looked at her intently, and then nodded. 'So do I. Sometimes the emotional factors help. I'll come back and see her again later, the nurses are keeping a very close watch on her, not just through the monitors. The problem is that she has no family or relatives at all. Sometimes people so alone have less reason to hang on. We have to give them that reason as best we can. But in the end, what happens is not our decision.' Was it hers then? Was it up to this frail girl to will herself to live? It seemed a lot to expect of her, and Melanie was silent as she followed Peter, almost dragging her feet. There was no further reason to linger here. Peter had his work to do and she had to move on, no matter how little the prospect appealed to her. Somehow she wanted to stick around now, to watch Pattie Lou, talk to Pearl, pray for Marie, drop in on the others she'd seen. But the issue was none of them, as she suspected now. It was Peter himself. She really didn't want to leave him. And he seemed to sense that too. He left the nurses and the charts and walked to where she stood.

'I'll take you downstairs, Mel.'

'Thank you.' She didn't decline. She wanted to be alone with him, but she wasn't even sure why. Maybe it was just his style that had got to her, the bedside manner, the warmth, yet she knew that it was something more. She was remarkably drawn to the man, but to what end? She lived in New York and he lived in LA. And if they had lived in the same town? She wasn't even sure of that as he walked her to her car in the parking lot, and she turned to face him again. 'Thank you for everything.'

'For what?' He smiled gently down at her.

'For saving Pattie Lou's life.'

'I did that for Pattie Lou, not for you.'

'Then for everything else. Your interest, your time, your cooperation, dinner, lunch . . .' She was suddenly at a loss for words and he looked amused.

'Anything else you want to add? Coffee in the hall?'

'All right, all right . . .' She smiled at him and he took her hand.

'I should be thanking you, Mel. You did a lot for me. You're the first person I've opened up to in two years. Thank you for that.' And then, before she could respond, 'Could I call you in New York sometime, or would that be out of line?'

'Not at all. I'd like that very much.' Her heart pounded in her chest, and she felt like a very young girl.

'I'll call you then. Have a good trip back.' He squeezed

102

her hand once more, and then turned, waved, and was gone. As simple as that. And as she drove towards Rodeo Drive, she couldn't help wondering if she would ever see him again.

CHAPTER 8

While Mel finished her shopping that afternoon, she found
that she had to push Peter Hallam from her head again and
again. It wasn't right that she should think so much about
him. What was he to her after all? An interesting man, the
subject of an interview, nothing more, no matter how
appealing he was. She tried to fill her mind with thoughts of
Val and Jess, and suddenly he would crop up. She was still
thinking of him as she threw her suitcase into the back of a
cab and headed for the airport at eight o'clock that night,
and suddenly in her mind's eye, she saw a crystal-clear
vision of Pam, a troubled, brokenhearted, lonely little girl.

'Shit.' She muttered out loud, and the driver glanced at
her.

'Something wrong?'

She had to laugh at herself, and shook her head. 'Sorry. I
was miles away.'

He nodded, nonplussed. He had heard it all before
anyway and as long as she gave him a decent tip, that was all
he cared about.

Once they had reached the airport she checked in,
bought three magazines, and sat down near the gate to wait
for her flight. It was already nine o'clock, and in twenty
minutes they would board. She looked around and realised
that the flight would be full, but as usual, she would be
travelling first class, so it probably wouldn't be too bad. She
flipped through the magazines waiting for the flight to be
called, keeping one ear alert for the flight number. It was
the last flight of the day headed for New York, familiarly
termed 'the red eye', because that was how one would arrive
at six o'clock the next morning, red-eyed and exhausted,
but at least one didn't lose an entire day flying.

As she listened, she suddenly started. She thought she

had heard her name, but decided that she had been mistaken. They called the flight, and she waited for the first crush of passengers to get on board, and then picked up the briefcase and handbag she was carrying and got in line with her ticket and her boarding pass in her hand, and again she heard her name. But this time, she was certain it was not her imagination.

'Melanie Adams, please come to the white courtesy phone . . . Melanie Adams . . . white courtesy phone, please . . . Melanie Adams . . .' Glancing at her watch to see how much time she had, she dashed for a white phone on the far wall and picked it up, identifying herself to the operator who answered.

'Hello, this is Melanie Adams. I believe you were paging me a moment ago.' She set her bags down on the floor next to her feet and listened intently.

'You had a call from a Dr Peter Hallam. He wants you to call him back immediately if you can.' And with that, she gave Mel his home number. She repeated it to herself, as she ran to the nearest phone booth, digging in her bag for a dime, and keeping one eye on the large clock hanging above. She had five minutes left to board her flight, and she couldn't afford to miss it. She had to be in New York by the next morning. The dime found, she slipped it into the slot in the phone and dialled the number.

'Hello?' Her heart pounded as he answered, wondering why he had called her.

'Peter, it's Mel. I only have a couple of minutes to catch my flight.'

'I don't have much more than that either.' His voice sounded terse. 'We just got a donor for Marie Dupret. I'm leaving for the hospital now, and I just thought I'd let you know on the off-chance that you'd want to stay.' Her mind raced as she listened, and for only the flash of a second she was disappointed. She had thought he had called her to say goodbye, but now she felt the adrenaline course through her system as she thought of the transplant. Now Marie had a chance. They had found a heart for her. 'I didn't know if you'd want to change your plans, but I thought I'd let you know, in case. I wasn't even sure what airline you were on and I took a wild guess.' His guess had been a good one.

'You just caught me.' And then she frowned. 'Could we film the transplant?' It would be a sensational addition to the story, and it would give her justification for staying another day.

There was a long pause. 'All right. Can you get a camera crew there right away?'

'I can try. I have to get clearance from New York to stay.' And the time it would take to call could cost her her flight. 'I don't know what I can do. I'll leave a message at the hospital for you either way.'

'Fine. I've got to go now. See you later.' His voice was businesslike and brusque and he hung up without saying more. Melanie stood in the phone booth for a second gathering her thoughts. The first thing she had to do was talk to the ground supervisor at the gate. She had done this before, and with any luck at all, they would hold the flight for five or ten minutes, which would give her time to call New York. She just hoped that she could reach someone OF sufficient rank in New York to get clearance. Grabbing her briefcase and handbag, she took off at a run for the gate, where she found a supervisor, and explained who she was, flashing her press card from the network.

'Can you hold the flight for me for ten minutes? I've got to call New York on a big story.' The supervisor didn't look pleased, but for people of Mel's rank they often did special favours, like finding them seats on fully booked flights, even if it meant bumping some unsuspecting passenger off the plane, or holding a flight just before takeoff, like this one.

'I'll give you ten minutes, but I can't give you much more than that.' It cost the airlines a fortune to pull stunts like that and delay on the ground. She turned away from Mel and then spoke into the small walkie-talkie she carried as Mel ran back to the pay phone, and put the call on her credit card. They got her through to the newsroom right away but it took four precious minutes to find an assistant producer and a story editor, who conferred with Mel on the phone.

'What's up?'

'A real break. One of the people I interviewed was a patient waiting for a transplant. And I just got a call from Hallam. They've got a donor, and they're going to operate now. Can I stay and take a camera crew back out to Center City to film the operation?' She was breathless from the excitement and from running to the phone.

'Didn't you shoot him in surgery before?'

'No.' She held her breath, knowing that could decide it all.

'Then stay. But get home tomorrow night.'

'Yes sir.' She grinned as she hung up the phone, and hurried back to the gate.

She told them she wasn't taking the flight and then called the local network for a camera crew. She hurried outside for a cab then, hoping that the airline would hold on to her bag in New York, as they'd promised to.

The camera crew was waiting for her in the lobby when she arrived, and they went straight upstairs to surgery. They all had to scrub, don masks and gowns, and they had been assigned a minuscule corner of the room to which they had to confine their equipment. Mel was vehement about following the rules because she was grateful that Peter let them be there at all and she didn't want to abuse the privilege.

At last, wheeled into the room on a stretcher with the side rails up, Marie appeared. Her eyes were closed, and she looked deathly pale. She didn't stir at all, until Peter walked in, in mask and gown, and spoke to her. He didn't even seem to see Mel then, although he glanced once at the camera crew, and seemed satisfied at where they stood. Then everything got underway, and Mel watched in fascination.

Peter frequently glanced at the monitors and gave a

constant series of orders to his team. They moved in total unison like an intricate ballet of hands, with instruments being passed to him from an enormous tray.

Melanie looked away when they made the first incision, but after that she was drawn to the intensity of the scene, and hour after hour she stood by and watched, praying silently for Marie's life, as they worked endlessly to replace her dying heart with the new one of the young woman who had died only hours before. It was fascinating to watch as they lifted the old one from her chest and placed it on a tray, and Melanie didn't even gasp as she watched them lower the new one into the cavity they had left. Valves, arteries and veins were hooked up and his hands moved ceaselessly over the woman's chest. Melanie held her breath, then suddenly the monitors came to life again, and the sound of the monitored heart beat leapt into the room like a drum in everyone's ears, and the cardiac team gave a cheer. It was truly amazing. The heart so lifeless since the death of its donor sprang to life again in Marie's body.

The surgery continued for another two hours, and at last the final incision was closed. Peter stood back, his back and chest drenched, his arms sore from the precise work, and he watched carefully as they slowly pushed her bed from the room again, into a nearby cubicle where she would be watched for several hours. He would remain close by for the next six or eight hours himself to make sure that all went well, but for the moment everything seemed to be under control. He walked out into the hall and took a deep breath of air, and Melanie followed him, feeling her legs shake. It had been an extraordinary experience watching him work, and she was deeply grateful for his call. He chatted for a few moments with the others, still in his cap and gown, his mask cast aside on a desk, and for a few minutes Mel conferred with the camera crew. They were ready to go home, and enormously impressed with what they'd seen.

'Christ, that guy's good.' The man in charge peeled off

his blue gown and lit a cigarette, wondering at the wisdom of it as he did, but all he could think of was what they'd got on film: the constantly moving hands of the doctors, working in pairs, sometimes two pairs together, never stopping, picking up tiny slivers of tissue to be repaired and veins barely thicker than hairs. 'It really makes you believe in miracles to see something like that.' He looked at Mel in awe, and he shook her hand. 'It was nice working with you.'

'Thank you for getting here so fast.' She smiled, and they glanced over some notes. He told her he'd have the film in New York the next day to add to the rest and then he and his crew left. She changed her clothes and was surprised to see Peter emerge in his street clothes too. Somehow she had assumed that he'd be sticking around in his operating-room garb, but she didn't know why she'd assumed that. It was strange to see him as just an ordinary mortal again. 'How did it go?' she asked him as they walked outside together into the hall. Something deep inside her leapt to see him again.

'Okay so far. The next twenty-four hours will be crucial for her though. We'll have to see how she holds up. She was terribly weak when we went in. Did you see that heart? It was like a piece of rock, it didn't have any give left at all. I don't think she'd have made it another twenty-four hours. She was damn lucky we got that donor in time.' Donor . . . donor . . . no face . . . no name . . . no past . . . just 'donor', an anonymous heart in a body one knew, with a face like Marie's. It was still difficult to absorb. Even after watching the operation performed for four hours.

Mel looked at her watch then and was surprised to see that it was well after six o'clock, and when she glanced outside she saw that the sun had come up. The night was gone, and Marie was alive. 'You must be beat.' He looked her over carefully and noticed the dark shadows under her eyes. 'Just standing there watching is a lot harder than doing the work.'

'I doubt that.' She yawned in spite of herself, and wondered how Marie would feel when she woke up. That was the worst of all and Melanie didn't envy her. She would have a lot to go through now, even more than she'd gone through before. She had the drugs to absorb, the rejection and infections to fight, and she would have the pain of having been cut almost in half as they worked. Mel almost shuddered at the thought, and Peter saw her grow pale, and without further ado, pushed her into the nearest chair. He'd seen the symptoms before, even before Mel herself knew she was growing faint. He gently pushed her head down towards her knees with his powerful hands and Mel was too surprised to speak.

'Take slow, deep breaths, and exhale through your mouth.' She was about to say something flip to him but suddenly found that she felt too sick to speak, and when she'd recovered again, she looked up at him in surprise.

'I didn't even feel that coming on.'

'Maybe not, my friend, but for a minute there, you turned an interesting shade of green. You ought to have something to eat downstairs, and go back to your hotel to sleep.' Then he remembered that she had checked out, and no longer had a room, and he thought of something. 'Why don't you go back to my place for a while? Mrs Hahn can put you in the guest room, and the kids won't even know you're there.' He looked at his watch, it was a few minutes before seven. 'I'll give her a call.'

'No, don't, I can go back to my hotel.'

'That's silly. Why go through all that, when you can sleep at my place? No one will bother you all day.' It was a generous offer, but she wasn't sure it was quite right. But she found that when she stood up, she was too tired to argue or even call her hotel for another room. He walked to a desk and picked up a phone and she sat watching him like an exhausted child. He came back to her looking as fresh as he had the morning before, although he had lost a night's sleep too, but he seemed to be used to it, and he was still exhilarated by his success. 'She'll be waiting for you when you arrive. The kids won't even be up till eight, except Mark who's already gone.' He glanced around and spoke rapidly to a nurse and then returned to Mel. 'Marie's doing fine, I'll take you downstairs and put you in a cab myself, and then I'll come back here to check on her.'

'You really don't have to . . . it's silly . . .' It was ridiculous, she had covered everything from mass murders to minor wars, and suddenly now she felt as though her entire body were going to melt, and she was grateful for his strong arm nearby as he led her downstairs. 'I must be getting old.' She smiled ruefully as they waited for the cab. 'I shouldn't be this tired.'

'It's the letdown. We all feel it eventually. It just hasn't hit me yet.'

'What'll you do?'

'Stay close, and catch a few hours of sleep here if I can. I called my secretary last night after I called you, and she'll cancel all my appointments today. Someone else on the team will cover for me this morning, and I'll do rounds myself this afternoon.' But she knew that he had to be dead on his feet now, not that it showed. He was as dynamic and alive as he had been hours before. He looked down at her gently as he put her in the cab. 'When are you going back to New York?'

'I'll have to go back tonight. They won't let me stay another day.'

He nodded, pleased that he'd caught her the night before. 'There won't be anything else for you to film anyway, Mel. From now on, we watch, and we juggle the doses of the medication to something she can tolerate. You saw everything there was to see last night.' She looked into his eyes again.

'Thank you for letting us be there.'

'It was good to have you there. Now go and get some sleep.' He gave the driver his address and closed the door before the cab disappeared into the Los Angeles traffic and headed in the direction of Bel-Air. As he watched her

111

drive away, he was suddenly grateful that she was still there, and that he would see her again in a few hours. He was as confused as Mel about what he felt. But he felt something for her. That was for sure.

CHAPTER 9

At the house in Bel-Air, Mrs Hahn was standing near a window, waiting for her, and with barely more than a hello, she led Mel upstairs to the guest room. Mel thanked her and looked around, starving and exhausted all at once, and longing for a hot bath, but too tired to do anything about any of it. She dropped her briefcase and her handbag beside the bed, wondering if she'd catch up with her suitcase again in New York, but right now she didn't really care. She lay down on the bed fully clothed and began to drift off to sleep thinking of Peter and Marie, just as she heard a soft knock on the door. She turned over in surprise, and pulled herself back to consciousness again. 'Yes?'

It was Mrs Hahn with a small wicker tray. 'The doctor thought you should have something to eat.' She felt like a patient as she eyed the plate of steaming scrambled eggs and toast, and a cup of chocolate that she could smell halfway across the room. 'I didn't bring you coffee so you would sleep.'

'Thank you so much.' It was embarrassing to be waited on, but the food looked wonderful to her as she sat up on the edge of the bed, her jacket rumpled, her shirt creased, her hair dishevelled from the way she had lain. And without another word, Mrs Hahn set the tray down on a small table beside the bed, and left the room again.

And as Mel devoured the eggs and toast, suddenly ravenous, she heard soft bumping sounds upstairs, and wondered if it was Matthew or Pam, getting ready for school. But she didn't have the strength to be polite and go upstairs to see them. She downed the hot chocolate, ate the last of the toast, and lay down again, sated, exhausted, pleased with her night's work. She closed her eyes and it was three o'clock in the afternoon when she awoke again. She looked at her watch in shock, and jumped off the bed, but she suddenly realised there was nowhere she had to go. She wondered what Mrs Hahn would think of her sleeping all day, and any minute the children would be home. And when she'd gone to sleep they had just been getting up to go to school. And then as she walked around the room, she began wondering how Marie had fared for the past seven hours. She saw a phone on a desk across the room, and walked to it in stockinged feet, looking down at the wrinkled clothes she wore. She dialled the hospital at once, asked for the cardiac floor, and then for Peter himself, and the woman who answered told her that he could not be called to the phone. Melanie wondered if he was asleep too.

'I was calling to see how Marie Dupret, the transplant patient, is.' There was a silence at the other end. 'This is Melanie Adams. I was in the operating room last night.' But she didn't need to say more. Everyone in the hospital knew who she was, and that she was doing a story on Peter Hallam and Pattie Lou Jones.

'Just a moment please.' The voice was crisp and she was put on hold, and then an instant later she heard a familiar voice.

'You're awake?'

'Barely, but I am. And mortified to have slept all afternoon.'

'Bull. You needed it. You were ready to pass out when you left here. Did Mrs Hahn give you something to eat?'

'She certainly did. This is the best hotel in town.' She smiled as she looked around the comfortable, well-decorated room, and imagined that here again all had been arranged by Anne. 'How's Marie?'

'She's doing great.' He sounded pleased. 'I couldn't take the time to explain it to you last night, but we tried a new technique, and it worked. I'll draw you a few sketches later, but suffice it to say for now that so far, so good. We won't know about rejection for at least a week.'

114

'How long before she's out of the woods?'

'A while.' The rest of her life, Mel knew. 'We think she'll do fine. She met all our criteria for a potential success.'

'I hope she keeps it up.'

'So do we.' She was struck again by how little of the credit he took for himself, and couldn't help but admire him again.

'Did you get any sleep?'

He sounded vague. 'Some. I decided to do rounds myself this morning, and I lay down for a while after that. I'll probably come home tonight for dinner with the kids. I can leave someone else in charge here by then.' And then he had a thought. 'I'll see you then, Mel.' He sounded so friendly and warm, and she was suddenly anxious to see him again.

'Your children are going to get awfully tired of me.'

'I doubt that. They'll be thrilled that you're still here, and so am I. What time's your plane, or have you thought about that yet?'

'I guess I'll take the same flight tonight.' She felt rested enough to tackle the red eye, after sleeping all day. 'I should leave here at eight o'clock.'

'That works out fine. Mrs Hahn feeds us at seven as a rule, and I'll be home by six if all goes well here. If anything comes up, I'll give you a call.' For a moment, she could almost imagine him saying the same thing to Anne; and it felt strange to listen to him, as though she were trying to take the dead woman's place, but she chided herself for being foolish as he said goodbye. There was nothing unusual about what he had said, and she was irritated with herself for fantasising again. And as though to wash away her thoughts of him, she walked into the shower and turned it on full blast, dropped her clothes on the bed, and stood beneath the steam. It occurred to her then that she could also swim in the pool but she didn't want to go outside yet. She needed time to wake up and clear her head. It had been a long night, and when she got out of the shower she realised that she had to call the studio in New York, and then Raquel. She had asked the story editor to call her home the night before, and she hoped they had. Raquel confirmed that to her when she reached her home number. The girls were disappointed that she hadn't come home that day, but she promised that the following morning she'd be there. And then she called the newsroom and told them that all was well. She reassured them that the transplant had been an enormous success, and they had got every moment of it on film.

'It's going to be a great piece, guys. You'll see.'

'Agreed. It'll be good to see you back, Mel.' But she didn't entirely agree. She wasn't anxious to leave LA, or Peter, and there seemed to be so many reasons to stay here: Pattie Lou, Peter, Marie . . . all excuses, she knew, but she just didn't want to go.

She put down the phone and dressed and then left her room to find Mrs Hahn. She found her in the kitchen, making pot roast for that night. She thanked her again for the breakfast she'd brought her when she arrived and apologised for sleeping all day.

Mrs Hahn looked unimpressed. 'The doctor said that was why you were coming here. Would you like something to eat?' She was efficient but not warm, and there was something intimidating about the way she spoke and moved. She was definitely not the kind of woman Mel would have wanted around her kids, and wondered that Peter did. He seemed warmer to her than that, and with no mother around . . . but again Mel remembered that she had been hired by Anne. Sacred Anne.

Mel settled for a cup of black coffee and made herself a piece of toast. She sat in the bright garden room filled with white wicker chairs.

To Mel, it seemed the sunniest room in the house, and the one she was most comfortable in. The formality of the other rooms put her off, but this one did not, and she lay down on a chaise longue and ate her toast, looking out at the peaceful view of the pool. She didn't even hear

116

footsteps and had no idea she wasn't alone until she heard the voice.

'What are you doing here?'

She jumped up with a start, spilling some of her coffee on her leg, but thanks to her black gabardine pants, she didn't get burned. She turned, she saw Pam. 'Hello. You surprised the hell out of me.' She smiled, but Pam did not.

'I thought you were in New York.'

'I almost was. But I stayed to watch your father do a transplant last night. It was fabulous.' Her eyes lit up again as she remembered Peter's deft hands, but his daughter looked unimpressed and disgruntled.

'Oh yeah.'

'How was school, Pam?'

She stared at Mel. 'This was my mother's favourite room.'

'I can understand that. I like it too, there's so much sunshine here.' But the comment had increased the awkwardness between them, just as Pam had intended.

Pam sat down slowly across the room from Mel, and glanced outside. 'She used to sit here every day and watch me play in the pool.' It was well set up for that and just a pleasant place to be. Mel watched the girl's face and the sadness she saw there and she decided to take the bull by the horns.

'You must miss her a lot.'

Something hardened in Pam's face, and she didn't answer for a long time. 'She could have had an operation, but she didn't trust my dad to do it.' It was a brutal thing to say, and inwardly Mel cringed if that was what she thought of Anne's decision.

'I don't think it was as simple as that.'

She jumped to her feet. 'What do you know about it, except what *he* told you?'

'It was a choice she had a right to make.' But Mel knew she was treading on delicate ground. 'Sometimes it's difficult to understand why other people do things.'

'He couldn't have saved her anyway.' She walked

117

nervously around the room as Mel watched. 'She'd have been dead by now, even with a transplanted heart.' Mel nodded slowly, most likely it was true.

'What would you have liked her to do?'

Pam shrugged and turned away and Mel saw her shoulders shake. Without giving it a second thought she went to her. 'Pam . . .' She turned her slowly around and saw the tears running down the young girl's face, she gently took her in her arms and let her cry. She stood there for a few minutes leaning against Mel, as Mel gently stroked her hair. 'I'm so sorry, Pam . . .'

'Yeah. Me too.' She pulled away at last and sat down again, wiping her face on her sleeve. She looked at Mel with misery in her face. 'I loved her so much.'

'I'm sure she loved you too.'

'Then why didn't she try? She'd have at least been here till now.'

'I don't know the answer to that, maybe no one does. I think your father asks himself the same thing all the time, but you have to go on. There isn't anything else you can do, as much as it hurts.' Pam nodded silently, and looked at Mel.

'I stopped eating for a while. I think I wanted to die too.' At least it was what the psychiatrist had said. 'Mark thinks I did it just to bug Dad, but I didn't. I couldn't help it.'

'Your father understands that. Do you feel better about things now than you did then?'

'Sometimes. I don't know . . .' She looked so desperately sad, and there was so little Mel could say to help. All one could do was be there for her. She had two brothers, neither of whom could be of much help to her, a hard-boiled German housekeeper who offered no warmth at all, and a father who was busy saving other people's lives. There was no doubt that this child needed someone else, but who? For a minute Mel wished that she could be there for her, but she had her own life to live three thousand miles away, her own children, problems, job.

118

'You know, Pam, I wish you'd come to visit me in New York sometime.'

'Your daughters would probably think I was dumb. My brothers do.' She sniffed loudly again and looked like a little girl.

Mel smiled gently at her. 'I hope they're smarter than that, and boys don't always understand. Mark is going through his own adjustments growing up, and Matt is too young to be much help.'

'No, I'm not,' a small voice piped up. Neither of them had seen him walk into the room. He had just come home from school, dropped off by the car pool he rode in every day. 'I make my bed, I take a bath myself, and I can cook soup.' Even Pam laughed at that, and Mel smiled at him.

'I know, you're a terrific kid.'

'You came back.' He looked pleased as he walked towards her and sat down.

'No, I just left a little later than I thought. How was your day, my friend?'

'Pretty good.' And then he stared at Pam. 'How come you're crying again?' And before she could answer he turned to Mel. 'She cries all the time. Girls are dumb.'

'No, they're not. Everyone cries. Even big men.'

'My dad never cries.' He said it with enormous pride, and Mel wondered if Peter played a macho game with him. 'I'll bet he does.'

'Nope.' He was firm, but Pam intervened.

'Yes he does. I saw him once. After . . .' But she didn't say the words. She didn't have to. They all understood, and Matt glared at her.

'That's not true. He's tough. So's Mark.' And with that, Mrs Hahn came into the room, and dragged Matthew away to wash his hands and face. He did his best to resist, but there was no swaying her, and Mel and Pam were alone again.

'Pam' – she reached out and touched her hand – 'if there's ever anything I can do for you, if you need a friend, call. I'll leave you my number when I go. Call me collect any time. I'm fairly good at listening, and New York isn't all that far away.' Pam looked at her with watchful eyes and then nodded her head.

'Thanks.'

'I mean it. Any time.'

Pam nodded and stood up. 'I'd better do my homework now. Are you leaving soon?' It was half hopeful, half not, as mixed as the rest of her feelings about Mel.

'I'm leaving for New York tonight. I'll probably hang around here till about eight o'clock.'

'Are you eating with us?' She looked annoyed, and Mel remembered what she had said.

'Maybe. I'm not sure. Would you mind that very much?'

'No, that's okay.' And as she stood in the doorway she turned back to ask, 'Do you want to borrow my bathing suit again?'

'I think I'll pass on that today, but thanks anyway.'

'Sure.' She nodded again and was gone, and a few minutes later Matthew bounded back into the room, bringing with him two books for her to read. It was obvious that they were both starved for attention as well as love, and he kept her busy and amused until Peter came home, and she saw that the day had finally taken its toll. He looked pale and tired, and she was sorry for him. There was so much for him to do here, as well, the children had such different needs, and his work used up so much of his energy and time. It was a wonder there was anything left for the children at all, but there was, whatever he could spare of himself at least.

'How's Marie?' Her eyes were full of concern and he smiled tiredly.

'Doing very well. Did Matthew drive you crazy all afternoon?'

'Not at all. And I had a nice talk with Pam.' He looked surprised.

'Well, that's something anyway. Want to come into the den for a glass of wine?'

'Sure.' She followed him across the house, and when they reached the den, she apologised again for taking advantage of his home.

'That's ridiculous. You put in a tough night last night. Why shouldn't you stay here for a day?'

'It was awfully nice.'

'Good.' He smiled at her and handed her a glass of wine. 'So are you.' He seemed warmer to her again. Like his daughter, he seemed to run hot and cold towards Mel, but she had the same conflicting emotions too, and she wasn't at all sure how to handle them. She just looked into his eyes and sipped her wine, and they reverted to small talk about the hospital which almost felt like her second home now, and before they had finished their second glass, Mrs Hahn knocked smartly on the door.

'Dinner is served, Doctor.'

'Thank you.' He stood up and Mel followed suit and walked beside him into the dining room, where they were rapidly joined by Pam, Matt and Mark, who came home just a few moments before. Mel found herself caught up in their banter once more. She felt surprisingly comfortable with them all and when it came time to leave to catch her plane, she was sorry to go. She gave Pam a hug, Matt a goodbye kiss, shook Mark's hand, thanked Mrs Hahn, and actually felt as though she were leaving old friends. She turned to Peter then, and shook his hand too.

'Thank you again. Today was really the best day of all.' She looked at his children standing nearby, and then back at him. 'And now I'd better call a cab, or you'll be stuck with me again.'

'Don't be ridiculous. I'll drive you to the airport myself.'

'I wouldn't think of it. You were up all night too. And you didn't sleep all day like me.'

'I slept enough. Come on, no nonsense now.' His voice was almost sharp. 'Where's your bag?'

Mel laughed. 'In New York, waiting for me, I hope.' He looked baffled and she explained. 'It was already checked

121

on to the plane last night when you called.' And then he laughed too.

'You really are a good sport.'

'Wrinkled, but a good sport and I wouldn't have missed that opportunity for anything in the world.' She looked down at the rumpled silk shirt and she had forgotten for the past few hours. The state of her dress didn't seem very important here. 'Anyway, don't be stubborn. Let me call a cab.' She looked at her watch. It was eight fifteen. 'I really have to go.'

He pulled his car keys out of his pocket and waved them at her. 'Come on, let's go.' He turned to the children and Mrs Hahn. 'If the hospital calls, I'll be home in an hour or two. I have my pager on me, so they can catch me if they have to.' Just to be safe, he called to check on both Marie and Pattie Lou again before they left, and the resident in charge said they were fine, and with that he escorted Mel to the door. She waved at the children for a last time, and they got into the car. She had the feeling that all her decisions were being made for her, but it was a pleasant change from constantly looking out for herself.

'There's something about you, Doctor. You seem to make up my mind for me and I can't even say I object.'

He laughed. 'I guess I'm used to giving orders most of the time.' He smiled at her. 'And being obeyed.'

'So am I.' She grinned. 'But it's kind of pleasant taking orders from someone else for a change, even about something so simple as not taking a cab.'

'It's the least I can do. You've been my shadow for the past four days, and done something absolutely marvellous, I suspect.'

'Don't say that until you see the finished film.'

'I can just tell from the way you work.'

'That's a lot of faith. I'm not sure I deserve all that.'

He looked at her again. 'Yes, you do.' And then he frowned. 'By the way, how was your talk with Pam?'

Mel sighed. 'Touching. She's not a very happy child, is she?'

'Unfortunately, that's all too true.'

'She's tormenting herself about Anne.' It seemed strange to say his wife's name, it felt awkward on her lips. 'I think she'll be all right in time. Mostly she needs someone to talk to.'

'I send her to a psychiatrist.' He said it defensively.

'She needs more than that. And . . .' She hesitated and then decided to go ahead. 'Mrs Hahn doesn't seem very warm.'

'She's not, at least not outwardly, but she loves those kids. And she's extremely competent.'

'She needs someone she can talk to, Peter, and so does Matt.'

'And what would you suggest?' He sounded bitter now. 'That I find a new wife just for them?'

'No. If you lead a normal life, you'll find one for yourself in time.'

'That's not what I have in mind.' She saw his jaw clench, and realised that they were both more tired than they knew.

'Why not? You were happily married before, you could be happily married again.'

'It would never be the same.' He looked sadly at Mel. 'I really don't want to get married again.'

'You can't stay alone for the rest of your life.'

'Why not? You never remarried. Why should I?' It was a good point.

'I'm not the marrying kind. You are.'

He laughed aloud at that. 'Well, that's a crock. Why not?'

'I'm just not. I'm too involved in my work to get tied down again.'

'I don't believe that. I think you're scared.' She almost flinched as he said the words; he had hit a nerve.

'Scared?' She sounded surprised nonetheless. 'Of what?'

'Commitment, love, being too close. I'm not sure. I don't know you that well.' But he had certainly seen into her. She didn't answer for a long time; she just stared into the night as they drove along and then she turned to him.

'You're probably right. But I'm too old to change now.'

'At thirty-two, four, five, whatever you are? That's crap.'

'No, it's not. And I'm thirty-five.' She smiled. 'But I like my life just as it is.'

'You won't when your daughters are gone.'

'That's something you should think of too. But in your case, your children need someone now, and so do you.' And then suddenly she began to laugh as she looked at him. 'This is crazy, here we are practically shouting at each other, that we should each get married. And we hardly know each other.'

He glanced over at her with a funny look on his face. 'The odd thing is that I feel as though we do. It seems as though you've been out here for years.'

She grew pensive then. 'I feel that way too, and it really doesn't make sense.' And then they were cast into the crowds and bright lights. He had tipped a porter so he could leave his car at the kerb, and he followed Mel inside, sorry that they hadn't had more time to talk alone. After last night he felt even closer to her than before. It was as though they had shared something special, the saving of a woman's life. It was like being combat buddies, or something more, and he was even sorrier now to see her go than he had been the day before.

'Well, let me know how the film looks.' They stood awkwardly at the gate as the flight was called, and she found herself itching to be held in his arms.

'I will. Take care. And give my love to the kids.' There was a feeling of *déjà vu* to the scene, but it was more poignant than before. 'And Marie and Pattie Lou.' Her voice was soft.

'Take care of yourself. Don't work too hard, Mel.'

'You too.' His eyes reached out to her, but there were no words for the confusion that he felt and he wasn't sure what to do. There was no privacy here, and he still wasn't sure what he felt for her.

'Thank you for everything.' And with that she shook him off guard by kissing his cheek, and walking through the gate, giving him a last wave, and then she was gone. He stood and stared, and then his beeper went off at his side, and he had to hurry to a phone. He couldn't wait for the plane to take off. He called the hospital, and the resident had a question about Marie. She was running a slight temperature, and he wanted to know if Peter wanted any of the doses of her medications varied. He made the necessary changes and walked back to his car, thinking not of Marie, but of Mel, just as her plane took off. The giant silver bird rose into the air and Mel stared down at the endless parking lots below, wondering where he was, and if she would ever see him or his children again. This time, there was no doubt in her mind. She was sad to leave, and sadder still to be going home. Tonight she didn't even try to convince herself that it wasn't true. She just sat staring out the window, thinking of him and the past four days, knowing that she liked him too much and it would get her nowhere. They led separate lives, in separate worlds, in cities three thousand miles apart, and that was just the way things were. And none of that would ever change.

CHAPTER 10

The flight to New York passed uneventfully. Mel took out a notebook and jotted down notes about the past few days while they were still fresh in her mind. There were a number of things she wanted to touch on in her commentary on the piece. Then at last, feeling drained, she closed the book and laid her head back against the seat and closed her eyes. The stewardess had offered her cocktails, wine, or champagne several times, but she had declined. She wanted to be left alone with her own thoughts, and after a while she drifted off to sleep for the last few hours of the flight. The trip from west to east always went too quickly to get much rest. With tail winds pushing the plane along, they made it to New York easily in just under five hours. She woke again with the sound of the landing announcement in her ears, and a stewardess touching her arm, asking her to fasten her seat belt before landing.

'Thank you.' She looked up at the stewardess sleepily and stifled a yawn, as she fastened her seat belt and then opened her bag to take out a comb. She felt as though she had been wearing the same clothes for days, and wondered again if she would find her suitcase waiting for her in New York. It seemed aeons since she had almost got on the plane in LA some thirty hours before, and been stopped by Peter's call. Then her mind drifted back to him again. His face seemed to come alive before her as she closed her eyes, and then forced herself to open them again as she felt the plane land on the runway in New York. She was home. And she had a mountain of work to do for the news and on the film she had done of him and Pattie Lou, and she had lots to do with the girls as well. She had her own life to lead, and yet there was the oddest feeling of regret to be back. She wished she could have stayed longer in LA, but

126

there was no need, and she could never have explained it to the network in New York.

She found her bag waiting for her in the special-services area of baggage claim, picked it up, walked outside, hailed a cab, and headed for New York City at full speed. There was no traffic at all at six thirty in the morning, and the sun shot darts of gold across the sky, which was reflected on the windows of the skyscrapers that lined the view. As they came across the bridge and headed south on the East River Drive, she felt something stir in her again. New York always did that to her. It was a splendid town. And suddenly it wasn't so bad to be home again. This was where she belonged. As she smiled to herself, she noticed the driver watching her in his rearview mirror with a curious look. As she often did to strangers, she looked familiar to him, and he wasn't sure why. Maybe he had had her in the cab before, he thought to himself, or she was the wife of some important man, a politician or a movie star and he'd seen her in the news. He knew he'd seen that face somewhere before, but he wasn't quite sure where.

'Been away long?' He continued to search his mind as he looked at her.

'Just a few days, on the West Coast.'

'Yeah,' he nodded, turning right at Seventy-ninth and heading west. 'I been out there once. But there ain't no place like New York.'

She smiled. New Yorkers were a breed unto themselves, loyal to the end, despite dog mess, debris, crime in the streets, pollution, overpopulation, and the city's myriad failings and sins. Nonetheless, it had a quality one found nowhere else, a certain electricity that touched one to the very core. And she could feel it even now, as she watched the city come alive, as they sped through its streets.

'It's a great town.' He voiced his passion for his hometown again, and Mel nodded her head.

'It sure is.' It really was good to be back, and a happy feeling stirred her soul, as they pulled up in front of her

127

house. She was excited about seeing the girls again, paid the cab, carried her bag inside, set it down in the front hall, and bounded upstairs to see them. They were both asleep, and she walked quietly into Jessica's room and sat down on the bed, looking at her. Her flame-coloured hair was spread out on the pillow like a dark red sheet, and she stirred as she heard her mother's voice and opened one eye. 'Hi, lazybones.' She bent down and kissed her cheek, and Jessie smiled.

'Hi, Mom. You're home.' She sat up and stretched and then hugged her mother with a sleepy smile. 'How was the trip?'

'Okay. It feels good to be back.' And this time she meant what she said. It did feel good. She had left California behind, along with Peter Hallam, and Marie Dupret and Center City Hospital, and all that she had done since she left New York. 'We did a terrific film.'

'Did you watch them operate?' Jessie was instantly intrigued. She would have given anything to have seen that, although her twin would have blanched at the thought.

'I did. I stayed to watch them do a transplant last night . . . no, the night before . . .' The time was all confused now in her head and she smiled. 'Whenever it was, it was a success. It was extraordinary, Jess.'

'Can I see the film?'

'Of course. You can come down to the station before we air the piece.'

'Thanks, Mom.' She climbed slowly out of bed, her long legs seeming longer beneath a short pink nightshirt, and Melanie left the room to see the other twin. In her room, Valerie was buried in her bed, fast asleep, and it took several gentle shoves and taps to move her at all. Melanie finally had to pull the blanket away from her and tug at the sheets, until at last Val woke up with a sleepy growl.

'Cut it out, Jess . . .' And then she opened her eyes and saw Melanie instead. She looked surprised and confused, forgetting that her mother was due back. 'How come you're home?'

'That's a nice welcome home. Last I heard, I live here.'

Valerie grinned sleepily and turned over on her side. 'I forgot you were coming back today.'

'So what were you planning to do? Sleep all day and cut school?' She didn't really worry about that, about either of them, although Valerie was sometimes the less conscientious of the two.

'That's a nice idea. After all, school's almost out.'

'Then what do you say you hang in for a couple more weeks?'

'Awww Mom . . .' She tried to go back to sleep and Melanie tickled her instead. 'Stop that!' She sat up with a shriek, defending herself against Mel's nimble hands. She knew all the places that tickled Valerie most, and a minute later they were laughing and Val was still shrieking as Jessica wandered into the room. With a single bound, she leapt into the bed, and helped Mel out, and then there was a pillow fight, which Valerie started in her own defence, and the three of them lay on the bed after a while, laughing and breathless. Mel felt her heart soar. Whatever she did, wherever she went, it was always so good to come home to them. And almost as soon as the thought crossed her mind, she found herself thinking of Pam in Los Angeles, and how different her life was from all this. How much she would have benefited from a life like the twins', and how lonely she was. Over breakfast, once the twins were dressed, she told them about the Hallam kids, especially Pam, and they seemed sorry for her when Mel explained to them about Anne's death.

'That must really be rough on her.' The more compassionate of the two, Val was the first to express concern, and then she grinned. 'And what's her brother like? I'll bet he's cute.'

'Val . . .' Jessie said it with a disapproving glance. 'That's all you think about.'

'So what? I'll bet he is.'

'Who cares? He doesn't live here. There are probably a lot of cute boys in LA. What's that going to do for you in New York?' Jessie looked annoyed and Mel was amused. She addressed her youngest daughter as she finished her tea. 'Does that mean you've exhausted the supply in New York?'

Val laughed. 'There's always room for one more.'

'I don't know how you keep their names straight.'

'I don't think she does,' Jessica was quick to add. In that one area, she disapproved of Val's style. She was more like Mel that way, independent, cool, cautious about getting involved with boys – too cautious at times – and it even worried Mel. Her life-style had clearly left its mark on the oldest twin. Maybe even on both. Perhaps that was why Val was always so anxious *not* to be without a beau. She didn't want to end up like Mel. 'She just oohs and smiles at them all in the halls at school, and I don't think they even care if she forgets their names.' It was more disapproval than jealousy at times like this, Mel knew. Val's passion for the opposite sex seemed trivial to Jess, who frequently had more important projects of an intellectual or scientific bent on her mind, but she had her share of boyfriends too. Mel reminded her of that when Val left the room to get her books for school. 'I know. But she acts like she doesn't have any sense. It's all she thinks about, Mom.'

'She'll get over it in a few years.'

'Yeah.' Jessie shrugged. 'Maybe.' And then they hurried off to school on Ninety-first Street, off Fifth, ten blocks away, and Melanie was left to gather her thoughts and unpack. She wanted to get to the station early that day to sort through her notes, and she had just stepped out of the shower at ten o'clock, when the phone rang, and she picked it up, still dripping wet. It was Grant, and she smiled to hear his voice.

'So you're back. I was beginning to think you'd left for good.'

'Nothing quite so dramatic as that. Although the last day was fairly dramatic, in a different way. They found a

130

donor for a transplant patient that was barely hanging on, and I missed my plane and went back to watch the surgery.'

'Your stomach is infinitely stronger than mine.'

'I'm not so sure about that, but it was fascinating to watch.' And again a vision of Peter flashed into her mind. 'It was a good trip all in all, and how are you?'

'No change. I called the girls a few times to make sure they were all right, and they were fine. I can't keep up with their social lives, I'm afraid.'

'Neither can I. But you were nice to call.'

'I told you I would.' He sounded happy to hear her voice, and she was equally so to hear his. 'How'd the little girl do?'

'Great. She looked brand-new the last time I saw her at the hospital. It's just amazing, Grant.'

'And the good doctor who did it all? Was he amazing too?' It was as though he already sensed what she felt, but she felt foolish admitting her feelings to him. She was too old for that. Sudden attractions like that were better left to Val.

'He was an interesting man.'

'That's all? One of the foremost cardiac surgeons in the country, and that's all you have to say?' And then suddenly he grinned. He knew her too well. 'Or is it that there's more?'

'There isn't more. I just had a very hectic few days.' She wanted to keep her feelings about Peter Hallam to herself. There was no point sharing them with anyone, not even Grant. Most likely she would never see him again, and the words were better left unsaid.

'Well, when you settle down, Mel, give me a call, and we'll go have drinks sometime.'

'You're on.' But she didn't even feel like doing that right now. She was in her own private haze and she didn't feel like emerging from it yet.

'See you later, kid.' And then after a moment's pause. 'I'm glad you're back.'

'Thanks, me too.' But it was a lie. Even the excitement of being back in New York didn't woo her this time.

As she left the house, she glanced at her watch, and saw that it was eleven o'clock. Peter would be in surgery by then. And suddenly she had an overwhelming urge to call the hospital and inquire about Marie, but she had to retreat back into her professional life now. She couldn't take on all their problems as though they were her own, Marie's heart, Peter's kids, Pam's empty, lonely life, little Matthew with the big blue eyes . . . suddenly she found herself longing for them again. Pushing them determinedly from her head, she hailed a cab and sailed downtown, looking at the city that she loved: people scurrying into Bloomingdale's and down into the ground to catch the subway, hailing cabs, or rushing in and out of skyscrapers on their way to work. It was like being part of a film just being there, and she felt buoyant and alive, even with almost no sleep, and she walked into the newsroom with a happy smile.

'What's with you?' The story editor growled at her as she rushed past, carrying two cans of films.

'I'm happy to be back.'

He shook his head, muttering, as he disappeared. 'Fool.'

She found a stack of mail on her desk, memos, summaries of major news items she'd missed while she was gone, and went out into the hall to watch the teletypes coming in for a while. There had been an earthquake in Brazil, a flood in Italy that had killed a hundred and sixty-four people, the President was going down to the Bahamas for a long weekend to fish. The news of the day didn't look overwhelmingly bad or good, and when her secretary came to tell her that there was a call for her, she went back into her office and picked up the phone without sitting down. She answered absentmindedly, glancing at the memos on her desk.

'Adams here.'

There was a moment's pause, as though she'd thrown

someone off with the brusque words, and she heard a long-distance purr. But she didn't even have time to wonder who it was. 'Is this a bad time?' She recognised the voice instantly and sat down, surprised to hear from him. Maybe, with some time to think in her absence, he was getting worried about the piece.

'Not at all. How are you?' Her voice was soft and at his end he felt the same mysterious stirring he'd felt in his soul since they met.

'I'm fine. I finished surgery early today and thought I'd call to make sure you got back all right. Did you find your bag in New York?' He sounded nervous, and she was pleased by the call.

'I did. How's Marie?' Maybe he had called to give her bad news.

'She's doing beautifully. She asked for you today in fact. And so did Pattie Lou. She's the real star around here.'

Mel felt tears sting her eyes, and once again she felt the same ache she'd felt on the plane, of wanting to be in LA and not New York. 'Tell her I send my love. Maybe when she's feeling a little better, I'll give her a call.'

'She'd love that. And how are your girls?' He seemed to be groping for something to say and Mel was both confused and touched.

'They're fine. I think Valerie fell in love a few more times while I was gone, and Jessica is desperately jealous that I got to watch the transplant. She's the more serious of the two.'

'She's the one who wants to go to med school, isn't she?' Melanie was surprised that he'd recalled and she smiled.

'That's the one. She read her sister the riot act this morning, about falling in love six times a week.'

Peter laughed from his little cubicle in the hospital on the West Coast. He had billed the call to his home phone. 'We used to have the same problem with Mark when he was about Pam's age. But in the last few years he's settled down.'

'Ah, but wait for Matt!' Mel laughed. 'That one's going to be the lady's man of all time.'

133

Peter laughed too. 'I have a sneaking suspicion that you're right.' There was a comfortable pause and then Mel filled the gap.

'How's Pam?'

'She's all right. Nothing new.' He sighed into the phone. 'You know, I think it did her good to talk to you. Just to be able to relate to someone other than Mrs Hahn.' Mel didn't dare tell him what she thought of the icy woman. She didn't feel it was her place to speak up.

'I enjoyed talking to her too.' Her emotional needs seemed so desperate, and there seemed to be a lot of anger to vent too. Mel couldn't resist asking him then. 'Did they get the little packages I sent yet?'

'Packages?' He sounded surprised. 'Did you send them gifts? You shouldn't have done that.'

'I couldn't resist. I saw something perfect for Pam, and I didn't want to leave Matthew and Mark out. Besides, they were very tolerant about letting me hang around. As you said, you haven't seen people much since . . . in the past year and a half' – she hastened to fill the awkward gap – 'so it must have seemed strange to them to have me appear. The least I could do was send them a little surprise to thank them for their hospitality.'

He was touched by the thought and his voice was soft. 'You didn't have to do that, Mel. We enjoyed having you here.' His words almost caressed her and she blushed. There was something deeply intimate about this man, even by phone, with three thousand miles in between, and she found herself thinking of him again in ways she hadn't wanted to. It was almost impossible not to be drawn to him. He was at the same time vulnerable and strong, humble and kind and yet so full of the miracles he wrought. It was a combination which, for Mel, had enormous appeal. She had always liked strong men, and yet too often she had shied away from them. It was easier to get involved with lesser lights than he.

'I really enjoyed working with you, you know.' She

wasn't sure what else to say, and still wasn't sure why he'd called.

'You stole my lines. That's what I was calling to tell you. I'd been very apprehensive about doing the interview. And you made me glad I decided to go through with it. Everyone here is.' But not as much as he was, though he didn't tell her that.

'Well, wait until you see it all on film. I hope you like it as much then.'

'I know I will.'

'I'm grateful for your faith in me.' And she truly was, but there was something more to what she felt as well, and she wasn't quite sure what it was.

'It's not just a matter of that, Mel. I . . .' He didn't quite know how to put his feelings into words, and suddenly wondered if he should have called. She was a woman who signed autographs and appeared on national TV. 'I just like you a hell of a lot.' He felt as awkward as a fifteen-year-old boy and they both smiled, in LA and New York.

'I like you too.' Maybe it was just as simple as that, and there was no harm in it. Why was she fighting so hard against what she felt? 'I liked working with you, meeting your kids, seeing your home.' And then she understood something else. 'I think I was especially touched that you let me into your private life.'

'I think I felt safe doing that with you. I didn't plan it that way. In fact, I told myself before you came that I wasn't going to tell you anything personal about myself . . . or Anne . . .' His voice grew very soft again.

Mel was quick to respond. 'I'm glad you did.'

'So am I.' 'I thought you handled the piece on Pattie Lou beautifully.'

'Thank you, Peter.' She liked what he had said. The trouble was that she liked too much about him. And then she heard him sigh softly at the other end. 'Well, I guess I should let you go back to work. I wasn't sure you'd be in after taking the red eye last night.'

She laughed softly at her end. 'The show must go on. And at six o'clock I have the news to do. I was just watching the teletypes come in when you called.'

'I hope I didn't interrupt.' He sounded contrite.

'No, it's kind of like watching the ticker tapes. After a while, you stop seeing what you read. And there's nothing major happening today, so far.'

'That's about the way it is here. I'm going to the office now. I have a lot of catching up to do, after keeping an eye on Marie and Pattie Lou for the past few days.' They were both back to their usual lives, their work, their kids, their responsibilities on separate coasts, and again she felt how much she had in common with him. He had as much resting on his shoulders as she on hers, in fact more. And it was comforting to know that there were other people in the world, carrying burdens and obligations as demanding as hers.

'You know, it's kind of nice knowing someone who works as hard as I do.' And he felt odd as she said the words. He had thought the same thing about her from the first. Even with Anne, it had bothered him sometimes that all she had to do was redecorate the house and buy antiques, work on the PTA and chauffeur children from here to there. 'I don't mean to sound presumptuous because my work doesn't include saving lives, but still, it's demanding as hell and most people don't understand that. Some nights I finish here and my brain is absolutely mush. I couldn't say an intelligent word to a living soul if my life depended on it when I got home.' It was one of the many reasons why she had never been tempted to marry again. She wasn't sure she could live up to the demands of it any more.

But he felt as relieved as she. 'I know exactly what you mean. But on the other hand, sometimes it's difficult not to have someone to share it with.'

'I never really have. As long as I've done well at my work, I've been alone, or more or less. I think it's easier like this.'

136

'Yes' – but he didn't sound convinced – 'but then there's no one to share the victories with.' Anne had always been good at that, and good at sharing the heartbreaks and tragedies too. It was just that her life had never been as full as his, but on the other hand maybe that had left her freer to support him. It was difficult to imagine a working wife, and yet he had always admired hardworking teams, doctors married to other doctors, lawyers married to bankers, professors and scientists. The combinations seemed to feed on themselves, giving each one a new impetus, although at times it could also be a double drain. 'I don't know the answers to all this, my friend. I just know it isn't always easy being alone.'

'Neither is being together.' She was convinced.

'No. But it has its rewards.' Of that he was sure. Especially when he looked at his kids.

'I guess that's true. I don't know the answers myself. I just know it's good talking to someone who understands what it's like to work like a mule, and then have to come home and be two parents instead of just one.' There had been times over the years when she thought she couldn't pull it off, but she had, and she had done well. Her job was secure, her success immense, her children happy and they were good kids.

'You've done a good job, Mel.' They were words that meant more to her than anything else.

'So have you.' Her voice was like silk to his ears.

'But I've only done it alone for a year and a half. You've been alone for fifteen. That really means something.'

'Only a few more grey hairs.' She laughed softly into the phone. Just then one of the editors signalled to her from the door. And she signalled back that she'd be with him in a few minutes, so he disappeared again. 'Well, it looks like they want me to go to work around here. One of the editors just showed up. I hope that means our film is in from LA.'

'So soon?'

'It's complicated to explain, but they do it all by

computers. We get it here within a day. I'll let you know how it looks.'

'I'd like that.'

And she had liked hearing from him. 'Thank you so much for calling me, Peter. I really miss you all.' The 'all' kept it safe. It meant she didn't just miss him. It was like listening to Val and Jess on the phone, fencing with their boyfriends, she chided herself and then smiled. 'I'll talk to you soon.'

'Good. We miss you too.' 'We' instead of 'I'. They were playing the same game and neither of them could figure out why, but they weren't ready for more. 'Take care.'

'Thanks. You too.' They rang off and Mel sat at her desk for a long moment, thinking of him. It was crazy, but she was excited that he'd called. As excited as a little girl. She hurried down the hall to the editing labs with a grin on her face that she just couldn't erase. A grin that stayed there until she saw the film. She saw herself looking at him, and Pattie Lou and Pearl and even Marie and her transplant done at two a.m., and she felt her heart race each time he spoke, each time the camera looked into his eyes and saw the decency and caring there. She felt almost breathless when at last they turned on the lights. It was a sensational piece of film.

In its pre-cut stage it went on for hours, it would need much cutting and editing. But all she could think of as she left the room, was him . . .

CHAPTER 11

That night, Melanie did the news again for the first time since she'd been back, and everything went as smoothly as it always did. She signed off with the pleasant, professional smile that people recognised everywhere across the entire United States, and as she walked off the set, she had no idea that Peter Hallam had been watching her intently in his den in LA. Halfway through it Pam had walked into the room and stood there and stared. Peter hadn't even known she was there.

'Someone shoot the President or something, Dad?'

He looked at her, annoyed, it had been a long day and he wanted to see Mel before she went off the air. He had watched her before, but it had never been quite like this. He knew her now, and suddenly it seemed terribly important to see her after their call that day. 'Pam, I'll come upstairs in a little while. I just want to be alone to watch the news.'

For a long moment, Pam stood there in the doorway, torn by her own feelings of anger and attraction to Mel. She had liked her when they met, but she didn't like the way her father looked when he saw her. 'Yeah, sure . . . okay . . .' But he didn't see the look on her face as she left the room and he sat staring at the set as Mel wound up for the day. He sat there for a little while longer, and then he turned off the set and went upstairs to see his children. He was truly exhausted. He had spent two hours with Marie that afternoon at the hospital. She seemed to be developing an infection, and was having a reaction to the medication. It was expected, but difficult anyway.

In New York, Mel hurried home after doing the news, and had dinner with the girls, and then went back to the studio to do the eleven-o'clock show. It was after that that

Mel saw Grant again for the first time. He was waiting for her on the set when she came off the air.

'You did a nice job tonight.' He looked down at her with a warm smile and could see how tired she was. But he saw something else too. Something that hadn't been there before, a kind of glow. 'How are you holding up with no sleep?'

'I'm beginning to fade,' she admitted with a tired smile, but she was glad to see him.

'Well, go home and get some rest.'

'Yes, Dad.'

'I'm old enough to be, so watch your step.'

'Yes, sir.' She saluted smartly, and a few minutes later she left, dozing sleepily in the cab.

She climbed the stairs to her room, peeled her clothes off and dropped them on the floor beside her bed. Five minutes later, she was sound asleep between her cool sheets, naked and peaceful, her mind empty at last of anything at all. And she didn't stir again until early next afternoon, when the phone rang and it was Peter again.

'Good morning. Is it too early to call?'

'Not at all.' She stifled a yawn and glanced at the clock. It was ten fifteen for him on the Coast. 'How's life in LA?'

'Busy. I've got two triple bypasses scheduled today.'

'How are Marie and Pattie Lou?' She sat up in bed and looked around her room in New York.

'They're both fine. Pattie Lou more so than Marie.' She really had been a victory for him. 'More importantly, how are you?'

'Honestly?' She smiled. 'I'm dead.'

'You ought to get some rest. You work too hard, Mel.'

'Look who's talking.' She tried to pretend that it was normal for him to call, but secretly she was thrilled. 'I'm going on holiday soon anyway.'

'You are?' He sounded surprised, she hadn't mentioned it before, but when had there been time during her few days in LA. 'Where?'

'Bermuda.' She sounded pleased. She'd been looking

140

forward to it for a long time. A television producer she knew had offered to rent her her house for a few days, and because it didn't coincide with any school holiday for the twins, she had just decided to go alone anyway.

He sounded nervous when he next spoke. 'Are you going with friends?'

'No. By myself.'

'You are?' He sounded both stunned and relieved. 'What an independent lady you are.' He admired her for that. He wasn't ready for a holiday alone yet. He would have been lost without the children, now that Anne was gone. But Mel had been alone for a lot longer than he.

'I just thought it might be fun. The girls are jealous as hell. But they have friends and a big prom that week.'

'I'm jealous too.'

'Don't be. It'll probably be very quiet.' But it wouldn't have been with him. She forced the thought from her mind. 'But it'll do me good.'

'Yes, it will.' He didn't begrudge her that. He just wished he could have been there with her, as crazy as the thought was. They were almost strangers to each other, although not nearly as much as they had been.

They talked on for a little while, and then he had to go off to surgery, and Mel wanted to go to the network to watch them edit some more of her film.

CHAPTER 12

The phone rang just as she was leaving the house the following Wednesday morning. She was in a hurry to get to Bloomingdale's because she desperately needed some more bathing suits for the trip to Bermuda that week. She had looked over the ones from the summer before and they were all badly worn and stretched and faded. She lived in her bathing suits for two months, and every year they took a beating.

'Hello?'

'It's me.' It was Grant.

'What's up? I was just running out to buy some new bathing suits for my trip.' She was finally beginning to look forward to it. And she was leaving in two days. 'Do you want me to pick anything up for you? I'm going to Bloomie's.'

'No, thanks. I forgot you were going down there. Need a butler or a male secretary while you're there?'

'No thank you.' She smiled at the phone, and he realised he'd hardly seen her since she got back from LA.

'I just wanted to ask you a question about Marcia Evans.' She was the grande dame of legitimate theatre and Mel had done an intimate interview with her six months before. 'I'm having her on the show tonight.'

Mel cringed. 'Good luck. She's a dragon.'

'Shit. That's what I thought. And the producer told me I had nothing to worry about. Any tips for my survival?'

'Bring along a snake-bite kit. She's the most venomous woman I've ever met. Just watch out that you don't piss her off. You'll see her coming.'

'That's a big help.' He didn't sound pleased, and he was furious with his producer for setting him up.

142

'I'll give it some more thought while I'm out shopping, and I'll call you when I get home.'

'Do you want to have dinner tonight, to give me courage?'

'Why don't you drop by to see the girls?'

'I'll try' – he grinned – 'if nothing else interferes.'

'You and tits, Grant.' She laughed.

'I can't help it if I'm weak. I'll call you later, kid.'

'Okay.' He hung up, and she looked in the mirror and picked up her handbag. She was wearing a white linen dress with a black silk jacket and black and white patent leather shoes she had bought in Rome the year before. She looked very chic and she felt good. They had worked like demons for a week, editing the film on Peter Hallam and Pattie Lou Jones and she was just loving what they got as they went along. As she reached the front door, the phone rang again, and she was tempted not to answer. It was probably the damn editor wanting her to come in, and for once she wanted some time to herself to do her shopping. But it rang so persistently that she gave in and walked into the living room and picked up the white phone she had concealed in a nook there.

'Yes?' She waited, afraid she'd hear the editor's voice again. He had already called twice that morning. But it wasn't the editor at all. It was Peter Hallam again. He called her often.

'Hello, Mel.' He sounded hesitant after her gruff response when she picked it up and she was embarrassed.

'Hi, Peter, I'm sorry if I barked. I was just running out, but . . .' She felt young again, and nervous, just as she had when he'd called before. He had a funny effect on her, which seemed to cancel out her success and her self-confidence. She was just a young girl again when she talked to him . . . or maybe 'just' a woman. '. . . it's nice to hear from you.' He hadn't called in a few days. 'How's Marie?' Suddenly she was afraid that he had called to give her bad news, but he was quick to reassure her.

'Much better. We had a problem last night, and I

143

thought she was going into a major rejection, but everything's under control again. We switched her medication. We think she might even be ready to go home in a few weeks.' It was something Melanie would have liked to see, but it didn't justify a trip West and her producer would never have let her go just for that.

'And the children?'

'They're fine. I just wondered how you were. I called you at the office but they said you weren't there.'

'I'm playing hooky.' She laughed and felt lighthearted and happy. 'This is the weekend I'm going to Bermuda, and I needed to shop for a few things.'

'That sounds like fun. We're staying here for a long weekend. Mark is playing in a tennis tournament and Matthew's going to a birthday party.'

'The girls are going to that prom I told you about, and then to Cape Cod with a friend and her parents.' They seemed to hide a lot in talk of their children, and Mel found herself wondering how *he* was, not Pam and Mark and Matthew. And then she decided to ask him. 'Are you all right, Peter? Not working too hard?'

'Of course I am,' he laughed, but he was pleased at the question. 'I wouldn't know how to do anything else, and neither would you.'

'That's true. When I get old and wrinkled and have to retire, I won't know what the hell to do with myself every morning.'

'You'll think of something.'

'Yeah, brain surgery maybe.' They both laughed, she sat down as Bloomingdale's and the bathing suits slipped her mind completely. 'Actually, I'd like to write a book then.'

'What about?'

'My memoirs.' She teased.

'No, really.'

It wasn't often that she confessed her dreams to anyone, but he was easy to talk to. 'I don't know, I think I'd write a book about being a woman in journalism. It was tough at

144

first, although it's a lot easier now, but not always. People resent it like hell when you make it. They're half glad, and half pissed. It's been interesting coping with that, and I think it's something a lot of women could relate to. It doesn't matter if you do what I do, or you do something else. The issue is crawling to the top, and I know what that's like, how much work it takes and what happens when you get there.'

'It sounds like an instant best seller.'

'Maybe not, but I'd like to try it.'

'I've always wanted to write a book about heart surgery for the layman, what it's like, what to expect, what to demand of your doctor, what the risks are in specific situations. I don't know if anyone would give a damn, but too many people are unprepared, and get screwed over by their doctors.'

'Now, that sounds like a good one.' She was impressed, there was a need for a book like that and it would be interesting to see what he did with it.

'Maybe we should run away to the South Pacific together, and write our books. When the kids grow up,' he added.

'Why wait?' It was an amusing fantasy, but it suddenly reminded her of the trip to Bermuda. 'I've never been to the South Pacific.' And she had been to Bermuda. It was tropical and it wasn't too far away but it was definitely not exciting. Or maybe it was that going alone didn't excite her. And Peter did? That question was frightening to answer.

'I've always wanted to go to Bora Bora,' he confessed, 'but I can never get away from my patients for long enough to make it worthwhile.'

'Maybe you don't want to.' It was something Anne had accused him of too, and it was probably true.

'You may be right.' Somehow it was easy to be honest with her. 'I'll have to save it till I retire.' There was a lot he had saved for that, and now that Anne was gone it would never be shared after all. He had put off so much for 'later' that he regretted now. There was no later. At least not for them. And he wondered at the wisdom of continuing to save things for 'later'. What if he had a stroke, if he died, if . . . 'Maybe I'll go sooner than that.'

'You ought to. You owe yourself something.' But what? All he wanted lately was her.

'Are you excited about your trip, Mel?'

'Yes and no.' She had been to romantic spots alone before. It had its drawbacks.

'Send me a postcard.'

'I will.'

And then, 'I'd better let you go. Call me when you get back from your trip. And rest!'

'You need it as much as I do. Probably more.'

'I doubt that.'

She looked at her watch then, wondering where he was. It was nine thirty in the morning in California. 'Aren't you in surgery today?'

'No. The last Wednesday of every month we have conferences to bring the whole team up to date on new techniques and procedures. We discuss what's being done all over the country, and what we've each tried to accomplish in surgery that month.'

'I wish I'd known. I would have loved to have that on film.' But she had enough without it.

'We start at ten o'clock. And I finished my rounds early.' He sounded boyish too then. 'Calling you is a treat I've been promising myself for days.' It was easier to say things like that on the phone, and he was suddenly grateful for the distance between them.

'I'm flattered.' He wanted to tell her that she should be, that he had never called another woman, in that sense, since marrying Anne, but he didn't say it. 'I've thought about calling you a few times too, to see how Marie was, but the time difference was always off.'

'That happened to me too. Anyway, I'm glad I called. Have a nice weekend in Bermuda.'

'Thank you. You have a nice one too. I'll call you when

146

I get back.' It was the first time she had promised that in just that way, and she was already looking forward to it. 'Our film is looking sensational, by the way.'

He smiled warmly. 'I'm glad.' But that wasn't why he had called. 'Take care of yourself, Mel.'

'I'll call you next week.' And suddenly she knew that a bond had formed between them that hadn't been there before, and as she left to go to Bloomingdale's, she felt young and excited and carefree.

She tried on two blue bathing suits, a black one, and a red one, but red had never been a good colour with her hair, and she bought a rich royal-blue one and the black one. They were a bit risqué, but she felt exotic today. As she stood at the counter smiling to herself, holding her charge card and the two bathing suits, waiting to be helped, she saw a woman in tears rush towards her. 'The President's been shot!' she screamed to anyone who would listen. 'He's been shot in the chest and the back, and he's dying!' The entire store seemed shot with an electric current as people shouted the news to each other and began running, as though their frenzied activity would help. But Mel, operating by reflex, dropped the bathing suits on the counter, and ran down three flights of stairs and out of the door. She climbed into the first cab she saw, breathlessly gave the studio address, and asked the driver to turn on the radio as they drove. Both she and the cabbie sat frozen in silence as they listened to the news. No one seemed to know yet for certain if the President was alive or not. He had been in Los Angeles for a day, conferring with the governor and assorted civic leaders in LA. He was rushed to the hospital in an ambulance moments before, critically wounded, as two Secret Servicemen lay dead on the pavement next to where he had stood. Mel's face was pale as she threw a ten-dollar bill into the driver's hands and hurtled through the double doors leading into the network building. Everything was already in total chaos there from the lobby to the newsroom, and as she flew towards the bureau chief's desk, he looked at her with relief.

'Christ, I hoped you'd get here, Mel.'

'I practically ran all the way from Bloomingdale's.' At least, she felt like she had. She knew that the one place she had to be was here.

'I want to put you on with the special bulletins right away.' He looked at what she was wearing and she looked fine, but he wouldn't have given a damn if she'd been stark naked. 'Get some makeup on and can you close your jacket a little? The dress is too white for the camera.'

'Sure. What's new now?'

'Nothing yet. He's in surgery, and it looks bad, Mel.'

'Shit.' She ran to her office, and where she kept her makeup, and five minutes later she was back, ready to go on the air. The producer followed her into the studio, and handed her a stack of papers for her to read quickly. She looked at him a moment later, with grim eyes. 'It doesn't look good, does it?' He'd been hit in the chest three times, and his spine seemed to have been affected, from the early reports. Even if he lived, he could be paralysed or worse yet, a complete vegetable. He was in Center City, undergoing surgery right then. And Mel suddenly wondered what Peter Hallam knew about it that the press didn't, but she didn't have time to call before she went on the air.

She went quickly to her desk, and began ad-libbing soberly into the camera as she went on beneath the hot lights and she delivered the news bulletins as they came on. All normal programming had been stopped to give the public the news as it came, but there wasn't a great deal to say yet. She had to wing it for most of the afternoon, and she didn't get a break for three hours, when she was relieved by one of the other anchors, the man who did the weekend news. They had all been called in, and there was endless discussion and surmise on the air between reports from the West Coast, and moments when they switched to the reporters in LA, standing in the lobby of Center City, so familiar now to Mel. She only wished that she were there, as she listened to the news. But by six o'clock there was still no news, except that he was still alive and had

148

survived surgery. They would have to play a waiting game, as would the First Lady, who was in the air on her way to LA now, and due to arrive at LA within the hour.

Mel did her usual show at six o'clock, and of course covered almost exclusively the news from LA and when she came off the air, the producer was waiting to confer with her.

'Mel.' He looked at her sombrely and handed her another sheaf of papers. 'I want you out there.' For a moment, she was stunned. 'Go home, get your stuff, come back and do the eleven o'clock, and we'll run you out to the airport. They're going to hold a flight for you, and you can start reporting from out there first thing tomorrow morning. By then, God only knows what will have happened.' The man who had shot him was already in custody, and lengthy profiles of his chequered past were on the air constantly, interspersed with interviews with major surgeons giving their opinions of the President's chances. 'Can you do it?' They both knew it was a rhetorical question. She had no choice. This was what they paid her for, and the coverage of national emergencies was part of it. She mentally ran over the list of what she had to do. She knew from experience that Raquel would take care of the girls, and she would see them when she went home between shows to pack.

At home, she found the twins and Raquel in tears in front of the TV, and Jessica was the first to approach her. 'What's going to happen, Mom?' Raquel loudly blew her nose.

'We don't know yet.' And then she told them the news. 'I have to go to California tonight. Will you guys be okay?' She turned to Raquel, knowing her answer would be yes.

'Of course.' She almost looked insulted.

'I'll be back as soon as all of this is over.'

She kissed them all and left for the network to do the late news, and as soon as she came off the air, she left in the wake of two cops who had been waiting to escort her to their car downstairs. They all listened intently to the radio as they sped to the airport with the sirens shrieking. It was a favour the police occasionally did for the station. They made it to JFK by twelve fifteen and the plane took off ten minutes after she boarded. Several times the stewardesses came to give her bulletins, transmitted by the pilots, as they got the news from towers and air controllers as they crossed the country. The President was still alive, but there was no way of telling for how long. It seemed an endless night and Mel finally disembarked feeling truly exhausted. She was met again by a police escort there, and she decided to go to Center City before going to her hotel and sleeping for a few hours. She would have to go to work at seven o'clock the next morning, and it was already four o'clock in the morning in LA. But when she reached Center City, there was no further news, and she got to her hotel just before five a.m. She figured that she could sleep for an hour or so before reporting for work. She was just going to have to drink a lot of black coffee, and she requested a wake-up from the hotel operator so she wouldn't oversleep. They had booked her into a hotel where she had never stayed, but it was close to Center City. And suddenly she realised how strange it was that she was back in LA again so soon, and wondered if she would have time to see Peter. Maybe when it was all over. Unless, of course, the President died. She might have to fly back simultaneously with *Air Force One* to attend the funeral in Washington, in which case she would never see him. But she hoped for the President's sake that wouldn't happen. And she desperately wanted to see Peter in the next few days. She wondered if he'd know she was there.

She woke up instantly when the operator called, all her senses alert, although her limbs ached and she felt as though she hadn't slept at all. But she would have to operate on black coffee and nervous energy and stay on her feet somehow. She had done it before, and she knew she could do it this time. Dressing quickly in a dark grey dress and high-heeled black shoes, she was out of the hotel and in the police car at six thirty and at the hospital ten minutes later, to get the latest details and go on the air. It was already almost ten o'clock in New York by then and the eastern portion of the country had been hungry for news for hours.

She saw the camera crew she had used before in the fray along with at least fifty other cameramen and two dozen reporters. They were camping out in the lobby and a hospital spokesman was giving them bulletins every half hour. And finally at eight o'clock, an hour after Mel went on the air, looking grave and impressive, the first bit of good news reached them. The President was conscious, and his spinal cord had been neither damaged nor severed. If he survived he would not be paralysed, and there had been no brain damage from what they could tell so far. But he was still critically ill and hovering between life and death. His survival was not yet assured, and three hours later the First Lady joined them and spoke a few words to the nation. Mel was able to get three minutes of her time. The poor woman looked grief-stricken and exhausted, but she stood speaking to Mel with dignity and a firm voice. One's heart went out to her as tears filled her eyes, but her voice never wavered. Mel let her speak, asked only a few questions, and assured her of the nation's prayers, and then miraculously was able to get a few moments later on with the President's surgeon. By six o'clock that night there was no additional news, and Mel was relieved by a local anchor, going on for the network. She was given five hours to go to her hotel and sleep, if she could. But by then she was so wound up, she couldn't sleep. She lay in the dark, thinking of a thousand things, and suddenly she reached for the phone, and dialled a local number.

Mrs Hahn answered the phone, and without friendly preamble Mel asked for Peter, and he was on the line a moment later.

'Mel?'

'Hi. I don't even know if I make sense, I'm so cross-eyed, but I just wanted to call and tell you I was here.'

He smiled gently then. She sounded exhausted. 'Remember me? I work at Center City too. Not to mention the fact that we do have a television set here. I saw you twice today, but you didn't see me. Are you holding up all right?'

'I'll do. I'm used to this. After a while, you just have to put your body on automatic pilot, and hope that you don't crash into a wall somewhere looking for a bathroom.'

'Where are you now?' She gave him the name of her hotel, and it struck him as remarkable that she was so near again. He had to admit that in spite of the horrendous circumstances, he liked it, although he wondered if he'd be able to see her. 'Is there anything I can do for you?'

'Not right now. But if there is, I'll let you know.'

He felt like a complete idiot asking her the next question, but he had to. 'Is there any chance that . . . I can see you sometime? I mean other than across a crowded lobby full of reporters?'

'I don't know yet.' She was honest with him. 'It depends on what happens.' And then she sighed. 'What do you think will happen, Peter? What are his chances really?' She should have asked him before, but she was so tired she didn't think of it till just now.

'Fair. Depends on what kind of shape he's in. His heart's not involved or they would have called me in. I was in the operating room when they operated, just in case. But they didn't need me.' She hadn't known that from the reports, but she suspected that there was a lot of information held back. The only thing they knew everything about was the assailant, a twenty-three-year-old man who had spent the last five years in a mental hospital and had told his sister two months before that he was going to kill the President. No one took him seriously since he thought that his roommate at the hospital was God and the head nurse was Marilyn Monroe. No one even thought he knew who the President was, but he did. He knew well enough to almost kill him, and maybe succeed after all. 'We'll know a lot more tomorrow, Mel.'

'If you get any inside leads, will you call me?'

'Sure. But why don't you get some sleep before you become the next patient?'

'I will, but I'm so damn keyed up I can't sleep.'

'Try. Just close your eyes and rest, don't think of sleeping.' His voice was soothing and she was glad she had called him. 'Do you want a ride to the hospital tomorrow?'

'Tomorrow?' She laughed. 'I have to be back at eleven o'clock tonight.'

'That's inhuman!' He was outraged.

'So is shooting the President.' They both agreed and she hung up, glad she had called. Melanie just hoped they could get together before she left LA. It would kill her to have been there and to leave without even seeing him once, but they both knew it could happen. And as Mel rolled over on the bed in her hotel room, she prayed that it wouldn't.

CHAPTER 13

On Friday, Mel and the rest of the press crew spent a long anxious day in the lobby of Center City. There were half a dozen people assigned to bring them sandwiches and coffee, and periodically they went on the air to give their assorted news stations the latest bulletins on the President's condition. But on the whole, nothing changed much from six in the morning until seven that evening. After coming back on duty at eleven o'clock on Thursday night, Mel didn't leave the hospital until eight o'clock Friday night, so exhausted that her head was throbbing and her eyes burning. She walked out into the parking lot and as she slid behind the wheel of the car that had been rented for her the previous night, her vision was so blurred that she was afraid to turn the key in the ignition and drive back to her hotel. The voice that she heard seemed to be coming at her out of the thick fog, as she turned to see who was standing beside the car and speaking to her.

'You're in no condition to drive, Miss Adams.' At first she thought it was a cop, but as she squinted she saw a familiar face, and she smiled and leaned her head back against the seat. The window was rolled down all the way. She knew she had needed as much air as she could get so she wouldn't fall asleep at the wheel on the way home.

'Well, I'll be damned. What are you doing here?' Even in her state of near collapse, she could see that his eyes were a deep blue, and it was wonderfully comforting just seeing him there.

'I work here, or did you forget?'

'But isn't it late for you to be here?'

He nodded and watched the look in her eyes. She was happy to see him too, but she was too exhausted to move. 'Move over. I'll drive you back to your hotel.'

'Don't be silly. I'm fine. I just have to . . .'

'Look, be practical, Mel. With the President here, when you wrap yourself around a tree in this car, they won't even give you a Band-Aid in the emergency room. Everyone in the whole place is rallying around him. So let's save ourselves a big headache, and let me drive you home. Agreed?' She didn't have the strength left to argue with him. She just smiled like a tired child, nodded her head, and slid over. 'That's a good girl.' He glanced at her to see if she'd object to the term and was relieved that she didn't. She just sat there looking glazed and didn't seem to object to his taking over. He drove expertly through the LA traffic, which was still heavy at that hour, and glanced over at her from time to time. At last he spoke again. 'You okay, Mel?'

'I'm just beat. I'll be okay with a little sleep.'

'When do you have to go back?'

'Not till six o'clock tomorrow morning, thank God.' And then she sat up a little straighter in her seat. 'Do you know anything I should know about the President's condition?' But he only shook his head. 'I hope he makes it.'

'So does everyone else in the country, so do I. You feel so helpless with something like this. But actually, you know, he was damn lucky. It could have been over right away. In fact, from the X-rays I saw it was very close. He came within a hair of losing his life, or his mind, or at best his ability to ever move from the neck down. If the bullet had ricocheted a little differently than it did . . .' He didn't have to finish the sentence. The surgeons working on the President were his friends, and he was painfully up to date.

'I feel so sorry for his wife. She's being brave, and she looks as though she's just barely hanging on to her last shred of hope.' She wasn't a young woman, and the last two days had been a terrible strain on her.

'She has a heart problem, you know. Only a slight one. But this is not exactly what the doctor ordered for her.'

Mel looked at him with a tired smile. 'At least you're around in case she has a problem.' And she was suddenly very grateful that he was around for her too. She realised now that she would never have made it across the obstacle course of the freeway. She said as much to him as they pulled up in front of her hotel.

'Don't be silly. I wouldn't have let you drive like that.'

'I'm just lucky you were there when I came out.' She felt slightly revived, but only barely. And she hadn't figured out that he'd been waiting for her, having foreseen the problem. It was something he had wanted to do for her, and he was glad that he had. 'Thanks so much, Peter.' They both got out of the car and he looked down at her.

'Will you get into the hotel all right?'

She smiled at the care he took of her. No one had been that preoccupied with her in years, if ever. 'I'm fine. I can walk. I just can't drive.' But she would have, if she'd had to.

'I'll pick you up tomorrow morning. Quarter to six?'

'I can't let you do that.'

'Why not? Normally, I'd be there by six thirty. What difference does half an hour make?'

'Really, I can drive myself.' She was almost embarrassed by the attention, but he held firm.

'I don't see why you should have to.'

And suddenly she had a thought. 'How are you going to get home from here?'

'Don't worry about that. I'll grab a cab back to the parking lot and pick up my car. Me, I'm wide awake. You're the one who's dead on your feet.'

'Oh, Peter, I didn't mean to . . .' But she yawned and cut off her own words and he laughed.

'Yes? Is there anything else you'd like to say to your public?' He was teasing and she was sorry she was so dazed by her long day.

'Just thank you.' Their eyes met and held for a moment outside the hotel. 'And it's nice to see you again.'

'No, it isn't, you can't even see. For all you know, a

perfect stranger just drove you home.' He guided her gently towards the door of her hotel and walked her into the lobby.

'All strangers should be so nice.' She mumbled softly.

'Now be good, and go up to your room and get some sleep. Have you eaten?'

'Enough. All I want now is my bed. Come to think of it, any bed will do.' The floor was even beginning to look good. He pressed the lift button for her and propelled her gently inside and before she could say more, he stepped back.

'See you in the morning.'

She would have objected, but the doors closed, and the lift deposited her on her floor. All she had to do was walk to her room, open the door, close it again, and make it to her bed. All of which she did, feeling like a zombie. She didn't even bother to take off her clothes, she called the operator before she passed out, and left a wake up for five o'clock in the morning, and the next thing she knew she was asleep, and the phone was ringing.

'Five o'clock, Miss Adams.'

'Already?' Her voice was hoarse and she was still half asleep. She had to shake herself awake, as she sat up with the phone in her hand. 'Have you heard any news? Is the President still alive?'

'I believe so.' But if he weren't, they would have called her from the hospital, or the network in LA.

Mel hung up and dialled the local station. The President was still alive, and there was no news since the night before. His condition was stable but still critical. She headed for the shower after that. It was too early to even order coffee. And then she went downstairs to stand outside the hotel at twenty to six, feeling that she should have insisted the night before that Peter not pick her up. There was no reason for him to chauffeur her around. It was silly really. But at exactly five forty-five, he picked her up, and opened the car door for her (he looked wide awake) and as she slid beside him, he offered her a thermos of coffee.

'Good God, this is the best limo service I've ever had.'

'There are sandwiches in that bag.' He pointed to a brown paper bag on the floor and smiled at her. 'Good morning.' He had correctly guessed that she hadn't eaten the night before, and he had made some sandwiches himself to bring to her.

'It sure is nice having a friend in LA.' She took a big bite of a turkey sandwich on white toast, and sank back gratefully against the seat of the Mercedes with a cup of coffee in her hand. 'This is the life.' And then she looked over at him with a shy smile. 'Somehow, when I left here two weeks ago, I didn't really think we'd see each other again. Or at least not for a long time.'

'That's what I thought too. I'm sorry it has to be over something as serious as this. But I'm glad you're here, Mel.'

'Know something?' She took another swig of the steaming coffee. 'So am I. That's awful to say, given why I'm here. But I don't know . . .' She looked away for a moment and then back at him. 'You've been on my mind a lot since I went back, and I wasn't sure why. Maybe coming back here will help me sort that out.'

He nodded. He had had the same problem. 'It's difficult to explain to you what I've been feeling. I keep wanting to call you to tell you things, to give you the latest news about Marie . . . or a surgery we just did . . . or something one of the children said.'

'I think you've just been terribly lonely and I opened a door. Now you don't know what to do with it.' He nodded, and Mel looked thoughtful. 'But the funny thing is that neither do I. You opened a door for me too, and I kept thinking of you when I went home. I was so glad when you called me that first time.'

'I didn't have any choice. I felt that I had to.'

'Why?' They were both looking for answers they didn't have.

'I don't know, Mel. It was actually a relief to know you were back. Maybe this time I'll find what I'm trying to say.' . . . or maybe I won't dare say it . . .

But Mel dared to ask the most difficult question. 'Does it scare you?'

'Yes.' His voice almost trembled and he didn't look at her as he drove. 'It scares me a lot.'

'If it's any consolation, it scares me too.'

'Why?' He glanced at her in surprise. 'You've been out there on your own for years. You know what you're doing. I don't.'

'That's the whole point. I've been out there alone for fifteen years. No one has ever come too close. If they did, I ran off. But there's something about you . . . I don't know what to make of you, and I was so damn drawn to you when I was here before.'

He stopped the car in the parking lot of Center City and turned to face her. 'You're the first woman I've been attracted to in twenty years, other than my wife. That scares the hell out of me, Mel.'

'Why?'

'I don't know. But it does. I've been hiding since she died. And all of a sudden I'm not sure I want to any more.' They sat in silence for a long time, and Mel broke the silence first.

'Why don't we just wait and see what happens. Not push anything. Neither of us has risked anything yet. You've made a couple of phone calls, and I'm out here because the President was shot. That's all there is to it for now.' She was trying to reassure herself as much as him, but neither of them was convinced.

'Are you sure that's all there is to it?' His eyes were gentle and she smiled at him.

'No, I'm not. That's the trouble. But maybe if we take it slow, we won't scare ourselves half to death.'

'I hope I don't scare you, Mel. I like you too much to want to frighten you away.'

'I scare myself more than you ever could. I never wanted to get hurt again, or to depend on anyone but myself. I've built a fortress around me, and if I let anyone in, they might destroy what I've built, and it took me so long to put it all together.' It was the most honest thing she could have told him, and there were tears in her eyes as he watched her.

'I won't hurt you, Mel, ever, if I can help it. If anything, I would want to take some of that load off your shoulders.'

'I'm not sure I want to give it up.'

'And I'm not sure I'm ready to take it on.'

'That's okay. It's better that way.' She sat back against the seat for one more moment before she had to leave him. 'The only thing that's too bad is that we're so far apart. You live here. I live there. We'll never find anything out like this.'

'Maybe we will while you're here.' He sounded hopeful, but she shook her head.

'That's not very likely while I'm working this hard.'

But he wasn't willing to be discouraged. Not yet. He needed to find out what he felt for this woman who appealed to him so much. He looked at the big green eyes he had remembered so well. 'The last time you were here, you followed me around while I was working. This time let me put myself at your disposal, as much as I can. Maybe we'll find a little spare time to talk.'

'I'd like that. But you see what it's like. I'm working day and night.'

'Let's just see. I'll see if I can ferret you out in the lobby later when I finish surgery and rounds. Maybe we can grab a sandwich.' She liked the idea, but she had no idea if she could get free.

'I'll do what I can to get away. But Peter, you have to understand that I may not be able to.'

'I understand that.' And then for the first time, he reached out and touched her hand. 'It's all right, Mel. I'm here. I'm not going anywhere.' But maybe she would. They both silently hoped that it wouldn't be too soon.

She smiled at him, enjoying the feel of his hand on hers. 'Thanks for the ride to work, Peter.'

'At your service, Ma'am.' He slid out and opened the door for her, and a moment later they were swallowed up by the crowd in the lobby. He turned back to glance at her once, but she was already deep in conversation with the other less important members of the press who had spent the night in the lobby, and the lift doors closed on him before she saw him again.

The news that Mel got was hopeful. The President was still alive, and half an hour before, a hospital spokesman had told them that there was some improvement in his condition.

At eight o'clock the First Lady returned. She was staying at the Bel-Air Hotel, and she was surrounded by Secret Servicemen who forced their way through the lobby. It was impossible to approach her although Mel and a host of others tried. The poor woman looked haggard and wan, and again Mel felt for her. At eight thirty she went on the air to New York, and again at nine for the noon news. All she could tell the nation was that the President was still alive. And she continued gathering bulletins throughout the day, without a moment to think of her own life, or Peter Hallam.

She didn't see him again until three o'clock, when suddenly he appeared beside her, looking impressive in his starched white coat and suddenly there was a surge of press around him. They thought he had arrived to give them news and it was almost impossible to shout above the din and explain that he was there to see a friend purely as a civilian. At last he and Mel escaped to a corner, although several members of the press thought she was getting a scoop on them. And finally in desperation, he pulled off the white coat and shoved it behind a waste bin in the lobby.

'Christ, I thought they would maul me.'

'They would, given half a chance. I'm sorry.' She smiled tiredly at him. She had worked for nine hours straight and the only food she'd had was the sandwich he'd given her in the car, although she had drunk gallons of coffee all day.

'Have you eaten?'

161

'Not yet.'

'Can you get away?'

She looked at her watch. 'I have to go on in ten minutes for the six o'clock in New York. But I should be able to get free after that.'

'How long do you have to stay?'

'A few more hours. I should be able to leave by six o'clock. I can always come back at eight if I have to, to cover the eleven o'clock in New York. In fact, I probably will have to. But after that, I hope I'm through, unless something new develops.'

He was thinking and then said, 'Why don't I leave here now, and come back for you at six o'clock. We can go somewhere quiet for dinner, and I'll get you back in here in time for you to do the bulletin for the eleven o'clock news in New York, and right after that I'll take you back to your hotel.'

'I'll probably be a zombie by then, and I may fall asleep in my dinner.'

'I don't mind. I've put people to sleep over dinner before. At least this time I can tell myself there might be an excuse.' He smiled at her, and felt an urge to pull her into his arms.

She smiled too. 'I'd like to see you tonight.'

'Good. See you at six then.' He hurried off to his office then, and he returned exactly three hours later. By then, Mel had dark circles under her eyes, and he could see when she got into his car that she was absolutely exhausted. She looked over at him with a tired smile.

'You know, Peter, any attraction you may feel for me right now practically amounts to necrophilia.'

He laughed at the horrifying suggestion and made a face. 'That was disgusting.'

'That's how I feel. How was work?'

'Fine. How's the President tonight?' He figured that now she knew more about it than he did. He was too busy with his own patients to worry about anyone else.

'He's holding his own. I'm beginning to think that he'll make it if he's held up for this long. What do you think?'

'I think you may be right.' And then he smiled. 'I just hope he doesn't spring to his feet in the morning, so that you have to fly home tomorrow.'

'I don't think there's any danger of that for the moment. Do you?'

'Honestly, no.' He looked pleased and glanced over at her as he drove her to a restaurant nearby.

'How are the kids, by the way?'

'Fine. They know you're here from what they see on the news, but I haven't had time to tell them I've seen you.'

She was quiet for a moment. 'Maybe you shouldn't.'

'Why not?' He looked surprised.

'Maybe it would make them nervous. Kids have remarkable antennae. I know mine do. Especially Jess. You can put something over on Val for a while, because she's always so wrapped up in herself. But Jessica almost senses things before they happen.'

'Pam's like that sometimes too. But the boys are different.'

'That's my point. And she has enough to contend with in her life, without worrying about me.'

'What makes you think she'd worry?'

'What makes you think she wouldn't? I mean, think of it, her whole world has been turned upside down in the last two years, but at least she knows she has you. And there have been no women for her to compete with, in her mind at least. And then I come on the scene, and I'm an instant threat.'

'What makes you think that?'

'I'm a woman. She's a girl, and you're her father. You belong to her.'

'My being interested in someone wouldn't change that.'

'Subtly, in some ways, it might. I'm sure your relationship with Pam was different when your wife was alive. You had less time for her, you had other things to do. Now suddenly you're all hers, or almost. Changing that back again, and for a stranger, won't be very welcome.'

He looked pensive as he stopped the car in front of a

little Italian restaurant. 'I never thought of it that way.' And then he smiled slowly at Mel. 'But I never had to. Maybe I should be a little cautious about what I tell her.'

'I think so.' She grinned. 'Hell, you may never want to see me again after the next few days. You're about to see me at my worst. After enough days of no sleep, I start to fall apart.'

'Don't we all.'

'I didn't think you did. You seem to hold up miraculously with all that you do.'

'I have my limits too.'

'Me too, and I hit mine about two days ago.'

'Come on, let's get you fed. That'll help.' They walked inside, and the headwaiter gave them a quiet table. 'Wine, Mel?' But she quickly shook her head.

'I'd pass out in my plate.' She laughed and ordered a small steak. She wasn't even hungry any more, but she knew that the protein would do her good. However, they enjoyed the dinner and the small talk, and she was amazed at how comfortable she was with him. He seemed interested in her work, and she already knew a great deal about his. It was a relaxing but stimulating conversation, and she sat back with her cup of coffee at the end, feeling content and sated. 'You are an absolute godsend. Do you know that?'

'I'm enjoying it too.'

'This is not at all what I expected when I came to LA.'

'I know.' He smiled. 'By now, you thought you'd be in Bermuda.'

'Is that what day this is?' She had lost track of time and she hadn't even talked to the girls since she'd arrived, but she knew they'd all understand. And the girls were in Cape Cod anyway for the long weekend. She hadn't even realised it had begun, but it had. It felt as though she had already been in LA for weeks. And in a way, she wished she had been. She had never felt that way before. Her whole life centred around New York, as a rule, but not right now. Her life was here.

'I'm sorry you missed the trip to Bermuda, Mel.'

'I'm not.' She looked frankly into his eyes. 'This is where I'd much rather be.' He wasn't quite sure how to respond, so he reached out and took her hand.

'I'm glad. I'm happy you're back, Mel. I'm just sorry you have to work so hard.'

Her eyes were deadly earnest as they looked into his. 'It's a small price to pay to see you.'

But Peter couldn't repress a sad thought. 'I'm sure the President doesn't feel that way.' They shared a serious moment and then Mel regretfully looked at her watch. It was time for her to go back to work. He offered to take her back to the hospital and wait but she protested for his sake. 'I can take a cab after I do the eleven o'clock,' which was only eight o'clock in LA.

'I told you. For as long as you're here, I'm your chauffeur.' He looked embarrassed then. 'Unless you'd rather not . . .'

This time she reached out and touched his hand. 'I love it.'

'Good.'

He paid the bill and they left and went back to Center City in time for her to announce to the viewers in New York that the President had a slight fever, but it was to be expected. And then half an hour later, Peter drove her back to her hotel, and dropped her outside, promising to be back early the following morning. Once again, she went inside and climbed into bed, but tonight it took her longer to fall asleep, and she was still awake when he called her half an hour later.

'Hello?' She was afraid it was bad news about the President.

'It's me.' It was Peter and she breathed a sigh of relief and told him why. 'I'm sorry if I scared you.'

'That's okay. Is something wrong?'

'No.' He hesitated and she could almost hear him breathing. 'I just want to tell you that I think you're terrific.' He had startled himself and could feel his heart beat faster. Melanie sat up in bed, feeling nervous and pleased all at once.

'I came to the same conclusion about you the last time I was here.'

He blushed, feeling silly and she smiled and they chatted for a little while, and then hung up at last, feeling both excited and scared and happy, like two kids. They were both taking tiny baby steps out on a limb, and it wasn't too late to turn back yet, but the balancing act got more delicate each day, and neither of them could figure out what would happen when she went back to New York, but it was too soon to worry about that. For the moment they were content.

CHAPTER 14

The next morning Peter picked her up again, and dropped her off at the hospital where she was told that the President was doing a little better. For the first time in days she found that she had a few minutes to herself in the middle of the day, and on a sudden whim, she called the cardiac unit, and asked if she could visit Marie. She took the lift to the sixth floor, and found her sitting up in bed looking pretty but pale, and her face had a new fullness to it. Melanie realised with sorrow that the unnatural bloating from the drugs was already setting in, but her eyes were bright and she looked happy to see Mel.

'What are you doing here?' She looked up at Melanie in surprise as she entered the room. There were still intravenous tubes in her arms, but she looked healthier than she had before the transplant.

'I came to see you. But not from New York, I'm afraid. I've been in the lobby for days, because of the President.' Marie nodded with a serious look in her eyes.

'What a terrible thing. Is he any better?'

'A little today. But he's not out of the woods yet,' and then suddenly she realised that it was a tactless thing to say, because Marie wasn't out of the woods yet either. She smiled gently at the young woman who was only a few years her junior, and whose life was held in such a delicate balance. 'He's not as lucky as you are, Marie.'

'That's because he's not a patient of Peter Hallam's.' There was a warm glow in her eyes as she said his name, and Mel watched her as understanding dawned. Peter Hallam had become a god of sorts to this girl. And Mel suspected that she had a crush on him. It was not an unnatural occurrence, given her dependence on the man, and the fact that he had saved her life by performing the

167

transplant. But it was only when Peter himself came into the room a little while later, and blushed as he saw Mel, that she saw something more. The remarkable communication between doctor and patient. He sat down beside Marie's bed, and talked to her in his quiet, soothing voice, and it was as though everyone in the room disappeared except them.

Mel suddenly felt like an intruder and left a little while later, returning to the mass of press still milling around the lobby. She didn't see Peter again until he drove her back to the hotel that night. As she had the night before, she had a two-hour break, and then she had to return to the hospital at eight o'clock to do a live report for the eleven o'clock news in New York. And it was on the way to dinner that she mentioned Marie to him.

'She absolutely worships you, Peter.'

'Don't be silly. She's no different from any other patient.' But he knew what Melanie meant, there was a special bond between him and each of his patients and maybe particularly with Marie, who had no one to stand beside her. 'She's a nice girl, Mel. And she needs someone to talk to while she goes through all this. You lie there all day and you think, sometimes too much. She needs someone to vent all that with.'

'And you are so eternally patient.' She smiled, wondering how he did it. He gave and he gave and he gave, almost beyond measure, of his skill, his heart, his time, his patience. It seemed incredible to her.

Halfway through dinner his pager went off, and he had to return to the hospital for an emergency.

'Marie?' Mel asked worriedly as they hurried to the car.

He shook his head. 'No, a man who came in last week. He needs a heart badly and we don't have a donor yet.' It seemed to be a never-ending problem for him, the absence of a heart when it was desperately needed.

'Will he make it?'

'I don't know. I hope so.' He wove his way expertly through the traffic and they were back at the hospital in less than ten minutes. It was the last she saw of him that night. She got a message in the lobby before she went on the air that Dr Hallam would be in surgery for several hours, and she wondered if that meant they had found a donor, or if Peter was trying to do whatever repair work he could in the meantime. She went back to her hotel alone in a cab, and she was surprised to find how much she missed him. She took a hot bath, and sat staring at the tile wall, sorry that she had questioned him about Marie. There had just been something in the woman's face when she said his name, and his tone with her had been so intimate. It almost made Mel jealous. She was in bed by nine thirty and slept soundly until her five o'clock call the next morning, and at five forty-five he was downstairs as always. But he looked tired this morning.

'Hi.' She slid into the car quickly and for an instant there had been almost a reflex reaction. She had been about to lean over and give him a kiss on the cheek, but at the last minute she didn't. She searched his eyes, and suddenly realised that something was wrong. 'You okay?'

'I'm fine.'

But she didn't believe him. 'How was last night?'

'We lost him.' He started the car and Mel watched his profile. There was something hard and lonely in his eyes. 'We did our best, but he was just too far gone.' And Mel suddenly understood something.

'You don't have to convince me.' Her voice was soft. 'I know how hard you tried.'

'Yeah. Maybe I just need to convince myself.'

She reached out and touched his arm then. 'Peter . . .'

'I'm sorry, Mel.' He glanced over at her with a tired smile, and she wished there were something she could do for him, but she wasn't sure what.

'Don't do that to yourself.'

'Yeah,' and then five minutes later, 'He had a young wife and three small kids.'

'Stop blaming yourself.'

'Who should I blame?' He turned to her with a flash of sudden anger.

'Has it ever occurred to you that you're not God. That you aren't to blame? That you don't give the gift of life?' They were harsh words, but she could see that he was listening. 'It's not in your hands, no matter how skilled you are.'

'He would have been a perfect candidate for a heart transplant, if we'd had a donor.'

'But you didn't. And it's over. Close the door.' They stopped in the hospital parking lot then, and he looked at her.

'You're right and I know it. After all these years, I shouldn't punish myself, but I always do.' He sighed softly. 'Do you have time for a cup of coffee?' There was something so comforting about her presence and he needed to be comforted.

She looked at her watch and frowned. 'Sure. I'll just check in. There's probably nothing new.' But when she walked in, there was news. A bulletin was due to be delivered on the air in three minutes. The President had just come off the critical list. When the news was announced, a cheer went up in the lobby. For most of the members of the press, it would mean that they would go home soon, and could stop camping in the lobby of Center City.

Mel went on the air to deliver the news to the East as Peter watched. While the whole country would rejoice, she and Peter felt strangely depressed. Their eyes met when she went off the air.

'Will you have to go home now?' It was a worried whisper.

'Not yet – I just got a memo. They want an interview with his wife today, if I can get it.' At that moment, Peter was paged, and he had to leave her.

Mel sent a note upstairs to the President's wife who had been sleeping in a room adjoining the President's for the past two days. A response came back a little while later.

170

The First Lady would grant Mel an exclusive interview at noon, in a private room on the third floor – which ruled out any hope of having lunch with Peter, but the interview went well and Mel was pleased, and that afternoon another encouraging bulletin was delivered. The President was out of the woods. By that evening when Peter drove her out for a bite to eat, the atmosphere of tension had greatly abated.

'How was your day?' She collapsed against the seat and looked over at him with a smile. 'Mine was a killer, but things are looking up.'

'I didn't stop all day. And Marie said to say hello.'

'Say hi for me.' But her mind was on other things. She was beginning to wonder how soon she would have to leave. There was a rumour that in a few days the President would be moved to Walter Reed Hospital in Washington DC, but the First Lady had been unable or unwilling to confirm it.

'What are you thinking about, Mel?' She noticed that he looked less depressed than he had that morning.

She smiled. 'Ten thousand things at once. We're hearing that they're going to send the President home soon. Do you think they can really move him?'

'Right now they'd be taking a chance, but if he continues to improve they could. And they can take all the equipment they'd need on *Air Force One*.' He didn't seem cheered by the thought and neither was Mel, but over dinner they forgot about it, and Peter began to tell her funny stories about Matt when he was two or three years old, and ridiculous episodes that had happened in the hospital when he was in training. From sheer exhaustion, they found themselves laughing like two kids, and when he drove her back to the hospital shortly before eight, she was in no mood to do the news with a serious face. Surprisingly they were both still in high spirits when they left Center City again half an hour later. There was something about being together that always buoyed them both and made life worth living.

'Do you want to come home with me for a drink?' He really didn't want to leave her yet, and suddenly he realised that she might be gone in a few days. He wanted to savour every moment of her presence.

'I don't think I should. I still think your kids would be upset.'

'What about me? Don't I have a right to see a friend?'

'Sure, but taking someone home can be a heavy trip. How do you think Pam would react to seeing me again?'

'Maybe that's an adjustment she'll just have to make.'

'Is it worth it for a few days?' Mel didn't think so. 'Why don't you come to my hotel for a drink instead? It's ugly as sin but the bar looks halfway decent.' Neither of them was interested in drinking. They just seemed to want to sit and talk for hours until they were ready to fall over from exhaustion.

'You know, I could sit here and talk to you all night.' He was still amazed at the range of conflicting emotions he felt for her, excitement, attraction, respect, trust, fear, distance, and closeness all at once. But whatever it was, he couldn't seem to get enough of it. The presence of Mel Adams in his life was apparently addictive. He was hooked, and he didn't know what to do about it.

'I feel the same way and the funny thing is that we hardly know each other, and I feel as though I've known you for years.' She had never enjoyed talking to anyone as much, and that still frightened her a little when she allowed herself to think of it. It was a subject neither of them discussed but both of them thought of. She was the brave one tonight, as she looked at him over their second Irish coffee. The drinks seemed to pick them up, while putting a soft edge on things. It was the mixture of coffee and whisky that did it, enhanced by the heady effect each of them had on the other. 'I'm going to miss you like crazy when I go back.'

He watched her carefully over his drink. 'So am I. I was thinking of it this morning after I dropped you off. What you said about the patient last night made a lot of sense.

You kind of took my day out of the ditch and picked me up again. I was headed for a real tailspin. It's going to be strange when I'm not picking you up at your hotel at six o'clock every morning.'

'You might even get some time to yourself again, and to spend with your kids. Are they complaining yet?'

'They seem to be wrapped up in their own lives.'

'So are the twins.' They were due back from Cape Cod that night. 'I'll have to call them if I can get the hour difference worked out right. When I wake up, they've left for school, and when I come home they're asleep.'

'You'll be home soon.' But he said the words with sorrow and she didn't answer for a time.

'It's a crazy life I lead, Peter.' She looked him straight in the eye as though asking him how he felt about it.

'But fulfilling, I suspect. We both seem to go nonstop, but it's not so bad if you like what you do.'

'That's how I've always felt.' She smiled, and he reached across the table for her hand. It was the only contact they ever had, but it was a comfortable gesture now. 'Thank you for everything you've done for me, Peter.'

'What? Drive you back and forth to the hospital a few times? That's hardly a monumental favour.'

'It's been nice though.' She smiled and he smiled in return.

'It has been for me too. It'll be strange when you're not here any more.'

She laughed. 'I'll probably be standing outside my house in New York at quarter to six every morning, waiting for you to come around the corner in your Mercedes.'

'I wish . . .' They fell silent then, and the bill arrived. He paid it, and they walked slowly into the lobby. It was late and they both had to get up early the next morning, and as they said good night to each other, Melanie found herself wishing they didn't have to.

'I'll see you tomorrow, Peter.' He nodded, and waved as

173

the lift doors closed. He went home, thinking about Mel, and wondering what life would be like again without her. He didn't even want to think of it. In her hotel room, Mel stood for a long time staring out the window, thinking of Peter, and the things they had said to each other in the past few days, and suddenly she felt an ache of loneliness well up in her, unlike any she had felt before. Suddenly she didn't want to go back to New York at all. But that was crazy. It was just what she had felt when she was in LA before, only more so. She went to bed with the uneasy feeling that night that Peter Hallam was deeper under her skin than she wanted him to be. And yet when she was with him, she didn't think of that. She just talked to him with the ease usually born of years of knowing someone. He made her feel that way each time she saw him, and she wondered for a moment, if that was only his bedside manner. She fell into an uneasy sleep that night, and was relieved to see him the next morning. She slipped quickly into the car, and they made the familiar drive to the hospital, chatting easily, and then suddenly Peter laughed and turned towards her.

'It's kind of like being married, isn't it?'

She felt herself go pale. 'What is?'

'Going to work together every day.' He looked sheepish. 'I have a confession to make. I like routine. I'm a creature of habit.'

'So am I.' She smiled back, feeling better again. For a moment she had been frightened. She settled back against the seat and watched the hospital loom towards them. 'I wonder what news awaits me today?' The President had been making steady progress, and they were just waiting for news of his being moved.

Nonetheless, when the announcement came that morning that the President was leaving for Washington the next day with a team of doctors, on *Air Force One*, she was stunned, and felt as though someone had delivered a blow to her solar plexus. The air whooshed out of her in one gasp – a barely audible 'No'. But it was true. He was

174

leaving. And once again, all was chaos in the lobby. Bulletins went on the air, interviews with doctors, Mel had to make a dozen calls to New York. They were asking for clearance for her for *Air Force One*, but thus far the only news was that six members of the press would be allowed on the plane. Silently, Mel found herself praying all day not to be among the lucky six, but at five o'clock she got a call from New York. She was among them. They were leaving at approximately noon the next day and she was expected to be at the hospital at nine o'clock, to cover all the preparations. When she met Peter in the parking lot that night, her whole body sagged as she got into the car.

'What's the matter, Mel?' He could see instantly that something was wrong. He had had a long day himself, in surgery for four hours, putting in a plastic heart, which he hadn't wanted to do in the first place. But in this particular case, there had been no other solution. They had already tried everything else, and there was no donor in sight for a transplant. But he knew how great a risk they ran now in regard to infection. And Marie had had a number of problems today too. But he didn't say anything to Mel as she turned to him with an unhappy look on her face.

'I'm leaving tomorrow.'

'Blast.' He stared at her for a long moment, and then nodded. 'Well, we knew you wouldn't be here forever.' It took him a few minutes to regain his composure and then he started the car. 'Do you have to come back tonight?'

She shook her head. 'I'm finished until nine o'clock tomorrow morning.'

At that he smiled more gamely and looked over at her with gentle eyes. 'Then I'll tell you what, why don't I drop you off at your hotel, let you relax for a while, and change if you want, and we'll go somewhere nice for dinner. How does that sound?'

'Lovely. You're sure you're not too tired?' She noticed now that he looked exhausted.

'Positive. I'd love it. Do you want to go back to the Bistro?'

'Yes' – she smiled finally – 'the only place I don't want to go back to is New York. Isn't that awful?' She would have been gone for only a week, but it felt like a year, and suddenly her life in New York loomed into perspective. The six- and eleven-o'clock news, the twins, her daily routine. At that precise moment, none of it was appealing, and she was still depressed when she went upstairs to change. The only thing that cheered her was when she saw Peter again, at seven thirty. He was wearing a dark grey flannel double-breasted suit, and she had never seen him look as handsome. All she had to wear was a beige silk dress with a heavy cream silk jacket that she had brought to wear on the air, but hadn't taken out yet.

They looked like a very distinguished pair as they walked into the Bistro, and the headwaiter gave them a lovely table. Peter ordered their drinks, and the waiter brought the chalkboard to the table, showing them the menu. But Mel wasn't even hungry. All she wanted to do was talk and be near Peter, and she found herself wanting to cling to him numerous times during the evening. Finally after the chocolate soufflé and the coffee, he ordered brandy for them both and looked at her sadly.

'I wish you weren't leaving, Mel.'

'So do I. It sounds crazy, but it's been a wonderful week, in spite of all the hard work.'

'You'll be back.' But God only knew when. She hadn't been to LA for over a year before she'd come to interview him. It was just a fluke that she had come back again so soon.

'I wish we didn't live so far away from each other.' She said it mournfully, like a little girl with a new best friend, and he smiled and put an arm around her shoulders.

'So do I.' And then, 'I'll call you.' But then what?

It was impossible to find the answers, they had lives at opposite ends of the country, with children, homes, careers, friends. None of it could be stashed into a suitcase and moved. The phone calls and occasional visits would have to be enough for Mel and Peter. It was almost more than she could bear to recognise that fact. They walked along Rodeo Drive after dinner, chatting.

'I wish our lives were different, Peter.'

'Do you?' He seemed surprised. 'How?'

'At least we could live in the same city.'

'I agree with you there. But otherwise, I'd say we're pretty lucky, now that we know each other. It's added a lot to my life.'

'Mine too.' She smiled and their hands knit tighter as they walked, each lost in thought for a little while.

He looked down at her, his hand still in hers. 'It's going to be damn lonely around here without you.' He heard the echo of his own words and couldn't believe he had said them, but he had, and he was less frightened of what he felt now. The brandy helped, and a week in her company had been like a gift he had never expected. He had grown fonder of her each day, and the prospect of seeing her go really depressed him, much more than he had expected.

Eventually they made their way slowly back to the car, and he took her back to her hotel, until at last they sat outside, and looked at each other in the lamplight. 'Will I see you tomorrow, Mel?'

'I don't have to be there until nine.'

'I'll be in surgery at seven. What time does the President's plane leave?'

'At noon.'

'Then I guess this is it.' They both sat sadly, looking at each other and then, without saying a word, he leaned towards her and gently took her face in his hands and kissed her. She closed her eyes and felt her lips melt into his, and she felt as though her insides trembled. She was almost dizzy when he stopped and she clung to him for a long moment. Then she looked at him and let her fingers touch his face, and then his lips, as he kissed the tips of her fingers. 'I'm going to miss you, Mel.'

'Me too.'

'I'll call you.' But then what? Neither of them had any answers.

And without saying anything more he pulled her close to him again and held her for a long time, and at last he walked her back into the lobby and kissed her one last time before she disappeared into the lift. Slowly, he walked back to his car, and drove away, feeling something heavy in his heart that he hadn't felt since he'd lost Anne. And he had never wanted to feel that again. It frightened him that he had come to care about her so much. It would have been so much easier if he hadn't.

CHAPTER 15

When Mel arrived at the hospital the next day, she was allowed to go upstairs with a two-man crew and speak to the First Lady briefly, while preparations were being made for the President's removal. They would be leaving the hospital at ten o'clock, arriving at Los Angeles International Airport shortly before eleven, and they would take off as soon as possible after that. The President was doing well, but the First Lady was obviously extremely worried. His condition was stable, but it was difficult to predict what might happen in the air. Nonetheless, he wanted to go back to Washington, and his physicians had approved the plan.

Mel completed the interview and waited in the hallway until forty-five minutes later when the President appeared on a stretcher. He waved his arm to the nurses and technicians lining the hall, and he smiled gamely and murmured greetings, but he still looked deathly pale, was heavily bandaged and there was an intravenous tube running into his arm. There was a fleet of Secret Servicemen surrounding the stretcher, interspersed with doctors and nurses who would be returning to Washington with him. Mel fell into step at a respectful distance, and took another lift to the lobby, where she joined up with the handful of other select reporters flying east on *Air Force One*. A separate limousine had been reserved for them, and she stepped into it with one glance back over her shoulder at Center City. She would have liked to have left a message at the desk for Peter before she left, but there was neither the opportunity nor the time, and a moment later they sped away towards the airport.

'How'd he look to you?' the reporter next to her asked briefly, checking some notes while lighting a cigarette with one hand. They were a relaxed group of pros, but nonetheless there was a faint hint of electricity and tension in the air. It had been an endless week for them all, and it would be good to get home and unwind. Most of them were returning to their home bases as soon as they reached Washington, and the network had already booked a seat to New York for Mel at ten o'clock that night. She would be picked up at LaGuardia at eleven and taken home. In a way, she felt as though she were returning from another planet. But she was not at all sure she wanted to go home now, and her mind lingered on Peter's words, and his face, the night before.

'Hm?' She hadn't heard the reporter's question.

'I said how did he look?' The older reporter looked annoyed and Mel narrowed her eyes, thinking of the President as he lay on the stretcher.

'Lousy, but he's alive.' And unless something drastic happened on the flight east, or he met with severe complications, it was unlikely that he would die now. He was a very lucky man, as they had all said again and again on the air. Other presidents had not been as lucky with assassination attempts as this one.

There was the usual banter between them on the way to the airport, dirty jokes, exchanged bits of gossip and old news. No one ever gave anything important away, but this was not as tense a trip as the one to LA had been for all of them. Mel thought back to the week before, and to seeing Peter again for the first time. She wondered now when she would see him next. She couldn't imagine another opportunity presenting itself in the near future, and the realisation of that depressed her.

The reporter sitting next to her glanced her way again. 'You look like the last week got you down, Mel.'

'No.' She shook her head, her eyes averted. 'I'm just tired, I guess.'

'Who isn't?'

And half an hour later they boarded the plane and sat in the passenger area in the rear. A sort of hospital-room arrangement had been made for the President towards the front, and none of them was allowed near it. Every hour or so, during the flight, the press secretary would join them and tell them how the President was doing, but it was an uneventful flight for them all and they reached Washington in four and a half hours and had the President settled at Walter Reed Hospital within an hour after that, and suddenly Mel realised that it was all over for her. The network's Washington correspondent had met them at the airport, and after accompanying the President to Walter Reed along with the others who had come from LA and glimpsing the First Lady once more, Mel stepped outside to the limousine waiting for her and went back to the airport. She had an hour left before her flight to New York, and she sat down, feeling as though she were in shock. The last week was beginning to seem like a dream and she wondered if she had imagined Peter and the time she had spent with him.

She walked slowly to a telephone booth at an adjacent gate, put a dime in the slot, and called her home collect. Jessie answered and for a moment, Mel felt tears fill her eyes, and she suddenly realised how exhausted she was.

'Hi, Jess.'

'Hi, Mom. Are you home?' She sounded like a child again as her voice filled with excitement.

'Almost, sweetheart. I'm at the Washington airport. I should be at the house by eleven thirty. God, I feel like I've been gone a year.'

'We've missed you like crazy.' She didn't even reproach her mother for not having called. She knew how impossible her schedule had been. 'Are you okay?'

'Wiped out. I can't wait to get home. But don't wait up. I'm going to crawl in and pass out.' It wasn't just the fatigue that was getting to her now. A kind of depression was setting in, as she realised how far away she was from Peter. And that was foolish too. But she couldn't seem to stop the feelings any more.

'Are you kidding?' Jess sounded outraged at her end.

'We haven't seen you in a week! Of course we'll wait up. We'll carry you upstairs if we have to.'

Tears filled Mel's eyes as she smiled at the phone. 'I love you, Jess.' And then, 'How's Val?'

'She's okay. We've both missed you.'

'I've missed you too, sweetheart.' But something important had been happening to her in California. There was a lot she needed to sort out, or at least absorb and the only people she wanted to see or talk to right now were the twins.

They were waiting in the living room when she got home, and fell into her arms one by one, delighted to have her home again. As Mel looked around, her house had never looked as good to her as it did now, or her children.

'Boy, it's good to be back, you guys!' But a tiny part of her said it wasn't. A tiny part of her said she wanted to be three thousand miles away, having dinner with Peter. But that was all behind her now and she had to forget it, at least for now.

'It must have been awful, Mom. It looked like you almost never left the hospital lobby from what we saw on the news.'

'Hardly ever except for a few hours' sleep here and there . . .' And time spent with Peter . . . She looked into their eyes, almost expecting them to see something different about her. But they didn't. There was nothing to see, except what she felt deep inside, and she kept that well hidden. 'Have you two been behaving all week?' Val brought her a Coca-Cola and she smiled gratefully at the voluptuous twin. 'Thanks, love.' And then she grinned. 'Are you in love again, young lady?'

'Not yet.' She laughed into her mother's eyes. 'But I'm working on it.' Mel rolled her eyes and they sat and chatted for a long time, and it was one o'clock in the morning by the time they all went upstairs. They kissed their mother goodnight outside her bedroom and went up to their own floor as Mel went to unpack her bag and take a hot shower. When she looked at the clock again, it was two o'clock in the morning . . . eleven o'clock on the West Coast . . . suddenly all that seemed to matter was where he was and what he was doing. It was like being constantly torn in two. She had a life to lead here in New York, and yet she had left a part of her three thousand miles away. It was going to be a difficult way to live, at least for now, and she still had to sort out what it all meant to her . . . what Peter Hallam meant to her . . . but, secretly, she already knew.

CHAPTER 16

The next morning, Grant called her just before noon, and woke her up, and his voice made her smile as she rolled over in bed and looked out at the brilliantly sunny June day.

'Welcome home, old girl. How was LA?'

'Oh, charming.' She smiled and stretched. 'I just sat around by the pool and soaked up the sun.' They both laughed, knowing what a rat race she'd been in. 'How've you been?'

'Busy, crazy, the usual. What about you?'

'What do you think with that insanity out there?'

'I think you must be dead on your feet.' But she didn't sound so bad.

'You're right. I am dead.'

'Are you coming in today?'

'Tonight, to do the six o'clock. I don't think I'll make it in before that.'

'Good enough. I'll keep an eye out for you. I've missed you, kid. Will you have time for a drink?' Time, yes, but the inclination, no. She still wanted some time to herself to sort things out. And she didn't feel like saying anything to Grant about it yet.

'Not tonight, love. Maybe next week.'

'Okay. See you later, Mel.'

As she got out of bed and stretched, she thought of Grant and smiled to herself. She was lucky to have a friend like him, and just as she went into the bathroom to turn on the shower, she heard the phone ring, and wondered if he was calling her back again. Not many people called her at home at noon, and hardly anyone knew she was back from the Coast yet. They wouldn't know that until they saw her on the news that night. Mel picked up the phone with a puzzled frown, hovering naked at her desk, looking out at the garden behind the house.

'Hello?'

'Hi, Mel.' He sounded faintly nervous and her heart seemed to give an enormous jerk as she heard his voice. It was Peter, and she could hear the hum of long distance. 'I wasn't sure if you'd be home, and I only had a few minutes, but I thought I'd call. Did you get home all right?'

'Yes . . . fine . . .' Her words seemed to tangle on her tongue and she closed her eyes, listening to his voice.

'We took a little break between surgeries today, and I just wanted to tell you how much I miss you.' And with one short sentence, he turned her heart upside down again and she didn't answer. 'Mel?'

'Yes . . . I was just thinking . . .' And then she threw all caution to the winds and sat down at her desk with a sigh. 'I miss you too. You sure turn my life topsy-turvy, Doctor.'

'I do?' He sounded relieved. She did the same to him. He had barely slept the night before, but he hadn't dared call and wake her up. He knew how exhausted she was when she left. 'Do you realise how crazy this is, Peter? God knows when we'll see each other again, and here we are like two kids, having a mad crush on each other.' But she felt happy again as they talked. All she had wanted was to hear him.

He laughed at her choice of words. 'Is that what this is? A crush? I wonder.'

'What do you think?' She wasn't sure what she was fishing for, and she was a little bit frightened of what she would get. She wasn't ready for declarations of passionate love from him, but he wasn't ready to give them either. She was still safe. But the worst of it was that she didn't even know if she wanted to be safe from him.

'I think that's about right. I'm in crush with you, Mel, is that how you say it?' They both laughed and Mel felt like a little girl again. He did that to her every time, and he was only nine years older than she was. 'How are the girls, by the way?'

'Fine. And your troupe?'

'They'll do. Matthew was complaining last night that he never sees me. We're going to go fishing or something this weekend if I can get away. But it depends on how this next surgery goes.'

'What are you doing?'

'A triple bypass, but there shouldn't be any complications.' And with that he glanced at the clock in the little room from which he'd called. 'Speaking of which, I'd better get back and scrub again. I'll be thinking of you though, Mel.'

'You'd better not. You'd better think of the patient.' But she was smiling. 'Maybe I should start ending the news with "And good night, Peter, wherever you are".'

'You know where I am.' His voice was so gentle it made her ache for him.

'Yeah. Three thousand miles away.' She looked sad.

'Why don't you come out for a weekend?'

'Are you crazy? I just left there.' But she loved the idea, as impossible as it was.

'That was different, you were working. Take some time off and come out for a visit.'

'Just like that?' She was amused.

'Sure. Why not?' But she suspected that it would have terrified them both if she'd done that, and she wasn't ready to take such a major step towards him.

'It may come as a shock to you, Dr Hallam, but I have a life here, and two children.'

'And you take July and August off every year. You told me that yourself. Take the girls to Disneyland or something.'

'Why don't you come visit us at Martha's Vineyard?' They were playing a game with each other and they both knew it, but it felt good to do it.

'First, my friend, I have to do a triple bypass.' End of round.

'Good luck. And thanks for calling.'

'I'll call you later, Mel. Will you be home tonight?'

'I'll be home, between shows.'

'I'll call you.' And he did, and her heart leapt again. She had finished dinner with the girls, and he had just got home from his office. It threw her into a tizzy until she left to do the eleven o'clock show, and she told herself it was crazy. She forced her mind back to the news and again as she delivered it, and she managed to keep her concentration until she went off the air, but when she saw Grant outside his studio she looked totally distracted.

'Hi, Mel. Something wrong?' He was going on in fifteen minutes and they didn't have much time to talk.

'No. Why?'

'You just look funny. You okay?'

'Sure.' But there was a dreamy look in her eyes and he felt as though she wasn't really there. And then suddenly he understood. He had seen a look faintly like it in her eyes once before, although she hadn't seemed as intensely stricken as she did now. He wondered who it was and couldn't figure out when she had found the time. Or where. New York or LA? He was somewhat intrigued, and Mel looked as though she was in a different world.

'Go home and get some sleep, kid. You look like you're still half out of it.'

'I guess I am.' She smiled at him and watched him walk into the set and then she left, but she realised that Peter's calls that day had set her back again. How on earth was she going to concentrate on her work? She could barely think straight.

She went home in a cab and let herself into the house. The girls were already in bed and Raquel had taken a few days off to make up for the previous week. Mel sprawled out on the living room couch, thinking of her life. She thought of Peter's suggestion to come out to LA, but that was crazy. The only answer was to hang in for the next few

187

weeks in New York, and get to Martha's Vineyard. Maybe then she could sort out her head as she did every year. Things would get back to normal with the sun and the sea and the totally relaxed life she led there.

CHAPTER 17

'Is everybody ready?' Melanie called upstairs from the hall, and looked around for a last time. She was closing the house in New York for the summer, and her two large suitcases were already in the hall, along with all three tennis rackets, two large straw hats belonging to the girls, (Mel was wearing hers), and Raquel's small green vinyl suitcase. She came with them every year for six weeks, and took the last two weeks off and returned to New York alone for her holiday. 'Come on, you guys! We have to be at the airport in half an hour!' But they were only going to LaGuardia, so she knew they would make it.

There was a wonderful upbeat feeling to their departure every year and she always felt like a young girl again as they left for Martha's Vineyard. She had signed off on the news the night before and she and Grant had gone out for a drink after his show to celebrate her temporary release, and things had been relaxed between them, but he could see in her eyes that she was still confused, and lately she had been tired and nervous. She had worked long hours at the station, finished the piece on heart surgery in California and done two major interviews and a feature before she left, so they'd have them to use during the summer. She was, as always, conscientious about her work, and lately it seemed to be taking more of a toll than it had before, but Grant had suspected that it was because of the emotional whirl she was in, although he still knew none of the details. In fact, Peter was still calling her every day, and Melanie had no idea what would ever come of it, if anything. Lately, she'd even been worrying about her contract which had to be renewed in October. There were a lot of political changes at the station, and there was talk of a new owner, and God only knew what that would mean. But Grant reassured her when they went out that she had absolutely nothing to worry about. Peter said the same when she confessed her concern to him. But nonetheless it had been on her mind, and now all of it could be packed up and put away for two months. She wouldn't think of work, or even Peter or Grant. She was just going to Martha's Vineyard, to relax with her daughters. But not if they didn't come soon, she told herself as she waited in the front hall with Raquel. Finally they came thundering down the stairs with assorted games and books and bags in their arms. Valerie was carrying an enormous stuffed bear.

'Val . . . for God's sake . . .'

'Mom, I have to. Josh gave him to me last week and his parents have a house in Chappaquiddick, he'll be coming over to see us and if I don't . . .'

'All right, all right. Just get all this junk put together please, and let's get in a cab or we'll never get there.' Going on a trip with the girls was always a challenge, but the cabdriver actually managed to get almost all of it squashed in his boot, and they finally took off with Mel and the girls in the back seat, Val carrying the enormous teddy, and Raquel in the front with the hats and the tennis rackets. As they sped along towards LaGuardia, Mel mentally ticked off a list, making sure that she had locked the garden door, and all the windows, turned on the burglar alarm, turned off the gas . . . there was always that sinking feeling that you'd forgotten something. But they were all in high spirits by the time they got on the plane, and as they left the ground, Mel had a feeling of relief that she hadn't had in weeks, as though she were leaving all her confusion behind in New York, and she would find peace in Martha's Vineyard.

Peter had been calling her once or twice a day, and as much as she enjoyed their conversations, she tormented herself about them. Why was he calling? When would they see each other again? And finally, what was the point? He admitted to the same confusions as she, but they seemed unable to stop moving inexorably forward on this path towards an unseen goal that still frightened them both and that they did their best not to talk about. They stuck to safe subjects, and now and then admitted how much they missed each other. But why, Mel asked herself too often, why do I miss him? She still didn't know the answer, or didn't want to.

'Mom, do you think my bike got rusty?' Valerie was staring into space on the plane, hugging her bear, and looking totally happy, as a man across the aisle stared at her in lustful fascination. Mel was just glad she hadn't let her wear the little blue French short shorts she had worn to breakfast, and threatened to wear on the trip to Martha's Vineyard.

'I don't know, love. We'll have to see when we get there.' The woman they rented the house from every year allowed them to leave a few things in the basement.

In Boston they rented a car and drove to Woods Hole where they took the ferry across to Vineyard Haven. The ferry was the part of the trip they all liked best. It gave one the impression of leaving the real world behind, and all its responsibilities with it. Melanie stood alone at the railing for a few minutes, letting the wind whip her hair, and feeling freer than she had in months. She realised suddenly how desperately she needed a holiday. And she enjoyed the few moments alone before the girls came to find her. They had left Raquel talking to some man on the lower deck, and when she joined them at last they teased her about it. Mel suddenly laughed at a mental image she had of Peter's Mrs Hahn, she could hardly imagine anyone teasing her, or her flirting with a man on a ferry. But for all Raquel's independent ways, they loved her, and she was pleased to see Jess give her a hug once before they landed. Even Raquel smiled. The Vineyard was a haven for them all, and when they reached the familiar house in Chilmark, the girls went running barefoot down on the beach, and chased each other as far as they could, while Mel watched them.

It was as easy settling in as it was every year, and by nightfall the four of them looked and felt as though they had been there for a month. They had got pink cheeks from the few hours they spent on the beach that afternoon, they were unpacked, and the teddy bear was ensconced in the rocking chair in Val's room. The house was comfortably furnished but there was nothing fancy about it. It looked like a grandmother's house, with a porch and a wicker swing, and flowered chintzes in all the rooms. At first it always had a musty smell which went away in a few days, and they no longer noticed. It was just part of the familiarity of Chilmark. The girls had been coming here since they were little, and, as Mel explained to Peter when he called that night, Chilmark was part of home.

'They love it here and so do I.'

'It sounds very New England, Mel.' He tried to envision it from her description. Long beaches, white sand, a casual life-style of shorts and sweat shirts and bare feet, and a smattering of intellectuals who came from New York, and gathered from time to time for lobster dinners and clambakes. 'We go to the mountains every year, to Aspen.' It was totally different from Martha's Vineyard, but sounded intriguing too as he described it. 'Why don't you come and bring the girls? We're going for the first ten days in August.'

'You couldn't pry them away from here for a million dollars or a date with their favourite rock star. Well . . .' She reconsidered the last and they both laughed. They had an easy telephone relationship going, but it seemed so unreal at times. They were disembodied voices lodged in the phone night after night, but never getting any nearer.

'I don't suppose I could pry you away.'

'I doubt it.' There was a strange silence then and Mel listened, wondering what was on his mind, but when he spoke again, he sounded as though he were teasing.

'That's too bad.'

'What is?' He wasn't making sense, and she was

192

wonderfully relaxed after dinner. She didn't want to play games on the phone, but he was obviously in a playful mood.

'That you don't want to leave there.'

'Why?' Her heart began to thump. He was making her oddly nervous.

'Because there's a conference I've been asked to attend in New York, to speak to a group of surgeons from all over the East Coast. They'll be gathering at Columbia Presbyterian.' She didn't answer for a moment as she held her breath and then she spoke in a rush.

'They will? And you're going?'

'I could. Normally I'd refuse, particularly at this time of year. New York in July is no treat, but I thought that maybe under the circumstances . . .' He was blushing furiously at his end, and Mel gasped. He continued, 'I told them yes at three o'clock this afternoon. Now what about you and Martha's Vineyard?'

'Shit' – she looked around the room with a grin – 'we just got here.'

He was quick to ask, 'Would you rather I not come? I don't have to.'

'For chrissake, don't be an ass. How long do you think we can go on like this? Calling each other twice a day and never seeing each other?' It had only been three and a half weeks since she'd left California, but it felt more like three years to them both, and they needed to get together again to resolve at least some of their feelings.

'That's what I thought too. So . . .' He laughed again, pleased with the prospect.

'When do you arrive?'

'Next Tuesday.' And then he added softly, 'I wish it was tomorrow.'

'So do I.' Her face sobered. And then she whistled. 'That's only six days away.'

'I know.' He grinned, he was as excited as a child. 'They took a reservation for me at the Plaza.' But as he spoke, Mel had a thought. She was hesitant to voice it, for fear of putting them both in an awkward spot, but if they could handle it, it might work out well.

'Why don't you stay at the house? The girl won't be there, and you could have their whole floor to yourself. It would be a lot more comfortable for you than a hotel.'

He was silent for an instant, weighing the pros and cons as she had before she asked. Staying under one roof could prove to be very awkward, and it was quite a commitment . . . but on a separate floor . . . 'You wouldn't mind? It would be easier, but I wouldn't want to put you out, or . . .' He bumbled over the words and she laughed and stretched out on her bed, still holding the phone to her ear.

'It makes me just as nervous as it makes you, but what the hell, we're grown-ups, we can handle it.'

'Can we?' He smiled at the phone. He wasn't sure he could. 'And can you leave the girls alone?'

'No, but Raquel is here, so that'll be fine.' She was suddenly wildly excited that he was coming. 'Oh, Peter, I can't wait!'

'Neither can I!'

The next six days dragged unbearably for them both. They spoke on the phone two or three times a day, and Raquel finally caught on that there was someone important calling Mel but the girls seemed not to see it. On Sunday night, Mel casually mentioned that she had to go to New York for a few days, and she'd be leaving on Tuesday morning, but the news was met with dropped jaws and staring eyes. She had never gone back to New York for anything, except the year Jess broke her arm and Mel wanted her to see an orthopaedic man in New York. But they had only stayed for two days, and that was important. This time Mel said she'd be back on Friday afternoon, which meant four days away. They found it hard to believe that she was going, but she insisted that there was a problem with one of her features at work and she had to go back and watch them edit. The girls were still amazed when they went back to the beach that night to meet some friends and build a fire, but Raquel eyed her shrewdly as they cleared the table.

'It's serious this time, huh?'

Mel avoided her eyes, and carried a stack of plates into the kitchen. 'What is?'

'You can't fool me. You got a new man.'

'That's not true at all. The man is a subject I did an interview with.' But she couldn't meet Raquel's eyes, and she knew that if she did, she couldn't convince her. 'Just keep an eye on the girls while I'm gone, especially Val. I notice that the Jacobs boy is all grown-up, and drools every time he sees her.'

'He won't do no harm. I'll watch them.' And then she watched Mel retreat into her room and walked into the kitchen with a grin and a cigarette. She was certainly no Mrs Hahn, but she was a sharp old woman and she loved them.

And on Tuesday morning, Mel took the ferry back, and flew from Boston to New York. She reached the house at four o'clock in the afternoon, which gave her plenty of time to air the place out, turn the air conditioning on, go around the corner to buy fresh flowers and whatever groceries they might need, and then come back and get ready to pick him up. His plane wasn't due in until nine, and she left for the airport at seven thirty to be cautious, which was just as well, because the traffic was heavy and cars were overheating left and right and it was eight forty-five when they got there. She had just enough time to check the gate at which he would arrive, hurry out there, and then stand tapping her foot nervously for the next half hour, as they were fifteen minutes late. At nine fifteen exactly, the big silver bird drew up at the gate, and passengers began disembarking. She stood watching intently as the people poured off, with California tans, and straw hats, and bare golden legs, and silk shirts open to the waist with gold chains, and then suddenly she saw a man who looked nothing like any of them, in a beige linen suit and a blue shirt and navy tie, his hair only slightly bleached from the sun, and his face tanned. But there was a serious air about him, as he walked towards Mel and looked down at her where she stood. Then without further ado he bent to kiss her. They stood there for what seemed like a very long time as people eddied around them like a river cascading past rocks, and then he looked at her and smiled.

'Hello.'

'How was the flight?'

'Not nearly as nice as this.' He grinned, and with that they walked hand in hand to pick up his baggage, and then went to find Mel's car in the enormous garage. But time and time again they stopped to kiss as they stood between the cars, and Mel wondered how she had ever survived without him. 'You look wonderful, Mel.' She had a deep tan which set off her green eyes and copper hair and she had worn a white silk dress with a flower in her hair and white high-heeled sandals. She looked summery and healthy and happy, and her eyes seemed to drink his as though she had waited for him for a lifetime.

'You know, I haven't been to New York in years.' He looked at the ugly scenery passing by as they drove into town, and shook his head. 'I always turn them down, but I figured this time . . .' He shrugged and leaned over to kiss her again as she drove. She hadn't expected him to be as bold, or herself to be as comfortable with it. But the endless conversations on the phone seemed to have given them an ease with each other they might otherwise not have had. They had only known each other for two months now, but it felt like two years, or twice that.

'I'm glad you didn't turn them down this time.' She smiled at him and then returned her gaze to the road. 'Are you hungry?'

'Not very.' For him it was only quarter to seven, but it was shortly before ten in New York.

'I've got food at the house, but we can go somewhere for a bite to eat, if you like.'

'Whatever makes you happy.' He couldn't take his eyes

off her. All else slipped his mind as he reached for her hand. 'I'm so happy to see you, Mel.' It almost seemed unreal that they should be together again.

'It's a little like a dream, isn't it?' She smiled as she asked.

'It is. Best dream I've had in years.' They fell silent again as they drove into town.

He smiled at her, and touched her neck with his hand. 'I figured I owed you at least one trip east, after all you've been to LA twice.' But still he had needed an excuse, a reason to come. He hadn't just got on a plane and come to see her. But it was easier for both of them this way, they could advance towards each other as they had been, by inches. 'The President's certainly made a remarkable recovery.'

'It's only been five weeks and he's on his feet and in the office a few hours a day.' Mel shook her head, still amazed at all that, and then she remembered something. 'How's Marie, by the way?'

'Fair.' A frown crossed his face, but he shook off the worry. 'I left two other men in charge while I'm gone. She's all right, but she had a terrible time with the steroids. Her face is bloated like a full moon now, and there isn't a damn thing we can do. We've juggled everything we could. But she never complains.' He looked unhappily at Mel. 'I wish it weren't so difficult for her.' For an instant, Mel tried to focus on Marie in her mind, but all she could really think of now was him. Everything else in their lives seemed unreal to them both. Children, patients, war, TV shows. All that mattered was Peter and Mel.

She drove down the FDR Drive and turned off at Seventy-ninth Street, and Peter watched the city streets drifting past them, curious about where she lived, about what her house would be like, about everything. In some ways, he knew so much, of what she felt and thought, and in other ways, he knew so little, mostly about her environment.

Mel smiled to herself, remembering the first time she had seen the house in Bel-Air, and been struck by its air of formality. She knew that he would find her house very different and she was right. He was enchanted as he stepped inside, and smelled the flowers she had bought, looked around at the bright colours everywhere, and out into the pretty little garden. He turned to her then with a delighted smile. 'This house is so you. I knew it would look like this.' He put his arms around her waist and she smiled.

'Do you like it?' But it was obvious that he did, even before he nodded.

'I love it.'

'Come on, I'll show you the rest.' She took his hand and led him upstairs, standing in the doorway of her own room, and den, and then taking him up to the girls' rooms, where she had prepared everything for him. Fresh flowers on the desk and near his bed, a silver thermos filled with ice water, stacks of thick towels next to the tub, and the lights were on invitingly as they came up the stairs. She had put him in Jessica's room, because Jessie was neater, and it was easier to make him comfortable there.

'This is absolutely lovely.' He sat down at the desk and looked around with delight, and then at Mel again. 'You have such a loving touch.' She thought the same of him, although it wasn't as apparent in his home, which still bore the chill trace of Anne, but as he reached out to her now there was such a gentle look in his eyes. She walked slowly towards him and he took her hand from where he sat. 'I'm so happy to see you again, Mel.' And then he pulled her down on his lap and kissed her again, and she was still breathless when they went back downstairs. They sat at the kitchen table, not caring to eat anything, and talked for hours, as they had for weeks now on the phone, and it was almost two o'clock when they finally went back up and said goodnight outside Mel's room with another endless kiss, and then with a smile and a wave he disappeared up the stairs to her daughter's room. Mel went into her own room, and thought of every word he had said to her that night. She realised again how happy she was with him. As she brushed her teeth and took off her dress, she couldn't stop thinking of him and she slid into her bed, glad that he had stayed at the house. Apparently, they could handle it with ease, and she liked hearing him walking around upstairs. With the time difference he wasn't tired yet, and the odd thing was that neither was she. All she could do was lie there and think of him, and it seemed hours later when she heard him padding softly down the stairs and past her room. She listened and heard the kitchen door close, and with a grin she got out of bed and followed him down. He was sitting at the kitchen table eating a ham and cheese sandwich and drinking beer.

'I told you we should eat!' She smiled and got a 7-Up for herself.

'What are you doing up, Mel?'

'I can't sleep. Just excited I guess.' She sat across from him and he smiled.

'Me too. I could sit here and talk to you all night, but then I'll fall asleep tomorrow when I have to speak.'

'Do you have a prepared speech?'

'More or less.' He explained to her what it was about. He was using slides of several surgeries, including Marie's. 'What about you? What are you doing this week?'

'Absolutely nothing. I don't have to work for two months, so I'll just hang around and play while you're here. Can I come and hear you speak?'

'Not tomorrow. But on Friday you can. Would you like to come?'

'Of course.' He looked surprised and she laughed. 'Remember me? I'm the lady who did the interview on you at Center City.'

He clapped a hand to his head with a look of surprise. 'So that's who you are! I knew we'd met before but I couldn't remember where.'

'Dummy.' She nibbled his ear and he swatted her behind. It was so comfortable sitting there together in the middle of the night, and at last they walked up the stairs again side by side, holding hands, as though they had lived together for years, and when she stopped outside her room, he bent to kiss her again.

'Goodnight, little friend.'

'Goodnight, my love.' The words just slipped out, and she looked up at him, her eyes wide, and with that he gently enfolded her in his arms again, and she felt so safe there.

'Goodnight.' He whispered the word, kissed her lips once more, and disappeared upstairs. She went into her room, turned off the light, and climbed into bed, thinking of him again and what she had just said. And the amazing thing was that she knew it was true. And as he lay in bed upstairs, he knew he loved her too.

CHAPTER 18

When Mel awoke the next day, Peter was already gone. She got up slowly and went upstairs to make his bed for him, but she found the room perfectly neat and when she went into the kitchen, she found a note he had left for her.

'Meet you here at six. Have a nice day. Love, P.' She smiled at the simple words, but it felt so good to read them. And she felt as though she were floating all day. She went to Bloomingdale's, and bought some things for herself and the house and the girls, and when she came home, there was that amazing feeling that in a few hours she wouldn't be alone.

She sat in the living room, cooling a bottle of wine, waiting for him, and at last he arrived, looking rumpled and tired and excited to see Mel. She rushed to her feet and quickly went to him. 'Hi, love, how was your day?'

'Wonderful now.' He walked into the living room with a smile. There were no lights on yet, and the room was filled with daylight and sun. 'How was yours?'

'Endless without you.' It was a very honest thing to say and she sat down again and patted the couch next to her. 'Come and sit down and tell me what you did today.' It was fun having someone to talk to at the end of the day, other than the girls. She told him what she had bought, where she had gone, and then sheepishly, she told him that she had literally counted the hours until she saw him again, and he looked pleased.

'I felt the same way. All I could think of was you. It does sound crazy, doesn't it?' And with that he put an arm around her shoulders and pulled her close. Their lips met and they kissed until they were both breathless. There seemed to be nothing to say when they stopped. All they wanted was to kiss again.

'Maybe I should start dinner or something?' Mel laughed, as though they needed a distraction from what they both felt.

'How about a cold shower, à deux?'

She smiled again. 'I'm not sure the "à deux" would help.' She got up and walked around but he pulled her into his arms again.

'I love you, Mel.' And then it was as though the whole world stood still for them both. He had never said that to any woman except Anne, and Mel had told herself for years that she never wanted to hear or say those words again. But this time it meant something to them both, and when he kissed her again she felt it sear her very soul, and she clung to him as though she would drown if she let go. He kissed her face, her lips, her neck and her hands, and then suddenly, without thinking about it, Mel stood up and gently led him upstairs, to her room. And then she turned to him.

'I love you too.' She spoke so softly that had he not been watching her, he would never have heard.

'Don't be afraid, Mel . . . please . . .' He walked to her and carefully unzipped her dress as she slowly unbuttoned his shirt, and when she was undressed he carefully laid her on the bed, and ran his hands slowly over her silky flesh, until at last she arched towards him, aching for his body on hers, and they pressed themselves close to each other, savouring each moment before he finally entered her and she gasped, and then it was almost as though he could hear her purr until at last she screamed and he groaned, and they lay in silence as the sunlight streamed across the floor. And when Peter looked down at her, there were tears coursing silently from her eyes. 'Oh baby, I'm sorry . . . I . . .' He was aghast, but she shook her head and kissed him again.

'I love you so much, it scares me sometimes.'

'It scares me too.' But he held her so close that night as they lay side by side, that it was impossible to believe that they would ever know anything except joy.

*

202

At nine o'clock they went downstairs, naked and hand in hand. She made sandwiches and they came back upstairs and watched TV and laughed. 'Just like married folk,' he teased, and she rolled her eyes and pretended to faint and he held her comfortably in his arms. And Mel realised that she had never been so happy with any man. They slept together in her bed that night, and awoke to make love several times. When he got up to go to his conference again, she got up with him, and made him coffee and scrambled eggs before he left. And when he was gone, she sat naked and alone, aching for the moment when he would return again.

CHAPTER 19

On Friday Mel went to the conference with Peter and listened to him speak, fascinated by what he said, and pleased for him by the reaction from the audience. His comments and slides and explanations of their latest techniques were met with continuous applause, and he was surrounded by his colleagues afterwards for almost an hour, as Mel stayed at a discreet distance and watched him with pride.

'Well, what did you think?' he asked her when they were finally alone again that night. They had opted for a quiet dinner at home, since he was leaving the next day, and they wanted some time to themselves.

'I think you're sensational.' She smiled happily at him as they shared a bottle of white wine. She had bought great big Maine lobsters that day, reminiscent of the dinners they would have eaten at Martha's Vineyard. She was going to serve them cold, with salad and garlic bread and chilled Pouilly Fumé. 'And I also thought their reaction was extremely good.'

He looked satisfied, and smiled. 'I thought so too.' He leaned towards her and gently kissed her lips. 'I'm glad you were there.'

'Me too.' And then a shadow crossed her eyes, thinking of the next day when he'd be gone. They were leaving for the airport together the next day at eight a.m. His flight was at ten, and he would be back in Los Angeles by one o'clock their time, in time to see Pam and spend some time with her before she left for camp the next day. And when she dropped him off, Mel was heading back to Martha's Vineyard and her girls.

'What's wrong, love?' He took her hand in his. 'You looked so sad just then.' He wondered for the hundredth time since they'd first made love if she regretted getting involved with him. He would be leaving after all, and neither of them knew when they would meet again. It seemed to be an uncertainty they constantly had to bear.

'I was just thinking of tomorrow when you leave.'

'So was I.' He put his wineglass down and took her hand in his. 'It's a crazy life we lead, you and I.' She nodded and they smiled. 'But we'll figure something else out.' And then he decided to pursue an idea he'd had before. 'What about coming to Aspen with your girls? We go in about three weeks, and Valerie and Jessica would love it, Mel. It's a wonderful place for kids . . . for us . . . for anyone, in fact.' His eyes lit up at the thought. 'And it would give us a chance to be together again.'

'But not like this.' She sighed and met his eyes with a rueful smile. 'Our children would probably all go nuts if they realised what was going on.' At least his daughter would, but she knew that it would startle hers as well. There had been no time to prepare them at all. Peter was a stranger to them, a name they'd almost never heard, except in the context of her work. And then suddenly, 'Zap! Guess what, girls, we're going to Aspen with him and his kids!' Melanie knew they'd have a fit.

'They'll adjust. And they don't have to know all the details.' He sounded so assured that Mel sat back and looked at him with a long, lazy, happy smile. For a man who had known no woman but his wife for the past twenty years, and no one at all since she had died, he seemed remarkably confident about things now, and Mel wasn't sure if it was indicative of what he felt for her, or simply a result of his constant poise.

'You're awfully relaxed about all this, beloved sir.'

He smiled at what she said. 'I've never felt like this before, Mel. But it all feels so right.' At least it did there, in New York, in her pretty little sun-filled house, alone with her. Perhaps it would be different when they were surrounded by kids, but he didn't think it would. 'I think our children will be able to handle it. Don't you?'

'I wish I were as sure. What about Pam?'

'She liked you when she met you in LA. And in Aspen, everyone has something to do, hiking, walking, swimming, tennis, fishing, the music festivals at night. The kids always seem to meet friends and have their own things to do.' But it sounded too easy to Mel, and she wondered how realistic he was. 'Besides' – he moved closer to her and held her tight – 'I don't think I can survive for more than a few weeks without you.'

'It seems like forever, doesn't it?' Her voice was soft and sad as she leaned her head against his chest and felt his warmth envelop her. 'But I don't know if we should come to Aspen, Peter. That's a lot to push at them all at once.'

'What? That we're friends?' He sounded both surprised and annoyed. 'Don't read something into it that they won't see.'

'They're not blind, Peter. They're all practically adults by now, except fot Matt. They won't be fooled.'

'Who's fooling them?' He pulled away from her for a moment to look into her eyes. 'I love you, Mel.' It was all he could think of each time he saw her face, every time she entered a room . . . whenever he thought of her.

'Do you want them to know that?'

He smiled. 'Eventually.'

'And then what? We go our separate ways, living our separate lives three thousand miles apart, and they know we've had an affair? Think of how they'll feel about it.' She thought for a moment, her mind filled with a picture of Pam's haunted face. 'Especially Pam.'

She sounded sincere and he sighed. 'You think too much.'

'I'm serious.'

'Well, don't be. Just come to Aspen and let's have some fun, without worrying about the kids. They'll be fine. Trust me.'

Mel was bemused by his innocence. Sometimes she was surprised at how naïve he was about his kids. But she had to admit that in spite of her reservations about the trip, she was anxious to see him again, and Aspen would provide a golden opportunity, if she could convince the twins to leave Martha's Vineyard for a week or two. She frowned as she considered what she would tell them when she went back.

'Don't worry so much, Mel. Just come.'

She smiled at him and they kissed and afterwards she sat pensively sipping her wine. 'I just don't know what to tell the girls about leaving Martha's Vineyard.'

'Tell them the mountains are better for their health.'

She laughed and looked at him with her head tilted to one side. 'Don't you like the beach?'

'Sure. But I love the mountains. All that good air, splendid views, good hikes.' She had never thought of him as being the outdoor type, but after the intensity of his work, it was easy to understand that he needed an outlet, and one on a grand scale. The mountains would provide that for him, but she had loved the beach since she was a child, and Martha's Vineyard was exactly what she wanted for her holidays with the girls.

'I could remind them about Mark;' – she grinned – 'that would convince Val anyway, but that headache we don't need.' He laughed at that.

'Maybe I should tell him about the twins before we go.' He didn't dare to ask her again that night if she was convinced, but the next morning, as they sat over coffee, he had to know. They were leaving the house in an hour for the airport, and his bags were already packed, and her little bag was too. She didn't plan to come back to the house in the city again until September. 'Well, Mel, are you coming?'

'I wish I were.'

He set down his cup and leaned over to kiss her. 'Will you come to Aspen at the end of the month, Mel?'

'I'll try. I have to think it out.' She had turned it over in her mind several times, and was still undecided. But if they didn't go, she might not see him again for months, and she didn't want that to happen either.

She set down her cup with a sigh, and looked him in the eye. 'I just don't know if it's a good idea for us to involve the children in what we feel.'

'Why not?' He looked upset.

'Because it may be too much for them to handle.'

'I think you're underestimating our children.'

'How are you going to explain our coming out there?'

'Does it have to be explained?'

'Oh, for God's sake, what do you think? Of course it does. How could you not explain it to them?'

'All right, all right. So we'll explain it. We'll tell them we're old friends.'

'Which they know damn well isn't true.' She seemed to be getting upset. He looked at his watch. It was seven thirty, and they had half an hour left. There wasn't much time to convince her. And if she didn't come, God only knew when he'd see her again.

'I don't give a damn what you tell them, Mel, your children or mine. But I want you to come to Aspen.' He was beginning to sound bullheaded about it and it annoyed her.

'I have to think it over.'

'No, you don't.' He towered over her, looking as immovable as a marble column. 'You've been making your own decisions for so damn long, that you don't know how to let yourself go and trust someone else.'

'That has nothing to do with this.' Their voices were rising. 'You're being naïve about how the children will react.'

'So what, for chrissake. Don't we have a right to a life too? Don't I have a right to love you?'

'Yes, but we don't have the right to screw up our kids for something that can't go anywhere, Peter.'

'And what makes you think that?' He was shouting now. 'Do you have other plans?'

'I happen to live in New York, and you live in LA, or don't you remember?'

'I remember perfectly, which was why I wanted to meet

you halfway three weeks from now, or is that too much to ask?'

'Oh for chrissake . . . all right!' She shouted the words 'All right! I'll come to Aspen.'

'Good!' He glanced at his watch then. It was five minutes after eight, and he suddenly reached out and pulled Mel towards him. Time was moving too fast. They were supposed to have left five minutes before, but he couldn't leave her now. He kissed the top of her head and stroked her hair, smiling at his own thoughts. 'I think we just had our first fight. You're a damn stubborn woman, Mel.'

'I know. I'm sorry.' She looked up at him and they kissed. 'I just want to do the right thing, and I don't want to upset our kids.'

He nodded. 'I know. But we have to think of ourselves now.'

'I haven't done that in a long time. Except to be sure I didn't get hurt.'

'I won't hurt you, Mel.' His voice was sad, it depressed him to think that she would defend herself against him too. 'I hope to hell I never do that.'

'You can't help it. When people care about each other, they get hurt. Unless you stay at a safe distance all the time.'

'That's not living.'

'No, it's not. But it's safe.'

'Screw safe.' He looked down at her seriously. 'I love you.'

'I love you too.' She still trembled when she said the words. 'I wish we didn't have to leave yet.' They were going to have to run like hell to catch his plane, and he looked at his watch and then at her.

'I have a suggestion.'

'What's that?'

'I'll call home and get someone to cover for me for another day. If they survived this long without me, they can hang on for another day. What do you think?'

She smiled like a little girl and let her whole body sag against him. 'I think it sounds wonderful.' And then she thought of something. 'What about Pam? Don't you want to see her before she goes to camp?'

'Yes, but maybe for the first time in almost two years, I'll do what I want to do for a change. I'll see her in three weeks when she comes home. She'll survive without me.'

'Are you sure?'

He looked very serious as he held her. 'What about you? Can you go back to the Vineyard tomorrow?'

'Are you serious, Peter?' She turned to face him, amazed at his decision. But she could see instantly that he was serious about staying.

'Yes. I don't want to leave you. Let's spend the weekend together.' A smile dawned slowly in her eyes and she hugged him to her.

'You are the most remarkable man.'

'In love with the most extraordinary woman. I'd say we make quite an impressive couple, wouldn't you?'

'Yes, I would.' Her voice was soft as they stood together in her kitchen. And then she looked up at him with a small smile. 'As long as you're not leaving right away, what do you say we go upstairs for a while, Doctor Hallam?'

'Excellent idea, Miss Adams.' She went upstairs and he followed her a moment later. He stayed in the kitchen, just long enough to call the doctor who was covering for him in LA and ask if he would mind staying on for two more days. His colleague teased him about it, but didn't seem to mind at all, and two minutes later Peter bounded up the stairs, taking them two at a time with his long legs and he burst into Melanie's bedroom with a boyish grin. 'I can stay!'

She didn't say a word in answer. She only walked towards him and took his clothes off one by one, and they fell onto her bed with an abandon that came from having taken one more step closer to each other.

CHAPTER 20

'But how come you're not coming home?' Pam's voice approached a whine when Peter called her before lunch. 'You don't have any patients in New York.' She sounded both angry and hurt and her voice was filled with accusation.

'I got delayed at the conference here, Pam. I'll be home tomorrow night.'

'But I'm leaving for camp tomorrow morning.'

'I know. But Mrs Hahn can take you to the bus. It's not like it's the first time you've gone.' It was odd how one had to defend oneself to one's children, Mel thought as she listened. 'This is your fourth year. You should be an old pro by now, Pam. And you'll be home in three weeks.'

'Yeah.' She sounded distant and gloomy and guilt pulled at his heartstrings, more so now that the decision was made and he had made love to Mel for the past two hours. Now it seemed less urgent that he stay, and Pam was bringing his responsibilities at home back into focus again. 'Okay.' She was shutting him out and he felt bad about it.

'Sweetheart, it couldn't be helped.' But it could have, which made him feel worse. Had he been wrong to stay? But dammit, didn't he have a right to his own life, and some time with Mel?

'It's okay, Daddy.' But he could already hear how despondent and depressed she sounded, and he knew from experience how unwise it was to upset her.

'Look, I'll come up to see you next weekend.' The camp was near Santa Barbara, and he could drive up easily from LA, and then he remembered that he would be on call all weekend. 'Damn, I can't. The next weekend then.'

'Never mind. Have a nice time.' She seemed suddenly

anxious to get off, and in New York, Mel watched Peter's face, easily reading the emotions there. When he hung up, she came and sat beside him.

'You can still catch a plane this afternoon, you know.'

But he shook his head with a dogged air. 'I don't think I should, Mel. What I said before is true. We have a right to some time together.'

'But she needs you too, and you feel torn.' It didn't take a psychic to see how he felt, and he nodded.

'Somehow she always makes me feel guilty. She's been doing it ever since Anne died. It's almost as if she holds me responsible for her death, and for the rest of time I'll have to atone for my sins and I'll never quite make it.'

'That's a heavy burden to bear. If you're willing to accept it.'

'What choice do I have?' He looked unhappy. 'She's had every emotional problem in the books since her mother died, from anorexia to skin problems and nightmares.'

'But traumas happen to everyone sooner or later. She's going to have to accept what happened, Peter. She can't make you pay for it forever.' But it looked like she was going to try. At least that was how it looked to Mel, but she didn't say anything further to Peter. He was determined to stay, and let her make the adjustment. And a little while later Mel called the twins and Raquel at the house in Chilmark.

The twins were both obviously disappointed that she wasn't coming home, Jessica more than Val, but they both said they'd see her the following night, and then turned the phone over to Raquel, who waited until they left the room before she made comment.

'Boy, he must be somethin' else!'

'Who?' Mel's face looked blank as Peter watched.

'The new boyfriend in New York.'

'What boyfriend?' But now she was blushing. 'Raquel, you're oversexed. How are the girls?'

'They're okay. Val has a new boyfriend she met on the

212

beach yesterday, and I think there's someone who's interested in Jessica, but she doesn't look too excited.'

Mel smiled. 'Sounds like everything there is normal. How's the weather?'

'Gorgeous. I look like a Jamaican.' The two women laughed and Mel closed her eyes, thinking of the Vineyard. She wished that she and Peter were there, and not stuck in New York on a Saturday in July. She knew that, even mountain lover that he was, he would love it.

'See you tomorrow, Raquel. And I'll be in and out of the house here if you need me.'

'We won't.'

'Thanks.' It was always so comforting to know that the girls were in good hands, and as she hung up she smiled to herself, trying to imagine that exchange with Peter's housekeeper, Mrs Hahn. It was beyond even Mel's imagination, and she laughed as she told him.

'You like your housekeeper a lot, don't you?'

Mel nodded. 'I'm damn grateful to her for all she's done. She's an ornery old bitch at times, but she loves those kids, and she even loves me.'

'That's not hard to do.' He kissed Mel full on the mouth and sat back to look at her. She handled her children differently than he did, spoke to her help in a way he never would, and her life seemed to run remarkably smoothly. For a minute, he asked himself if he would only disrupt it, and she saw the look in his eyes as she got up and stretched. They had had a wonderful morning, and it was like an extra gift, since they hadn't expected to be together, and it made them appreciate the time even more.

'What were you thinking then, Peter?' She was always curious about his thoughts, and always intrigued by what he told her.

'I was thinking how well organised your life is, and how long it's all been running on the same track. I was wondering if I'm more of a disruption than an asset.'

'What do you think?' She sprawled on the chaise longue in her room, naked, and he found himself longing for her

213

again. It was amazing how constantly his body hungered for her.

'I think I can't think straight when I see you without your clothes on.'

'Neither can I.' She grinned and beckoned to him with one finger, as he approached and lay down on the chaise beside her, and a moment later he rolled slowly over her, pulling her long thin figure on top of his body.

'I'm crazy about you, Mel.'

She could hardly breathe she wanted him again so badly. 'Me too . . .' And then they made love again, and forgot their troubles and guilts and responsibilities, and even their children.

It was one thirty before they had showered and got dressed and Melanie looked like a contented cat as they strolled out of the house into the hot sunshine. 'We sure are lazy.'

'Why not? We both work so damned hard, I can't remember ever having a weekend like this.' He smiled down at her and she laughed.

'Neither can I. Or I'd be too tired to work.'

'Good. Maybe I need to keep you too tired to work, so you don't think of that fancy job of yours all the time.'

She was surprised at his comment. 'Do I do that?' She wasn't aware of thinking of work all the time, and wondered what he meant by it.

'Not really. But there's a certain awareness that you have another life, not just your kids and your house, and a husband.'

'Ah.' Understanding was beginning to dawn. 'You mean I'm not just a housewife. Do you mind that?'

'No.' He shook his head slowly, thinking about it, as they wandered down Lexington Avenue with no particular destination in mind. It was just a hot, sunny day, and they were happy to be together. 'I respect who you are. But it's different than if you were just . . .' He looked for the words and smiled down at her. 'An ordinary mortal.'

'Bullshit. What's different about it?'

'You couldn't just leave for Europe with me for six months, could you?'

'No, my contract wouldn't exactly melt into thin air, not without a hefty lawsuit. But you couldn't do that either.'

'That's different. I'm a man.'

'Oh, Peter!' She hooted. 'You are a rotten chauvinist.'

'Yes' – he looked down at her proudly – 'I am. But I still respect your job. So long as you stay as feminine as you are and can manage all the womanly stuff too.'

'What does that mean?' She was suddenly vastly amused by him. From anyone else it might have annoyed her, but it didn't from him. 'You mean like wax floors and bake cheesecake?'

'No, be a good mother, have babies, care about the man in your life, without putting your work first. I was always happy that Anne didn't work because it meant she was there for me. It would bother me if the woman I loved weren't.'

'No one's there all the time, Peter. No woman and no man. But if you care enough about someone you can juggle things most of the time, so you're there when they really need you. It's a question of good organisation, and a sense of priorities. I've been there for the girls most of the time, in fact almost always.'

'I know you have.' He had sensed that about her from the first. 'But you haven't wanted to be there for a man.'

'No, I haven't.' She was honest with him.

'And now?' He looked worried as he asked the question, like a little boy who was afraid he wouldn't find his mommy.

'What are you asking me, Peter?' There was a sudden silence between them. There was a potential which they both sensed, which still frightened them both, but Peter was bravest about pointing to it, and now he suddenly wanted to know where Mel stood, but he didn't want to scare her off. Maybe it was too soon to be asking these questions. She sensed his concern and leaned towards him. 'Don't worry so much.'

215

'I just wonder what all this means to you sometimes.'

'The same thing it means to you. Something beautiful and wonderful that's never happened to me before. And if you want to know where it's going, I can't tell you.'

He nodded. 'I know. And that bothers me too. It's like in surgery, I don't like to wing it, I like to know where I'm going, what's the next step.' He smiled at her. 'I'm a planner, Mel.'

'So am I. But you can't plan these things.' And she smiled at him, the mood lightened between them.

'Why not?' He was teasing now and she grinned.

'What do you want, a contract from me?'

'Sure. A contract for that gorgeous body of yours any time I want it.'

They held hands and swung their arms, and Mel looked at him happily. 'I'm so glad you stayed for the weekend.'

'So am I.'

They went to Central Park and wandered around until five and then walked up Fifth Avenue to the Stanhope Hotel and had a drink at the outdoor café. Then they walked the few blocks back to her house again, ready to sequester themselves in her comfortable little house. They lay on the bed and made love, and sat watching the sunset at eight o'clock, and then they showered and went to Elaine's for dinner. The place was full and Mel knew half the people there, even though most of the people she knew left town for the weekend in summer. One instantly sensed how much a part of her life this was; the celebrities whom she knew and who knew her, the recognition, and the whole electricity of New York seemed to suit her. There was a milieu like that in LA too but it had never been a part of his life. He was too busy with his own doings, his family, and his patients.

'So, Doctor, what do you think of New York?' They were walking arm in arm down Second Avenue, back towards her house.

'I think you love it, and it loves you.'

'I think you're right.' She smiled happily. 'But I happen to love you too.'

'Even though I'm not a talk show host, or a politician or a writer?'

'You're better than all that, Peter. You're real.'

He smiled at the compliment. 'Thank you. But so are they.'

'It's not the same thing with them. They only touch half my life, Peter. There's another part they never come near. I've never really found anyone who understood both halves of my life before. My family life and my professional life are both important to me, and they're so diametrically different.'

'You seem to manage both.'

She smiled, and nodded. 'It's not always easy though.'

'What is?' He was suddenly thinking of his daughter's reaction to his staying in New York, and he suspected that she'd make him pay for it when she saw him again. She always did.

But Mel looked at him then with a smile and they turned west on Eighty-first Street, and went back to her house to lie in bed and talk until two in the morning.

The next morning, they had brunch at the Tavern-on-the-Green, and then they went down to Greenwich Village for a street fair. There wasn't a great deal to do in New York in the summertime, but neither of them seemed to care. They just wanted to be together, and they walked for hours, talking of their pasts, their lives, their work, their children, themselves. It was as though each couldn't get enough of the other, and at five o'clock they regretfully went back to Mel's house, and made love for a last time. At seven o'clock they took a cab to the airport. And suddenly the time moved all too quickly. It seemed only minutes later when they had to say goodbye and they clung to each other at the gate for their final moments.

'I'm going to miss you so much.' He looked down at her, infinitely glad he had come to New York. He sensed that it had changed the course of his whole life and he wasn't even afraid any more. He put a finger under her chin and tipped her face up to his. 'You promise, you're coming to Aspen?'

She smiled and fought back the tears she felt welling up in her throat. 'We'll be there.' But she still didn't know how she'd tell the twins.

'You'd better.' He held her close and kissed her one last time before boarding the plane with a wave, and as he left, Mel felt as though he had taken her heart with him.

It was a long lonely trip back to Martha's Vineyard that night and she didn't arrive at the house in Chilmark until after midnight, and everyone was asleep. She was relieved that they were. She didn't want to talk to a soul in the world except Peter Hallam, and he was still on a plane heading west to Los Angeles.

Mel sat for a long time on the porch of the house that night, listening to the sound of the ocean, and feeling the gentle breeze on her face. There was a wonderful, peaceful feeling just being there, and she was sorry he hadn't been able to be there with her. But for now, it was just as well. They had needed to be alone. And being in Aspen with his children and hers was going to be enough of a challenge. She still hadn't decided when or how to tell the girls, but she decided the next morning at breakfast that it would be best to give them all the time she could to get used to the idea. They had never left the Vineyard in the middle of the summer before, and she knew they would find it strange. More than that, they would find it suspicious.

'Aspen?' Jessica stared at her in amazement. 'Why would we be going to Aspen?'

Mel attempted to look nonchalant, but she could feel her heart beating faster. Partly because they were putting her on the spot, and partly because she was about to tell a lie. 'Because it's a very exciting invitation, and we've never been there.' Raquel snorted as she went back to the kitchen for the maple syrup, and Val looked at her mother in horror.

'But we can't leave. Everything's happening here, and we don't know anybody in Aspen.'

Mel looked at the youngest twin calmly. She would be easier to convince than her sister. 'Relax, Val, they have boys in Aspen too.'

'But that's different. And we know everyone here!' She looked as though she were going to cry, but Mel held firm.

'I just think it's an opportunity we shouldn't miss.' Or did she mean 'I'? She felt guilty for what they didn't know.

'Why?' Jessica was watching her every move. 'What's in Aspen?'

'Nothing . . . I mean . . . oh, for chrissake, Jess, stop acting like the official investigative team. It's a fabulous place, the mountains are wonderful, there are loads of kids and things to do, pack trips, horses, hiking, fishing . . .'

'Blyearghk!' Valerie interrupted with disgust. 'I hate all that stuff.'

'It'll do you good.'

But this time Jessica intervened, ever practical. 'But that means we'll miss part of the summer here. And we rented the house for both months.'

'We'll only be gone for two weeks. You'll still have six weeks here.'

'I just don't understand it.' Jessica left the table in obvious annoyance and Val burst into tears and hurried to her room.

'I won't go! It's the best summer I've ever had, and you're trying to wreck it!'

'I am not trying to – ' But the door slammed before she could finish, and she looked at Raquel in obvious irritation as she cleared the table.

'It must be serious.' She shook her head wisely and Mel got up with a groan of aggravation.

'Oh, for chrissake, Raquel.'

'All right, all right. Don't tell me. But wait and see, six months from now you gonna get married. I never seen you leave the Vineyard before.'

'This will be a fabulous trip.' She was trying to convince

219

them all, including herself, and wishing it were a little bit easier.

'I know. And what about me? Do I have to go too?' She didn't look any more thrilled than the girls.

'Why don't you take your holiday then instead of waiting until the end of the summer?'

'Sounds good to me.'

At least that was one worry behind her. Val didn't come out of her room for two hours, and then emerged, red-eyed and red-nosed, to meet her friends on the beach, and she was obviously not speaking to her mother. Jessica came to find Mel alone on the porch half an hour later, answering some letters. She sat down on the steps near Mel's feet, and waited until her mother looked up from what she was writing.

'How come we're going to Aspen, Mom?' She looked Mel straight in the eyes and it was difficult not to tell her the truth . . . because I've fallen in love with this man and he goes there in the summer.

'I thought it might be a nice change for us, Jess.' But she didn't quite look Jessica in the eyes, and didn't see how carefully she was watching her mother.

'Is there another reason?'

'Like what?' She was stalling for time, her pen poised over her paper.

'I don't know. I just don't understand why you'd want to go to Aspen.'

'We were invited by friends.' At least it was a half-truth, but this was turning out to be as difficult as Mel had feared, and if Peter thought his group was going to be any easier, he was crazy.

'What friends?' Jessica looked at her more intently, and Mel took a deep breath. There was no point lying to her, she'd find out soon enough.

'A man named Peter Hallam and his family.'

Jessica looked shocked. 'The doctor you interviewed in California?' Mel nodded. 'Why would he invite us to Aspen?'

'Because we're both alone with our children, and he was very nice to interview and we got to be friends. He has three children more or less your ages.'

'So what?' Jessica sounded even more suspicious now.

'So it might be fun.'

'For whom?' Touché. She was outraged now, and Mel felt suddenly exhausted. Maybe it was stupid to push to go to Aspen.

'Look, Jess, I just don't want to argue about this with you. We're going and that's it!'

'What is this?' She stood up with her hands on her hips, glaring at her mother. 'A dictatorship or a democracy?'

'Call it what you like. We're going to Aspen in three weeks. I hope you'll enjoy it, if not, call it two weeks out of a very long pleasant summer. I might remind you that you're going to have one hell of a nice time here, get to do everything you want for almost two months, and you and Val are having quite an elaborate birthday party next week. I don't think you have much to complain about.' But apparently Jessica did, as she stomped off in a huff without saying another word to her mother.

Things didn't improve much in the next two weeks despite the clambake on the beach for seventy-five kids for Jessie's and Val's sixteenth birthday. It was a wonderful party and everyone had a great time, which made them even more resentful that they had to leave the following week. By then, Mel was sick to death of hearing them complain about it.

'What about you, love?' She lay on her bed talking to Peter one night. They were still talking to each other twice a day, and dying to see each other, in spite of the children.

'I haven't told them yet. There's time.'

'Are you kidding? We're meeting you next week.' She sounded aghast. She had taken two weeks of abuse from the twins, and he hadn't even started dealing with it at his end.

'You have to be casual about these things.' He sounded extremely nonchalant and Mel thought he was crazy.

'Peter, you've got to give them time to adjust to the idea that we're meeting you there, or else they're going to be awfully surprised and probably very angry.'

'They'll be fine. Now tell me about you.' She told him about what she'd been doing, and he reported on the technique he had tried in surgery that morning. Marie was doing extremely well, despite a minor setback and she was due to leave the hospital in a few days, later than expected but in high spirits.

'I can't wait to see you, love.'

'Me too.' He smiled at the thought, and they chatted on for a little while. But he wasn't smiling when he faced Pam four days later.

'What do you mean we've invited friends to Aspen this year?' She looked livid as she faced him across the dinner table. He had told Mark the night before, just casually, as he was going out, and Mark had looked surprised but he hadn't had time to discuss it. And he was going to tell Matthew after he told Pam. But Pam looked as though she were about to go through the roof as she looked at her father. 'What friends?'

'A family I thought you'd enjoy.' He could feel sweat drip slowly down his sides, and was annoyed with himself for it. Why did he let her make him so nervous? 'There are two girls almost your age.' He was stalling, and they both knew it but he was terrified to tell her it was Mel. What if she went off the deep end again?

'How old?'

'Sixteen.' He looked hopeful, but his hopes were quickly dashed.

'They're probably creeps and they'll snub me because I'm younger than they are.'

'I doubt that.'

'I won't go.'

'Pam . . . for heaven's sake . . .'

'I'll stay here with Mrs Hahn.' She seemed as movable as granite.

'She's taking her holiday.'

'Then I'll go with her. I won't go to Aspen with you unless you get rid of these people. Who are they anyway?'

'Mel Adams, and her twins.' It had to be said, and Pam's eyes opened wide.

'*Her?* I won't go!' Something about the way she said it finally got to him, and before he could stop himself, he slammed a fist into the dining table.

'You'll do what I tell you, do you understand? And if I say you're going to Aspen, that's exactly what you'll do! Is that clear?' But she said not a single word in answer; she took her empty plate and threw it against the wall, where it shattered in a dozen pieces on the floor. She flew from the room and he watched her. If Anne had been alive, she would have forced her to come back and clean up the mess, but he didn't have the heart to do that to her. She was a child without a mother. Instead, he sat in the dining room, staring at his plate, and then a few moments later, he left the room and closed himself in his den. It took him half an hour to get up the courage to call Mel. He just needed to hear her voice, but he didn't tell her anything of what had happened.

The next morning, Pam did not come down to breakfast and Matthew quizzed him with a look of interest. He had returned from his grandmother's house the night before after dinner.

'Who's coming to Aspen with us, Dad?'

With a belligerent air, Peter looked him straight in the eye. 'Miss Adams. The lady who had dinner with us here one night, and her two daughters.' He sat braced for war since that was what he'd met in the first round, but Matthew's face exploded with joy at the news.

'She is! Wow! When is she coming?'

Peter relaxed in his chair with a smile and looked at his youngest child in relief. Thank God one of them was decent about it. He still hadn't heard from Mark, but maybe he would behave as strangely as Pam, although that was unlikely. Mark was too involved in his own life these days to be much trouble. 'She's meeting us in Aspen, Matt. All three of them are.'

223

'Why don't they come here and we can fly together?'

'Fly where?' Mark entered the room with a sleepy scowl. He had been out late the night before and had to get to work in a hurry now, but he was starving. He had already asked Mrs Hahn for fried eggs, bacon, toast, orange juice, and coffee.

'We were talking about Aspen.' Peter looked defensively at Mark, and waited for the now-expected explosion. 'He was thinking that Mel Adams and her daughters should meet us here.' There was no immediate reaction and he turned back to Matt. 'But they're coming from the East and it's easier for them to fly to Denver and then Aspen.'

'Are they cute?'

'Who?' Peter looked blank. He couldn't keep up with them all these days and he was still unnerved by Pam's reaction the night before. She had yet to emerge from her room, and the door had been locked when he tried it the night before and there had been no answer when he called her name. He decided to leave her alone to cool off for a day. He'd talk to her tonight after he came home from the office.

'Are her daughters cute?' Mark looked at his father as though he were extremely stupid, and Peter sat back in his chair and laughed, just as Mark's gargantuan repast arrived.

'Good God, who's all that for?'

'Me. Well, are they?'

'Are they what? Oh . . . oh . . . sorry . . . I don't know. I assume so. She's a good-looking woman, her daughters must be too.'

'Hmmm . . .' Mark was torn between attending to his breakfast and discussing the prospects of Mel's daughters. 'I hope they're not dull.'

'You're a jerk.' Matt looked at him in disgust. 'They're probably gorgeous.'

And with that, Peter stood up with a grin. 'And on that note, gentlemen, I bid you good morning. If you see your sister, give her my love. I'll see you all tonight. Mark, will you be home?'

He nodded, gobbling half a piece of toast, one eye on the clock, worried about being even later for work. 'I think so, Dad.'

'Don't forget to tell Mrs Hahn your plans.'

'I won't.' With that, Peter left them and went to the hospital to do rounds. They weren't doing any surgeries that morning. Another special meeting had been called to discuss techniques, among them Peter's newest which he explained in great detail to Mel later that afternoon when he called her. And when he had finished, he decided to be honest with her about Pam's reaction.

'She'll be all right. I think it's just very threatening to her.'

'Do you still want us to come?'

'Are you kidding?' He sounded horrified that she would even ask. 'I wouldn't even consider going without you. What about your brood? Are they adjusting?'

'Grudgingly.'

The 'casual' reception he had hoped for had vanished into thin air. Mel had been right, about Pam at least. 'Matt is thrilled. And I'm afraid that Mark is already contemplating the twins with a somewhat eager eye. But he's harmless.'

'Don't tell me that!' Mel laughed. 'Wait till you see Val!'

'She can't be as exotic as all that.' Mel was always talking about the girl's voluptuous figure and sex-kitten allure. But she was probably viewing the child with a far from objective eye, as the girl's mother.

'Peter.' Mel's voice was firm. 'Valerie is not exotic. She's just downright sexy. You'd better start putting saltpetre in Mark's food right now.'

'Poor kid. I think he's still a virgin, but working really hard to change his status. He turns eighteen next month, starts college in September, and the last thing he wants to be is a virgin.'

'Well, tell him to practise on someone other than my daughter.'

'That's a deal, as long as I can practise on her mother.' They both laughed then, and said they were looking forward to Aspen in spite of their children.

'Think we'll survive it, Peter?'

'I have not a single doubt, my love. We're all going to have a great time.'

'You think Pam will be okay?'

'I'm certain of it. And the fact is we have to think of ourselves too. I love you, Mel.' She responded in kind and they hung up at last.

But his diagnosis seemed to be a trifle optimistic as they boarded the plane to Denver from LAX a few days later.

'Come on, sourpuss, it's time to board.' Mark found Pam unbearable when she sulked, as she had been for days. She wasn't speaking at all to their father. 'You're going to make it a great holiday for all of us, aren't you?'

'Up yours.' She spoke to her older brother in a tone that would have curled anyone's hair, and Mark looked as though he would have liked to hit her.

'Come on, you two.' Peter was wearing chino slacks, a plaid shirt, and a red sweater over his shoulders, carrying a small back-pack. He had everyone's boarding passes in one hand, and was holding on to Matt's hand with the other. Matthew was in such high spirits that he amply made up for Pam, who found a seat by herself across the aisle when they boarded. The men sat three abreast, with Matthew on the window side so he could look out, and Peter on the aisle so he could keep an eye on Pam, but she turned her face away, and looked out the window for the first half of the flight and then she read a book until lunch was served, but she did no more than pick at her food before the tray was picked up again. Peter concealed his worry. Later, when Peter broke out the candy he had brought for the kids, he passed some to her too, but she declined it without looking at him.

'She's really being stupid, Dad.' Mark said it sotto voce to his father before they landed in Denver.

'She'll be all right. Mel's girls will distract her. She's probably just feeling threatened because she won't be the queen bee for a while. She's used to being the only girl around the three of us, and here come three new ones. It's bound to be a bit of a jolt at first.'

'She just likes getting her way. She has ever since Mom died.' He looked reproachfully at their father. 'Mom would never have let her get away with this.'

'Maybe not.' But even that reproach hurt Peter. He tried so damn hard, and why did they always think Anne had done it all better?

But then Matthew reclaimed his attention as they landed, and they had to run to change planes, and catch the flight to Aspen. It was a short bumpy ride over the mountains and they made a spectacular landing, dipping in between the mountains to the tiny airport filled with Lear jets and small private planes. Aspen was a magnet to the very rich, and also to a more varied, interesting crowd. There seemed to be everything there, all kinds of people, which was one of the reasons why Peter liked it. It was one of the many traditions he had shared with Anne, that he still kept up now, because they had shared happy times during their holidays there, in winter and summer.

'We're here!' He said it with joy in his voice and the four of them disembarked and rented a car at the airport, to go to a condo much like the one they had rented for the past five years. It seemed time for a new one this time, and even Pam seemed more excited as they approached town. As usual, nothing had changed, including the spectacular view of the mountains. They had just enough time to settle in and unpack, and go to the supermarket for some food, before Peter had to go to the airport to meet Mel's plane. He looked around the group unpacking the food before he left and made one of his seemingly 'casual' offers. 'Anyone want to come?'

'I'll come.' Mark was quick to drop what he was doing,

227

and put his Topsiders on his bare feet. He was wearing khaki shorts and a red T-shirt, and with his deep tan from LA and his hair bleached from the sun, even Peter had to notice that the boy was strikingly handsome. Mel's twins would melt, and if they didn't there was something wrong with them, he grinned to himself, proud of his oldest son.

'Me too!' Matt piped up, grabbing his favourite space gun.

'Do you need that thing?' Peter glanced at the gun, it made a noise that drove him crazy.

'Sure, we might be invaded by creatures from outer space.'

'They're coming in on the next flight?' Pam asked pointedly and Peter glared.

'That's enough! In fact' – he looked angrily at Pam – 'I think you should come too. We're a family, and we do things together.'

'How touching.' She stood firmly in the kitchen. 'I think I'll stay.'

'Come on, idiot.' Mark pushed her towards the door and she pushed him back. Peter roared.

'God damn it! I want you to behave, now!' Pam seemed suddenly mollified by the roar from her father, and the four of them drove to the airport in silence. Peter worried about what Pam would say to Mel and her daughters. But as he saw Mel step off the plane, all he could think of was how much he loved her and how desperately he wanted to pull her into his arms. But they had to remain in control in front of the kids. She came towards him, with her red hair tied in a loose knot, a straw hat shielding her eyes, and a pretty cream-coloured linen dress and sandals. 'It's good to see you, Mel.' He took her hand as the children watched, and she kissed his cheek lightly and turned at once to his children. It took every ounce of self-restraint she had not to kiss him full on the mouth.

'Hi, Pam, it's nice to see you again.' She lightly touched her shoulder and bent to kiss Matt who threw his arms around her neck, and then at last she turned to say hello to

Mark, but he was staring intently at a young woman behind her. 'Let me introduce my daughters to you. This is Jessica.' It was easy to see that they were mother and daughter from the red hair, but it was Valerie who had riveted Mark's attention. 'And this is Valerie.'

Both girls said hello quietly, and Mel introduced them both to Peter, who had to fight not to burst into laughter. His oldest son looked as though he were going to fall into a dead faint at Val's feet, and as he and Mel went to gather their bags he looked at her with a grin and shook his head.

'You were right. I'm not even sure that saltpetre would have made a difference.' The girl had a voluptuous quality that almost defied description, even more so because she appeared so fresh and naïve. 'You ought to keep her off the streets, Mel.'

'I try, love, I try.' She turned to him then. 'How are you? Did the trip go okay?'

'Fine.'

'How's Pam?' She glanced at her out of the corner of her eye and saw that Jessie was talking to her. Matt stared up at Jess in blatant adoration. 'I'd say some of the dynamics are going to work out okay.' Val and Mark were talking animatedly and Pam seemed to be answering Jess, as Jessica took Matt's small hand in her own, and admired the space gun between spurts of conversation with his sister. 'They're all good kids, that should help.'

'So is their mother.'

'I love you,' she mouthed silently to him, with her back turned to the children, and he longed to take her in his arms.

'I love you too.' He said it close to her ear, and a porter helped them with their bags. It was a good thing they had a station wagon. With seven of them and the Adams' bags, the car was crammed to the gills on the way back to the condo. Everyone seemed to be talking at once – even Pam seemed to be slowly coming out of her shell, with Jessica devoting her attention to her.

She didn't even seem to object as vehemently as Peter

229

had feared when he explained the sleeping arrangements. Pam, Jess, and Val would share the room with two sets of bunk beds. It was cramped, but the girls didn't seem to mind it. Pam was actually laughing by then, as Jessica teased her about something. The two boys shared a room with twin beds, and Peter and Mel took the two smallest rooms, with a single bed in each. Usually, Peter's children had their own rooms, but this year it had taken a little creative arranging to fit them all in and manage separate bedrooms for himself and Mel, but that was crucial on this first trip with the children.

'Everybody all set?'

'We're fine,' Valerie was quick to answer, looking admiringly at Peter, and later she whispered to her mother, 'He's cute,' as Mel laughed. Unfortunately, she also clearly thought his son was. But Mel had already warned her that another romance would only complicate everyone's life for the next two weeks. Val had dutifully agreed on the flight to Denver, but by the time they were all cooking dinner that night, she and Mark were in charge of the salad and the baked potatoes, and Mel was beginning to lose hope of dashing a potential romance. She only hoped they'd get good and tired of each other in the next two weeks. 'Val wasn't known for the length of her romances,' Jessica said to Pam with a laugh as they sat near the fire, after she had helped Pam put Matthew to bed. She seemed sensitive to Pam's threatened feelings.

'I don't think Mark has uncrossed his eyes since you two got here.' Peter grinned, appreciating the efforts of the older twin to put his daughter at ease. She seemed like a very special girl, and he remembered much of what Mel had said about her. It was funny to see them now after hearing so much about them, but they were very much as Mel had described, especially Val, whom one would almost imagine as a centrefold in *Playboy*, instead of a junior in high school. But there was a pleasing innocence about the girl, despite her spectacular body. 'I

hear you're interested in going to medical school, Jess.'
Her eyes lit up at his question and Pam looked bored.

'How disgusting.'

'I know.' She looked placatingly at Pam. 'Everyone thinks that. I want to be a gynaecologist or a paediatrician.'

'They're both good specialities, but very demanding.'

'I want to be a model,' Pam assumed an aloof stance and Jess smiled.

'I wish I could be, but I don't have your looks.' It was not true, but Jessica genuinely believed it. She had lived too long in Val's shadow.

'You can be anything you choose to, Jess.' Mel was sitting by the fire, relaxed, and happy just to be near Peter again. It seemed a thousand years since she had last seen him.

'Anyone for a walk?' Mark bounded into the room with the suggestion, and after working on them all for a while, the whole group agreed, except Matt who was sound asleep in his bed.

'Will he be all right here alone?' Mel looked concerned, and Peter nodded with a smile.

'He'll be fine. He sleeps like a rock. Mountain air does that to him. Anne always said . . .' He stopped, visibly pale. Mel felt a tremor up her spine. It was odd to be following in Anne's footsteps, to be here with her children now that his wife was no longer alive. She wondered if that was part of Pam's reaction, and made a point of trying to talk to her as they wandered in the cool mountain air, but Pam seemed much more interested in chatting with Jessie, and they walked in three comfortable pairs for about half an hour, Val and Mark, Jessie and Pam, and Melanie and Peter.

'See? It all worked out fine, didn't it?' He sounded supercilious and Mel laughed.

'Don't count your chickens yet. We just got here.'

'Don't be silly. What could happen now?'

She pretended to shield her head from the wrath of the

231

gods, and then glanced at Peter. 'Are you kidding? Anything. Let's just hope there are no murders, broken bones, or unwanted pregnancies after this little adventure.'

'Such an optimist you are.' And with that he pulled her behind a tree and kissed her quickly, unseen by the children, and they giggled softly as they began walking again. It felt so good just to be together again, and there was something nice about seeing their children together, no matter what horrors Mel predicted.

They returned at last to the condo, happy, relaxed, tired from their trip and from settling in, and everyone went to their assigned rooms, apparently without problem. Each room had its own basin, so there was no massive lineup to brush teeth, and Mel could hear the girls giggling in their room after the lights were turned out. She was dying to tiptoe down the hall to Peter, but she didn't think it was wise. Not yet. Not with the children so close. Just as she lay in bed, thinking of their time together in New York, she saw her door open and a shadow cross the room. She sat up in bed in surprise, just as he slipped beneath her covers.

'Peter!' She was startled to see him.

'How do you know?' He was smiling in the dark and she put her arms around his neck and kissed him.

'You shouldn't . . . what if the children . . .'

'Never mind the children . . . the girls are too busy thinking we don't hear them, and Mark is probably as dead to the world as Matt by now . . . it's time for us now, kiddo.' He put his arms around her and let his hand slip beneath her nightgown as she fought not to make a sound. 'God, how I've missed you.'

But Mel said not a single word, and what she showed him told him that she had missed him too. Their bodies blended in exquisite pleasure for hours, and then, reluctantly, he left her. She tiptoed to the door to kiss him goodnight and watched him pad softly down the hall. There was no sound from the children's rooms. They were all sound asleep, and she couldn't remember ever being so happy. She tiptoed back to her bed, which still bore the sweet smell of their passion, and drifted off to sleep, holding her pillow.

CHAPTER 21

The next day they went on a five-mile hike, and picnicked on the way. They stopped beside a small stream, and went wading and Matt caught a snake for Mark, which sent all three of the girls screaming back to Peter and Mel, who laughed at them. But eventually Matthew let the snake go, and they continued their hike until the late afternoon, when they went back to the condo for a swim in the pool, and the kids cavorted like old friends, but Mel noticed that whenever Jessica wasn't talking to Pam, Pam was watching her with Peter.

'They make a nice group, don't they, Mel?'

There was no denying that. A handsome one too. They were all beautiful children, but there was still that unhappy light in Pam's eyes, particularly whenever she saw Mel with her father. Mel was particularly grateful to Jessie for keeping her distracted. And of course Valerie and Mark had been inseparable since breakfast that morning. 'They do make a nice group,' Mel agreed with a tired smile. 'But one that bears watching.'

'There you go again. What are you worrying about now?' He was amused by her reactions. She seemed to be ever watchful over their joint brood, but he liked that about her too. He could easily see that she was a wonderful mother.

'I'm not worried about anything. But I'm keeping an eye on things.' She grinned, and Peter glanced at Val and Mark.

'I think they're harmless. All that energy and young flesh, but fortunately neither of them is quite sure what to do about it all yet. Next year we might not be as lucky.'

'Oh, Christ' – Mel rolled her eyes – 'I hope that's not true. I wish I had married that child off when she was twelve. I don't think I can stand watching her for another four or five years.'

'I don't think you really have to. She's an awfully nice girl.'

Mel nodded, but she looked cautious. 'But much too trusting. She's an entirely different character from Jessie.'

He nodded in agreement. He had seen that already. 'Pam seems to be very fond of Jess.'

'She's good with younger kids.'

'I know.' He smiled happily, it was the happiest he had been in two years. 'Matt adores her.' And then he lowered his voice and bent near Mel's ear. 'And I adore you. Do you suppose we could stay here forever?'

'I'd love it.' But that wasn't entirely true either. She missed their time alone in New York. Here, she was not free to be herself. She had to keep an eye on the children, and she wasn't afraid to put her foot down when she had to. She let the four older ones go to the cinema that night, while she and Peter stayed home with Matt, but when Mark and Val wanted to go out alone after they'd brought Jessie and Pam home, Mel vetoed the idea without question. 'It wouldn't be nice to the others, you two. We're here as a group.' And there were other reasons, which she didn't go into. Reasons why she kept a close vigil every day, as they went for walks, and rode horses, and had picnics in fields full of flowers. There was something so natural and sensual about it all, in their tight T-shirts, and short shorts, and skimpy bathing suits, with the fresh mountain air, and the constant proximity in the condo. She had never seen Val quite so taken with any boy, and it worried her more than she admitted to Peter. She said something to Jess about it when they were alone one day, and Jessie had noticed it too.

'You think she's okay, Mom?' There was a strong bond between the twins, and Jessica always worried about her sister.

'I do. But I think she bears watching.'

'Do you think she . . .' Jessie felt uncomfortable accusing her sister to her mother. 'I don't think she'd . . .'

235

Mel smiled. 'I don't think she would either, but I think it's easy to get carried away in fields of wild flowers, with snow on the mountains, or at night if you're alone. I think Mark is more intense than a lot of boys she's used to. And I just want to be sure that she doesn't do anything foolish. I don't really think she would though, Jess.'

'She's not saying much to me this time, Mom,' and that was very unusual for Val. Usually she told Jess everything that happened in her life, particularly what concerned boys. But about Mark she was strangely quiet.

'Maybe she thinks it's more serious than it is. First love.' Mel smiled again.

'Just so she doesn't do anything stupid.'

'She won't.' Mel looked confident in both her own vigil and her daughter's wisdom. 'What about Pam? How do you think she is, Jess?' She trusted her daughter's judgment almost more than anyone else's, except now maybe Peter's, and he was hardly objective about his only daughter.

'I don't think she's a really happy kid, to say the least. We've talked about a lot of stuff, and she opens up a lot sometimes, and other times she's all locked up. I think she really misses her mother. Maybe more than the others. Mark is older, and Matthew was pretty little when she died, but Pam feels ripped off. She gets angry at her father sometimes about it.'

'Is that what she said, Jess?' Mel's voice was soft and filled with concern.

'More or less. I think mostly she's confused. It's not an easy age, Mom.' Jessica looked older and wiser than her years as she spoke and Mel was touched by it.

'I know. And you've been nice to her. Thank you, Jess.'

'I like her.' She said it honestly. 'She's a real bright kid. A little mixed up sometimes, but smart as hell. I invited her to come and see us in New York sometime, and she said yes.' Mel looked surprised. 'Would you mind that?'

'Not at all. All the Hallams are welcome any time they'd like.'

Jess fell silent for a moment and then looked at her mother. 'What's happening with you and Dr Hallam, Mom?'

'Not much. We're good friends.' But she felt as though Jessica already knew much more. 'I like him, Jess.'

'A lot?' Jessica searched Mel's eyes, and she knew she had to be honest with the child.

'Yes.'

'Are you in love with him?'

Mel held her breath. What did those words mean? What did Jess want to know? The truth, Mel told herself. Only that. She had to tell her the truth. 'Yes, I think I am.' Jessica looked as though she had received a physical blow.

'Oh.'

'Are you surprised?'

'Sort of yes and sort of no. I suspected it before, but I wasn't sure. It's different when you actually hear someone else say it.' And then she sighed and looked at Mel. 'I like him.'

'I'm glad.'

'Do you think you two will get married?'

But this time Mel shook her head. 'No, I don't.'

'Why not?'

'Because our lives are too far apart. I can't quit my job and move to L.A. and he can't move to New York. And we both have too much keeping us where we are.'

'That's sad.' Jessica searched her eyes. 'If you lived in the same town, do you think you'd get married?'

'I don't know. It can't be an issue for us. So it's nice to enjoy whatever time we have.' Mel reached out and touched her daughter's hand. 'I love you, Jess.'

She smiled. 'I love you too, Mom. And I'm glad we came after all. I'm sorry I gave you such a hard time before.'

'That's okay. I'm glad it all worked out.'

'Am I interrupting anything?' Peter wandered into the room and saw them both, and the two of them holding hands, but Mel shook her head.

237

'We just had a nice talk.'

'That's nice.' He seemed pleased and smiled at Jess. 'Where's everyone else?'

'I don't know.' It was about five o'clock and Mel had just come back from the store when she started talking to Jess. She assumed the other kids were at the pool, as they had been at that hour, every day for the past week.

'Val and Mark took a walk with Matt.'

'They did?' Mel was surprised. 'Then where's Pam?'

'In our room, asleep. She had a headache this afternoon. I thought you knew.' But Mel still looked surprised, and Peter patted her arm.

'Mark will take care of Val and Matt. Don't worry about them, Mel.' But when they weren't back at seven o'clock, Mel was seriously concerned, and Peter didn't look as confident as he had before.

He stopped in to see Jess and Pam in their room. 'Do you know where they went?' Jessica shook her head and Pam looked blank.

'I was asleep when they left.'

He nodded and went back to Mel. It was still light outside but he wanted to have a look around. 'I'll be back in a little while.' But when he didn't come back in an hour either, Mel was as frightened as the girls.

'What do you suppose happened, Mom?' Jessica whispered. Pam was sitting white-faced in their room.

'I don't know, love. Peter will find them.' But on the hillsides behind the house, he was wandering aimlessly, having abandoned the trails, calling out their names. And it was dark when he found Val and Mark at last, scratched and frightened and alone.

'Where's Matt?' He spoke directly to his son, with fear and tension in his voice, as he noticed that Val's face was covered with tears and scratches.

Mark looked as though he were about to cry too. 'We don't know.'

'When did you see him last?' Peter felt his jaw go tense.

'About two or three hours ago. We were just walking

along and then all of a sudden we turned around, and he wasn't there.' Val began to cry incoherently giving her version of the tale, and Peter saw that Mark was still holding her hand and he began to suspect what had happened and why they had lost track of Matthew.

'Were you two making out?' He was blunt with the words, which only made Val cry more, and sheepishly Mark hung his head, but not before his father's hand cracked across his face. 'You little sonofabitch, you had a responsibility to your brother if you took him out with you!'

'I know, Dad.' Tears began to slide down his face now, but the next hour of their search yielded nothing more, and Peter led them back to the trail they had left, and back to the condo far down the mountainside. They had to call the sheriff and begin the search for Matthew. He found Mel pale-faced with the girls, and when he returned with only Val and Mark, the three girls burst into tears. He went quickly to the phone with Mel at his side, and the search party arrived in less than half an hour, with ropes and stretchers, a paramedic team, and enormous searchlights.

'We'll take helicopters up tomorrow, if we don't find him tonight.' But Peter didn't want him out alone all night, and he was already terrified that the child might have fallen into a ravine, and broken a leg or worse. He could be unconscious somewhere. Peter left with the other man, and the girls stayed with Mel and Mark below. Mark was crying openly now, as Mel tried to reassure him, but there was no way of soothing the guilt he felt and Mel had managed to say almost nothing to Val. It was well after ten o'clock by now, and there was still no sight of the child, as suddenly Pam exploded at Val and shrieked at her.

'It's all your fault, you horny bitch, if you hadn't been out kissing Mark, my little brother wouldn't have got lost.' To which Val found no response, and she collapsed in Jessie's arms, sobbing hysterically. It was only then that Mel heard a shout and a bleat of horns well up the mountainside; lights were flashed and it seemed moments later when the entire crew came down, victorious, with Matthew in their arms, and Peter fighting back tears of relief as he waved at them.

'Is he all right?' Mel ran to Peter's side, and the tears escaped his eyes at last. He stood there for a long time, holding her, as he sobbed. Matthew was still a little way behind in the arms of one of the sheriff's men. They had found him just outside a cave, frightened and cold and unharmed. He said he had wandered off by himself for a little while, and got lost. And he claimed to have seen a bear.

'Oh, Mel' – Peter couldn't let go of her – 'I thought we'd lost him.'

She nodded, tears pouring down her own face. 'Thank God he's all right.' She saw him being carried into their midst, filthy dirty, his face scratched and his clothes torn, and she could see that he had fallen a few times, but he looked very excited to be with the sheriff's men and he was wearing someone's hat. Mel scooped him into her arms and held him there. 'You scared us to death, Matt.'

'I'm okay, Mel.' He looked suddenly very grown-up and brave.

'I'm glad.' She kissed his cheek and handed him to his father then, who thanked all the sheriff's men, and at last they all went back inside and collapsed in the living room. Mark was hugging his little brother to his chest, and Valerie was still crying but she was smiling now as well, and even Pam had cried with relief. Everyone fussed over him, and it was midnight before they all settled down, and Pam had apologised to Val, and Mark had sworn that they would never go off alone again. As they all sat by the fire, finishing the hamburgers that Mel had made for them all, Peter spoke to them.

'I want one thing clear right now. I think tonight has taught us all something.' He looked pointedly at Val and Mark. 'We can all have a wonderful time while we're here. But you can't kid around, you can get lost in the woods, you can get bitten by snakes and God knows what. And I want you each to feel responsible for the rest of the group. From now on, I want to see all five of you together or not at all. If anyone goes somewhere, the rest of you go too. Is that clear?' He looked at his oldest son again, who nodded his head shamefacedly. He had been so intent on Val that he had entirely forgotten about Matthew. And when they had caught their breath again, he had gone. 'If I see anyone paired off here, they're going home that day, and I don't care who it is.' But they all knew he meant Val and Mark. 'Now I want everyone to go to bed and get some sleep, it's been a tough night for everyone.' They were quick to disband and go to their rooms, but there was a new camaraderie between them now.

'Christ, Mel, I thought I'd die out there on that hill with no goddamn sign of him.' He lay in her bed that night, thinking of it all again and she held him again and felt him tremble in her arms.

'It's all over, my love. He's safe, and it won't happen again.'

They didn't even make love that night. They held each other close, and Mel lay awake beside him for most of the night, watching him sleep until the sky lit up with the first light of dawn. She woke him gently then, and he went back to his own bed, and then she slept at last. But all she thought of all night was how much she loved him – loved them all – and how desperately she wanted nothing awful to happen to any of them again. It was the first time she had realised how *much* she loved them and how deeply they were lodged in her heart. When they all awoke the next day, they truly seemed like one family. The five children became inseparable from that moment on, and although Mel frequently saw Mark holding Val's hand, or looking into her eyes with that special glance that lit up her face, they never went off alone again and the remaining week slid by them much too quickly.

On their last night there, Peter took them all out, and they had a wonderful time, laughing and talking like old

241

friends. To look at them one would never have known that they hadn't grown up under one roof, and no one would have believed the extent to which they had fought the trip at first. Peter smiled at Mel several times. It had been a perfect holiday, despite that one ghastly night of looking for Matt, but even that seemed to be forgotten now.

They sat by the fire until late that night, even Matt, who finally fell asleep on Jessica's lap, and she put him in his bed with Pam's help. When they all parted at last, it was with regret to end their happy time, and Mel and Peter lay awake for hours, both of them sad to be leaving.

'I can't believe I'm leaving you again.' He was leaning on one elbow, looking down at her, after they'd made love.

'It can't be helped.' And then suddenly she had a thought, and she looked at him with a hopeful smile.

'Why don't you all spend the Labor Day weekend at Martha's Vineyard with us?'

'That's a hell of a long trip for three days, Mel.' He looked dubious, but he wanted to cling to any hope he could.

'Then stay a week.' Stay a month . . . stay a year . . .

'I can't.'

'But the kids could.' It seemed like a great idea to her. 'Pam and Matt could. Mark will be through his job around then too. He could fly back for the weekend with you. The other two could come ahead.'

'It's a thought.' He smiled at her; not really thinking of the kids just then, but only of her. He wanted desperately to stay with her, but there was no way they could. 'I love you so much, Mel.'

'I love you too.' And they lay back in each other's arms again and made love on and off until the dawn. They both looked depressed the next morning when they got up in their separate rooms. There would be no lovemaking again that night, no long walks in the woods or in the fields of flowers. It was time to go home again. Back to reality, and clinging to him on the phone. But she brought up her idea for Labor Day and the kids cheered. 'That does it then.'

242

She looked victoriously at Peter and he laughed. He looked happy about the holiday too.

'All right. You win. We'll come.'

'Hurray!' You could hear their shouts halfway up the mountainside, and they chattered all the way from Aspen to Denver on the flight. The kids sat in one row straight across, and Peter and Mel sat alone for the last time. And in Denver, everybody cried, and Peter looked into Mel's eyes and whispered to her.

'I love you, Mel. Don't ever forget that.'

'Remember that I love you too.' The kids pretended not to watch, but Val and Mark smiled, and Pam turned away so as not to see, but she and Jessica were holding hands, which gave Pam some comfort. And Matt gave Mel a great big goodbye kiss.

'I love you, Mel!'

'I love you too.' She tore her eyes from his, and kissed each of the children, and told Pam, looking into her eyes. 'Take good care of your dad.' She wanted to add 'for me'.

'I will.' There was a new gentleness in Pam's voice, and they were all subdued as they went their separate ways and Matthew cried openly as his father led him to their plane.

'I want them to come with us.'

'You'll be seeing them again soon.'

'When?'

'In a few weeks, Matt.' Peter glanced at Mark then and saw a dreamy expression on his face. He wondered just how much had happened between him and Val but figured it couldn't be much. On the plane that left for Boston at the same time as the flight to LA, Jessica and Val barely spoke, and Mel looked out the window seeing nothing there except a vision of Peter's face. Three weeks till Labor Day seemed endless to her, and then what? An endless year until Aspen again? It was madness they had inflicted on themselves, but Mel knew, as well as Peter did on the flight to LA, that for them it was too late to turn back now.

243

CHAPTER 22

The weeks at Martha's Vineyard seemed to drag by for them all once they returned from Aspen. It was nothing like their time there in July, when they threw themselves wholeheartedly into the amusements of the summer. Instead, once they got back, Val seemed to spend all her time staring into space, and Mel spent most of hers on the phone, and Jessica teased them both.

'Boy, you two sure are a lot of fun.' Valerie almost killed herself getting to the mailbox every day to check for letters from Mark, and each time Mel left the house she would come back and casually ask, 'Anyone call?' and both girls would laugh. Only Raquel seemed to treat it all like a serious illness that had descended on their home. She warned them all that in six months . . . they'd see! She never finished her warnings, but they sounded ominous to everyone, and Mel always listened to her with amusement.

'Now, Raquel, relax!'

'This time it's serious, Mrs Mel.'

'Yes, it is. But serious and terminal aren't the same.'

Grant called too to say hello. He was madly in love with the weather girl on Channel 5, and there was also a cute little redheaded female jockey in White Plains, not to mention some staggeringly sexy Cuban girl. Mel teased him about it and told him to act his age, and she finally told him about Peter, or rather the girls did. He sounded hurt when Mel got back on the phone.

'You couldn't have told me yourself? I thought we were friends.'

'We are, but I needed time to think this thing out.'

Grant sounded surprised. 'Is it as serious as that?'

'It could be, but we haven't solved the problem of distance yet.'

'Distance?' And then suddenly, all the pieces fell into place. 'You little minx, it's the heart surgeon on the West Coast, isn't it?'

She grinned like a little kid and giggled into the phone.

'You jerk. Now what are you going to do? You're here, he's there.'

'I haven't figured that out yet.'

'What's to figure out, Mel? You've done it again, found yourself the "Impossible Dream". Neither of you is going to quit your job for chrissake, and you're both anchored where you are. My friend, you've done it again. You're playing it safe.'

His words depressed her long after she got off the phone, and she spent days wondering if what he said was true. Was she really involved in just another impossible romance?

As if to validate her feelings she dialled Peter in California.

He was excited about Marie's progress, having seen her that day and she was doing very well. Mel found herself praying that no new transplant patient would come on the scene in the next week, or he wouldn't be able to fly east for the Labor Day weekend.

He reported that Pam and Matt were ready for the trip east, and Matthew was so excited he could hardly see straight.

'What about Pam?'

'She's more outwardly subdued than Matt, but she's just as excited as he is.'

'So are the girls. They can hardly wait until they get here.' They had made dozens of plans to include Pam, and Mel was going to take charge of Matthew. Even Raquel was excited about the prospective visits, although she pretended to complain about the extra work. They had spent hours trying to work out the sleeping arrangements and finally decided that Mark would sleep on a sleeping bag on the living room couch, Pam would sleep on a rollaway bed in the twins' room, Matt would sleep in the twin bed in Raquel's, and when he came, Peter would have the guest room. It had taken some doing, but the house could accommodate them all.

When Pam and Matthew arrived, there was an aura of festivity throughout the whole house, and all the children went down on the beach as Mel watched them join the others they met there every day. The boy Val had discovered at the beginning of the summer no longer held an interest for her, and there were half a dozen madly in love with Jess, who wouldn't give any of them the time of day. One or two of them thought Pam a remarkably attractive girl, and no one could believe she was only fourteen. She was so tall and looked so much older, and for the whole week, Mel was happy with her brood of four and reported to Peter twice a day.

'I wish you'd hurry up and get here.'

'So do I. Mark is practically catatonic with anticipation.' But the night before they were due to leave LA the whole trip almost went down the drain. A young woman came in with rejection of the transplant that had been done four months before, and a severe infection. Mel heard the news with a sinking feeling in the pit of her stomach, but she didn't press Peter about the trip, or urge him to leave the woman in the care of his very capable colleagues. As it turned out, the poor woman died before morning. He called Mel about it the next day and was very depressed.

'There was nothing we could do.' But it always got him down anyway.

'I'm sure there wasn't. It'll do you good to get away now.'

'I guess it will.' But it took some of the shine out of the trip for him, and he was quiet as he and Mark flew to Boston. But on the second leg of the trip, he seemed to revive and he and Mark chatted about Mel and her daughters.

'They're really nice, Dad.' Mark blushed as he tried to sound nonchalant, and Peter smiled at his son.

'I'm glad you think so, I think so too.' It was going to be

246

wonderful to see her again, and suddenly it was all he could think of as the small plane landed on the narrow airstrip, and he hastened off the plane behind Mark, who was practically jet propelled out the door, and down the rickety metal stairway. He came to a screeching halt in front of Val, not sure whether to shake hands or kiss her or just say hi. He stood there stumbling over his own feet and blushing furiously as Val did the same, and Peter pulled Mel into his arms with a ferocious grip and held her, and then he dutifully kissed Pam, and Jess and Val, and then Matt. Val and Mark headed towards the baggage claim together, and Peter saw Mark stealthily take her hand and he grinned at Mel.

'There they go again.'

She smiled, glancing at the two lovebirds far ahead. 'At least here they can't get lost in the mountains.' But they seemed to go off in a sailboat much of the time over the Labor Day weekend, and Peter had to remind them again about the group rules he had insisted on in Aspen.

'The same rules apply here.'

'Oh, Dad.' It was Mark who objected, almost whining as he hadn't in years, but he wanted so much to be alone with Val. They had so much to tell each other. 'We just want to talk.'

'Then do it with the others.'

'Yuck.' Pam rolled her eyes and held her nose. 'You should hear the junk they say to each other.' But Mel had noticed that there was a fourteen-year-old boy from down the beach whom Pam had not found particularly 'yucky'. Only Jess and Matthew seemed to have maintained their sanity by the end of the weekend. Jessica was already thinking ahead to the first day of school, and Matt was so happy with Mel and his father that he was no trouble at all. He had longed for that kind of security for years, without actually understanding what was missing. And Peter chuckled at Raquel, who obviously approved of him and spent a lot of time telling him how lucky he was to have Mel, how all she'd needed was a good man, and what she needed now was to get married. Mel was horrified when he told her as they lay on the beach on Sunday.

'Are you kidding? She said that?'

'She did. Maybe she's right. Maybe that is what you need. A good husband, to keep you barefoot and pregnant.' He seemed amused by it all, and even more so to watch the children living out their end-of-summer madness. He was keeping a good eye on Mark. He didn't want him getting out of line with Val, and he could see that their hormones were pumping furiously throughout the weekend. Peter turned back to Mel then, remembering what Raquel had said. 'What do you say to that?'

'I'm sure the network would be thrilled.' She was amused at the suggestion, but didn't consider it a real threat. All she cared about right now was being with him for the weekend. She'd think about the future later, about what they would do about seeing each other again, and when. And then she remembered something else. 'You just reminded me, I have to call my lawyer after the Labor Day weekend.'

'How come?'

'My contract is up in October, and I like getting started nice and early outlining what I want for the next one.' He admired the way she handled her work. In fact, there was a lot more than that he admired about her.

'You must be able to call your own shots by now.'

'To some extent. Not entirely. But anyway, I want to sit down with him some time in the next couple of weeks and see what he thinks.'

Peter grinned, in a silly mood, the end-of-summer madness was beginning to touch them all. 'Why don't you just quit?'

'And do what?' She didn't find the idea quite as funny as he did.

'Move to California.'

'And sell tacos on the beach?'

'No, this may come as a shock to you, but we have television there now too. We even have news.' He was

248

smiling and she thought he had never looked more handsome.

'Do you? How intriguing.' But she didn't take the suggestion seriously for a moment until he reached out and touched her arm, and she saw that he was looking at her strangely.

'You know, you could do that.'

'What?' A chill ran down her spine despite the brilliant sunshine and hot weather.

'Quit and move to California. Someone would put you on the air there.'

She sat up very straight and stared down at him lying in the sand. 'Do you have any idea how many years it took me to get where I am here at the network? Do you have even the remotest idea of what Buffalo was like at twenty below, or Chicago? I worked like hell for this job, and I'm not giving it up now, so please don't joke about it, Peter. Ever.' She was still upset when she lay down in the sand beside him again. She didn't find the suggestion even remotely amusing. 'Why don't you give up your practice and start fresh in New York?'

She saw that he was looking at her intently, and she was sorry her tone had been as sharp. He looked hurt. 'I would if I could, Mel. I'd do anything to be near you.' And the accusation was that she wouldn't, which wasn't fair.

'Do you understand that it's no easier for me?' Her voice was gentler now. 'Leaving New York would be a step down for me now, wherever I went.'

'Even to LA?' He looked suddenly depressed. Their situation was hopeless.

'Even to LA.' And then after a moment's silence when they both stared out to sea licking their wounds, 'We'll just have to find some way to be together.'

'What do you suggest? Weekends in Kansas City?' This time it was Peter who sounded angry and bitter, and he looked down at her now with fire in his eyes. 'What do you think this will be when it grows up, Mel? A holiday romance? We meet for long weekends with our kids?'

'I don't know what to suggest. I can fly to LA, you know, and you can come here.'

'You know how rarely I can leave my patients.' And she couldn't leave the girls all the time, and they both knew it.

'So what are you telling me? That I should give up now? Is that what you want?' Suddenly, she was frightened by the gist of their conversation. 'I don't have the answers, Peter.'

'Well, neither do I. And something tells me you don't want to find them.'

'That's not true. But the reality is that we both have important jobs at opposite ends of the country, and neither one of us can just dump what we're doing and move, nor would we want to. And we're not ready to yet, anyway.'

'Aren't we?' He looked angry again. 'Why not?'

'Because we've only known each other for four months, and I don't know about you, but that doesn't seem like very long to me.'

'I'd have married Anne five minutes after I met her and I was right.'

'That was Anne.' She was shouting at him now, but they were alone on the beach. The children had all gone to play volleyball somewhere else and Matt was with Raquel looking for seashells. 'I'm not Anne, Peter, I'm me. And I'm not going to follow in her goddamn footsteps. Even if you did take me to Aspen, which is where you went with her every year.'

'So what, dammit. Didn't you like it?'

'Yes, I did. But only after I overcame the creepy feeling I had every time I thought that you'd been over every inch of that place with her, and probably even slept in the same bed.'

He was on his feet now and so was she. 'It may interest you to know that this time I ordered a different condo. I'm not as totally insensitive as you seem to think, Miss Adams.' And after that they both stood very still, and suddenly Mel hung her head.

'I'm sorry . . . I didn't mean to hurt you . . .' She

looked up at him again then. 'It's difficult, sometimes, knowing how attached you were to her.'

Peter pulled her slowly towards him. 'I was married to her for eighteen years, Mel.'

'I know . . . but I feel like I'm always being compared to her. The perfect wife. The Perfect Woman. And I'm not perfect. I'm me.'

'Who compares you?' He looked shocked. He had never said anything like that. But he hadn't had to.

Mel shrugged as they sat very close on the sand again. 'You . . . the children . . . maybe Mrs Hahn.'

Peter was watching her closely. 'You don't like Mrs Hahn, do you? Why?'

'Maybe because she was Anne's. Or because she's so cold. I don't think she likes me either.' Mel smiled, thinking of Raquel, and Peter laughed, knowing what she was thinking.

'No, she certainly isn't Raquel, but no one is. Except Raquel herself.' He had come to like her too, but he wasn't sure he could live with her loose tongue in his household. He liked Mrs Hahn's restraint and the way she controlled the children. Raquel was more like a friend with a mop in one hand, and a microphone in the other.

'Were you serious about me moving to California, Peter?' She looked worried as she asked, and slowly he shook his head.

'I guess not. Just dreaming. I know you can't give up your job here. I wouldn't want you to anyway. But I wish there were a way we could be together. This is going to be a terrible strain commuting back and forth.' Grant's words echoed in her ears . . . dead end . . . dead end . . . And she didn't want it to be.

'I know it's a strain to come here. I'll do my best to come to LA as much as I can.'

'So will I.' But they both knew that she would do most of the commuting. There was just no other way. She could leave the twins more easily than he could leave his patients, and sometimes she could bring them too. As though to illustrate the point, he got a call late Sunday night. One of his old transplant patients had had a major heart attack. He gave all the suggestions he could over the phone, but the transplant had been two years before, and the man's chances weren't great, whether Peter was there or not. He stayed awake all night, worrying about his patient, and feeling that he should have been there with him. 'I have a responsibility to these people, Mel. It doesn't just end when I pull off the mask and gown after the surgery. It goes on, as long as they live. At least that's how I feel.'

'That's why you're good at what you do.' Mel sat next to him on the porch, hugging her knees as they watched the sun come up, and an hour later they got the call from LA that his patient had died. They took a long walk on the beach then, saying little, and Mel held his hand, and when they came back to the house he felt better. It was all that he would miss when he went back to LA again. He needed her with him.

Monday was their last day together at the Vineyard. The kids had plans for the entire day, and Raquel was busy cleaning up before they closed the house. Mel had encouraged everyone to pack the day before so they didn't have to waste their last day packing. And they had already decided that they wouldn't leave until Tuesday morning. Peter and his children would leave as they had come, on a seven a.m. flight out of the Vineyard, which coordinated with a nine a.m. flight to Los Angeles from Boston, which arrived in the morning in LA The time difference worked in their favour, and Peter could go straight to the hospital and do rounds, after dropping the kids off at home. Pam and Matthew didn't start school until the following week and Mark had three weeks before he started college.

Mel and the twins would take the ferry to Woods Hole, drive to Boston, return their rented car, and then fly to New York, getting to their home actually later than the group flying to LA But as they contemplated leaving on Monday night, there was silence. It was sad to be leaving each other again, they were really a group now. Pam was the first to express her sorrow to be leaving, and Mark quickly seconded his sister's view, holding tightly on to Valerie's hand, a sight they were all beginning to get used to.

'Can't you ever prise those two apart?' Peter was still mildly worried, but Mel was beginning to relax about it as they lay in bed on their last night.

'They're all right. I think the less fuss we make, the quicker they'll get bored with it.'

'Just so no one gets pregnant.'

'Don't worry, I'm keeping an eye on Val, and so is Jess. And frankly, I think Mark is a very responsible boy. I don't think he'd take advantage of Val. Not even if she tempted him, which I'm praying she won't.'

'I hope you're not overestimating him, Mel.' He put an arm around her shoulders and thought back over the weekend. And then he looked at her with a tender smile. 'So when do you come to LA?'

'I go back to work in two days, let me see what's happening there and we'll talk about it. Maybe weekend after next, or the weekend after that?' She sounded hopeful, but he looked depressed.

'That's practically October.'

'I'll do my best.'

He nodded, not wanting to argue with her, but her best still wasn't going to be what he wanted. He wanted her there all the time and he couldn't see how he was going to get that. He wasn't ready to give her up either. Suddenly in the last month he had come to feel that he couldn't live without her. He knew that was crazy, but it was how he felt. He needed her near him to share the joys and burdens of his daily life, the funny things said by Matt, the patients who died, the tears shed by Pam, the beauty, the traumas, all of it. It meant nothing without her, but there was no way that he could take her to LA with him. And as they made love that night he wanted to drink her spirit and swallow her soul and remember every nook and cranny of her body.

'Sure you won't come with me?' he whispered before he boarded the plane to Boston.

'I wish I could. But I'll be there soon.'

'I'll call you tonight.' But just the idea of having to call her again, and not see her, depressed him. He had finally found the woman he wanted and he couldn't have her, not because another man did, but because a network thought they owned her, and worse yet, she liked it. Yet he knew that she loved him. It was a lousy situation, but he hoped that in time something would happen to resolve it. He smiled to himself. Maybe she would decide that she couldn't live without him. 'I love you, Mel.'

'I love you more,' she whispered, and out of the corner of their eyes they saw Val and Mark kissing and holding each other tight, and Pam made a horrible face.

'Yuck. They're disgusting.' But the boy she had liked on the beach had come to say goodbye to her, and she blushed furiously as she said goodbye to him. Only Matt was left out of the romantic scene, and everyone kissed him goodbye half a dozen times.

'Come out soon,' Peter said to Mel.

'I promise.'

The two tribes waved as the Californian contingent boarded the small plane, unsuccessfully trying not to shed tears en masse, and then the Adams got into their car and drove toward the ferry, the twins waving handkerchiefs and crying openly, as Mel tried to conceal her aching heart.

CHAPTER 23

The interview that Melanie had done of Peter when they met aired the first week in September and was hailed as one of the most extraordinary documentaries that had been done in the history of television. Everyone felt sure that Mel would win an award for it, and suddenly everyone seemed to be talking about Dr Peter Hallam. And better yet, since the surgery, Pattie Lou Jones had bloomed. There was a brief film clip of a follow-up on her.

Everyone in LA called to tell Peter again and again what a marvellous interview it was, and what a breakthrough for heart transplants and greater public acceptance of them. But repeatedly, Peter gave Mel the credit, and said what a remarkable job she'd done. So much so that when she finally came out to Los Angeles for the last weekend in September, everyone in the hospital seemed to treat her like an old friend, as did Matthew and Mark; Pam still showed a little reserve, and Mrs Hahn was no friendlier than she had been before.

'It's almost like coming home, Peter.' She smiled happily as he drove her to her hotel. She was staying at the Bel-Air, because it was close to his house and she liked the seclusion. He was spending the night with her and they could hardly wait. They felt like two kids sneaking off to a hotel, and Mel giggled at the thought. He was going to tell the children the next day that he had stayed at the hospital with a patient, but all his medical contacts knew where he was, in case he was needed during the night. 'It's so good to be back.' She strutted around the large, cheerful room, peeled off her dress, and sat happily in her slip looking at Peter. It had been three and a half weeks since she'd seen him, but she just hadn't been able to come out sooner, no matter how lonely she'd been for him. And she was. There

had been one emergency at the station, Jessica had go'
sick, and it had taken more time than she had thought tc
reorganise their life in the autumn. It always did, but this
year she was in more of a hurry than usual. She was
absolutely desperate to get to LA to be with him.

'It's so good to see you, Mel. It's awful being three
thousand miles apart.'

'I know.' But there was no solution to that, and they
both knew it. They ordered room service and enjoyed
staying in their room alone, and they had already made
love once when Peter asked her how the sketching of the
new contract was going. 'We know what we want at least.
The question now is will we get it.' It was a bit like his own
plight with her and he smiled, and kissed her softly on the
lips.

'They're crazy if they don't give you everything you
want. You're the best thing they've got and they know it.'

Mel smiled at the lavish praise. 'Maybe I should have
you negotiating this instead of my lawyer.'

'When do you start actually negotiating this?'

'In about two weeks.'

He looked sad, but almost resigned now. 'That means I
don't see you for another month, I imagine.'

She couldn't deny that. Contract negotiation was a tense
time for her, and she wanted to be on hand every moment.
She wouldn't be in the mood to go anywhere, not even to
see him. 'Can you come east?'

He shook his head. 'I doubt it. We've done two heart-
transplant patients in the last month' – she knew that
much already – 'and we're waiting to do another heart-
lung. I'm not going to be able to go anywhere for quite a
while.'

'Able,' she reminded him, 'but not willing. There's a
difference.' But she understood the reasons why. They
were both trapped by their jobs and their lives and their
children. It was crazy, almost like being married to
separate people, and they had to take what they could
while they could get it.

Mel didn't even see his children again until Sunday afternoon, the night before she took the red eye. They had stayed almost in hiding at the Bel-Air. They wanted to be alone every moment they possibly could, and Mel thought it was best if they didn't see too much of the children. She could already sense that now that Pam was back on her own turf, she was not as warm to Mel. She felt more secure here, and she had her father to herself again. But the boys hadn't changed. Mark pumped her for every possible bit of news of Val, and all Matthew wanted to do was sit on her lap and hug her. The afternoon and evening went too quickly, and it seemed only hours after she arrived that she was back at the airport with Peter, waiting for her plane, with tears in her eyes. She didn't want to leave him, but she had to.

'It's a crazy life we lead, isn't it?'

'It is.' His pager went off then and he rushed to a nearby phone. There was a problem with one of his transplants, and he had to leave at once. For a second, it reminded him of the night he had operated on Marie, and had called her at the airport just before she got on the plane. But this time she wasn't invited, and she wasn't on a story, and she had to get back to New York by the next morning. He couldn't even wait for her flight. He had to kiss her then, and run down the long terminal hall, turning to wave once or twice before he disappeared, and she was left alone. It was awful having two careers as demanding as theirs, she thought to herself as she boarded the plane in the first class section, and she decided that if anyone asked for an autograph she would break their arm. She wasn't in the mood to be nice to anyone, but fortunately no one spoke to her from Los Angeles to New York, and she walked into her house at six thirty the next morning, feeling tired and depressed. When she called Peter at the hospital, at seven a.m. his time, she was told that he had just gone back into surgery. It was a lonely existence for both of them, but it couldn't be helped.

And as it turned out, she didn't get back out to see him

257

at all in October. The negotiations for the new contract were hard going.

'Have you forgotten me entirely, or is there any hope for the coming month?' Peter was beginning to complain daily on the phone, and Mel thought that if she saw another flowery envelope from Mark to Val she would scream. He must have bought her every corny card in the state of California by then, and it drove her crazy, but Val loved it.

'I promise, I'll be out this month.'

'That's what you said last month.'

'It's the damn contract, besides which, you know I worked two weekends.' This was when the Soviet premier and his wife had arrived for an unexpected visit, and Mel had been dispatched to Washington, D.C., to interview the Russian counterpart of America's First Lady. She had actually liked her. The following weekend she had done a follow-up interview on the President's recovery. 'I can't help it, Peter.'

'I know, but I have no one else to moan to.'

She smiled. There were times when she felt the same way about his patients. 'I promise. I'll be out next weekend.' And she kept her word, but he spent most of it in surgery with Marie, who was suddenly failing. They had operated on her twice in the past month, but she was having every possible complication typical of transplants. Mel spent most of the weekend shopping and taking his children out. She took Pam with her when she shopped for the girls, and they had lunch at the Polo Lounge at the Beverly Hills Hotel, which Pam loved although she didn't admit it. Her eyes grew as wide as saucers whenever someone approached Mel for an autograph, which they did four or five times before lunch was over. After that she took Matt to a film. And finally on Sunday, she got some time with Peter, but he was distracted, listening for the phone with one ear, and thinking about Marie the entire time.

'You know, if she weren't so damn sick, I'd be jealous.' She tried to joke with him about it, but neither of them was really in the mood.

'She's a very sick girl, Mel.'

'I know she is. But it's hard sharing you with her, when we wait so long between visits.' But that reminded him of something he'd been meaning to ask her.

'What about Thanksgiving?'

'What about it?' She looked blank.

'I've been wanting to ask you if you and the girls would come out here. We do a traditional Thanksgiving every year, and we'd all love to have you. It would make it a real family event for us.'

'That's about three weeks away, isn't it?' He consulted his calendar and nodded. 'Then we should have closed the contract by then.'

'Is everything determined by that, Mel, even Thanksgiving?' He looked upset and she tried to soothe his ruffled feathers with a kiss.

'It puts a lot of pressure on me, that's all. But we should have wrapped it up by then.'

'Then you'll come?'

'Yes.' He looked first thrilled, then worried.

'What if the contract doesn't close before Thanksgiving?'

'Then I'll come anyway. What do you think I am? A monster?'

'No, a damn busy woman. And too important by half.'

'Do you love me in spite of that?' Now and then she worried that it would get to him and he'd throw in the towel. It was something she had always worried about, that success would cost her the love of a decent man like him.

But he put his arms around her now and held her close. 'I love you more than ever.' And tonight when he took her to the plane he stayed until it took off.

When she told Jess and Val the next morning, Valerie gave a squeal of delight and rushed upstairs to dash off a note to Mark before she left for school. Mel stared at the stairs in annoyance and then addressed herself to her oldest daughter.

'Doesn't she think of anything else any more?'

259

'Hardly ever,' Jessica answered honestly.

'I can't wait to see her grades at half-term.' Jessica didn't say a word, she knew just how bad they were going to be. The constant letter writing to Mark had taken its toll on her sister's homework.

'It'll be fun to go to California for Thanksgiving.'

'I hope so.' Mel smiled tiredly, and kissed the girls when they went to school. Before she unpacked from the weekend, she called her lawyer. She knew he went to the office before eight o'clock every morning. But the news he gave her wasn't good. The network was still stalling on the contract, hoping she'd give up some of what she wanted. But he reminded Mel that she didn't have to, that they'd probably give in to her demands, and if they didn't, a dozen other offers would come in a matter of moments, if she even hinted that she was open to offers.

'But I'm really not, George. I want to stay where I am.'

'Then hang tough.'

'I intend to. Any chance we get it wrapped up before Thanksgiving?'

'I'll do my best.'

But as it turned out, his best didn't do it. And when they took the plane to LA three weeks later, nothing was settled. Mel's lawyer insisted that they were at the eleventh hour, but nothing was signed yet, and it was driving her crazy. Peter could see just from the nervous way she walked off the plane that it was all getting to her, but they would have four days together now, and he hoped she would unwind. He just prayed that the President didn't get shot and no one needed a heart transplant over Thanksgiving. His prayers were answered. They spent a peaceful Thanksgiving, with all five children happy to be together again. Mrs Hahn outdid herself nobly with a Thanksgiving feast which left everyone barely able to leave the table.

'My God, I can't move.' Val stared down at her stomach in despair. Mark came to her rescue, and pulled her out of her seat, as Pam and Jess went upstairs to play chess. Matthew curled up near the fire with his favourite blanket and his teddy bear and went to sleep. Peter and Mel repaired to his den to relax and talk. There was a feeling of homecoming about it all, and Peter had insisted that they not sleep at a hotel, but stay there at the house, in the guest room. Because Jess was there Mel felt that Pam wouldn't be as upset at their staying there. She was in effect Mel's guarantee of safe passage.

'It was a beautiful dinner, Peter.'

'I'm glad you're all here.' He looked at her searchingly and saw the tired lines around her eyes. They didn't show on camera with her makeup, but he knew they were there, and it bothered him to see them. She shouldn't have been working that hard, or been under that much pressure. 'You've been pushing too hard, my love.'

'What makes you say that?' She stretched her legs out towards the fire.

'You've lost weight and you look tired.'

'I suppose I do . . . It's a tough business.' She smiled at him. She knew he'd had a rough time too, with two new transplants and Marie, who was developing problems with the steroids again, but she was doing better.

'Nothing new on the contract?'

'George says it's a matter of hours. They ought to sign it on Monday when I go back.'

Peter didn't say anything for a long time and then he looked at Mel. He didn't know how to begin to approach it, but the time was now or never. It might be his last chance forever, or at least a year. He had to. 'Mel . . .'

'Hmm?' She had been staring into the fire in the silence, and now she looked up with a smile, relaxing at last after weeks of tension. 'Yes, Doctor?'

He wanted to move closer to her, but he didn't. 'I've got something to ask you.'

'Something wrong?' Maybe something about Pam, but she had been all right lately. Better than Val surely, whose grades, Mel had discovered, had never been lower. But she was going to speak to Peter about that later in the weekend. They were going to have to put some kind of restrictions on the two lovebirds before Val flunked out of school completely, and Mel wanted Peter's support. But there was no rush to talk about that yet. 'What's up, love?'

'Something I've been wanting to discuss with you for a long time. About your contract.'

She looked surprised. So far he'd stayed away from advising her about her work, and she thought it just as well. He didn't know her field any better than she knew his, and all they could offer each other was moral support, which was what they both needed. 'What about it?'

'What if you don't sign it?'

She smiled. 'The problem isn't me, it's them. I'd sign it in a minute, if the bastards would give us all the conditions we want. And I think they will. But it's been a war of nerves till now.'

'I know it has. But what if you don't sign it . . .' He held his breath and then went on a moment later, 'And sign with someone else instead?'

'I may have to if I don't get what I want.' But she hadn't got the point yet. It was the farthest thing from her mind. 'Why? What did you have in mind?' He was obviously telling her something but she wasn't sure what yet.

He looked her straight in the eye and said it in a single word. 'Marriage.' There was a total blank on her face and then a look of shock as she went pale, staring at him.

'What do you mean?' Her voice was no more than a whisper.

'I mean I want to marry you, Mel. I've been trying to get up the guts to ask you for months, but I didn't want to screw up your career. But with your contract taking this long to get signed, I just thought . . . I wondered . . .' She got up and stalked across the room, to stand near the fire with her back to him, and then at last she turned slowly.

'I don't know what to say to you, Peter.'

He tried to smile, but he was so desperately afraid he couldn't. 'A simple yes will do.'

262

'But I can't do that. I can't give up everything I've built in New York. I just can't . . .' Her eyes filled with tears. 'I love you, but I can't do that . . .' She started to tremble all over and he went to her and took her in his arms, with tears that she could not see filling his eyes as he held her.

'It's all right, Mel. I understand. But I had to ask you.'

She pulled away from him so she could see him, and there were tears pouring down her cheeks as well as his now. 'I love you . . . oh God, don't ask me to do that, Peter. Don't make me prove something I can't prove to you.'

'You don't have to prove anything to me, Mel.' He wiped his cheeks and sat down on the couch. There was no kidding themselves either, they couldn't go on flying across the country to see each other forever. The end was inevitable, and they both knew that. He looked at her now, his eyes boring into hers and shook his head slowly. 'I used to think we were both such lucky people, good kids, good careers, and we found each other.' He smiled ruefully. 'Now I don't think we're so lucky.'

Mel didn't answer and at last she blew her nose and wiped the tears from her cheeks. 'I don't know what to say to you, Peter.'

'Don't say anything. Just know that if you change your mind I'm here and I love you. I want to marry you. I'll support everything you do, within reason. You could work as hard as you want and as much as you want at any of the LA networks.'

'But LA's not New York.' He wanted to ask her then if New York meant more to her than he did, but it wasn't a fair question and he knew it.

'I know that. We don't need to discuss it. I just had to ask you.'

'It looks like I'm choosing work instead of you, and that's so ugly.'

'Sometimes the truth is ugly.' It had to be faced between them.

'Will you still want to continue . . . with . . . us . . .

with me . . . if I sign my new contract and stay in New York?' She trembled at the question. What would she have now if she lost him? Nothing.

'Yes, we'll continue for as long as we can both stand it. But it can't go on forever and we both know that. And when it ends, Mel, we're both losing something wonderful, something that we both need desperately. I've never loved anyone more than I love you.' Tears spilled down her cheeks again then and she couldn't bear it any longer. She went outside for some air, and a little while later Peter joined her. 'I'm sorry I asked you, Mel. I didn't mean to make you unhappy.'

'You didn't. It's just that sometimes' – her eyes filled with tears and her voice broke – 'life is full of such tough choices. All I wanted was a better contract and now I feel like I'm breaking your heart if I sign it.'

'You're not.' He held her close to him. 'You're doing what you have to do for you, Mel, and that's terribly important. I respect that.'

'Why the hell did we have to be so unlucky?' She was openly sobbing. 'Why couldn't we both have lived in the same city?'

He smiled, accepting their fate now. She was what she had been from the beginning and he had been wrong to try to change that. 'Because life is full of challenges, Mel. We'll make it. Hell, if I had to travel five times that distance, I would still want to see you.' And then he looked at her again in the soft darkness. 'Will you come back out here for Christmas?'

'Yes, if I'm not working.'

'Okay.' He tried to feel satisfied with that, but he wasn't. He had no choice though, and as they lay side by side that night they were both thinking, and the heavy mood was still on them the next day and the day after.

And the children didn't help them. Val and Mark seemed to have plans for every moment of the weekend, and Jess and Pam and Matthew went to films, visited friends, did errands. Peter didn't even insist this time that they all stick together, he had too much on his own mind. And Mel looked even more upset when they left than she had when they'd arrived, and her lawyer's call the next morning did nothing to soothe her.

'Well, we got it.' He almost crowed with victory when he called at eleven o'clock that morning. She had been quietly pacing her room, thinking of Peter's face when she left him. He looked devastated and she felt worse, but there had been no choice to make and he knew it.

'Got what?' Mel was almost too nervous this morning to think straight. And she had sent the girls off to school despite their return on the red eye.

'Good God. What did you do in California, Mel? Spend the whole weekend on dope or LSD? You got your *contract!*' He was as nervous and exhausted as she was. It had been a long fight this time, but it was worth it. She had had the guts to hold out, and had got everything she wanted. Not too many of his clients had the gall to do that, but she did. 'We sign at noon today. Can you be there by then?'

'Hell, yes.' She grinned, it was what they had waited two months for, but somehow when she hung up the phone, she found that the thrill was gone. The victory was empty now, thanks to Peter. When she signed the contract, she would feel that she had betrayed him.

But at noon she was at the network and George and all of the officials were waiting. There were ten people in the room, and Mel was the last to arrive, dressed in a black Dior suit, with a mink coat over her arm and a black hat with a veil, which suited her humour. She looked like a widow in an old film, going to the reading of a will. She made a dramatic entrance and the network men seemed pleased. They always got their money's worth with Mel Adams, and even they respected her for the long battle. She cast smiles around the room and sat down with a look at George, who nodded. He could hardly wait to call the press and announce this one. It was a knock-out contract for Mel and everyone in the room knew it, including Mel herself. She glanced over the conditions, pen in hand. The network officials had already signed it, and all that was missing was her signature on the dotted line. She picked up her pen, and held it, feeling her palms damp, her face grow white, as suddenly she seemed to see Peter's face before her. She stopped, silent, pale, thinking, and looked at George. He nodded again.

'Everything's just fine, Mel.' He was smiling, looking ghoulish and suddenly she knew that she couldn't do it. She stood up, the pen still clutched in her hand, and shook her head at them, looking at the men she had worked for.

'I'm sorry. I can't do it.'

'But what's wrong?' They were stupefied. Was she crazy? She would have told them that she was if they had asked her. 'It's all there, Mel. Everything you asked for.'

'I know.' She sat down again, looking broken. 'I can't explain it. But I can't sign the contract.'

As a single body, they began to look ugly, and George with them. 'What the hell . . .'

She looked up at each one of them, still shaking, and tears stung her eyes, but she couldn't cry now. She wanted it so badly she could taste it, but there was something else she wanted more and which she knew would last a lifetime, not just a year. And he was right. She could work in LA. Her career wouldn't be over just because she left New York. She stood up again and said in a strong voice, 'Gentlemen, I'm moving to California.'

The room was stunned into silence. 'You signed with the network there?' Now they knew she was crazy. They couldn't have offered her more money. Or had they? The flashy creeps. But Mel had always had more class than that. No one understood what had happened, least of all her own lawyer. She gulped then, and spoke to no one in particular.

'I'm getting married.' And then without another word, she strode from the room, rushed into the lift, and left the building before anyone could stop her. She walked all the way home, and when she got there she found that she felt a

266

little better. She had just thrown her whole career out of the window, but she thought that he was worth it. She just hoped she wasn't wrong, as she picked up the phone and dialled his number. The operator in the hospital paged him, and found him. He was on the phone in less than a minute, busy and distracted, but happy to get the call.

'Are you okay?' He was only half listening to her answer.

'No. I'm not.'

And then he heard her, and the strangeness of her voice. God, something had happened. He had sounded like that when Anne died . . . the twins . . . 'What is it?' His heart pounded as he waited.

'I went to sign the contract . . .' She sounded numb. 'And I didn't.'

'You didn't what?'

'I didn't sign it.'

'You what?' His legs turned to jelly beneath him. 'Are you crazy?'

'That's what they said.' And suddenly she panicked, terrified that he had changed his mind and now it was too late. She had thrown everything out the window. She almost whispered. 'Am I?'

And then he understood what she had done and why, as tears came to his eyes. 'Oh, baby, no you aren't . . . yes, you are . . . oh God, I love you. Do you mean it?'

'I think so. I just threw away a million bucks for the year. I think maybe I must mean it.' She sat down and started to laugh, and suddenly she couldn't stop laughing and he couldn't stop either. She took off her hat and veil and tossed them in the air. 'Doctor Hallam, as of the thirty-first of December, which happens to be New Year's Eve, I'm unemployed. Practically a vagrant.'

'Terrific. I've always wanted to marry a vagrant.'

The laughter at her end died into silence. 'Do you still?'

His voice was very gentle. 'Yes. Will you marry me, Mel?' She nodded and he waited, terrified. 'I can't hear you.'

'I said yes.' And then, desperately nervous, 'Do you think they'll hire me in LA?'

'Are you kidding?' He laughed again. 'By tonight, they'll be beating your door down.' But there were other things on his mind. 'Mel, let's get married at Christmas.'

'Okay.' She was still in a kind of stupor, and everything he said sounded fine to her now. 'When at Christmas?' It was all like a dream, and she wasn't sure yet how long she'd been dreaming. She remembered a room full of men in dark suits, and her refusing to sign a contract, but after that everything was a blur except this phone call. She could hardly remember how she had got home now. Had she walked? Taken a cab? Flown?

'How about Christmas Eve?'

'Sure. When's that?'

'In about three and a half weeks. Is that okay?'

'Yes.' She nodded slowly. And then, 'Peter, do you think I'm crazy?'

'No, I think you're the bravest woman I've ever met, and I love you for it.'

'I'm scared.'

'Don't be. You'll get a great job out here, and we'll be happy. Everything is going to be wonderful.' She hoped he was right. All she could think of now was what she had done by refusing to sign the contract, but if they had asked her again, she would have refused again. She had made her decision, and now she would have to live by it, whatever that took, and of that she wasn't sure yet.

'What'll I do with my house?'

'Sell it.'

'Can't I rent it?' She felt sick at the thought of giving it up forever. She had to take such giant steps now.

'Are you planning to move back there?'

'Of course not, unless you do.'

'Then why keep it? Sell it, Mel. You can use the money to invest in something out here.'

'Will we be buying a new house?' She felt confusion begin to sweep over her as she sat staring into space and she heard the doorbell ringing in the distance but she didn't answer. It was Raquel's day off and there was no one she wanted to see now, particularly reporters, if they'd heard the news.

'We don't need a new house, Mel. We have this one.' He sounded so happy, but as she listened she knew she didn't want to live there. It was Anne's house . . . their house . . . not her house . . . but maybe just in the beginning . . . 'Look, you just relax. Have a drink or something. I've got to get back to work here. I'll call you later. And remember. I love you.'

'I love you too.' But her voice was only a whisper, and she didn't move from the chair for an hour as she contemplated what she'd done, and when George called she attempted to explain it. He told her that he thought she was crazy, but it was an intensely personal decision. He agreed to sound out the LA networks, and by that night she had three offers, and by the following week she had a contract, for the same money she had wanted in New York, and had had to wait two months for. But of course this was LA, and not New York. But the furore she had created was beyond measure, and it was an agony to go into work now. They had asked her to stay until December 15, and then she could leave two weeks before the end of her contract. But everywhere she was treated like a traitor, even Grant came to see her to tell her that she was crazy, that it would never work, that she was meant for the big time in New York, not the LA market, and marriage wasn't her life-style. She felt as though she were drifting through a nightmare, and the twins kept looking at her as though she had betrayed them.

'Did you know you were going to do it?' Jess asked when she told them, meaning accept Peter's proposal. But it sounded as though she were asking her if she knew she was going to commit murder.

'No, I didn't.'

'When did he ask you?'

'On Thanksgiving.' The reproach she felt was in her

eyes each time she looked at her mother, and Valerie was so nervous that she seemed ready to throw up each time Mel looked at her. Even she wasn't totally pleased to be moving. They had to change schools mid-year, leave their home, their friends. And when Mel put the house on the market, she thought it would kill her. It sold on the first weekend, and when she got word, she sat down on the stairs and cried. Everything was happening much too quickly. Only Raquel seemed to know what was going on, as she packed endless boxes for California.

'I tole you, Mrs Mel . . . I tole you last summer . . . in six months . . .'

'Oh, for chrissake, Raquel, shut up.' But halfway through the packing, Mel realised that she didn't know what she was going to do with Raquel. There was no room for her at Peter's, and the woman had been with her for years. She called him in a panic one night at midnight in California, 3 a.m. in New York.

'What am I going to do with Raquel?'

'Is she sick?' He had been half asleep when she called him. But Mel was wide awake.

'No. I mean about bringing her.'

'You can't bring her, Mel.'

'Why not?' She bridled.

'There's no room, and Mrs Hahn would kill her.'

'Personally, I'd prefer it if Raquel killed Mrs Hahn.'

'Mrs Hahn is devoted to my children.' It was the first time he had spoken to her in that tone of voice and Mel didn't like it.

'Raquel is devoted to mine. Now what?'

'Be reasonable.' How reasonable did she have to be? She had given up a job, a house, her children had given up friends and schools, just how much more did he want her to leave behind her? Raquel too?

'If she doesn't come, Peter, neither do I, or the children.'

'Oh, for God's sake.' And then he decided it was too late to argue. 'All right. We'll rent her a flat.'

'Thank you.' Mel announced the news to Raquel the

next morning, still feeling annoyed at Peter, but this time Raquel surprised her.

'To California? You crazy? I live here, in New York.' She smiled at Mel and kissed her cheek. 'But thank you. I gonna miss you. But I just don' want to move to California. You gonna have a good life now. You got a good husband. But me, I got a boyfriend here. Maybe sooner or later I'll get married too.' She looked hopeful, and determined not to go to California.

'We're going to miss you too.' They would have nothing familiar except each other. Even her furniture was going into storage. There was no room for it in his house. And as the days progressed, Mel realised that this was not going to be easy.

On the fifteenth of December, two weeks earlier than her contract required, she did the eleven o'clock news for the last time, from New York. And she knew that approximately two weeks later, she would be coming on the air, on another network, from LA, but this era in her life was over. Gone forever. She cried as she put down her mike, and walked out of the studio, and outside Grant was waiting. He hugged her, and she cried in his arms, as he shook his head, like an astonished father, but he was proud of her too. She had done something good for herself, and he was glad. Peter Hallam was a fine man. Grant just hoped that everything would work: the careers, the kids, the move. It was a lot to ask. But Mel could handle it, if anyone could.

'Good luck, Mel. We'll miss you.' They had wanted to give her a party, but she had refused. She couldn't bear it. Her emotions were too raw now. She promised to come back and visit, and introduce everyone to Peter. To them it was a fairy story. She had gone to do an interview and fallen in love with the handsome doctor, but it all hurt so much now. Leaving them, closing the house, leaving New York.

'Goodbye, Grant. Take care.' She kissed his cheek, and walked away with tears running down her face. She was leaving all that was familiar to her and all her old friends, and five minutes later she left the building, the building where she had aspired to so much and gone so far. Now she was leaving, and when she got home that night, all she saw was a mountain of boxes. The movers were coming the next morning, and it would be Raquel's last day as well. They would stay at the Carlyle Hotel for the weekend, and on Monday they would close the house, she would pick up the white wool Bill Blass dress she'd bought at Bendel's, and the day after, on December 19, they'd fly to LA, five days before the wedding . . . her wedding . . . she sat up in the dark, feeling it all close in around her. Her wedding. She was getting married . . .

'Oh my God.' She sat in bed and looked at the chaos around her, and the tears slid slowly down her face, as she wondered what madness had overtaken her life. Even the thought of Peter waiting for her in LA didn't console her.

CHAPTER 24

On Saturday the sixteenth of December, Mel stood in her bedroom on East Eighty-first Street for the very last time. The moving men had ransacked the house, and the last truck had just rumbled down the street, to carry her 'goods', as they called them, to California, where everything but her clothes and a few small treasures she loved would go into storage. The rest simply wouldn't fit into Peter's house, he had told her.

The girls were waiting downstairs for her with Raquel, in the front hall, but she had wanted to see the view from her bedroom one last time. Never again would she lie in bed in the morning, looking out the window, listening to the birds in the small garden. There would be other birds in California, another garden, a whole different life. But it was impossible not to think of how much it had meant to her when she bought this house. It was a lot to give up for a man she loved, and yet it was only a house after all.

'Mom?' Val shouted up to her from the front hall. 'You coming down?'

'I'll be right there,' she shouted back, her eyes dragging across the room for a last time, and then she ran quickly down the stairs, and found them waiting for her, their arms loaded with the gifts they had exchanged with Raquel, standing next to the cases they were taking to the hotel. When Mel went outside to hail a cab she saw that there was a light snowfall settling on the ground. It took her almost half an hour to find a cab, and when she came back to get the girls, she found them in tears, locked in Raquel's arms.

'I gonna miss you guys.' Raquel looked into Mel's eyes and smiled through her tears. 'But you did okay, Mrs Mel. He's a nice man.'

Mel nodded, unable to speak for a moment, and then she kissed Raquel's cheek and looked at the twins. 'The cab's outside, girls, why don't you put your stuff in the front seat?' They trundled outside in their boots and parkas and jeans and warm scarves, and Mel found herself thinking that those days were over too, except when they went skiing somewhere, from now on.

'Raquel' – Mel's voice was hoarse from the emotion she felt – 'we love you, remember that. And if ever you need anything, or if you change your mind about coming to LA . . .' Her eyes filled with tears, and the two women embraced.

'It's gonna be okay, *hija* . . . you gonna be happy out there . . . don' cry . . .' But she was crying too. They had shared so many years, and together they had raised the girls. And it was all over now. Mel had given everything up for her new life, even Raquel.

'We're going to miss you so much.' A horn honked outside, and Mel hugged Raquel once more and looked around the darkened house. The sale would be completed on Monday, and the new people were moving in the following day, and everything would be different. They would paint and paper the whole house, redo the kitchen, knock out some walls. She shuddered at the thought as Raquel watched her.

'Come on, Mrs Mel, let's go.' She gently took Mel by the hand and they walked outside. Mel turned to lock her front door for the last time, feeling everything inside her go taut. But this was what she had wanted, and there was no turning back now.

They stood on the pavement side by side, Raquel in the new coat they had bought her as a Christmas gift that she had decided to open early this year, and Mel walked towards the cab. Mel had also given her a cheque that would tide her over for a month or two, and a reference that would win her any job. She pulled open the door of the cab and slid in beside the girls, and waved to Raquel as they drove away, all three of them crying in the back seat and Raquel crying and waving as she stood in the falling snow.

Once they got to the hotel, the girls were excited by the elaborate suite. They ordered room service, turned on the TV, got on the phone to their friends; Mel finally had a little time to herself. She called Peter from the separate phone in her room.

'Hi, love.'

'You sound beat. Are you all right?'

'Yeah, it was awful saying goodbye to Raquel and selling the house.'

'You'll be out here soon and that'll all be behind you, Mel.' He told her that he had got a stack of papers for her from the station in LA that day. She was due to start on the first of January, and they wanted to see her briefly at the station the minute she arrived.

'I'll call them on Tuesday when I come out.'

'That's what I told them too. Are you all right, sweetheart?' He knew how hard it was for her to leave New York, and he admired her for the courageous thing she had done. Even though he had asked her to marry him, he had had almost no hope of her doing that. It had all seemed like a dream to him, and now the dream was coming true.

'I'm okay, love. Just tired.' And depressed, but she didn't want to tell him that. It would be better once she was with him again, then the anguish of the change wouldn't be quite as sharp as it was now. 'How's work?'

'Intense just now. We seem to have a house full of patients needing transplants, and no hearts. It's like a juggling act keeping ten balls in the air at once.' But she knew how well he did that, and she smiled to herself, and realised again how much she missed him. She hadn't seen him since their Thanksgiving trip to LA, she hadn't even seen him since she accepted his proposal.

'How's Marie?'

'Doing better again. I think she'll be fine.' He was obviously in high spirits, and Mel felt better again when she got off the phone. That night she and the girls ordered dinner in their rooms, and they went to bed early, and when they woke up the next day there was a foot of snow outside.

'Look, Mom!' For once, Jessica forgot her serious thoughts and she squealed like a little child. 'Let's go to the park and have a snowball fight.' Which was exactly what they did, and afterwards Mel suggested they rent skates, and they skated at Wollman Rink, laughing and teasing, gliding, and falling down. Val didn't seem as enchanted with the plan as her mother and her twin, but in the end she was game and they all had a wonderful time, and they walked slowly back to the hotel, and had steaming cups of hot chocolate and whipped cream.

'I guess we're just tourists now.' Mel smiled. And the three of them went to the cinema that night. The girls had plans to see their friends the next day, but they had nothing planned for that night. And on Monday morning, Mel gave in the keys for the house, and then stopped at Bendel's to pick up her wedding dress, as planned. It was a simple white wool dress with a jacket that matched, in a beautiful textured wool by Bill Blass. The girls came with her and picked out dresses for themselves in a pale blue, and at Mel's suggestion, they bought an identical dress for Pam.

They were getting married on Christmas Eve at St Albans Church in Beverly Hills on Hilgard Avenue across from UCLA, and there would be only a handful of guests, all of them Peter's friends, since Mel knew no one in LA.

'It's going to be weird with none of our friends there, isn't it, Mom?' Val looked concerned and Mel smiled.

'It's going to be that way for a while, until Peter's friends are our friends too.' Val nodded, and Jessica looked downcast. It reminded her again that they didn't know a soul in LA and had to go to a new school. She wasn't looking forward to that. Only Val didn't mind quite so much, it was easier for her because of Mark.

And on Monday night, Mel took them both to 21 for

their last dinner in New York, and a limousine took them back to the hotel for their last night. The three of them stood looking out at the skyline before they went to bed, and Mel felt tears sting her eyes again. 'We'll be back to visit, you know.' But she wasn't sure if she was reassuring herself or the girls. 'And maybe you'll want to come to college here.' That was only two years away for them, but for her . . . except for visits, there would be no coming back. She had made an enormous step in every way.

The next day, leaving the Carlyle was not as painful as leaving the house had been. There was a sense of an adventure begun as they left, and the girls were in high spirits as they left for the airport in a limousine, and then boarded the plane. Two college students going home to LA had already spotted Jess and Val, and once the plane took off Mel hardly saw them again until they landed.

'Where have you two been?' She wasn't particularly concerned as they came back to their seats to land. There wasn't very far for them to go on a plane.

'Playing bridge in the back with two kids from LA. They go to Columbia and they're going home for Christmas and they invited us to a party tomorrow night in Malibu.' Val's eyes shone and Jessica laughed and looked at Mel.

'Yeah, and I bet Mom will really let us do that.' She was wise to her mother's rules, and Mel laughed.

But Val tried again. 'We could take Mark.'

'I think we're going to have some settling in to do.'

'Oh, Mom . . .'

But the plane touched the ground then, and it was bright and sunny outside, and the three of them looked around anxiously as they came off the plane, wondering which Hallams had come to the airport, but then Val gave a whoop as she saw Mark, and Mel saw that they were all there, even Matthew. She rushed into Peter's arms and he held her tight, and in that single moment she knew that she had done the right thing. She knew that with every ounce of her being, she loved him.

CHAPTER 25

Mel and the girls stayed at the Bel-Air until December twenty-fourth, and at five in the afternoon, a rented limousine came to pick them up, and drove them to the church. She looked beautiful in the white wool dress, and the girls looked lovely in their blue ones. Mel was carrying a bouquet of white freesia mixed with white cymbidium orchids and baby's breath, Jess and Val had small bouquets of white stephanotis, mixed in with tiny spring flowers, and there were tiny knots of the same flowers woven into their shining hair.

Mel looked at them one last time before they got out of the car, and approved of what she saw. 'You look beautiful, girls.'

'So do you, Mom.' Jessica's eyes shone as she searched her mother's eyes. 'Are you scared?'

She hesitated and then grinned. 'To death.'

Jessica smiled, and then a worried look crossed her eyes, maybe they would go home again. 'Are you going to chicken out?'

But at that, Mel laughed. 'Hell no. You know what they say, "You can't go home again."' But as she said the words, a shadow crossed Jessie's eyes, and Mel was sorry she had been flippant. She reached out and touched the pretty young redhead's hand. 'I'm sorry, Jess.' And then in a soft voice, 'This will be home to us soon.' But she knew that of all of them, the move had been hardest on Jess, and yet the girl never seemed to complain. She had spent the last five days helping Pam reorganise her room, and helping Val move their things into the guest room. She and her twin were going to share the guest room, and it would be strange to no longer have their own rooms.

'I wouldn't mind if she weren't such a slob,' Jess

confided to Pam, and then shrugged. There simply wasn't enough room in the house to give them separate rooms, and Jessica accepted that. She accepted everything. Even the chilly reception by Mrs Hahn, who continually looked into their suitcases and the closets with discerning glances. And the last of their things waited now in suitcases at the Bel-Air Hotel, where they would be picked up that night and moved to the Hallam house. Mel hadn't wanted any of them to move in until the wedding day.

'Well' – Jess glanced out the car window at the pretty little church – 'I guess this is it.'

Mel fell silent and simply looked and Val gasped as she saw Mark go into the church, he looked so handsome and young and strong. Peter and Matt were already inside, and Pam was waiting for them in the vestibule. She was going to go up the aisle first in her blue dress that matched the girls', carrying a similar bouquet and then Valerie would follow Pam, and Jessica behind her, and after a moment's pause, Mel. Peter and the boys would be waiting at the altar for them, and on the way out, Pam and Matt would hold hands, leading the entourage down the aisle, and Mark would walk behind them, and then Peter and Mel. They had planned it all in a matter of weeks, Mel had ordered the invitations she liked in New York, and Peter's secretary had sent them out to his closest friends.

Mel looked around the church as she walked down the aisle, she realised that there was not a single soul there she knew. Here she was getting married, with not a single friend there, only her twins. And as she approached the altar, she looked deathly pale, anticipation and excitement were draining her, and her eyes went to Peter's, as he stepped forward and quietly took her arm. Suddenly nothing mattered in the world, except him, and a soft rose glow brought life to her face. He whispered softly to her before the ceremony began.

'I love you, Mel. Everything's going to be fine.'

'I love you, too.' It was all she could say.

And then the minister reminded the congregation of

why they were there. 'Dearly beloved, we are gathered here today, on Christmas Eve, on this holy day' – he smiled – 'to join this woman and this man in the bond of holy matrimony . . .' Mel could hear her heart pound, and every minute or two Peter would gently pat her hand, and then the moment came to exchange their vows and their rings. He had ordered hers without her being there, a simple circlet of diamonds in a narrow band. She had insisted that she didn't want an engagement ring. As she looked down at the ring now she felt tears fill her eyes, so that she could barely see him as she slipped on a simple gold wedding band.

'To have and to hold from this day forward . . . for better or worse . . . until death do you part . . .' A shiver ran down her spine. After all this she couldn't bear losing him. And yet he had survived losing Anne, and now here they were. She looked into his face, looking up at the man who was her husband now. 'I now pronounce you man and wife.' The organ sprang to life, and a choir sang 'Silent Night', and as Mel looked into Peter's eyes she felt as though she were going to melt. 'You may kiss the bride,' the portly minister said to the groom, and smiled at Mel. Peter did, and then they seemed to float down the aisle, and for the next hour she shook hands with dozens of people she had never seen, their faces all strange to her, but she found a minute to kiss Mark, Matthew and Pam and tell them how happy she was, and in the distance she glimpsed Mrs Hahn. Even on their wedding day, Mel thought the woman looked sour, but Peter made a point of going to shake her hand, and then Mel saw her smile. And she wondered if Mrs Hahn disapproved of her. Perhaps she still missed Anne. Seeing her there suddenly brought back visions of Raquel, and Mel wished she were there to see her wedding day. With no family of her own, Raquel had been almost a mother to her.

The seven of them hopped in a limousine afterwards to go to the Bel-Air Hotel, where the reception was being held, and Mel suddenly became aware that her wedding party was larger than she had thought it would be. The invitations to the reception had been for six o'clock, with dinner scheduled for seven thirty, and as they entered the enormous facilities of the club, Mel realised that there were at least a hundred people there. A seven-man band began to play 'Here Comes the Bride' and Peter stopped her right there and kissed her full on the mouth.

'Hello, Mrs Hallam.' Suddenly it all felt crazy and wonderful to Mel, and it didn't matter who the people were, strangers or not, or even people she would never see again. They were all sharing in the happiest moment of her life. People came up to her constantly and shook her hand, told her how much they enjoyed seeing her on TV, and how lucky Peter was. So they didn't seem so much like strangers any more.

'No, I'm the lucky one,' she insisted again and again, and there was only one moment to mar the fun, when she thought she glimpsed Val talking to Mark, crying softly in the corner of the dining room. By the time she got to where they sat, Val seemed to have recovered, and she smiled and hugged Mel. Jessica watched, and then took her mother in her arms too.

'We love you, Mom. And we're so happy for you.' But she could see in Jessie's eyes that there was pain there too. It was going to take them all time, even Mel with Peter at her side. But she felt certain that she had done the right thing for all of them, especially Peter and herself, and the girls would have to adjust to that. But she knew that to them it still seemed brutal, and she was just grateful that they hadn't taken it out on Peter. That could have been a possibility with children less supportive than hers.

She had noticed once or twice how snappy Pam was with her. But she would take care of that slowly, when Pam was used to the idea of her father being married again. All in good time, Mel reminded herself again and again.

The romance between Val and Mark still seemed to be on, although they didn't seem quite as happy as they had

281

been before. Mel suspected that living together would take the bloom off the rose for both of them. Once he saw what a 'slob' she was, as Jess said, and she had him around all the time, the romance was bound to cool. At least Mel hoped it would. She turned her thoughts from them to Matt, who bowed and invited her to dance She did a sort of little jig with him as people smiled and watched, and at the very end, Peter cut in, and swept her off in a waltz.

'Do you have any idea how beautiful you are?'

'No, but do you know how happy I am?' She beamed at him.

'Tell me. I want to hear.' He looked as happy as she. But the changes had been easier for him. They were all happening to Mel, giving up her job, pulling her kids out of school, selling her house, letting Raquel go, leaving New York . . .

'I've never been happier in my life.'

'Good. That's how it should be.' He glanced around the room as they twirled. 'Our kids look pretty happy too.' Pam was laughing at something Jess had said, and Mark was dancing with Val, as Matthew entertained the guests.

'I think they are. Except Mrs Hahn, she doesn't look too thrilled.'

'Give her time. She's a little stiff.' That was the understatement of the year, but Mel didn't comment on it. 'She loves you too, and so do all my friends.'

'They look nice.' But they could have been members of a wedding anywhere, sent by central casting to eat, dance, and beam.

'Later, when things settle down, I'll arrange some quiet evenings so you can meet people in small groups. I know how hard this must be.'

'It isn't really.' She smiled into his eyes. 'Because of you. You're all I care about here, you know, except the kids.'

He looked pleased, but he wanted her to like his friends too. They already knew who she was, but now she needed to meet them. 'You'll get to like them, too.' The dance ended, and one of Peter's colleagues cut in, and they spoke of the interview she had done of Peter earlier in the year. He had been in the operating room when they did the transplant on Marie, and Mel remembered him.

She danced with dozens of people she didn't know, laughed at jokes, shook hands, tried to remember names and then gave up, knowing she never would, and at last at eleven o'clock they all went home. The limousine took them to Peter's house on Copa de Oro Drive in Bel-Air and the children filed in. Mark was carrying Matt who had fallen asleep in the car, and the girls were still chatting between yawns, as Peter took Mel's arm and stopped her from walking in the door.

'Just a minute, please.'

'Something wrong?' She looked surprised. The chauffeur was going in with their bags, but Peter was smiling at her, and then he suddenly swept her into his arms, and carried her over the threshold, depositing her inside near the Christmas tree.

'Welcome home, my love.' They stood and kissed and the kids tiptoed upstairs, but the only one who really smiled was Mark. All three girls looked tense as they tried not to think what this day meant. It was no longer a game. It was for real. Pam and the twins quietly said goodnight, and went upstairs to their rooms, and closed their doors. Pam didn't like seeing Mel in Peter's arms, any more than the twins liked realising that their mother was no longer solely theirs. The lines had been drawn.

Peter and Mel lingered downstairs for a while, talking about their wedding day. It had been a lovely party and they'd had a good time. He poured her another glass of champagne from his bar, some Cristal he had saved, and he toasted her as the clock on the mantelpiece chimed. 'Merry Christmas, Mel.' She stood up and set down her glass, and they kissed for a long, long time and then he swept her into his arms, wedding dress and all, and carried her upstairs.

283

Peter and Mel spent Christmas with their children in the house on Copa de Oro Drive, and Mrs Hahn cooked them a wonderful Christmas dinner, of goose and wild rice, a chestnut purée, little peas and onions, and mince pie and plum pudding for dessert.

'No turkey this year?' Jessica looked surprised as they came down to dinner, and when she got one whiff of the goose, Val burst into tears and ran upstairs, but when Mel started to go to comfort her, Mark stopped her.

'I'll do it, Mel.' He seemed strangely quiet, but no one except Jessica noticed. Val seemed to cry a lot lately, or Jess thought so at least, and she had heard her crying in her bed the night before, but Val wouldn't tell her what was wrong, and Jessie didn't want to upset her mother, who hadn't seemed to notice anything wrong with Val.

'Thanks, Mark.' And then she turned to Peter, 'I'm sorry. I think everyone's tired.'

He nodded, not looking worried. Their traditions were new to the twins. They had goose every year, thanks to Mrs Hahn in recent times and Anne before that. They only ate turkey on Thanksgiving. And on Easter they had ham.

But when Mrs Hahn served the mince pie Jessie and Val only picked at it, longing for the hot apple pie they always had in New York at Christmas. Even the tree looked strange to them. There were tiny flashing lights on it and only large gold balls. All of their antique Christmas decorations they had spent years collecting and loved, and multi-coloured lights, had gone into storage with the rest of their things.

'I'm full.' Mel looked at Peter in despair as they left the table. The only good thing she could say about Mrs Hahn was that her cooking was superb. It had been a lavish meal, and they all felt full as they went to sit in the living room. And then, as Mel looked around at her new home, she realised that there were still all the same pictures of Anne around, and one oil portrait over a narrow French table. Peter noticed her looking at the photos of Anne, and he tensed for a moment, wondering if she would say something. But she didn't. She silently made a mental note to put them away when they came back from their honeymoon on the morning of New Year's Eve.

Peter had suggested Puerto Vallarta, one of his favourite places, and they were taking all five children with them, although Mel was nervous about taking Matt to Mexico, in case he got sick. The others were old enough to be careful, but she'd have to watch Matt. They had decided that it wouldn't be diplomatic to leave the children so soon. They could take a trip alone later, maybe to Europe, or Hawaii, depending on when they could get away. Under her new contract, Mel no longer had two months off as she had in New York. She had only one and a maternity leave. She had been amused when they insisted in putting it in the contract. She had had all the babies she was going to have, and all at once too. She had laughed again when she told Peter about it, and he teased her about getting pregnant if she didn't behave. In answer to which she had teasingly menaced him with pinking shears.

As they sat in the living room on Christmas night, Mel groaned at the thought of packing again. It seemed as though she had done nothing but for the past month. At least she wouldn't need much in Puerto Vallarta, and all the children were excited about going. That night there was much scurrying between rooms as they giggled and teased and took things from each other. Matt bounced on Val's bed, and Pam tried on some of Jessica's sweaters, at her new sister's invitation.

Peter and Mel could hear the racket from their room and Mel smiled. 'I think they're going to make it.' But she was still aware of a certain mild tension between the two

285

groups. There was something very real about all this, and there was no escaping it now.

'You worry about them too much, Mel. They're fine,' he told her with a smile as he answered the ringing telephone. Then he sat down at his desk with a frown, with the phone still in his hand as he asked a series of rapid-fire questions. He set the phone down again and grabbed his jacket from a chair, explaining quickly to Mel what had happened. 'It's Marie. She's rejecting again.'

'Is it serious?'

He nodded, his face pale. 'She's in a coma. I don't know why they didn't call me earlier today. They gave me some bullshit story about it being Christmas and not wanting to disturb me since I wasn't on call. God damn it.' He stood in the doorway looking unhappily at Mel. 'I'll be home when I can.'

As he left, she saw their trip to Mexico going out the window. When the children came to say goodnight a while later, she didn't say anything, not wanting to upset them. She said only that he'd gone to the hospital to check on a patient. But once they'd left the room again, she found herself thinking about Marie, and praying for her. Peter never called to give her any news. At two thirty Mel gave up and went to bed, hoping he'd be able to leave on the trip. Otherwise they would have to cancel it. She didn't want to leave without him. This was their honeymoon.

She felt him slip into bed beside her just after five o'clock, and when she reached out to him he felt distant and stiff. It was so unlike him that she opened an eye, and then moved closer to him.

'Hi, sweetheart. Everything all right?' He didn't answer, and she opened both eyes. Something was wrong. 'Peter?'

'She died at four o'clock. We opened her up and she was just too far gone. She had the worst case of hardening of the arteries I've ever seen, and with a new heart, dammit.' It was obvious that he blamed himself. They had given her seven months and no more, but it was seven months more than she would have had without it.

'I'm sorry.' There seemed to be so little she could say, and he was shutting her out. He resisted all her efforts to console him. And finally at six o'clock he got out of bed. 'You should try to get some sleep before we leave.' Her voice was gentle and she was obviously worried about him. But she felt it too. Marie had been someone important to them both, right from the first. Mel had watched the transplant. And she felt the girl's loss now. But she was not prepared for what Peter said next. He sounded like an angry unhappy child.

'I'm not going. You take the children.' He looked petulant and upset as he sat down heavily in a chair in their bedroom, and as it was still dark outside, Mel turned on a light to see him better. He looked exhausted and there were dark circles under his eyes. It was a hell of a final note to their wedding and a rotten beginning for their honeymoon.

'There's nothing you can do here. And we won't go without you.'

'I'm not in the mood, Mel.'

'That's not fair. The children will be so disappointed, and it's our honeymoon.' He was being unreasonable, but she knew that he was too tired to make much sense. 'Peter, please . . .'

'Dammit' – he leapt to his feet, glaring at her – 'how would you feel? Seven lousy months, that's all . . . that's all I gave her.'

'You're not God, Peter. You did what you know how to do, and you did it brilliantly. But God makes those decisions, you don't.'

'Bullshit! We should have done better than that.'

'Well, you didn't, dammit, and she's dead.' Now Mel was shouting too. 'And you can't stay here and sulk about it, you have a responsibility to us too.' He glared at her and stalked out of the room, but he came back half an hour later with two cups of coffee. They didn't have to be at the airport until noon so there was still time to convince him. He handed Mel a cup of the steaming brew with a sour look and she looked into his eyes as she thanked him.

287

'I'm sorry, Mel . . . I just . . . I can't ever feel good about it when I lose a patient, and she was such a sweet girl . . . it's not fair . . .' His voice drifted off and Mel set down her cup and put her arms around his shoulders.

'You're not in a fair business, sweetheart. You know that. You know the odds each time you go in. You try to forget them, but they're still there.' He nodded, she was right. She knew him well. He turned to her then with a sad smile.

'I'm a lucky man.'

'And a brilliant surgeon. Don't ever forget that.' She didn't ask him about Mexico again until after he'd had breakfast with the children; he was strangely subdued and Mark asked Mel about it as they walked back upstairs side by side.

'What's wrong with Dad?'

'He lost a patient last night.'

Mark nodded, understanding. 'He always takes that hard, especially if they're transplant patients. Was it?'

'Yes. The one he did when I interviewd him in May.' Mark nodded again and looked questioningly at Mel.

'Are we still leaving for Mexico?'

'I hope so.'

Mark didn't look too sure. 'You don't know how he gets with this kind of thing. We may not be going.'

'I'll do my best.'

He looked at her then and seemed about to say something else but Matt came along and interrupted them. He couldn't find his flippers and wanted to know if Mel had seen them.

'No, I haven't, but I'll look around. Did you check out at the pool?' He nodded, and Mel went on to her own room after he went his way and she found Peter there, sitting in a chair and staring into space, looking suddenly older than his years. His oldest son knew him well. He was taking Marie's death very hard, and Mel was beginning to doubt that they would be going anywhere that day. 'Well, sweetheart' – she sat down near him on the edge of the bed – 'what'll we do?'

'About what?' He looked blank, he was thinking of how her heart had looked when they'd opened her up.

'The trip. Shall we go or stay?'

He hesitated for a long moment, looking into Mel's eyes. 'I don't know.' He seemed incapable of making that decision at the moment.

'I think it would do you good, and the kids too. We've all been through a lot lately, a lot of adjustments, a lot of changes, and there are more to come. It seems to me that a trip might be just what the doctor ordered.' She smiled and didn't point out to him that she was starting work at the new network in a week and would be under tremendous pressure herself. She needed a holiday even more than he did.

'All right. We'll go. I guess you're right. We can't disappoint the children, and I've already arranged for someone to cover for me.' She put her arms around him and hugged him tight.

'Thank you.' But he barely responded, and he spoke to no one on the way to the airport. Once or twice Mel's and Mark's eyes met, but they said nothing until they were alone for a moment on the plane, after takeoff.

Mark filled her in on what to expect. 'He could be like this for a while, you know.'

'How long does it usually last?'

'A week, sometimes two. Sometimes even a month, it depends on how responsible he feels and how close he was to the patient.'

Mel nodded. It didn't give her much to look forward to, certainly not on their honeymoon. And Mark was right. They landed in Puerto Vallarta and piled into two jeeps to take them to their hotel where they had three rooms reserved, which looked out over the beach and water. There was an enormous open-air bar downstairs just below their windows, and three swimming pools filled with laughing, shouting people. Above all the other noises were the sounds of a steel band, interspersed from time to time with mariachis. It was a festive atmosphere and the children were thrilled, especially Jessica and Val who had never been to Mexico before. Mark took them all downstairs to swim and have a soda in the bar, but Peter insisted on staying in their room. Mel tried to woo him out of his mood.

'How about a walk on the beach, love?'

'I don't feel like it, Mel. I'd really like to be alone. Why don't you join the children?' She wanted to snap at him that it was their honeymoon, not the children's, but she decided that it was wisest to say nothing at all. Maybe he would snap out of it quicker. So she left him.

But as the days rolled on, he didn't seem to improve. She went shopping in town with Pam and the twins and they bought beautiful embroidered blouses and dresses to wear in LA at the pool, and Mark took Matthew fishing twice. She took everyone except Matt to Carlos O'Brien's for Cokes and people-watching several times and she even took the older ones to a disco one night, but Peter never joined them at all. He was obsessed with what had happened to Marie, and several times a day he would spend an hour in the room trying to get a line to L.A. to check on his current patients.

'It really wasn't worth coming, for you to sit in your room all week long, calling Center City,' Mel finally snapped at him towards the end of their stay, but he only looked at her with empty eyes.

'I told you that at home, you didn't want to disappoint the children.'

'This is our honeymoon, not theirs.' She had finally said it. She was bitterly disappointed. He had made no effort all week, and they hadn't even made love since Marie had died. A honeymoon to remember it was not.

'I'm sorry, Mel. It was just rotten timing. I'll make it up to you later.' But she wondered if he ever could. And suddenly she realised that she didn't even have her own home to return to when the trip was over. She missed the house in New York more than ever, and thinking of it reminded her of the photographs of Anne she wanted to put away when they returned. She wondered what Peter would do with her portrait. It was her house now too, and she didn't want to look at Anne every time she turned around. That seemed normal, at least to Mel, but she wasn't going to broach the subject until they returned to Los Angeles. She still called it LA whenever she spoke of it, and never home, because it wasn't home yet. New York was. She noticed that with the twins too; when they were at Carlos O'Brien's, some boys asked Jessica where they were from and she answered 'New York' without thinking and then Mark teased her and she explained that they had just moved to LA But other adjustments came more quickly. Mel noticed that they referred to each other as brothers and sisters, except for Mark and Val who had reason not to adopt those titles.

The only one to get sick was Valerie, on the last day. She bought an ice cream on the beach, and when Mel heard what she'd done she groaned as she stood by Val, while she threw up for hours and then had diarrhoea all night. Peter wanted to give her something but she absolutely refused to take it, and when Mel finally came to bed at four in the morning, he awoke, his medical instincts alert.

'How is she?'

'Asleep at last. Poor child. I've never seen anyone so sick. I don't know why she wouldn't take the Lomotil you offered her, she isn't usually that stubborn.'

'Mel, is she all right?' He was frowning and thinking of something.

'What do you mean?'

'I don't know. I don't know her that well. But she looks different than she did in Aspen, and at Thanksgiving.'

'Different how?'

'I'm not sure what I mean, to tell you the truth. Just a feeling. Has she had a checkup lately?'

'You're making me nervous. What are you suspecting?'

291

She expected nothing less than the threat of leukaemia, but he shook his head.

'Anaemia maybe. She seems to sleep a lot, and Pam says she threw up after Christmas dinner.'

Mel sighed. 'I think it's nerves. Jess looks lousy to me too. I think the move was a big change for them, and they're at a tough age for that. But maybe you're right. I'll take them both to the doctor when we get back.'

'I'll give you the name of the doctor we use. But don't worry about it.' He kissed her for the first time in days. 'I don't think it's serious, and I think you may be right. Girls at that age tend to nervous upsets. It's just that ever since Pam had anorexia last year, my antennae go up every time something seems off to me. It's probably nothing.'

But in Pam's room, Mark was sitting beside her bed. He had waited for hours for Mel to leave, and Val was awake now, and terribly weak from her bout with tourista. She was crying softly and Mark was stroking her hair, as they both whispered so as not to wake Jessie or Pam.

'Do you think it'll hurt the baby?' Val whispered to Mark, and he looked at her miserably. She had found out two days after she arrived from New York. He had taken her for a pregnancy test. And they both knew when it had happened. When they finally made love for the first time, on Thanksgiving. Val looked terrified now. They hadn't decided what to do about it yet, but if they decided to have it, she didn't want to have a deformed baby.

'I don't know. Did you take any medicine?'

'No,' she whispered. 'Your dad tried to give me some, but I wouldn't take it.' Mark nodded, but that was the least of their problems. She was only five weeks pregnant, but that meant that they had less than two months to do something about it, if she would.

'Do you think you can sleep now?' She nodded, her eyes already half closed and he bent to kiss her, and then tiptoed out of the room. He had wanted to tell his dad, but he couldn't with Christmas and the wedding and everything, and Val had begged him not to. He had to take her to a good doctor, if she was going to get an abortion, not to some crummy clinic, but he was waiting to talk to her about it until they got back to LA. There was no point discussing it here. There was nothing they could do, and it would just make her more nervous.

'Mark?' Jessica turned in her bed as he was about to leave the room. His departing noises had awoken her. 'What's wrong?' She sat up and glanced from him to her sister.

'I just came to see how Val was.' Val was already sleeping and he didn't approach from the doorway.

'Is something wrong?' She must have been totally out of it, Mark decided, if she didn't remember how sick Val had been all day with the tourista.

'She got sick from something she ate.'

'I mean, more than that.'

'No, she's okay.' But he was shaking when he got back to his own room. Jessie sensed something, and he knew what they said about twins, that they were practically psychic about each other. All he needed was for her to say something to his dad, or their mother and all hell would break loose. He wanted to take care of it himself. He had to. There was no other way.

CHAPTER 27

They left for LA the morning of New Year's Eve with Val still weak, but well enough to go home. And they got back to the house at four in the afternoon, tired and suntanned and happy with their trip. Peter had finally consented to come out of seclusion for the last day, and a good time was had by all. Even Mel. Although it hadn't been much of a honeymoon for her, to say the least. He apologised to her on the flight home, and she told him she understood. At least she had got some rest before she started work at the network in LA She had to report at noon the next day, on New Year's Day, and at six o'clock that night she would begin co-anchoring with Paul Stevens. He had been at the station for years, and although he had some devoted fans, his ratings were starting to slip, and they were bringing Mel in to pull him up again. The network felt that together they should make an unbeatable team. He was tall, grey-haired, and blue-eyed, with a resonant deep voice, and a style which appealed to the ladies, according to the surveys. Mel had a strong female draw too, and the surveys all showed that men loved her as well. With the two of them on the air, the network knew that they had a prize show, and even if Stevens slipped farther, Mel could carry him. But it was the first time Paul Stevens had ever co-anchored, and he was less than thrilled, and for Mel it was a step down too, as she had been sole anchor now for years. It was going to be a humbling experience for both, she knew, and a lesson in diplomacy, working with him.

Peter and Mel decided to stay home on New Year's Eve, and drink champagne by the fire. Mark took Val and Jessie out to a party he'd been invited to. Mel was pleased that he had included Jessie as well, although she didn't look too thrilled to go and Val wasn't on top form yet. Mel suggested that they not stay out too late, and warned them to be careful driving, and then she went upstairs to check on Pam, who had a friend sleeping over. Matt was asleep in his bed with a noisemaker beside him. He wanted someone to wake him up at midnight so he could blow his horn, but Mel correctly assumed that there would be no one awake in the house by midnight to wake him up. She was half tempted to wait up for Mark and the twins but she and Peter were exhausted. As he sat in bed reading some of his medical journals, Mel wandered around the house, trying to make herself feel as though it were her home too, but it just didn't feel like it yet. She saw the photographs of Anne in the silver frames, and began gathering them up one by one There was a grand total of twenty-three, and she put them all in a drawer in Peter's study, and as she crossed the living room with the last batch in her arms, she saw Pam standing in the doorway.

'What are you doing?'

'Putting some pictures away.' There was a strange exchange of looks and Mel saw that Pam was rigid as she stood there.

'Of who?'

'Your mother.' Mel's voice didn't waver.

'Put them back!' Her voice was almost a snarl, and Mel saw that the friend who was sleeping overnight was standing just behind her.

'Excuse me?'

'I said, put them back. This is my mother's house, not yours.' If Mel didn't know her better she would have said she was drunk. But she wasn't. She was just extremely angry and upset, so much so that she was shaking where she stood.

'I think we can discuss this some other time, Pam. When we're alone.' Mel was determined not to lose her cool, but she found that she was shaking too.

'Give me those!' And then suddenly, Pam lunged at her, but Mel saw her coming and dropped the pictures into a chair and grabbed Pam's arms before she could do any damage. She held her fast and spoke to her in a stern voice.

'Go to your room. Right now!' It was nothing different than she would have said to the twins. But Pam ignored her and frantically picked up all the framed photographs Mel had dropped into a chair. And she stood glaring at Mel with her arms full.

'I hate you!'

'You're welcome to all the photographs you like. I put the rest in your father's study.'

Pam ignored her. 'This is our house, *ours*, and my mother's, and don't you forget it!' Mel's palm itched to slap her, but it seemed unwise in the presence of her friend. Instead, she took a firm grip on Pam's shoulder and propelled her to the door.

'Go upstairs to your room right now, Pam. Or I'm going to call your friend's mother and ask her to pick her up. Is that clear?' Pam said not a word, she trundled upstairs with the photographs of her mother, and her embarrassed friend Joan trailing behind her, as Mel stayed long enough to turn off the lights downstairs and then went up to her bedroom, where Peter was still happily reading his journals. Mel stood staring at him for a long moment, aware that at least some of what Pam had said was true. It was their house. Mel hadn't even been allowed to put her furniture in it. And it still had Anne's mark on it everywhere. Still trembling from her encounter with Pam, Mel stared at Peter as he looked up. 'I want that portrait taken down tomorrow.'

'What portrait?' He looked at her as though she were crazy, and she almost looked it.

'The one of your late wife.' She spoke through clenched teeth and he was totally baffled. Maybe the champagne had gone to her head.

'Why?'

'Because this is my house now too, not hers. And I want it taken down. I immediately!' She was almost shouting at him.

'It's by a very famous artist.' He started to stiffen too. Her attitude seemed totally uncalled for and he knew nothing of the exchange with Pam.

'I don't care who it's by. Get rid of it. Throw it out. Burn it. Give it away. Do whatever the hell you want with it, but get it out of my living room!' She was suddenly on the verge of tears as he stared at her in disbelief.

'What in hell is wrong with you, Mel?'

'What's wrong with me? What's *wrong* with me? You move me into a house where not so much as a hat pin is mine, where everything belongs to you and your children and you've got photographs of your first wife all over the house, and I'm supposed to feel at home?'

He was beginning to understand, or so he thought, but she still sounded irrational. And why now? 'Then put the photographs away if you want to. But you didn't object to them before.'

'I didn't live here before. But I do now.'

'Apparently.' He was getting annoyed. 'I suppose you don't find the decor adequate for you?' There was suddenly a nasty tone in his voice.

'It's perfectly adequate, if you don't mind living in Versailles. Personally, I'd rather live in a house, a home, something a little warmer and on a slightly more human scale.'

'Like that dollhouse you had in New York, I suppose?'

'Precisely.' They stood across the room from each other as each one steamed.

'Fine. Then put the photographs away if you want. But the portrait stays.' He said it just to annoy her, because he didn't like the way she'd broached the subject at all, and Mel's mouth almost fell open.

'The hell it does.' And then, 'It goes or I do.'

'Doesn't that sound ridiculous to you? You're behaving like an idiot, or aren't you aware of that?'

'And you're selfish. You expect all the adjustments to be mine, and you don't change a thing, not even the photographs of your wife.'

'Then have some photographs taken of yourself and we'll put those around too.' He was being nasty now and he knew it, but he was tired of hearing her bitch about Anne's pictures. He had thought of putting them away once or twice himself, but the thought depressed him and he didn't want to upset the children. He reminded her of that now. 'I don't suppose you've thought of what reaction you'd get if you threw that portrait out.'

'Oh, yes, I already know that.' She advanced on him with a vicious look. 'I was just putting the photographs in question in your study, and your daughter informed me that this is your house and not mine, or more exactly, her mother's.'

And suddenly Peter understood it all. He sat down with drooping shoulders and looked up at Mel. He could just imagine the scene with Pam, and that explained Mel's behaviour to him. It hadn't made any sense before. He didn't think she was given to rages. 'Did she say that, Mel?' His voice was kinder now, and his eyes were too.

'She did.' Mel's eyes filled with tears and she still did not approach her husband.

'I'm sorry.' He beckoned to her but she didn't approach and she was crying openly now. He went to her and put his arms around her. 'I'm so sorry, love. You know this is your home too.' He held her and she began to sob. 'I'll take the portrait down tomorrow, it was stupid of me.'

'No, no, it's not that . . . it's just . . .'

'I know . . .'

'It's so hard to get used to living in someone else's house. I'm so used to having my own.' He sat her down beside him on the bed.

'I know . . . but this is your home now too.'

She looked up at him and sniffed. 'No, it's not. Everything is yours and Anne's . . . I don't even have any of my own things around.' Peter looked pensive as he listened to her.

'Everything I have is yours, Mel.' But she wanted her own, not his.

'Just give me time. I'll get used to it all. I'm just tired, and there's been so much going on, and Pam upset me with what she said just now.' Peter kissed his wife and stood up.

'I'll go up and talk to her.'

'No! Let me handle that. If you intervene, she'll just resent me more.'

'She loves you. I know she does.' But there was worry in his eyes.

'But it's different now. I was just a guest before, and now I'm an intruder in her house.'

Peter looked even more upset at that. Was that how she felt?

'You're not an intruder. You're my wife. I hope you remember that.'

She smiled through her tears. 'I do! There's just a lot going on at once, and tomorrow I start my new job.'

'I know.' He understood, but it made him sad to see her cry, and he vowed to himself to take Anne's portrait down the next day. She was right. 'Why don't we both go to bed early tonight? We're both tired and it's been a rough week.' Mel didn't disagree. Moving from New York, their wedding, honeymoon, Marie's death . . . They brushed their teeth and went to bed and he held her close to him in the dark, feeling her warm flesh next to him. This was what he had longed for in the past six months . . . more than that, the last two years . . . and even before that, it had never been like that with Anne. She had been so much more distant than Mel. Mel seemed almost like a part of him, and for the first time in a week he felt something deep inside him stir, and as he held her close, he wanted her as never before. And when the old year became the new, he was making love to her.

299

CHAPTER 28

As per her new contract, negotiated while she was still in New York, the car arrived for Mel in the early afternoon, and drove her to the station where she would work. She walked inside, aware of a hundred stares. There was incredible curiosity about her. Mel Adams was starting work. She was introduced to the producers, assistant producers and directors and cameramen and editors and grips, and suddenly despite the new surroundings, Mel felt as though she were in a familiar world. It was no different for New York or Chicago or Buffalo before that. A studio was a studio, and as she looked around the office she was assigned, she suddenly sighed and sat down. In a way, it felt like coming home. She spent the entire afternoon familiarising herself with the people who came and went, the features and interviews recently done. She had a glass of wine with the producer amd his crew, and at five thirty Paul Stevens arrived. The producer introduced them at once, and Mel smiled as they shook hands.

'It'll be nice working with you, Paul.'

'Wish I could say the same.' He shook her hand and walked away, as the producer attempted to fill the awkward gap and Mel raised an eyebrow and turned away.

'Well, at least I know where I stand.' She grinned ruefully. But it wasn't going to be easy working with him. He was furious to have a female share his spot, and he was going to make Mel pay for it in every way he could. She discovered that the instant they went on the air that night. He was saccharine sweet whenever he spoke to her, but he undercut her and upstaged her in every way he could, trying to make her nervous, throw her off, and generally drive her insane. It was obvious to her that his outrage was so acute that when they went off the air, she stood in front of Paul's desk and looked down at him. 'Is there anything we ought to talk about right now, before this thing gets out of hand?'

'Sure. How would you like to split your pay cheque with me? I'm splitting my spot with you, that seems only fair.' His eyes glittered evilly, and Mel understood what the problem was. The papers had long since leaked what her contract was, and it was probably three times what they paid him, but that wasn't her fault.

'I can't help the arrangements the network made with me, Paul. It was a price war with New York. You know what that's like.'

'No, but I'd like to try.' He had been trying to get to New York for years, and she had just thrown it away, and come to breathe down his neck. He hated the bitch, no matter how good they said she was. He didn't need her co-anchoring with him. He stood up now and almost snarled at her. 'Just stay out of my face, and we'll do okay. Got that?'

She looked at him sadly and turned and walked away. It wasn't going to be easy working with him, and she thought about it all the way home. She only had to do the six o'clock here, for the same money she'd been offered to do the six and eleven in New York. LA had really done well by her. And Paul Stevens hated her for it.

'How'd it go? You looked great.' Peter looked proud of her when she came home, and everyone was still gathered around the set, but Mel didn't look pleased.

'I've got a co-anchor who hates my guts. That ought to make work fun.' That, and Pam reminding her that she lived in Peter and Anne's home, she thought, as she hung up her coat.

'He'll mellow out.'

She didn't look as sure. 'I wouldn't bet on that. I think he's hoping I drop dead or go back to New York.' Mel's eyes drifted to Pam, wondering what she'd see there, but the girl's eyes were blank. And when Mel glanced at the living room wall, she saw that the portrait was gone, and she was thrilled. She threw her arms around Peter's neck, feeling better after all, and whispered in his ear. 'Thank you, my love.' Pam knew what they were talking about. She got up and left the room as the others watched, and Peter spoke in a normal voice.

'I hung Anne's portrait in the hall.'

Mel froze. 'You did? I thought you said you'd put it away.'

'It won't bother anybody there.' Oh, no? Their eyes met and held. 'You don't mind, do you?'

She spoke in a very quiet voice. 'As a matter of fact, I do. That wasn't what we agreed.'

'I know . . .' And then he turned to her, 'It's a little rough on the kids to do everything at once. All the photographs are gone.' Mel nodded and didn't say a word, she went upstairs to her room to wash her face and hands, and then joined them at dinner, and afterwards she knocked on Pam's door.

'Who is it?'

'Your wicked stepmother.' She smiled at the door.

'Who?'

'Mel.'

'What do you want?'

'I've got something to give you.' And when Pam cautiously opened the door to her, Mel handed her a dozen photographs of Anne in silver frames. 'I thought you'd like these for your room.'

Pam glanced at them and then took them from her. 'Thanks.' But she said nothing more. She simply turned and closed the door in Mel's face and Mel went back downstairs.

'Were you upstairs with Pam?' Peter was pleased as she walked into their room. He was reading his medical journals again. He had to keep abreast of what was new.

'Yes. I took her some of the photographs of Anne.'

'You know, that really shouldn't be such an issue with you, Mel.'

'Oh, no?' He really didn't understand and she was too tired to argue about it with him. 'Why not?'

'Because she's gone.' He said it so quietly, Mel had to strain to hear.

'I know. But it's difficult living here with her photographs staring at me all the time.'

'You're exaggerating. There weren't that many around.'

'I put twenty-three of them in your study last night. That's not bad. I just gave a dozen of them to Pam. And I thought I'd put some in Matt's and Mark's rooms. That's where they belong.' Peter didn't answer and went back to the journals on his lap, as Mel stretched out on the bed. The producer had suggested she do as many special features as she could in the next month. They were desperate to pull their ratings up, and historically her interviews had worked miracles for the news show in New York. She had promised to do her best, and had already made notes about half a dozen subjects that interested her. But she could just imagine what Paul Stevens was going to say when he got wind of that. Maybe all she could do was ignore the man, but the following night, he was rude to her as she came on the set, and despite his charm while they were on the air, she had the feeling that he would have liked to punch her out when they went off. It was really an untenable way to work, and not what she was used to at all. But she submitted her list of possible interviews to the producer that night, and he loved almost all of them, which was both good news and bad. It meant that she would be working overtime for the next month or two, but maybe that was one way to settle in. It was always strange working for a network at first. It was just a little stranger for her this time because she was feeling her way around at home as well.

'Busy day today?' Peter looked at her distractedly as he came in and she smiled. She had got home at seven fifteen, and he was even later than that. It was almost eight o'clock.

'Pretty much.' She was in a quiet mood. The hassles with Paul Stevens wore her out.

'Is that guy behaving any better than before? Paul What's His Name?'

She smiled. Everyone in LA knew his name, whether they liked him or not. 'No. I think he was a little worse.'

'Sonofabitch.'

'What about you?' The kids had gone back to school, and had eaten dinner at six. Mel and Peter were eating at eight.

'Three bypasses in a row. It wasn't a very exciting day.'

'I'm doing an interview with Louisa Garp.' She was the biggest star in Hollywood.

'You are?'

'I am.'

'When?'

'Next week. She accepted today.' Mel looked pleased and Peter was obviously impressed. 'Hell, I even did Dr Peter Hallam once.' She smiled and he reached out and took her hand. They were both so busy now, both had such hectic jobs. He hoped it didn't mean they'd never be able to spend time with each other. That wasn't the kind of life he liked. He liked knowing that his wife was there for him. And he wanted to be there for her too.

'I missed you today, Mel.'

'I missed you too.' But she also knew what the next two months would be like. She was going to scarcely see him at all. But maybe after that things would settle down.

They sat in the living room after dinner and talked for a while and Pam came down. Peter stretched an arm out to her. 'How's my girl?' She came to him with a smile. 'Did you know that Mel is doing an interview with Louisa Garp?'

'So?' She seemed to be bitchy all the time now, as though Mel were a real threat to her, and Peter looked annoyed.

'That's not a very pleasant thing to say.'

'Oh yeah?' She was asking for it, but Mel didn't say a word. 'So what? I got an A on my art history paper today.'

'That's great!' Peter let the second comment slide by.

Mel was furious and when the girl left she told him so. 'What did you want me to say? Last year the kid was flunking out, now she tells me she has got an A.'

'Terrific. But that doesn't cancel out her being rude to me.'

'For chrissake, Mel, give her time to adjust.' He was tired now. He'd had a long day. And he didn't want to come home to argue with Mel. 'Let's go upstairs to our room and close the door.' But as soon as they did, Jess came in, and Mel gently asked her to leave.

'Why?' She looked shocked.

'Because I haven't seen Peter all day, and we want to talk.'

'I haven't seen you either.' She was clearly hurt.

'I know. But we can talk in the morning, Jess. Peter will be at the hospital by then.' He left the room to take a shower and Mel kissed her cheek but Jess drew away.

'Never mind.'

'Jess, come on . . . it's hard cutting myself into pieces for everyone. Give me a chance.'

'Yeah, sure.'

'How's Val?'

'How do I know? Ask her. She doesn't talk to me any more, and you don't seem to have time to talk to us.'

'That's not fair.'

'Isn't it? It's true though. I take it he comes first.' She nodded towards the bathroom door.

'Jess, I'm married now. If I'd been married all these years, it would have been different than it was.'

'So I gather. Personally, I preferred it before.'

'Jessie . . .' Mel felt agonised as she looked at her oldest child. 'What's the matter with you?'

'Nothing.' But tears filled her eyes, and she sat down on her mother's bed, trying not to cry. 'It's just . . . I don't know . . .' She shook her head in despair and looked up at Mel. 'It's everything . . . a new school, a new room . . . I'll never see any of my friends again . . . I have to share a room with Val and she's such a pig. She takes all my stuff

305

and she never gives it back.' They were big problems to her and Mel's heart went out to her. 'And she cries all the time.'

'She does?' And just saying it made Mel think. She realised that Val had been crying a lot in the last few weeks. Maybe Peter had been right, and Val was sick. 'Is she all right, Jess?'

'I don't know. She acts weird. And she's always with Mark.' Mel made a mental note to say something again about that.

'I'll talk to them again.'

'It won't change anything. She's in his room all the time.'

Mel frowned. 'I specifically told her not to do that.' But there were other things that Mel had also specifically told her not to do, and Jess knew perfectly well that she did, but she would never have told her mother that. Mel put her arms around Jessica then and kissed her cheek and Jessie looked at her with a sad smile.

'I'm sorry if I was a bitch.'

'It's hard on all of us at first, but we'll get used to it. I'm sure it's hard on Pam and Mark and Matt to have us in the house too. Let's give everyone a little time to settle down.'

'What's all this?' Peter came out of the shower with a towel wrapped around his waist and smiled at Jess. 'Hi, Jess. Everything okay?'

'Sure.' She smiled and stood up. She knew she should leave them alone. She turned to Mel. 'Goodnight, Mom.' And as she left the room, it tore at Mel's heart to see her so sad. She didn't say anything to Peter about their exchange but it was one more burden on her heart as she went back to work the next day, and had to deal with Paul Stevens again, and that night when she came home, Peter called. There was an emergency he had to take care of himself, he'd be home in a 'while', and a while turned out to be eleven o'clock.

They never seemed to get off the merry-go-round any more, and for the next three weeks she was constantly out doing interviews, fighting with Paul Stevens before or after the show, or listening to Jessie's and Val's complaints when she got home. Mrs Hahn wouldn't let them in the kitchen for a snack. Pam was taking their clothes, Jess said that Val and Mark were locked in his room all the time, and to top it off at the end of January, Mel got a call from Matt's school. He had fallen out of a swing in the playground and broken his arm. Peter met them in the emergency room with an orthopaedist friend, and Mel joked tiredly that it was the first time they'd seen each other in weeks. He had had emergencies almost every night, endless bypasses to do, and two potential transplant patients had died for lack of donors' hearts.

'Do you think we'll survive, Mel?'

She collapsed on their bed in exhaustion one night. 'Some days I'm not sure. I've never done so many goddamn interviews in my life.' And she still felt as though she were living in someone else's home, which didn't help, but she hadn't had time to do anything about it yet. And she hadn't even had time to tackle the frozen Mrs Hahn. 'I wish you'd get rid of her,' Mel finally admitted to Peter one afternoon.

'Mrs Hahn?' He looked shocked. 'She's been with us for years.'

'Well, she's making life very tough for Val and Jess, and she certainly isn't pleasant to me. This might be a good time for a change.' There were a lot of changes she wanted to make around the house, but she didn't have time.

'That's an insane idea, Mel.' He looked angry at the mere thought. 'She's part of this family.'

'So was Raquel part of ours, and I had to leave her in New York.'

'And you resent me for that?' He was wondering if in transplanting Mel, he had asked too much. She was testy with him now all the time, and he knew that she wasn't crazy about her job. The money was fabulous, there was no denying that, but the conditions weren't as good as those she had known before, there was the endless prob-

307

lem with Paul Stevens, she said. 'You blame everything on me, don't you?' He was looking for a fight. For no reason he could explain, that morning a perfectly decent bypass patient had died.

'I'm not blaming anything on you.' She looked desperately tired as they talked. 'But the fact is that we both have enormous jobs that make tremendous demands on us, five kids, and a very demanding life. I want to make things easier in every possible way. And Mrs Hahn is complicating things.'

'Maybe for you, but not for the rest of us.' He looked stubbornly at Mel and she wanted to scream.

'And don't I live here too? Christ, between you and Pam . . .'

'Now what?' The remark didn't miss its mark.

'Nothing. She just resents our being here. I expected that.'

'And you don't think your daughters resent me? You're crazy if you think they don't. They're used to having a hundred per cent of your time, and every time we close our bedroom door now, they get pissed off.'

'I can't help that, any more than you can change Pam. They all need time to adjust, but Jess and Val have had the biggest change in their lives.'

'The hell they did. Pam lost her mom.'

'I'm sorry.' There was no talking about it with him, or touching the sacred subject of Anne. Mel had noticed that a few of Anne's pictures had gone back up, but she hadn't brought up the subject again, and her portrait was still in the hall.

'So am I.'

'No, you're not.' Mel wouldn't let the argument die, which was not wise. 'You expect us to make all the adjustments around here.'

'Is that right? Well, just exactly what do you think I ought to do? Move to New York?'

'No.' She looked him straight in the eye. 'Move to a new house.'

'That's absurd.'

'No, it's not, but changes scare you to death. When I came along, you were still sitting around with everything the same, waiting for Anne to come home. And now you've moved me into her house. It's okay for me to turn my whole life upside down, but you want everything just the way it was. And guess what? That doesn't work.'

'Maybe it's the marriage you want to move out of, Mel, and not the house.'

She stood staring at him from across the room, in total frustration and despair. 'Are you ready to quit?'

He sat down heavily in his favourite chair. 'Sometimes I am.' He looked up at her honestly. 'Why do you want to change everything, Mel? Mrs Hahn, the house, why can't you leave things as they are?'

'Because everything here is changed, whether you want to admit that or not. I'm not Anne, I'm me, Mel, and I want a life that's ours, not borrowed from someone else.'

'This is a new life.' But he didn't sound convinced.

'In an old house. Jess and Val and I feel like intruders here.'

'Maybe you're just looking for an excuse to go back to New York.' His face was grim, and Mel wanted to cry.

'Is that what you think?'

'Sometimes.' He was being honest with her.

'Well, let me explain something to you. I have a contract here. If you and I called it quits tonight, I'd still be stuck here for two years, like it or not. I can't go back to New York.'

'And you hate me for that.' It was a statement of his view of the facts.

'I don't hate you for anything. I love you.' She came and knelt beside his chair. 'And I want this to work, but it isn't going to happen by itself. We both have to be willing to change.' She reached up and gently touched his face.

'I guess . . .' Tears suddenly began to fill his eyes and he turned his head away and then looked back again. 'I

309

guess I thought . . . we could keep a lot of things . . . the same . . .'

'I know.' She reached up and kissed him. 'And I love you so much, but there's so much going on that my head spins sometimes.'

'I know.' Somehow they always found each other after the fights, but there were so many fights these days. 'I should have made you sign the contract in New York, Mel. It wasn't fair to drag you out here.'

'Yes, it was.' She smiled through her own tears. 'And you didn't drag me anywhere. I didn't want to stay in New York. All I wanted was to be here with you.'

'And now?' He looked frightened of what she would say.

'I'm glad we came. And in a while, it'll all fall into place.'

He took her hand then and led her gently to the bed and they made love as they had before, and Mel knew she had found him again. She didn't regret any of what she had done, but it had taken its toll, and there were pressures on all of them. She just hoped they'd all survive it, but with Peter strong at her side, she knew they would.

The only misery he couldn't seem to protect her from was at work, and in February he looked at her one night as she came home almost in tears.

'My God, if you only knew what a creep that man is.' Paul Stevens was driving her insane. 'One of these nights I'm going to kill him right on the set, when we're on the air.'

'Now that would be news.' He looked sympathetically at her. For once, things were a little quieter for him at work. 'I have an idea.'

'A hit man. That's the only thing I want to hear.'

'Better than that.'

'Cement shoes.'

Peter laughed. 'Let's all go skiing this weekend. It'll do everyone good. I'm not on call, and I hear the snow is great.' Mel looked wan at the thought. Just the idea of packing them all up exhausted her. 'What do you think?'

'I don't know.' She hated to be a spoilsport and for once Peter was in such a good mood. She smiled at him and he put his arms around her. 'Okay.' At least they'd get away from the problems in the house.

'Is it a deal?'

'Yes, Doctor.' She grinned, and went upstairs to tell the kids, but she found that Val was in bed with what looked like a bad case of flu. She was deathly pale, half asleep in bed, and when Mel touched her forehead, she felt terribly hot. And Mark was sitting worriedly near her bed. It didn't look any different from the flu's she had got so frequently in New York. She was made of much less rugged stuff than Jess. 'I've got good news,' she told Mark and the twins in the girls' room. 'Peter's taking us all skiing this weekend.' They all looked pleased but their reaction was subdued. Mark seemed terribly involved with Val, and Jessie seemed vague as she glanced at her twin.

'That's nice.' Val was the first to speak, but her voice sounded terribly weak.

'You okay, love?' She sat down on Val's bed, and the girl winced.

'I'm fine. Just the flu.'

Mel nodded, but she was still worried about Val. 'You think you'll be okay by this weekend, Val?'

'Sure.'

Mel went down the hall then to tell Pam and Matt and then came back with some aspirin and juice for Val, and then she went back downstairs.

'Everyone pleased?'

'I think so. But Val's sick.'

'What's she got?' He looked concerned. 'Should I go have a look?'

Mel smiled, but she knew her daughter better than that. 'I think she'd be embarrassed if you did. It's just the flu.'

He nodded. 'She'll be all right by the end of the week.'

'I still have to get her to that doctor you mentioned to

me.' But every time she had suggested it to Val, she had burst into tears and insisted she was fine. When they flew to Reno at the end of the week, and piled into a van for Squaw Valley, Val still looked terribly pale, but all of her other symptoms seemed to be gone, and Mel had other worries by then. Paul Stevens had made a major scene on the set just before they went on the air the night before she left for Reno. It was becoming an agony to go to work, and she dreaded each day more, but she was determined to stick it out no matter what. The weekends were a blessed relief now, especially this ski trip to Squaw Valley.

Peter had rented a van for them at the Reno airport, and they piled into it in high spirits, singing songs, helping each other with skis and bags. Peter stopped to kiss Mel before they climbed in the van, and the kids all hung out of the windows and hooted and cheered. Even Pam seemed in better spirits than she had been in over a month, and Val had a little colour in her cheeks, as they took off for Squaw Valley, and by the time they got there, everyone was laughing and joking and Mel was delighted that they had come. It would do them all good to leave LA and the house which was becoming such a source of contention between her and Peter.

He had found them a pleasant little condo, in a place where he and his children had stayed before. It was small but adequate for them. They slept as they had in Mexico, the girls in one room, the boys in another, and Mel and Peter in a third. And by lunchtime they were on the slopes, whooping and laughing and chasing each other down the mountain. As usual, Mark stayed close to Val, but there seemed to be less frivolity between them than there had been before, and Jess and Pam raced down the steepest trails with Matt just behind them.

At the end of their first run, Mel stopped breathlessly at the foot of the mountain and stood beside Peter as they waited for the others. It was exhilarating just to be there in the fresh mountain air, and Mel felt younger than she had in a long, long time. She looked at Peter with joy, and watched their children coming down the hill from over his shoulder.

'Aren't you glad we came up, Mel?'

She looked happily into his eyes. He was handsomer than ever, his blue eyes bright, his cheeks pink, his whole body filled with life. 'You know, you make me so damn happy.'

'Do I?' He looked hopeful, he loved her so much. He had never wanted to make her unhappy, but now and then he feared that he had, just by the very fact that he had brought her west and indirectly forced her into another job. Sort of like a mail-order bride. He smiled at the thought. 'I hope so. There's so much I want to do with you, and give you.'

'I know.' She understood him better than he knew. 'But we have so little time. Maybe as time goes on, we'll get better at juggling it all.' But there would always be interviews and features and news reports she had to do, and there would always be people who needed new hearts, or their old ones repaired. 'At least the children will settle down.'

'I wouldn't bet on that.' He laughed as he watched the five of them zoom towards them, with Matthew bringing up the rear, but not by much. He was almost as swift as the others. 'Not bad, you guys. Shall we try it one more time? Or do you want to stop for lunch now?' They had eaten on the plane, and bought sandwiches to eat in the van in Reno, but Jess was quick to speak up.

'I think Val should eat.' Mel was touched at how she still looked after her twin, and then noticed how pale the child was. She moved towards her, still on skis, and touched her forehead. She had no fever.

'You feeling okay, Val?'

'Sure, Mom.' But her eyes seemed a little vague, and on their way back up the mountain, Mel mentioned it to Peter again on the chair lift.

'I've got to get her to the doctor when we get home, no matter how much she cries and screams. I don't know why she's so dead set against going to a new doctor.'

Peter smiled as they floated through the air, past the

enormous pine trees on the way up the mountain. 'Two years ago I had to take Pam to her paediatrician for a checkup for school, and she ran all around the room, screaming so he couldn't give her her tetanus booster. The truth is that no matter how tall they are, or how adult they think they are, they're all kids. It's easy to forget it sometimes, because they seem so sophisticated. But it's all veneer. Underneath, they're no more mature than Matthew.'

Mel smiled her agreement as their skis dangled crazily in midair. 'You're right about Val, but I don't think that's true of Jessie. That kid has been an old soul from the day she was born, and she's always looked out for her sister. Sometimes I think I rely on her too much.'

Peter looked at her and spoke very gently. 'Sometimes I think you do too. She's been looking upset since you got out here. Is it me, or is she jealous of Val and Mark?' She hadn't been aware of the tension emanating from Jessie like barbed wire, and Mel was surprised that he had noticed. He was amazingly perceptive, particularly considering how little he saw of them because of his long hours in the hospital and in his office.

'I think it may be a little bit of both. She's used to having me to herself more than she does now. And I've been trying to iron things out with Pam, and Matthew needs me more than the others. He's been hungry for some loving for two years.'

Peter looked hurt. 'I tried.'

'I know you did. But you're not . . .' She leaned over and kissed him, and they sped off the lift at the top of the mountain. It was nice having time to talk to her husband. They had too little of it in LA, and they were both always exhausted. But here, even in a few hours, she felt as though they had made contact again. And she glanced back once or twice as they skied down the slopes, to make sure that the others were all there. She recognised them all by their colour combinations and their outfits. Jessica and Val in matching yellow ski suits, Mark in black and red,

Pam in red from head to toe, and Matthew in royal blue and yellow. She had worn a fur jacket and hat and black ski pants, and Peter was entirely clad in a navy blue stretch suit. They were a colourful bunch.

Towards the end of the afternoon, they all went inside for cups of hot chocolate, and then they went back out to the slopes. And this time the young people took a different trail from Mel and Peter, but by then Mel was confident that they were all good skiers and could take care of themselves, even Matthew, and she knew that Jessie would keep an eye on him, if Pam didn't. It was heavenly skiing beside Peter in the crisp mountain air, and on their last run they raced each other down the trail. Peter won by several yards and Mel was breathless and laughing when she joined him at last.

'You're terrific!' She gazed at him with admiration. He seemed able to tackle anything he wanted, and to do it well.

'Not any more. I was on the ski team in college, but it's been years since I took it seriously.'

'I'm glad I only met you now. I could never have kept up.'

'You're not bad.' He smiled and swatted her behind with a leather glove, and she giggled and they kissed, and then they left the slopes and took off their skis, and waited for the kids at the bottom. It seemed a long wait, but eventually, they all came down, Val in the rear this time. She seemed much slower than the others, and Jess turned back several times to watch her, as Mel narrowed her eyes and watched them.

'Is she all right?'

'Who?' He had been watching Matt. The boy was making amazing progress.

'Val.'

'Right behind Mark?' He couldn't see the colour of her hair in the white woolly hat, and he had mistaken Jess for her sister.

'No, she's the last one, still a little ways up, in the same

315

suit as Jess.' He looked and they both saw that she faltered once or twice, stumbled, caught herself, and then continued downhill, narrowly missing two skiers and flying between them. 'Peter . . .' Instinctively Mel grabbed his arm as they watched. 'Something's wrong.' But almost as she said it, Val seemed to loop crazily for a moment, regain her balance, and then she began weaving as all of them watched, and suddenly she fell just before the end of the slope; she fell sideways and her bindings released, but she lay face down in the snow, as Mel rushed to where she lay and Peter followed. He knelt quickly beside the unconscious girl, pulled her eyelids up, looked at her eyes, felt her pulse, and looked at Mel, unable to comprehend what had happened to her.

'She's in shock.' Without saying more, he unzipped his jacket and put it on her, and by reflex Jess did the same and handed hers to Peter, as the others stared at her in disbelief and Jess knelt beside her and held her hand. Peter looked around the group, hoping that the ski patrol would see them soon. 'Does anyone know what happened? Did she have a bad fall, hit her head? Could she have broken something? Even a bad sprain?' Mark was strangely silent and Pam shook her head as Matt began to cry and clung to Mel. And then suddenly Mel gave a shout as she watched her daughter's inert form; there was a huge red stain spreading up from where her trouser legs met, and even the snow around her was red.

'Peter, oh my God . . .' She pulled off her gloves and touched Val's face; it was like ice, but it was a cold that came from within.

Peter looked at his wife, and then down at his stepdaughter. 'She's having a haemorrhage.' Mercifully at that moment the ski patrol arrived, and two powerful young men wearing red and white arm bands knelt beside Peter.

'Bad fall?'

'No, I'm a doctor. She's having a haemorrhage. How fast can you get a stretcher for her?' One of them pulled out a small walkie-talkie and gave a red alert and their exact location.

'It should be here pretty quickly.' And almost before he had finished speaking, a stretcher on a sled appeared in the distance, with two men skiing with it. Mel was kneeling beside Val, her own jacket on top of the unconscious girl now, and she could see that in spite of their efforts her lips were turning blue. Mel eyed Peter frantically.

'Can't you do anything?' They were eyes filled with tears and accusations, and he looked at Mel almost with desperation. If they lost her, Mel would never forgive him. But he was absolutely helpless.

'We have to stop the bleeding, and get her a transfusion as quickly as we can.' He turned to the boy from the ski patrol then. 'How close is the nearest first-aid station?' The patrolman pointed to the very foot of the hill. It was barely more than a minute from where they stood. 'Have you got plasma?'

'Yes, sir.' Val was already on the sled, and she had left a huge puddle of blood in the snow behind her, as the whole family followed the sled to the little shelter.

Peter turned to Mel again. 'What's her blood type?'

'O, positive.'

Jessie was crying softly by then, as was Pam, and Mark looked as though he would be the next one in need of the sled. They unloaded Val as quickly as they could and carried her inside. There was a trained nurse there, and a doctor had been called. He was out on the slopes, bringing down a man with a broken leg, but Peter quickly propped Val's hips higher than her head, and the nurse helped him pull off her clothes as the others stood by. They began the plasma and an I.V., but Val showed no sign of coming round, and Mel's face was grim and filled with terror.

'My God, Peter . . .' There seemed to be blood everywhere and she turned to Jess suddenly, remembering Matthew, staring wide-eyed at his stepsister. 'Pam, take your brother outside.' She nodded dumbly and left as Mark and Jessica stood by, clinging to each other with a

317

vicelike grip, as Peter and the nurse fought to save Val's life and Mel watched.

The doctor arrived only minutes later, and added his efforts to Peter's. An ambulance had been called, and they had to get her to the hospital at once, it was obviously a gynaecological haemorrhage, but there was no way of knowing how it had started or why.

'Does anyone know . . .' The doctor began, and Mark stunned them all by stepping forward and speaking in a trembling voice.

'She had an abortion on Tuesday.'

'She what?' Mel felt the room spin around her as she stared at Mark and then Peter. He caught her just before she fell. The nurse brought smelling salts, and the doctor continued to work on Val. But it was obvious that only surgery would stop the bleeding, and even that wasn't sure now. She had lost massive amounts of blood, and Peter looked at his son in horror.

'Who in God's name did this?'

Tears stood out in Mark's eyes and his voice trembled hideously as he faced his father. 'We didn't want to go to anyone you knew, and that ruled out just about everyone in LA. Val wanted to go to a clinic. We went to one in West LA.'

'Oh, for chrissake . . . do you realise they may have killed her?' Peter was shouting in the tiny room and Mel began to sob as Jess clung to her mother.

'She's going to die . . . oh my God . . . she's going to die . . .' Jessica had totally lost control at the sight of her dying twin, and it brought Mel to her senses to see what was happening around her.

She spoke to Jess in a brutal voice, and hers was the only voice one heard in the tiny shelter. 'She's *not* going to die, do you hear me? She's not going to die!' She said it as much to God as to those in the shelter. And she glanced from Mark to Jess in sudden fury. 'Why in hell didn't any of you tell me?' There was only silence as she looked at Mark. It would have been too much to expect of them, to

318

tell her, and then she turned to Jess. 'And you! You knew!' It was a vicious accusation.

'I guessed. They never told me.' But her tone was as filled with fury as her mother's. 'And what difference would it have made if we had told you? You're always too busy with your job and your husband, and Pam and Matt. You might as well have left us in New York, you might as well – ' But she was silenced by a sharp crack across the face from her mother which sent her sobbing into the corner. The shriek of the ambulance suddenly echoed in the distance, and a moment later they were busy bundling Val into it, with two attendants and Mel beside her.

Peter spoke quickly to his wife. 'I'll follow you in the van.' He ran outside, leaving all their skis at the shelter. They could come back later, that was the least of their problems now. He started the engine, and the others silently hopped in. Jess and Mark beside him in the front, and Pam and Matthew in the back. No one said a word as they drove to the hospital in Truckee. It was Peter who first broke the silence.

'You should have told me, Mark.' It was a quiet voice in the silent car, and he could only begin to imagine what his son was going through.

'I know. Dad, will she make it?' His voice trembled and there were tears pouring down his face.

'I think so, if they get her there quickly. She's lost a lot of blood, but the plasma will help.' Jessica sat between them in stony silence, the mark of her mother's hand still on her face, and then Peter looked down at her, and touched her knee with one hand. 'She'll be all right, Jess. It looks worse than it is. It's impressive as hell when you see a lot of blood like that.' Jessica nodded and said nothing. And when they reached the hospital in Truckee, they all piled out of the car, but the young people got no farther than the waiting room. Peter and Mel went inside with Val while they prepped her, and Peter opted not to scrub and watch the surgery so he could stay with Mel while they waited. A gynaecological surgeon had been called, and Peter assumed he knew what he was doing. They were told only that she was in grave danger, and that there was a possibility that a hysterectomy would have to be performed. They wouldn't know till they got inside how bad the damage was. Mel nodded dumbly and Peter led her outside to wait with the others. She stayed noticeably away from Mark, and Jess kept her distance from her, and after a while, Peter went to his oldest son and gave him twenty dollars and told him to take the others to the cafeteria and get something to eat. Mark nodded and left, with the rest of the group in tow, but none of them was hungry. All they could think of was Val on the operating-room table. When they were gone, Mel turned to Peter with tears streaming from her eyes and sank onto his chest with a wail of despair. It was a scene he saw every day in the halls of Center City, but now it was happening to them . . . to Mel . . . to Val, and he had the same feeling he had had when Anne had died, of being utterly helpless. At least now he could help Mel. He held her tight in his arms, and made soft soothing noises.

'She'll be all right, Mel . . . she'll be – '

'What if she can never have babies?' Mel was sobbing uncontrollably in his arms.

'Then at least she'll be alive and we'll have her.' That would be something to be grateful for at least.

'Why didn't she tell me?'

'They were afraid to, I guess. They wanted to work it out for themselves.' It had been admirable but foolish.

'But she's only sixteen.'

'I know, Mel . . . I know . . .' He had suspected a while before that she and Mark had finally made love, but he hadn't wanted to say anything to upset Mel. And he realised now that he should have had a talk with Mark. He sat thinking about it all as they came back from the cafeteria and Mark slowly approached Mel and his father. Mel looked up at him miserably and continued to cry and he sat down and looked at her in as much pain as she.

'I don't know what to say . . . I'm sorry . . . I . . . I

never thought . . . I would never have let her . . .' He bowed his head in lonely grief as the sobs racked him, and Peter's heart went out to him as he took him in his arms with Mel, and suddenly Mel and Mark were clinging to each other and crying, and then Jessica was there too, and Pam and Matthew. It was a hideous scene, and the doctor came out and looked at them with a groan. Peter saw him first and disengaged himself from the others. He went to speak to the surgeon quietly, as Mel watched with terrified eyes.

'How did it go?'

The surgeon nodded, and Mel held her breath. 'She was lucky. We didn't have to remove her uterus. She just had a monstrous haemorrhage, but there's no permanent damage. I wouldn't suggest she try an abortion again though.' Peter nodded. Hopefully not.

'Thank you.' He extended a hand, and the two surgeons shook hands.

'I was told you're a doctor.'

'I am. Cardiac surgery. We're from LA.' The other surgeon narrowed his eyes, clapped a hand to his head and grinned.

'Oh, yes. I know who you are. You're Hallam!' He was so excited he could hardly stand it. And then he laughed. 'I'm glad I didn't know that before we went in. I'd have been a nervous wreck.'

'You shouldn't. I couldn't have done what you just did.'

'Well, I'm glad to have helped.' He shook Peter's hand again. 'Honoured.' Peter knew then that there would be no bill, and he was sorry, the man had done a fine job and he had saved Val's life and the lives of her future children, and maybe even Mark's. He wondered if this would end the romance now, or if it would pull them together closer. It had certainly pulled the family together in the last hour, and as they sat and waited for Val to come out of the anaesthetic, they began to come alive again. They talked and joked a little, but the atmosphere was generally subdued. It had been a heavy dose of reality for them all to live through. And before Val ever woke up, he took Pam and Matthew back to the condo. Mark and Jess had insisted on staying with Mel, and they wanted to see Val, but the other two looked worse than Val by then. Peter had insisted on taking them home no matter how much they protested.

'We want to see Val,' Matthew whined.

'They won't let you, and it's late, Matt.' His father was gentle but firm. 'You'll see her tomorrow, if it's allowed.'

'I want to see her tonight.' He led him outside and Pam followed with a last look at the others, and when Peter returned Val had just woken up and was back in her room, but she was too groggy to understand what they said to her. She just smiled and drifted off and when she saw Mark, she reached for his hand and whispered, 'I'm sorry . . . I . . .' And then she went back to sleep, and an hour later they all left and went back to the condo. It was almost midnight and everyone was exhausted.

Mel kissed Jessie goodnight and held her close for a long moment before she went to bed, and Jessica looked at her mother with sad eyes. 'I'm sorry I said what I did.'

'Maybe some of it was true. Maybe I have been too busy with the others.'

'There are a lot of us now, and there's a lot of pressure on you. I know that, Mom . . .' Her voice drifted off, remembering another time, another place . . . when they didn't have to share quite as much as they did now.

'That's no excuse, Jess. I'll try to do better from now on.' But how much better could she do? How many more hours were there in a day? How could she give each one what they needed, do her job, and even have time to breathe? She was a mother of five now, and the wife of an illustrious surgeon, not to mention co-anchor-woman on a TV news show. It barely left her time to breathe. And her daughter had accused her of being more interested in her stepchildren than in her own. Maybe she was trying too hard to please them all. She kissed Mark goodnight too, and then fell into bed with Peter, but as tired as she was, she couldn't sleep. She lay awake for hours thinking of what Jess had said, and of Val lying in the snow covered with blood. Peter felt her shudder beside him.

'I'll never forgive myself for not knowing what was going on.'

'You can't know everything, Mel. They're almost grown-up people now.'

'That's not what you said today. You said they were as grown up as Matthew.'

'Maybe I was wrong.' It had shocked him to realise that his son had almost become a father. But Mark had turned eighteen in August. In truth, he was a man. 'I know they're young, and they're too young to be doing what they are, making love, and getting pregnant and having abortions, but it happens, Mel.' He sat up on one elbow and looked down at his wife. 'They tried to work it out, you have to give them credit for that.' She wasn't ready to give them credit for a damn thing, nor herself.

'Some of what Jessie said was true, you know. I've been so involved with you, and Pam and Matthew, I haven't had much time for them.'

'You have five children now, and a job, and a bigger house to run, and me. Just how much can you expect of yourself, Mel?'

'More, I guess.' But she was exhausted at the thought.

'How much more can you do?'

'I don't know. But apparently I'm not doing enough, or this would never have happened to Val. I should have seen what was going on. I should have known, without being told.'

'What do you want to do? Play policeman? Give up your job, so you can drive car pools?'

It wasn't a very appealing thought, and they both knew it, but a little while later Mel answered in a small voice. 'That's what Anne did though, isn't it?'

'Yes, but you and she are different women, Mel. And I don't think she ever really felt fulfilled, if you want to know the truth. The difference is that you do. It makes

323

you a happier person.' It was a nice thing to have said, and she turned to him with a smile as they lay in the dark, with only the moonlight outside, casting soft shadows on them.

'You know, you make me feel better, Peter. About a lot of things. Most of all myself.'

'I hope I do. You make me feel better about me. I always feel that you respect what I do.' He took a deep breath. 'Anne never really approved of what I did.' He looked at Mel with a small smile. 'She thought transplants were disgusting and wrong. Her mother had been a Christian Scientist, and she always had a basic distrust the medical profession.'

'That must have been hard on you.' He had never told her before, and she was intrigued by the information.

'It was. I never fully felt I had her approval.'

'You have mine, you know, Peter.'

'I know that. And it means a lot to me. I think that was one of the first things I liked about you. I respected you, and I could feel that you respected me.' He smiled and kissed the tip of her nose. 'And then I fell in love with your sexy legs and here we are.'

She laughed softly in the darkness, amazed at how strange life was at times. Only hours before she had been hysterical, sure that she was about to lose her daughter, and now they were lying in the dark exchanging confidences and talking. But she realised something that she hadn't been aware of before. She and Peter had become friends over the past few months, best friends, and she had never been as close to anyone, woman or man. He had broken through the walls she had built over the years, and she hadn't even noticed. 'I love you, Peter Hallam, much, much more than you know.' And with that, she yawned, and fell asleep in his arms, and when he looked down at her, he saw that she was smiling.

CHAPTER 29

Peter took Mark and Jess and Matthew home on Sunday night, and Mel stayed in Truckee with Val. They gave up the condo and she took a room in a motel, and walked to the hospital every day, and on Wednesday the doctor said Val could fly home with her mother. Surprisingly, it was a nice time for both of them, and they talked to each other as they hadn't in years, about life, about boys, about Mark, about sex, about marriage and Peter, and Mel's life. When they landed in Los Angeles on Wednesday night, Mel felt that she knew Val as she never had before. And she only wished that she had that kind of time with them more often, without having to go through the trauma that they had just endured.

Val seemed in pretty good shape mentally as well. She felt terrible about having done away with an unborn child, but she had decided that having a baby at sixteen would have ruined her life and Mel couldn't disagree with her. It would have changed her whole life, and forced her into a lasting relationship with Mark, which may not have been what she would want later. She had admitted to her mother that she was ready to let go of him for a while, and see other boys. The intensity of their relationship scared her, and she didn't want the same thing to happen again. Mel was pleased with her conclusions, and maybe it had been a costly lesson that would serve her well for the rest of her life. She would never be cavalier about birth control, or getting involved in a sexual relationship without giving it serious thought. But she was sorry that she had to go through such misery. She had described the abortion to Mel, and Mel was astounded by her courage, and she told her as much.

'I don't think I could have done it.'

'I didn't feel like I had a choice. And Mark was there.' She tried to shrug it off, but they both knew she never would. Mel had held her close and they had cried, as Val told her.

'I'm sorry, baby.'

'Me too, Mom . . . I'm sorry . . .' She returned to LA contrite, and Mel noticed that night at dinner that she treated Mark more like a brother now, and he didn't seem to mind. There had already been a subtle change between them, and it was for the best. Peter had noticed it too, and mentioned it to Mel that night. 'I know.' She nodded. 'I think the big romance is over.'

'That's just as well.' Peter smiled tiredly. He had had a long day, and been in surgery for five hours that morning. He had come back to real life and a mountain of work waiting for him at Center City. 'We can let him loose on the neighbourhood now and wish him luck. I never realised what an agony it was to have daughters.' Even though he had done his share of worrying about Pam, but not in quite the same way as one worried about Val. It was that damn body of hers that worried one so. 'It's a damn shame she's not ugly.'

Mel grinned. 'Tell me about it. I've been getting grey hair over it for years.'

But by the next day she was back to getting grey hair in the newsroom. Paul Stevens had created all kinds of chaos while she was gone. She had called in sick for three days, and when she came back on Thursday morning, he had done everything he could to sabotage her. Fortunately, the producer knew what Stevens had in mind, that he hated Mel with a passion, so he hadn't done any real damage. But it was depressing to hear the gossip he had circulated about her, and to hear the trouble he had tried to create, by claiming she was hailed as a royal bitch in New York, and everyone there had hated her guts, that she had slept her way to the top, and any other bit of filth he could think of. Mel reported it all to Peter that night, and he was livid for her.

'Why, that little sonofabitch . . .' He had clenched a fist and Mel smiled tiredly at his reaction.

'He really is a bastard.'

'I'm sorry you have to go through that.'

'So am I. But there it is.'

'Why does he hate you so much?'

'Mainly, the difference in money, and also because he doesn't want to share the limelight. He hadn't had a co-anchor in years and he doesn't want one. Neither have I, but I figure you have to adapt to the situation. I'd like nothing better than to get rid of him, but I figure that it's not worth the aggravation.'

'Too bad he doesn't figure the same thing.'

'Isn't that the truth.'

And on and on it went for the next month, so much so that Mel began to feel ill most of the time. She had headaches, and a knot in her stomach that never went away, and she began to dread going to the station. She did as many interviews as she could, just to get away, but nowadays she was also trying to spend more time with the girls, particularly the twins. Jessica's speech hadn't gone unheeded at the time of Val's abortion. She had accused her mother of being more interested in Peter's children than them and now she was trying to shift the balance. But she sensed that Pam seemed to feel put aside, and she noticed her ganging up on her with Mrs Hahn whenever she could, and to alleviate that, Mel attempted to include Pam with the twins whenever possible, but it was difficult to keep everyone happy, and lately she had been feeling so lousy that it was difficult to meet their needs and hers too. She was out shopping with Matt one day when she actually had to sit down and catch her breath. She was so dizzy and nauseous that she thought she was going to faint in Safeway. She made him promise not to tell his father, but he was so upset he told Jess, who immediately told Peter when he came home. He glanced thoughtfully at Mel over dinner and then questioned her about it that night.

'You sick, Mel?'

'No, why?' She turned away so he wouldn't see her face.

'I don't know. A little bird told me that you didn't feel so hot today.' He was looking worriedly at her when she turned around.

'And what did the little bird say?' She wanted to feel out how much Peter knew.

'That you almost fainted at the grocery store.' He pulled her down on the bed next to him and looked closely at her. 'Is that true, Mel?'

'More or less.'

'What's wrong?'

She sighed and stared at the floor and then back at him. 'That Paul Stevens has been driving me crazy. I think I might have an ulcer, and I've been feeling lousy for the past few weeks.'

Peter looked at her unhappily. 'Mel, will you promise me you'll have it checked out?'

'Yeah,' she sighed, but she didn't sound sure. 'I really don't have time though.'

He grabbed her arm. 'Make time then.' He had lost one wife, and couldn't bear the thought of losing another. 'I mean it, Mel! Either that or I'll check you in the hospital myself.'

'Don't be silly. I just got dizzy.'

'Had you eaten?'

'Not in a while.'

'Then it might have been that. But I want you to check it out anyway.' And he noticed now that she had lost weight, her face was drawn and she looked pale. 'You look like hell.'

'Gee, thanks.'

He leaned over and took her hand. 'I'm just worried about you, Mel.' He pulled her close. 'I love you so damn much. Now will you call tomorrow and have someone check you out?'

'Okay, okay.' And the next morning he gave her a list of names, of doctors and specialists. 'You want me to see all of them?' She looked horrified and he smiled.

'One or two will do. Why don't you start with Sam Jones, and let him figure out who else you should see.'

'Why don't you just check me into the Mayo Clinic for a week?' She was teasing but he was not amused. She looked even worse than she had the night before.

'I just might.'

'The hell you will.'

She made an appointment with Sam Jones for that afternoon. It would have been a four-week wait, except that when she told the nurse who she was, miraculously, they found a spot for her that day. She stopped in at two P.M., and she had to be at work by four. Jones used every minute that he could, to take blood, do urine tests, go over her, take down a history, listen to her lungs, take her blood pressure. She felt as though he had touched and prodded every inch of her by the time he was through.

'Well, so far, you look all right to me. Tired maybe, but basically healthy. But let's see what all the lab tests say. Have you been feeling run-down for very long?' She told him all the symptoms she'd had, the queasiness, headaches, the pressure she was under at work, the move from New York, the change of jobs, Val's abortion, getting married, and adjusting to a whole new set of kids, while living with the ghost of Peter's late wife, in the house she still didn't feel at home in.

'Stop!' He fell back in his chair with a groan, clapping a hand to his head. 'I'm beginning to feel queasy too. I think you've just given your own diagnosis, my friend. I don't think you needed me at all. You need six weeks on a sandy beach.'

She smiled at him. 'I wish. But I told Peter all it was was nerves.'

'You may be right.' He offered her Valium, Librium, or sleeping pills and she declined them all. When she saw Peter that night, she told him what Sam Jones had said.

'See, there's nothing wrong with me. I'm just over-worked.' They both knew that anyway, but he still wasn't convinced. He was inclined to be overly cautious about her, and Mel knew that.

'Let's see what the lab tests say.'

She rolled her eyes and went to put Matthew to bed. Pam was listening to her stereo, and the girls were doing homework in their room. Mark was out. The grapevine had told Mel a few days before that he had a new girlfriend, a freshman at UCLA, and Val didn't seem bothered at all. There was a boy in her class she said was 'really cute', and Jessica had finally found someone she liked who had taken her out on two dates. All was well with all of them for once. She returned to Peter with a happy sigh. 'All's quiet on the Western Front at least.' She reported on them all and he was pleased. Things were finally settling down after all, or so he thought. But neither of them was prepared for the news they got the next day.

Mel forgot to call Dr Jones before she left for work, and there was a message for her to call him at home when she got in. Peter saw the message first and called Sam himself, but his old colleague and friend would say nothing at all to him. 'Have your wife call me when she gets home, Pete.'

'For chrissake, Sam, what's wrong?' He was terrified but Jones would not relent, and Peter pounced on Mel the moment she walked through the door. 'Call Jones!'

'Now? Why? I just walked in, can I at least hang up my coat?'

'For chrissake, Mel . . .'

'Jesus.' She looked at the worried look in his eyes, wondering what he wasn't telling her. 'What's wrong?'

'I don't know. He won't tell me a thing.'

'Did you call him?' She looked annoyed.

He confessed. 'Yes. But he wouldn't tell me anything.'

'Good.'

'For chrissake . . .'

'All right, all right.' She dialled the home number he had left, and Mrs Jones went to get her husband. Peter hovered over Mel but she waved him away. She and the doctor went through the usual small talk before getting down to why he had called her.

'I didn't want to tell Peter before I told you.' He sounded serious and Mel held her breath. Maybe Peter was right. Maybe something awful was wrong with her. 'You're pregnant, Mel, but I thought you'd like to tell him that yourself.' He was beaming at his end, but Mel was not at hers. She wore a glazed expression and Peter stared at her, convinced it was bad news. He sank slowly into a chair and waited until she hung up.

'Well?'

It was difficult to fend him off. He was just sitting there, watching.

'What did he say?'

'Nothing much.'

'Bullshit!' Peter leapt to his feet in the front hall. 'I saw your face. Now are you going to tell me yourself or am I going to call him back?'

'He won't tell you a thing.'

'The hell he won't.' Peter was beginning to steam, and Mel felt as though she were in shock. She stared at him and stood up.

'Could we go in your study and talk?' He said not a word but followed her in and shut the door. She sat down again and stared at him. 'I don't understand it.'

'Tell me what he said, and I'll try and explain it to you, Mel, but for God's sake tell me what's wrong.'

And this time, she smiled. He was expecting complicated results, but there was nothing complicated about what Jones had told her. The only thing complicated about it was what it was going to do to her life. 'I'm pregnant.'

'You're what?' He stared at her in disbelief. 'You're not?'

'I am.'

And suddenly he grinned. 'Well, I'll be damned. You are?'

'I am.' She looked as though she'd just been run over by

331

a train, and he came to her side and pulled her into his arms.

'That's the best news I've had in years.'

'It is?' She still looked shocked.

'Hell, yes.'

'For chrissake, Peter, that's all we need. We're already drowning in the responsibilities we have. And a baby? Now? I'm thirty-six years old, we have five children between the two of us . . .' She was horrified at the thought, and he looked crushed.

He tried to sound matter-of-fact as he asked, 'Will you abort it?'

She stared into space remembering what Val had said about going to the abortion clinic with Mark. 'I don't know. I don't know if I could.'

'Then there's no decision to be made, is there?'

'You make it sound awfully simple.' She stared at him unhappily. 'But it isn't as simple as all that.'

'Sure it is. You have a maternity clause in your contract. You told me so.'

'Christ. I forgot.' And then she began to laugh as she remembered how amused she had been at that. And suddenly it all seemed very funny to her. She began to laugh and laugh and laugh and Peter kissed her cheek and took a bottle of champagne from the bar. He popped the cork, and poured a glass for each of them and toasted her.

'To us.' And then, 'To our baby.'

She took a sip and set it down again rapidly. It made her queasy almost at once. 'I can't.' She literally turned green before his eyes, and he set down his own glass and came to her.

'Sweetheart, are you all right?'

'I'm fine.' She smiled and leaned against him, still unable to believe the irony of it all. 'I have daughters who are almost seventeen, and I'm pregnant. Would you believe . . .' She began to laugh again. 'I can't even figure out how it happened, unless you put a hole in my diaphragm.'

'Who cares? Look at it as a gift.' He looked soberly at his

wife. 'Mel, I deal with death every day of the week. I fight it, I hate it, I try to outsmart it by putting plastic hearts in people's chests, pig's valves, and valves from sheep, I do transplants, I do anything I can to cheat that old boy death always watching over me. And here you are, with a precious gift of life, given to us gratuitously. It would be criminal not to appreciate that.'

She nodded quietly, touched by what he had said. What right did she have to question such a gift? 'What'll we tell the kids?'

'That we're having a baby, and we're thrilled. Hell, I thought you were sick.'

'So did I.' She smiled, feeling better again now that the champagne was far from her lips. 'I'm glad I'm not.'

'Not half as glad as I am, Mel. I couldn't live without you.'

'Well, you won't even have to try.' And with that, Matthew came and pounded on the door to announce that it was dinnertime and before they went into the dining room to eat, Peter called them all into the living room and made a little speech.

'We have something exciting to tell you all.' Peter beamed and looked at Mel.

'We're going to Disneyland next week!' Matt filled in and everyone laughed and began to offer their best guess. Mark thought they were building a tennis court, Pam thought they were buying a yacht, the twins decided on a Rolls-Royce, and a trip to Honolulu, an idea of which everyone approved, and each time Peter shook his head.

'Nope. Not quite. Although Honolulu does sound nice. Maybe at Easter time. But we have something much more important to tell you than that.'

'Come on, Dad, what is it?' Matthew was dying to know, and Peter looked straight at him.

'We're having a baby, Matt.' He looked at them all, and Mel watched their faces too, but they were no more prepared for the reactions they got from the kids than they had been for the test results from Sam Jones.

'You're what?' Pam leapt to her feet, clearly horrified, and she stared at Mel in disbelief. 'That's the most disgusting thing I've ever heard.' And with that she burst into tears and fled to her room, as Matthew looked at them with trembling lip.

'We don't need another kid around here. We've already got five.'

'But it might make a nice friend for you, Matt.' Peter looked at him as tears filled the child's eyes. 'The others are so much older than you are.'

'I like it like that.' He followed his sister to his room, and Mel turned to her own children, to see Val dissolve in tears.

'Don't expect me to be pleased for you, Mom.' She stood up and her copious bosom heaved. 'I just killed my baby two months ago, and now I suppose you expect me to be pleased about yours?' She ran from the room in tears, and Mark shrugged, but he didn't seem to think it was much of an idea either. Jessica simply stared at them, stricken. It was as though she knew how much they already had on their backs, and couldn't understand how they could even consider taking on more. And the worst of it was that Mel thought she was right. She went upstairs with the excuse of checking on her twin and Mark disappeared too. They sat alone in the living room, as Mel wiped tears from her own eyes.

'Well, so much for that.'

'They'll come round.' He put an arm around his wife, and looked up to see Hilda Hahn staring at them.

'The dinner is getting cold.' She looked fierce, and Mel stood up, obviously depressed. The children were all in an uproar at the prospect of another child, and she was still having problems at work. Somehow it all seemed like more than she could cope with right now, and they went in to dinner, as Mel felt her heart drag. And she looked up to see Mrs Hahn staring at her.

'I couldn't help overhearing the news.' Her heavy German accent always grated on Mel's nerves, there was nothing warm or kindly about the way she spoke, unlike the other German women Mel had known. And she stared at Mel again now. 'Isn't it dangerous to have a baby at your age?'

'Not at all' – Mel smiled sweetly – 'I'm only fifty-two.' Knowing full well that Mrs Hahn was fifty-one. Peter smiled at her. Anything that Mel did now was okay with him. And he didn't give a damn how their kids behaved, he was thrilled and he wanted Mel to know it. But she couldn't eat dinner, all she could think of was the children and their reactions. She went up to see them, but all doors were closed and nowhere did she get a warm reception. When she came downstairs to their bedroom, Peter insisted that she lie down, and she laughed at him. 'I'm only about four or five weeks pregnant, for chrissake.'

'Never mind. You might as well start out right.'

'I think we did that in the living room about two hours ago.' She sighed as she lay on their bed. 'That was some reception we got, wasn't it?' Their reactions had cut her to the quick, and left her feeling unprotected and unwanted and alone.

'Give them a chance. The only ones who really have grounds to be upset are Val and Matt, and I'm sure they'll both survive the shock.'

'Poor Matt.' Mel smiled thinking of him. 'He wants to be our baby, and I don't blame him a bit.'

'Maybe it'll be a girl.' Peter looked thrilled and Mel groaned.

'Not another one. We already have three.' She was already adjusting to the idea and the miracle of it seemed remarkable to her. They talked about it that night for hours, and he kissed her tenderly the next morning before he left. But when she went down to breakfast and saw Matt and Pam and the twins, she felt as though she had ventured into the enemy camp. She looked around at them and felt despair wash over her. They would never adjust.

'I'm sorry you all feel this way.' Val wouldn't look her in

the face, and Jess looked intensely depressed, Matthew wouldn't touch anything on his plate, and when Mel looked into Pam's eyes she was terrified by what she saw there – hatred and fury mixed with terror. It was as though she had run away to a distant place in her head where Mel could no longer reach her.

Of all of them, Pam was by far the most upset. Mel tried to talk to her about it that day when she came home from school, but when Mel went up to her room, she slammed the door in her face, and locked the door. Even when Mel pounded on it, she wouldn't open it again.

Theirs became a house filled with grief, and hurt and anger. It was as though they each wanted to punish her, each in their own way, Mark by never being home, to his father's despair, the twins by keeping away from her and shutting her out, Matt by whining all the time and having trouble at school, and Pam by turning off and skipping school. They called Mel four times in as many weeks that Pam had disappeared before her second class, and when she questioned the child about it, she shrugged and went upstairs and locked her door. Her final act of viciousness was to hang her mother's portrait boldly over the bed in Mel and Peter's room. When Mel came home one day and saw it there, she gasped and stared.

'Did you see her do this?' she asked Mrs Hahn, as she held the portrait of Anne in trembling hands.

'I see nothing, Mrs Hallam.' But Mel knew that she had. When they called Mel from Pam's school again to tell her that she had cut class again, she decided to stay home that day and wait for her to turn up. But by four o'clock she still had not. And this time Mel began to wonder if there was a boy involved. At five o'clock, she sauntered in with a grin on her face, amused that Mel had waited for her all day long, and when Mel took a good look at her, she could see that the girl was stoned. She sent her to her room after confronting her, then left for the newsroom. Later, she told Peter what she thought.

'I really doubt that, Mel. She's never done that before.'

'Take my word for it.' But he shook his head. He didn't believe his wife, and when he questioned Pam, she denied everything Mel said. Pam was beginning to cause a serious rift between them, and Mel felt she was losing her only ally now. Peter always took Pam's side against her. Her home was filled with enemies, and it wasn't even her home, and now Peter was on his daughter's side. 'Peter, I know that she was stoned.'

'I just don't think she was.'

'I think you should talk to her school.' When Mel attempted to discuss it with Val and Jess, they were distant but polite. They didn't want to get involved, nor did Mark. Mel was a pariah now, to all of them, because of the unborn child she was carrying. She had betrayed them.

And two weeks later when the L.A.P.D. called, it was an empty victory. She had been right. Pam had been caught buying a lid of grass from some kids downtown when she should have been in school. Peter went right through the roof and threatened to send her to boarding school, but again the child turned on Mel. 'You turned him against me. You want me sent away.'

'I want no such thing. But I want you to behave, and I think it's about time you did, time you stopped cutting school every other day, and smoking grass, and behaving like a little beast around this house. This is your home and we love you, but you can't behave any way you want. In every society, in every community, in every home, there are rules.'

But as usual, Peter let Pam off the hook, put her on restriction for a week and let it go at that. He didn't back the position Mel took, and two weeks later, Pam was picked up again. This time she got even more attention than before, and Peter called up her old psychiatrist. A series of appointments were set up and he asked Mel if she could get Pam there. And the result of that was that Mel had to almost drag her there four times a week, break her neck to get to work, and run home again at night, trying to pay some attention to Matt and the twins. All she wanted to do was sleep, between throwing up the heavy meals persistently prepared by Mrs Hahn.

'This is what the doctor likes,' she'd say as she put another plate of sauerkraut in front of Mel, and finally after a month of it, she wound up in the hospital one Friday night with bleeding and cramps, and her obstetrician looked at her soberly.

'If you don't slow down, you're going to lose the baby, Mel.'

Tears filled her eyes. Everything was a fight these days. 'I don't think anyone would give a damn.'

'Would you?'

She nodded her head, tired, sad. 'Yeah, I'm beginning to think I would.'

'Then you better tell everyone around you to shape up.'

Peter came to see her the next day, and looked mournfully at her. 'You don't really want the baby, do you, Mel?'

'Do you think I'm trying to get rid of it?'

'That's what Pam says. She says you went horseback riding last week.'

'*What?* Are you crazy? Do you think I'd do that?'

'I don't know. I know this interferes with your work, or you think it will.' She stared at him in disbelief, got out of bed, and packed her bag. 'Where are you going?'

She turned to look at him. 'Home. To kick your daughter.'

'Mel, come on . . . please . . .' But she checked out of the hospital, and went home, climbed into bed, despite all of Peter's apologies, and that afternoon she went downstairs and ordered Mrs Hahn to make chicken and rice that night, something *she* could eat for a change, and she literally lay in wait until all of the children came home. By six o'clock they were all there, surprised to see her again. And when they came downstairs to eat, she was waiting at the table, with eyes of fire.

338

'Good evening, Pam.' She started with her. 'How was your day?'

'Fine.' She attempted to look confident, but she kept glancing nervously at Mel. 'I understand that you told your father I went horseback riding last week. Is that true?' There was dead silence in the room. 'I repeat. Is that true?'

Her voice was low. 'No.'

'I can't hear you, Pam.'

'No!' She shouted at Mel, and Peter reached for his wife's arm.

'Mel, please, don't upset yourself . . .'

Mel looked him right in the eye. 'We need to clear the air. Did you hear what she said?'

'I did.'

Mel turned back to Pam. 'Why did you tell your father a lie? Did you want to make trouble for us?' Pam shrugged. 'Why, Pam?' She reached out and touched the girl's hand. 'Because I'm having a baby? Is that so awful that you have to punish me? Well, I'll tell you something, no matter how many babies we have, we'll still love you.' She saw Pam's eyes fill with tears while Peter kept his grip on her arm. 'But if you don't knock off the trouble you've been pulling ever since I moved in, I'm going to kick your behind from here to the other side of town.' Pam smiled through her tears and looked at Mel.

'Would you really do that?' She sounded almost pleased. It told her they cared about her, still.

'I would.'

Mel looked around the rest of the table then. 'And that goes for the rest of you too.' She softened her voice as she looked at Matt. 'You're always going to be our baby, Matt. This one will never take your place.' But he didn't look as though he believed her. Then she turned to the twins. 'And you two.' She looked specifically at Val. 'I didn't plan the timing of this to hurt you, Val. I couldn't know what was going to happen any more than you planned what happened to you, and the two of you have been totally insensitive about how I feel, and I think it's lousy of you.' She turned to Mark then, 'And frankly, Mark, I'm surprised to see you here tonight. We don't seem to see much of you any more. Did you run out of funds so you had to eat here for a change?'

'Yeah.' He grinned.

'Well, I think you ought to keep in mind that as long as you're living at home, you have a responsibility to this family to be here more than once a month. We expect to see a little more of you than we have lately.'

He looked startled by what she said, and subdued as Peter watched. 'Yes, ma'am.'

'And Pam' – Peter's only girl looked at her cautiously – 'from now on you take yourself to the psychiatrist. You can take the bus just like everyone else. I'm not going to drive you all over town. If you want to see him, you can get there by yourself, but I'm not going to drag you there by the hair. You're almost fifteen years old. It's time you took some responsibility for yourself.'

'Do I have to take the bus home from school?' Matt piped up hopefully. He loved the bus, but Mel smiled and shook her head.

'No, you don't.' She looked around the table then. 'I hope I've made myself clear to all of you. For your own reasons, you've all behaved like little beasts since your father and I told you that I was pregnant, and personally I think it stinks. I can't change what you feel, but I can change how you act, and I'm not willing to accept the way you've been treating me, all of you' – her eyes even took in Mrs Hahn – 'there's room for everyone here, for you, for me, for your father, this baby, but we have to be nice to each other. And I'm not going to let you go on punishing me' – tears suddenly sprang to her eyes and overflowed – 'for this unborn child.' And with that she threw down her napkin and went upstairs, not having touched a morsel of food, but at least she had proved a point with that too, and Mrs Hahn had actually produced salad, and roasted chicken, and rice. Peter looked around at all of them.

They looked embarrassed and subdued, as well they should have, and they knew it.

'She's right, you know. You've all been rotten to her.'

Pam tried to stare him down, but it didn't work, and Mark squirmed uncomfortably in his seat, as Val hung her head. 'I didn't mean to . . .'

Jess spoke up too. 'Yes, you did. We all did. We were mad at her.'

'It isn't fair to take it out on her like that.'

'It's okay, Dad. We'll be good now.' Matt patted his father's arm and they all smiled, and a few minutes later Peter took a plate up to their room where she lay crying on the bed.

'Come on, sweetheart, don't get so upset. I brought you something to eat.'

'I don't want to eat. I feel sick.'

'You shouldn't get excited like that, it's bad for you.' She turned around to look at him in disbelief.

'Bad for me? Do you ever think how bad for me it is to have everyone in this house treat me like dirt?'

'They'll shape up now.' She didn't answer him. 'And you shouldn't be so hard on them, Mel. They're just kids.'

She narrowed her eyes and looked at him. 'I don't count Matt because he's six years old and he has a right to be mad about this, but the others are practically adults, and they've stomped all over me for the past month. Pam even told you a blatant lie so that you'd think I was trying to lose our child, and you believed her!' Suddenly she was raging at him, and he hung his head, and then finally he looked at her.

'Well, I know this baby will interfere with your work, and you didn't want it at first.'

'I'm not even sure I want it now. But it's there for chrissake, and that's another thing. Just where do you think we're going to put it in this house?'

'I hadn't thought of that.'

'I didn't think you had.' She looked depressed. She didn't want to fight with him, but in his own way he was

341

hurting her too. She spoke more quietly to him. 'Can we finally sell this place?'

He looked horrified. 'Are you out of your mind? This is my children's home.'

'And you built it with Anne.'

'That's beside the point.'

'It's not to me. And there's no room for our baby here.'

'We'll add on a wing.'

'Where? Above the swimming pool?' It was an absurd idea and he knew that.

'I'll call my architect and see what he suggests.'

'You're not married to him.'

'And I'm not married to you. You're married to that job you bitch about so much.'

'That's not fair.'

His rage continued. 'And you wouldn't give it up for a day, would you? Even if it cost you our child . . .' You could hear their voices across the house.

'It won't.' She leapt off the bed and confronted him. 'But you and the children will if you don't all get off my back and start doing something for me for a change. They want to take it out on me for daring to get pregnant, and you want to squash me into your old life, while your daughter puts her mother's portrait over my bed.'

'Once. Big deal.' He looked unimpressed.

'That thing shouldn't even be in this house.' And then she stared at him. It had gone too far. 'And neither should I. In fact' – she stalked to the closet, pulled out a case and threw it on the bed, then marched to her chest of drawers and began throwing things into the open suitcase – 'I'm getting out until you all think this out. Those kids, all of them, damn well better behave, and you'd better stop treating Pam like a little wilting flower with a head of glass or she's going to wind up a junkie or some other crazy thing by the time she's sixteen. There's nothing wrong with that kid that a whole lot of discipline won't cure.'

'May I remind you that *my* daughter is not the one who got pregnant earlier this year.' It was a low blow and he

342

knew it as soon as the words were out. But it was too late to turn back now.

Mel stared at him with hatred in her eyes. 'Touché. And we can thank your son for that.'

'Look, Mel . . . why don't we calm down and talk . . .' He was suddenly frightened by the look in her eyes, and he knew she wasn't supposed to get upset, but she had made him so angry.

'You're half right at least. I'm going to calm down, but we are not going to talk. Not now anyway. I'm walking out of here tonight, and you can manage the kids on your own. In fact, you can sit here and figure out what you want to do about them, this house, and me.'

'Is that an ultimatum, Mel?' His voice was strangely still.

'Yes, it is.'

'And what do you do in the meantime?'

'I'm going away to make up my mind about a few things myself. What I want to do about living in this house, whether or not I want to quit my job, and if I want to get rid of this kid.'

'Are you serious?' He looked shocked, but she suddenly looked frighteningly calm.

'I am.'

'You'd get rid of our child?'

'I might. You all seem to assume that I have to do as I'm told, what's expected of me. I have to be here day after day, I have to put up with Mrs Hahn, I have to take anything the kids dish out, I have to live with Anne's pictures staring me in the face, I have to drive Pam to the psychiatrist day after day, I have to have this baby no matter what . . . Well, guess what? I don't. I have choices to make too.'

'And I have nothing to say about any of it?' He looked furious again.

'You've said enough. You defend Pam every time I open my mouth. You tell me how marvellous Mrs Hahn is and I tell you I hate her guts, and you tell me this is your house,

343

and you assume that I have to have our child. Well, I don't. I'm thirty-six years old and frankly I think I'm too old for this. And I'm much too old to be taking this kind of dirt from anyone, you, or the kids.'

'I wasn't aware I'd been giving you dirt, Mel.'

She looked sadly at him. 'I've changed my whole life for you in the past six months, given up my job, my home, my town, my independence. I have a job out here which may or may not work out, but is something of a step down for me, and working with a real sonofabitch. You don't seem to appreciate any of that. And for you, everything is status quo. Your kids still have their own rooms, own house, pictures of their mom everywhere, their housekeeper, their dad. The only inconvenience is that now they have to put up with me. Well, if any of you expect me to stick around, maybe you'd all better start thinking about what changes you're going to make. Or I may make a few big changes and go home.'

He looked terrified but his voice was firm. 'Mel, are you leaving me?'

'No, I'm not. But I'm going away for a week to think things out for myself, and decide what I want to do.'

'Will you have the abortion while you're gone?'

She shook her head and fought back tears. 'I wouldn't do that to you. If that's what I decide, I'll tell you first.'

'It's getting awfully late for that. There would be a risk involved.'

'Then I'll have to take that into consideration too. But right now, I'm going to think about what *I* want, not what you want, or you expect, or what makes you comfortable or the kids need. I have needs too, and no one has given two dots about them in a long time, not even me.' He nodded slowly; devastated that she would leave, even for a week.

'Will you let me know where you are?'

'I don't know.'

'Do you know where you're going?'

'No, I don't. I'm going to get in the car and drive, and

344

I'll see you in a week.' She was leaving him with a lot to think about. She wasn't going to be the only one thinking things out that week.

'What about your work?'

'I'll tell them I'm sick again. I'm sure Paul Stevens will be thrilled.'

And he knew that he had to say something to her then, before she left, before she threw it all away in her head. 'I won't be, Mel. I'll miss you terribly.'

She looked sad as she walked away with her case. 'So will I. But maybe that's the whole point of this. Maybe it's time we both figured out how much this all means to us, how much it's worth, how much we're willing to pay for what we want. I don't know any more, I thought I did, but suddenly I wonder about it all, and I need to think it out.' He nodded, and watched as she walked out the door, and a moment later he heard the front door close behind her. He had wanted to take her in his arms, to tell her he loved her more than life itself, that he wanted their child, but he had been too proud, he had only stood there. And now she was gone. For a week. For longer? Forever?

'Where's Mom?' Val looked in, in surprise, as she passed their room.

'Out.' He stared at her. 'Gone.' He decided to tell her the truth. He would tell them all. They deserved to know. They had played a part in it too. They were all responsible for how she felt. He wouldn't take the blame alone, although he realised now that a good part of it was his. He had been so damn stubborn about the house, about everything. She had made all the changes required for their new life, and he had made none. She was right, it wasn't fair. He looked sadly at Val now, who didn't seem to understand.

'Gone? Gone where?'

'I don't know. She'll be back in a week.' And then Val simply stood and stared at him. She understood. They'd all gone too far. But they had all been so damn mad at her, and she had been too. It didn't seem worth it now.

'Will she be okay?'

'I hope so, Val.' He walked into the hall and put an arm around her as Jess came up the stairs and looked at them.

'Did Mom go out?'

'Yeah.' Val answered for him. 'She left for a week.' And as the rest of them came up the stairs, they heard what Val said, and they simply stood where they were and stared at him.

CHAPTER 30

When Mel left the house that night, she simply got in the car and drove, with no set plan of where to go, no one she wanted to see. All she wanted to do was get away, from her house, her job, their kids, and him. And for the first fifty miles, all she thought of was where she was leaving from, not where she was going to.

But after that, she began to relax, and suddenly after almost two hours, she stopped for petrol, and grinned to herself. She had never done anything quite as outrageous in her life. But she couldn't take any more. Everyone was pushing her, and it was time she thought of herself instead of all of them. Even as far as this baby was concerned. She didn't have to do a damn thing she didn't want to. Hell, she made a million bucks a year, she could buy her own goddamn house, she told herself. She didn't have to live with Anne's ghost, if she didn't want to, and she already knew that she did not. And as she began driving again, with a full tank of petrol, she began thinking of all the changes she had made in her life in the last six months, and how few changes had been required of Peter. He still worked in the same place, with the same people who respected his work, slept in the same bed he had slept in for a number of years. His children hadn't been moved out of their home. He even had the same housekeeper. The only thing that had changed for him was the face he kissed before he left the house for work, and maybe he didn't even notice that. And as Mel pulled into Santa Barbara, she began to steam again, and was glad she'd left. She was only sorry she hadn't done it before, but who had time, between driving Pam to her psychiatrist, trying to pacify the twins, keep a remote eye on Mark, and play Mommy to Matthew, hold Peter's hand when his transplant patients died, not to mention doing interviews, specials, and the six-o'clock news every night? It was a wonder she had time to dress and comb her hair. To hell with all of them. Peter, the kids, and Paul Stevens. Let him anchor alone for a while, they could always say that she was sick. To hell with them. She didn't care.

She pulled into a motel and paid for a room, which looked like it could have been anywhere in the world, from Beirut to New Orleans, when she glanced at the rust-coloured shag rug on the floor, the orange vinyl chairs, the spotless white tile bathroom, the rust-coloured bedspread. It was definitely not the Bel-Air, or even the Santa Barbara Biltmore where she had stayed years before, and she didn't give a damn. She took a hot bath, turned on the TV, watched the news when it came on at eleven o'clock, by habit more than desire, and turned out the light without calling home. Screw them all, she thought to herself, and for the first time in months she felt free, to do what she wanted to do, to be herself, to make up her own mind without considering a living, breathing soul.

As she lay in bed, she thought of what was inside her, and realised that even here she wasn't totally alone. The baby had come with her . . . the baby . . . as though it were already a person separate from herself . . . She laid a hand on her stomach, which had been so flat a month before, and now there was a small but distinct bulge where the hollow between her hip bones had been. It was odd to think what would happen if she went on with the pregnancy. The baby would become real to her, she would feel it move in about six weeks . . . for a tiny moment, there was a tender feeling deep inside her, and then she let it go. She didn't want to think of that right now. She didn't want to think of anything. She closed her eyes and went to sleep, without dreaming of Peter, or the children or their unborn child, or anything. She just lay in bed in the motel room and slept, and when she woke up the next day, the sun was streaming into her room, and she couldn't remember where she was at first. When she looked around and realised where she was, she laughed to herself. She felt good, and strong, and free.

When Peter woke up that morning in Bel-Air, he reached over to the other side of the bed, instinctively feeling for her, and when his hand and leg met smooth, empty sheets, he opened one eye, and remembered with a sinking heart that she was gone. He turned over and lay staring up at the ceiling for a long time, wondering where she was, and remembering why she had gone. It was really all his fault, he told himself, you couldn't blame the kids, or Paul Stevens at her job, or Mrs Hahn. It was that he had done everything wrong from the first. He had expected too much of her, expected her to change her entire life . . . for him. And he knew she regretted everything she'd done. He lay there reproaching himself, thinking of how much she loved her life in New York, and wondering how he had even dared to think she could give that up. A job that any man in the country would have drooled to have, a house she loved, her friends, her life, her town . . .

And as Melanie began driving slowly north, she thought of Peter's face the first time they had met, those endless first days during the interview, the exhausting hours they shared when the President had been shot . . . his first trip to New York. She began to think not so much of what she'd had there, but what she'd got in exchange . . . the first time Matt had climbed into her lap . . . a look in Pam's eyes once or twice . . . the moments when Mark had clung to her and cried when Val almost died on their skiing trip. Suddenly it was difficult to exorcise them all from her life. Her anger now was directed more at the twins, at Jess for expecting too much of her, for expecting her to be there for everyone and especially for her, at Val for resenting this baby in her mother's life because she hadn't been able to have her own.

She owed them more than that. But how much more did she have to give? No more than she had already given them, that was the tragedy of it, and it wasn't enough, she knew. And now there was one more pair of eyes to look into hers one day and tell her that she didn't have enough to give to him, or her . . . and there was nothing at all left of herself. It exhausted her to think of it, and she was relieved when she saw Carmel at last. All she wanted to do was check into another motel and go back to sleep again . . . to get away . . . to dream . . . to escape . . .

'When's Mommy coming back?' Matthew stared glumly at his plate, and then at the rest of them. No one had said a word since they had sat down to dinner that night. It didn't feel like Sunday night without her. It was Mrs Hahn's day off, and usually Mel made them all something they liked to eat. She talked and laughed and listened to them, kept an eye on everyone, and spoke about what she had lined up in the week ahead, knowing full well that everything would change before the week was halfway out. But she would tease and joke, and manage to include everyone, or try to. Matthew looked up at Peter then, his eyes filled with reproach. 'Why did you make her go away?'

'She'll be back.' Jessica was the first to speak, as tears filled her eyes. 'She just went away for a little rest.'

'Why can't she rest here?' He looked accusingly at her. She was the only one who would speak to him. The rest of them seemed to have been struck dumb, but Mark addressed him now.

'Because we all wear her out, Matt. We expect too goddamn much of her.' Mark looked pointedly at Pam, and then let his glance take in everyone, and after dinner Peter heard him shouting at Val. 'You blamed her for goddamn everything . . . that you had to leave New York . . . your friends . . . your school . . . you even blamed her for what happened to us. It wasn't her fault, Val.' But the pretty little blonde sat down and cried so hard that he didn't have the heart to go on. Peter walked slowly up the stairs to Val's room, and found them all sitting there except for Pam who was lying on her bed, staring at the ceiling with the radio on. She had wanted her to go. She admitted it to herself, even if she wouldn't have told her psychiatrist. She wanted her own mother back. But she understood now that that was never going to be. It was either Mel or this incredible emptiness, the same way it had been when her mom was first gone, with only Mrs Hahn there for them, and suddenly Pam knew that wasn't what she wanted, for them, or for herself. She got up and walked into the twins' room and found the others there, even Matt, sitting sadly on the floor.

'Boy, this room is small.' She looked around. Her room was twice that size. Val and Jess didn't say anything, but they turned as they saw Peter in the doorway.

'Yes, it is.' But it only reminded him of what Mel had said, that the twins had never shared a room in their life. And here, they were squashed in like orphans, while Pam had a room twice the size. Had everything she said been true? Most of it, he told himself. Not all of it. But too much for him to be able to discard all that she had said.

'A double room?' The man at the motel in Carmel asked.

'No.' She smiled tiredly. 'A single will be fine.' He looked at her sorrowfully. They always said that, and then a guy and two kids would make a mad dash into the room, thinking he wouldn't know that they were there. And they probably had a large slobbering dog. But this time he was wrong. She took her small overnight bag out of the car, walked inside and closed the door, and lay down on the bed without looking around. It was almost identical to the room she'd had the night before. There was a sameness to everything new as she lay down in another orange vinyl room with a rust-coloured shag rug, and went to sleep from sheer exhaustion.

'Dr Hallam?'

'Hmmm?' A nurse had spoken to him, and he sat in a cubicle with a stack of charts, grateful that they had only had two bypasses to do that morning.

'Is something wrong?' She was terrified of him. He was a great man and if she made a mistake, her neck would be on the line, but he only looked at her and shook his head with a tired smile.

'Everything is fine. What about Iris Lee? Is there any reaction to the drugs yet?'

'Not yet.' She had had the transplant two weeks before, and everything seemed to be going well, but Peter didn't have a lot of hope for her. They hadn't got a heart in time, and had had to put a child's heart piggyback with her own. Sometimes the technique had worked well for him, but Iris had been so frail, in her case it had been a desperate move, and he had been expecting the worst for days. This time, Mel wouldn't be there for him. It was like in the days after Anne's death. He was alone now. And even lonelier than he had been when Anne died.

'Jess?'

'Yeah?'

Val lay on her bed after school, while Jessie sat at the desk in their room. 'Do you ever wish we'd go back to New York?'

'Sure.' She turned to look at her twin. 'Lots of times. There's nothing wrong with that. We lived there for a long time.'

'Do you suppose that's where Mom went?' She had been thinking about it all day.

'I don't know. I don't know where she'd go. She might even be in LA.'

'And not call us?' Val looked horrified and Jessie smiled.

'Would you call us if you felt like that?'

Val shook her head. 'I guess not.'

'Neither would I.' She stared out the window then with a small sigh. 'I blamed everything on her, Val. Everything. It was so unfair, but all the decisions were hers. She always used to ask us what we thought about things, and this time she just went ahead, and pulled us out of school, moved out here . . .' She thought about it for a long time. 'I guess I was annoyed at her for taking the decisions out of our hands.'

'She must have thought she was doing the right thing.' Val looked sad and Jess nodded her head and looked at her.

'The bitch of it is that she did. I like Peter, don't you?'

Val nodded her head again. 'All I could think of when I heard we were moving out here was Mark.'

Jess smiled. 'I know that. It sure didn't help me much while we were leaving New York. Mom had Peter, you had Mark. And I had nothing.' She grinned. It didn't seem so awful now. She liked their school, and she had met a nice boy a month or so before. For the first time in her life, she had met someone she really cared about. He was twenty-one, and she had a feeling that her mom was going to have a fit, especially after what had happened with Val and Mark. But she knew that this was going to be someone special to her, and she sat staring into space with a distant smile.

'What are you grinning about?' Val had been watching her. 'And you sit there with a happy smile. What's up?'

'Nothing much.'

But instantly Val knew. Jess might have got better grades, but Val knew men. She zeroed in on her sister with narrowed eyes. 'Are you in love?'

Jess looked at her with a smile. She hadn't wanted to tell her yet. 'Not yet. But I met someone nice.'

'You?' Val looked stunned, and Jessie nodded, unwilling to say more. But Val didn't look impressed. 'Just watch out.' They both knew what she meant, and Val had been right. She'd learned one of the toughest lessons of life, and she wouldn't forget.

Mrs Hahn served them dinner silently that night, and Peter didn't get home till nine o'clock. Matthew was already in bed, tucked in by Jess, Pam, and Val and Peter went upstairs to check on them. 'Everyone all right?' They were a quiet group, but everyone nodded as he went

353

from room to room. He had had a rough day but there was no one to tell, he stopped in the twins' room and stared at Jess. 'Any word from your mom?' She only shook her head and he went back downstairs, just as Mel drove up San Francisco's California Street on Nob Hill, and checked into the Stanford Court Hotel. It was a refreshing change from the motels she'd been staying at, and the room was all done in grey velvets and silks and moiré, and she collapsed on the bed with a tired groan. She felt as though she had been driving for days and days and days, and she reminded herself to slow down a bit. She hadn't made her mind up yet, and she didn't want to lose the baby before she did. She had a responsibility to it, if it was going to live. She lay awake thinking about it that night, about how angry Val had been, Jess's fury over just how many changes she expected them to make . . . Pam's hostility and ploys for attention for herself, even poor little Matt's hurt, and Peter's expectation that she would have the baby in spite of it all, as an antidote to his constant bouts with death in the operating room. It all seemed terribly unfair. She had to have it, or not have it, for all of them. Once again, the issue was them and not herself.

She walked through Chinatown the next day, and then drove to Golden Gate Park, and wandered through the flowers. It was almost May . . . May . . . she had met Peter almost a year before, and now here she was, and when she got back to the hotel, she took her little phone book out of her bag, dialled 8 for long distance, and called Raquel. It was eight o'clock in New York and they hadn't heard from her in months, Mel didn't even know if she had a job. Or she could have been out, but she picked the phone up on the first ring.

'Hello?' She sounded as suspicious as she always did and on her end Mel grinned.

'Hi, Raquel, it's me.' It was like calling home from far away in the old days, and she had to remind herself not to ask how the twins were. 'How are you?'

'Mrs Mel?'

'Of course.'

'Is something wrong?'

'No, I just thought I'd call and see how you were.'

'I'm fine.' She sounded pleased. 'How are the girls?'

'They're wonderful.' She wouldn't tell her about Val. She was all right now. 'They like their school, everything seems to be working out.' But as she said it, her voice trembled and tears filled her eyes.

'Something's wrong!' It was an accusation this time, and Mel felt tears rise in her throat.

'Absolutely not. I was in San Francisco for a few days and I got lonely for you.'

'What you doing there? You still working too hard?'

'No, it's not as bad. I only have to do the six o'clock.' She didn't tell her what an agony the job had been. 'And I'm just here to take it easy for a few days.'

'Why? You sick?' She had always been to the point and Mel smiled. What was the point of fooling her?

'To tell you the truth, you old witch, I ran away.'

'From who?' She sounded shocked.

'Everyone. Peter, the kids, my job, myself.'

'What's happening to you?' It was obvious that she disapproved.

'I don't know. I guess I just needed some time to think.'

'About what?' She sounded angry at Mel now. 'You always think too much. You don't need to think.' And then, 'Is your husband there?'

'No, I'm here alone.' She could just see Raquel's face, and she wondered why she had called, but she had wanted to hear a familiar voice and she didn't want to call home.

'You go home right now!'

'I will in a few days.'

'I mean now. What's wrong with you? You going crazy out there?'

'A little bit.' She didn't want to tell her about the baby yet. She still needed time to make a decision about that. And there was no point telling anyone if she was going to get rid of it. In LA, she could always say that she lost it

355

because she worked too hard, and no one knew at work yet. 'I just wanted to know if you were all right.'

'I'm fine. Now you go home.'

'I will. Don't worry about me, Raquel. I send you a big kiss.'

'Don't kiss me, go home and kiss him. Tell him you're sorry you ran away.'

'I will. And write to me sometime.'

'Okay, okay. And give my love to the twins.'

'I will.' They hung up then and Mel lay on the bed for a long time. Raquel didn't understand any better than they did. In her mind, Mel belonged at home, no matter what they said or did. It was her place. And the truth was that she thought so too.

She ordered room service that night, had a hot bath, and watched a couple of hours of TV. She didn't feel like going out. There was nowhere she wanted to go, and at eleven o'clock, before the news came on, she dialled, got a long-distance line, and held the phone in her hand for a long time. Maybe Raquel was right . . . but she didn't want to call unless she wanted to . . . She dialled the number, not sure yet if she'd hang up or speak to him, but when she heard his voice, her heart leapt as it had almost a year before.

'Hello?' She could tell that he hadn't been asleep yet. And she hesitated for one beat.

'Hi.' It was a cautious sound.

'Mel?'

'No. Chicken Delight. Yeah, it's me.'

'For God's sake, are you all right? I've been worried sick.'

'I'm okay.'

He didn't dare to ask, but he had to know. 'The baby? Did you . . . did you get rid of it?'

She sounded hurt. 'I told you I wouldn't do that until I told you what I'd decided to do.'

'And did you decide?'

'Not yet. I haven't really given it a lot of thought.'

356

'Then what the hell have you been thinking about?'

'Us.'

There was a long pause. 'Oh.' And then, 'So have I. I've been a real sonofabitch, Mel. The kids think so too.'

'No, they don't.' She smiled. He had been breast-beating while she was gone, and that really wasn't the point. 'That's silly, Peter. We both had a lot of adjustments to make.'

'Yeah, and I let you make them all.'

'That's not entirely true.' But it was in part, and he knew it now. She didn't totally want to take the truth from him. 'One of us had to move, ourselves, our kids, had to give up our old lives. And it was impossible for you. It was my choice.'

'And I let it go at that. I let everything fall on you. I even expected you to step into Anne's shoes. It makes me sick when I think about it now.'

She sighed. He wasn't entirely wrong, but there was more to it than that, and she knew that now. 'And in a way, I think I expected to continue my old independent life, to make all my decisions for myself without consulting you, bring up my kids the way I want, and coincidentally yours too. I expected you and your children to throw out all your old ways at once because I told you to. And that wasn't right.'

'It wasn't wrong.' He sounded desperately contrite and she was touched.

'Maybe we were both half right and half wrong.' She smiled.

He wasn't smiling yet. She wasn't home. And he still didn't know where she was. 'Where does that leave us now?'

'A little wiser than we were.'

He wasn't sure what she meant. 'And you, Mel? Are you going back to New York?' He heard her gasp.

'Are you crazy?' And then, 'Are you throwing me out?'

This time he laughed. 'I don't know if you remember this, but last time I looked you ran away. In fact, I don't even know where you are.'

357

She smiled at that. She had forgotten to tell him when she first called. 'I'm in San Francisco.'

'How did you get there?' He seemed surprised.

'I drove.'

'That's too far, Mel.' He was thinking of the pregnancy, but he didn't want to tell her that.

'I stopped in Santa Barbara and Carmel on the way up.'

'Do you feel all right?'

'I'm fine.' And then she smiled as she lay on her bed at the Stanford Court. 'I miss you a lot.'

'Well, that's nice to hear.' And then he finally dared to ask. 'When are you coming home?'

'Why?' She sounded suspicious again and he groaned.

'Because I want you to clean the place and mow the lawn, you idiot. Why do you think? Because I miss you too.' And then he had an idea. 'Why don't you stay there for a few more days, and I'll meet you there.'

Melanie's face suddenly burst into a smile. 'That's a nice idea, love.' It was the first time she had called him that in a long while and he beamed.

'I love you so much, Mel. And I've been such a fool.'

'No, you haven't. We've both been. So much happened in so little time and our work puts so much pressure on us both.' He couldn't disagree with that.

'What do you want to do about the house? Do you still want to move? I will if you want us to.' He had thought about it a lot in the past few days, and he didn't want to give up the house he loved, but if it meant that much to her, and there really wasn't enough room for the twins, unless maybe they exchanged rooms with Pam, and he knew she'd have a fit. 'What do you think?'

'I think we should stay where we are for a while, and let everyone settle down before we make any more changes at all, and that goes for Mrs Hahn too.' He was relieved at what she said and he thought she was right. They all needed time to settle down now. So everything was resolved, except her miseries at her job, and what to do about their unborn child. 'Do you really want to come up here?'

358

'Yes, I do. I feel like we haven't been alone for years. We even took the kids to Mexico on our honeymoon.'

She laughed at that. 'Whose idea was that?'

'All right . . . mea culpa . . . but anyway, a romantic weekend sounds fabulous to me right now.'

'I'll do my best. Keep your fingers crossed.'

She did and he called her back the next day. He had got two surgeons on the team to split the weekend and cover for him. It had taken a little negotiation, but he had been so intense about it that they had both agreed.

'I'll be there in two days.'

'Good.' And she needed that much time to herself to think about whether she wanted an abortion or not. She really wasn't sure. 'How are the kids, by the way?'

'Fine. And really beginning to appreciate you.' And so was he. He could hardly wait to see her on Friday night. It was like the days when she was living in New York, only worse, because he knew what he was missing now. And he told her so. 'I miss you too, Mel, more than you know.' It had been a ghastly week for him. And Iris Lee had died that day, but he had expected it. He didn't tell Mel. They had their own problems now, without adding another thing. He was more worried about her than his patients now. 'Are you feeling all right?'

'I'm fine.'

He didn't ask her if she'd made up her mind yet. The next day she took a long walk in Muir Woods, and tried to think about what she wanted to do. Again and again she came back to what she had told Val . . . 'I don't know if I could have done what you did . . .' It was not a condemnation, whatever Val might have thought at the time. There was something about aborting a child at her age, married to a man she loved, with plenty of money between them both. There was no reason for it, no way she could explain it to herself, and perhaps there would be no way she could live with it. 'But do you want the child?' she asked herself, and that was where she got hung up. She wasn't sure. But what an ugly luxury to dispose of a life because she wasn't in the mood, it didn't fit in with her job, it annoyed her other kids . . . and there they were again . . . the all-powerful others in her life, husband, children . . . what she owed *them*. What did she owe *herself*? And suddenly she heard her own voice in the woods. 'I want this child.' She was so startled that she looked around, as though to see who had spoken these words, but she knew she had. She felt a thousand-pound weight lift off her heart and she smiled. She looked at her watch. It was time for lunch. She had to take care of the baby if she were having it . . . *I want this child* . . . the words had been so strong and sure, and so was she as she made her way back to her car, walking through the woods.

CHAPTER 31

As she stood at the gate waiting for him, Mel felt dampness in her palms, and the same nervousness she had felt a year before. It was like starting all over again, except that it would be better this time. He was the third one off the plane and she flew into his arms. It had been an endless week.

'Oh, Mel . . .' Tears filled his eyes and he was beyond words as he clung to her. He didn't even care what she did about the baby now. He wanted her and only her . . . and no more so than she wanted him.

'God, I missed you so much.' But as she pulled away from him, smiling and with tears in her eyes, he saw that she looked better than she had in months. She looked rested and relaxed and the frown between her brows was gone.

'You look wonderful, Mel.'

'So do you.' And then she looked down at the zipper in her slacks that had barely closed and was straining now. 'I've gained a little weight here and there.' He wasn't sure what to say and she smiled at him. 'I've decided that . . .' She felt strange saying the words. Who was she to decide about a life. It was what she had said to him a long time ago. God decided that, he didn't, and neither did she. 'The baby's going to be fine.'

'Is it?' He wanted to be sure he understood what she meant.

'Yes.' She beamed.

'Are you sure?'

'I am.'

'For me?' He didn't want her to do that. She had to want it too, and it was a lot to ask, given the fact that they had five others at home, and the ultra-demanding job she had.

'For myself, for you, for us . . . for all of us . . .' She blushed and he took her hand. 'But mostly for me.' She told him what had happened when she was walking in the woods and tears filled his eyes as he pulled her close to him again.

'Oh, Mel.'

'I love you.' It was all she could say, and arm in arm they walked outside, and shared a weekend like no other they had ever shared.

They started the drive home slowly Sunday afternoon, and took Route 5 so it wouldn't be quite as long. By ten o'clock they were home, and as she looked at the house, Mel felt as though she had been gone for years. She stood outside for a moment or two and just smiled, but Peter took her hand and walked her inside. 'Come on, kiddo, let's get you to bed. That's a long drive for you.' He was treating her like Venetian glass and she smiled at him.

'I think I'll live.' But as soon as she stepped inside the house, there was an explosion of sound. The' kids had heard them drive up, and Pam had looked outside and given a horrendous squeal.

'They're home!' She was first down the stairs, and threw her arms around Mel. 'Welcome back!' It wasn't welcome home, but it was close. The twins hugged her, and Mark, and Matthew woke up from all the noise and wanted to sleep in her bed that night. When they had all finally returned to their rooms again after almost an hour of clatter and noise and talk, Mel lay on their bed and looked at Peter with a happy smile.

'They're all good kids, aren't they?'

'They have a good mother.' He sat down on the edge of the bed and took her hand in his. 'I promise, Mel. I'll do everything I can to make things easier for you.' But there was only so much he could do, and that night he got a call at two a.m. He was back on call, and one of his bypasses needed him at once. The next time Mel saw him was when he came home at noon to change his clothes. She had the house back in control, had told Mrs Hahn what she wanted served for dinner that night, and Peter noticed with a grin that Mrs Hahn did not look pleased, but she

362

made no complaint to him. Peter changed his clothes and hurried off to work, just as Mel left. She smiled and waved as they pulled out of the driveway in their separate cars. Pam was getting herself to the psychiatrist alone that day, as she had done the week before when Mel was absent. Mark had said he'd be home after dinner but not too late, since he had exams the next day, the twins were playing tennis with friends, but would be in by five o'clock. Mrs Hahn was picking Matthew up at school, as she had a year before, and Mel was off to work for the first time in a week, and when she got in, even Paul Stevens's viciousness couldn't dampen her spirits today. Everything felt too good.

But at six forty-five, after she had done the news, the producer sought her out and found her in her office, jotting down some notes before she went home. He walked in and closed the door, and Mel looked up.

'Hi, Tom. Is something wrong?'

He hesitated and Mel felt a chill. Were they firing her? Could they? Had Stevens finally won? 'Mel, I have to talk to you.' Oh dear.

'Sure. Sit down.' She waved him to a chair. The office didn't feel like home yet but it was all she had there.

'I don't know how to tell you this, Mel . . .' Her heart stopped. My God, she was being canned. She had been the biggest newsroom star at the network in New York, she had won four prizes for the documentary interviews she'd done and that little horror had got her canned.

'Yes?' She might as well make it easy for him, she just hoped she didn't cry, and all she wanted was to go home to Peter now. To hell with their job and their lousy show. She'd go home and have the baby and take care of their kids.

'I don't want to frighten you.' That didn't make sense. 'But we've had several threats . . .' She looked blank. 'They started coming in during the week you were gone. And they began again today.'

'What kind of threats?' She didn't understand. Was that

363

little sonofabitch threatening to quit? Let him then. The ratings would soar. But she didn't want to tell Tom that yet.

'Threats on your life, Mel.' She stared at him.

'On me?' It had happened once in New York, years ago, some kook didn't like a piece she'd done and called the network for months, threatening to strangle her, but eventually he'd got bored or given up. Mel looked amused. 'At least someone's watching out there.'

'I'm serious, Mel. We've had problems like this before. This is California, not New York. We've had several assassination attempts on presidents out here.'

She couldn't help but smile. 'I'm flattered, Tom, but I'm hardly in those leagues.'

'You're important to us.'

She was touched. 'Thank you, Tom.'

'And we've hired a bodyguard for you.'

'You've what? Oh that's ridiculous . . . you don't really think . . .'

'You have children, Mel. Do you want to take that chance?' His question stopped her dead.

'No, I don't, but . . .'

'We didn't want to frighten your husband while you were gone, but we think it's serious.'

'Why?' She still looked amused. It happened in their business all the time.

'Because we got a call last week, and the man said there was a bomb in your desk. There was, Mel. It would have gone off in exactly one hour, when you opened your desk, and blown us all to kingdom come, if you'd been here.' Suddenly she felt sick.

'They think they might know who it is. But in the meantime, while they figure it out, we want you safe. We were very glad that you were gone last week.'

'So am I.' She felt an unconscious twitch in her left eye as she spoke, and she looked up to see a tall stern-looking man walk into the room. Tom introduced him at once. He was her bodyguard, and two others had been hired as well.

They wanted her escorted whenever she came and went, and they left it up to her, but they thought she should have them at home as well. It was no secret who she was married to, and anyone could look them up. The bodyguard's name was Timothy Frank and as he left the building at her side, she felt as though she had a wall with her. He was the biggest, broadest, toughest man she'd ever seen. And she thanked him when he got her home. She had been asked to leave her car at the station that night, and go home with Tim in the limousine. As she rolled up, she saw that Peter was home.

'Hi.' He looked up from some papers he was going through and smiled. It was good to have her home again, but the frown was back, and she looked extremely strained.

'Trouble at work?'

'You might say that.' She looked dazed. Tim had left again with the limousine.

'What's wrong?' She told him then about the bomb and he stared at her. 'My God, Mel. You can't live like that, and neither can we.'

'What do you expect me to do?'

He hated to say the words, but she was pregnant now, and it was just too much strain for her. Even if they caught the guy in a week or two, just knowing that it could happen again would put too much pressure on her, and on him. He didn't want her going through that. And if they didn't catch the guy . . . He shuddered at the thought, and stood up to close his study door. He stood there, looking down at her. 'I think you should quit.'

'I can't.' Her face turned to rock. 'It happened once in New York and I didn't quit then. I won't do it for a reason like that.'

'What reason do you need?' He was shouting at her. Life never seemed to get off their backs, patients dying, unruly kids, bomb threats, unexpected pregnancies. It was almost more than he could stand to think about as he looked at her. 'What if someone bombs this house and one of the children is killed?'

She winced at his words and turned a faint shade of green. 'We'll have bodyguards round the clock.'

'For five kids?'

'God damn it, I don't know . . .' She leapt to her feet. 'I'll stay in a hotel if you want me to. But I won't quit my job, because of some lunatic. For all I know it's Paul Stevens just trying to scare me off.'

'Is that what the police think?'

She had to be honest with him. 'No, they don't. But they also think they know who the guy is.'

'Then take a leave until they pick him up.'

'I can't, Peter. I can't, dammit. I have a job to do.'

He walked over and grabbed her arm. 'You'll get killed.'

'I've taken that chance before.' Her eyes blazed. He couldn't make her quit her job, not after all these years. It was part of who she was, and he had promised to respect that, for better or worse.

'You've never taken that chance with my child's life. Think of that.'

'I can't think of anything any more.'

'Except yourself.'

'Damn you.' She walked out of the room and slammed the door, and went upstairs, and he didn't speak to her again that night. Things were off to a great start again, and the children sensed the tension in the house. She called the producer of the show that night, and accepted his offer of bodyguards, for herself, her husband, and the kids. It would take an army to keep them safe, but the station was willing to pay for it. And she told Peter about it when they went to bed. 'They start tomorrow morning, at six.'

'That's ridiculous. What am I supposed to do? Do rounds with a bodyguard?'

'I don't think the problem is you. Maybe he could just go with you when you go outdoors. The real problem is me.'

'I'm aware of that.' He felt sick at the thought. And the next morning, at breakfast, she explained it to the kids.

Their eyes were wide as she explained, and she assured them that they'd all be safe and in a few days the man would be caught. It was just something they had to live with for a little while. Matt thought it was fabulous, Mark was embarrassed to have to take a bodyguard to college with him, and the girls looked terrified. But as they each left for school with the policeman assigned to the task, Mrs Hahn sought Mel out upstairs.

'Mrs Hallum?' She always pronounced it that way, and Mel turned to speak to her.

'Yes, Mrs Hahn?' Peter called her Hilda now and then, but Mel never did. And there was no 'Mrs Mel' as there had been in New York with Raquel.

'I wanted to tell you that due to the circumstances, I quit.'

Mel stared at her. 'You do?' Peter would be shocked, and possibly even angry at her. She was wreaking havoc on their house and it was not her fault.

'I really don't think that you're in any danger here, and as I explained to the children this morning, there will be full protection here at all times.'

'I've never worked in a house where there had to be police before.'

'I'm sure you haven't, Mrs Hahn. But if you'll be patient for a little while . . .' She owed it to Peter at least to try.

'No.' She shook her head decidedly. 'I won't. I'm leaving now.'

'With no notice at all?'

She shook her head, looking at Mel accusingly. 'Nothing like this ever happened before when the doctor's wife was here.' The doctor's wife being Anne of course, the *real* Mrs Hallam as opposed to Mel. And now Mel couldn't help pushing her a little, with a barely concealed grin. She was hardly heartbroken to see the woman go. She had hated her from the first.

'Things must have been pretty dull here then.' She looked nonchalant and Hilda Hahn was clearly horrified. She didn't even offer to shake Mel's hand.

'Goodbye. I left the doctor a letter in my room.'

'I'll see that he gets it then. You don't want to stay long enough to say goodbye to the children yourself?' That seemed mean to Mel, but she knew that they'd survive.

'I don't want to be in this house for another hour.'

'Fine.' Mel looked unperturbed and watched her go, and she almost shouted hallelujah as the front door closed. But that night, Peter was a little less than thrilled.

'Who's going to run this place Mel? You don't have time.' She searched his eyes for accusation, but it was more concern.

'We'll find someone else.' She called Raquel, but she still refused to come out, and she urged Mel to be careful with the girls. 'In the meantime, I can do it myself with the kids.'

'That's great. Someone is out there planting bombs with your name on them and you have to worry about doing laundry and making beds.'

'You can help too.' She smiled.

'I have other things to do.' And a bodyguard to endure. The entire situation wore on his nerves as the days went on and the bomber wasn't caught. There had been four more threats, and a defective bomb was found in Mel's desk. At long last even Paul Stevens felt sorry for her. He knew she was pregnant now, and there were dark circles under her eyes from lying awake at night, wondering if the man would be caught. He would in time, they always were, but how long would that be?

'I'm sorry this is happening to you, Mel.' He finally called a truce one day and held out a hand.

'So am I.' She smiled tiredly after they went off the air. The bodyguard had stood close by during the entire time. She was constantly aware of him, and in the morning when the kids left for school, the house seemed to be full of cops. It was driving Peter nuts and they were fighting all the time. He had almost got used to his own man, but the others seemed 'de trop' for him. 'It goes with the turf, I guess,' she told Paul.

He looked sadly at her. 'You know, I used to envy you.'

'I know.' She smiled. And she knew why. 'But at least you don't have to contend with this.'

'I don't know how the hell you stand the strain.'

'Mostly, I worry about the kids . . . my own . . . his . . . if something happens to one of them, I'll never forgive myself.' It had been going on for a month by now, and she was seriously beginning to think she ought to give in and leave. She hadn't said anything to Peter yet, because she didn't want to get him started, or let him think that it was sure. But she had promised herself that if the bomber wasn't caught in the next two weeks, she would quit.

Paul Stevens looked horrified as he contemplated it all. 'If there's anything that I can do . . .' She shook her head and said goodnight, and went home to her family, but it wasn't the casual group it used to be. There were unmarked police cars outside, and inside the house everyone was aware of the danger that lurked near them every day.

'Do you think they'll catch him, Mom?' Matthew asked her that night.

'I hope so, Matt.' She held him on her lap, praying that the danger would not touch him . . . or any of them . . . she looked from him to Pam to the twins. Mark was out. And that night Peter talked to her about it again.

'Why don't you resign?'

She didn't want to tell him that she was thinking the same thing. 'I'm not a quitter, that's why.' But she had thought of something else. 'What if we go away?'

'Where?'

It was June by then, and she thought of it with a sigh, as she looked at Peter hopefully. 'What about taking everyone to Martha's Vineyard for a while?' She hadn't rented the house this year, but maybe she could still get it for a few weeks, or rent another one. But he shook his head.

'That's too far away for you.' She was four months pregnant by then, and just beginning to show. 'And I'll never see you if you go there. Why not something nearby?'

'That defeats the whole purpose of the trip.' She was

exhausted by the whole idea, and she was staggered by what the station was spending on bodyguards, but nobody begrudged them to her. It certainly wasn't their fault they got on her nerves. That morning as she poured a glass of milk for Matt, one of the men had asked her to 'Step back from the window, please.' It certainly reminded one day and night of what was going on, and the threat to their lives. 'What about Aspen again?' She looked hopelessly at Peter then.

'I don't think the altitude is good for you.'

'Neither is the tension here.'

'I don't know. I'll think about it today.' And so did she. Suddenly all she wanted to do was run away again. She had lived with the nightmare for a month, and she couldn't stand it any more. She went to work that afternoon, and sat at her desk, her bodyguard just outside the room and suddenly she looked up and saw the producer staring down at her with a smile.

'Mel, we've got good news for you.'

'You're sending me to Europe for a year?' She smiled, and for the first time, she thought she felt the baby move. They hadn't mentioned her pregnancy on the show because they were afraid that the madman who was hunting her would do something even worse to her if he found out. So the secret she was carrying remained invisible and unknown beneath the desk.

'Better news than that.' The smile grew wider and she saw Paul Stevens in the hall looking at her benevolently.

'You're giving Paul my job.' Paul grinned and nodded yes as Mel laughed. They were almost friends now, as a result of the agonies of the past month.

'They caught the lunatic who's been threatening you.'

'They did?' Her eyes grew wide and filled with tears. 'It's all over then?' He nodded and she began to shake.

'Oh my God.' She put her head down on her desk and began to sob.

CHAPTER 32

'Well, my love,' Peter looked happily across at her, as they sat beside their pool; all the kids were out, and they had peace again. 'What'll we do for fun this week?' He smiled at her. 'No one can accuse us of having a dull life at least.'

'God forbid.' She lay back and closed her eyes. She knew what she wanted to do. She wanted to go to Martha's Vineyard and lie in the hot sand, but all the kids had other plans by then, Peter was tied up with his work, and she had agreed to forfeit her holiday that year, and take maternity leave instead. The baby was due around Thanksgiving, and she was leaving on October first.

'I have an idea, Mel.'

'If it involves anything more than falling into the pool, don't tell me now.' Her eyes were closed as he smiled at her, and walked slowly over to where she sat.

'Why don't we look at some houses today?' She opened one eye.

'You're kidding of course.'

'I'm serious.'

She looked absolutely amazed. 'You are?'

'Well, much as I hate to admit it, there's nowhere to put the new baby, except maybe in the garage, and I think a whole lot of construction would drive us nuts. The twins need their own rooms . . .' Mel knew how hard it was for him to admit mistakes, and she held out her arms. He knew how badly she had wanted to move out of Anne's house, and she had long since given up.

'Wouldn't you rather stay here? I really wouldn't mind. We can figure something out for a couple of years, and Mark will be gone soon.' He had decided to go east to college for his junior and senior two years, which meant he had only one more year at home, and Jess already knew she wanted to go to Yale if she could get in . . . 'The kids are practically grown-up.'

'That's nice for them. I wish I could say the same for me.'

'You're the nicest man I know.' She kissed him gently on the lips and he let his fingers drift up her leg. 'Hmm . . . Do you suppose anyone can see us here?'

'Only a neighbour or two, and what's a little passion between friends?'

He took her inside then, and their lovemaking renewed the bond between them. Afterwards he brought her lunch on a tray, and she lay in bed looking comfortable and happy and relaxed. 'Why are you so good to me?'

'I don't know. I must love you a lot.'

'Me too.' She smiled happily. 'Did you really mean that about a new house?' The idea delighted her, but she didn't want to push. She knew how much the old one meant to him and how much effort he had put into it, standing behind Anne. But in Mel's mind, it would always be Anne's house, not even his, but Anne's. Even now.

'Yes, I did.' She beamed and finished lunch, and then they got up and went for a drive, and here and there they saw a house they liked, but none of them was for sale.

'You know, it could take us years to find the right place.'

'We have the time.'

She nodded, feeling relaxed, and enjoying the Sunday afternoon. The next weekend was the Fourth of July. And it was then that they saw the perfect house for them. 'My God' – Mel looked at Peter as they walked around for a second time – 'it's huge.'

'This may come as a shock to you, Mrs Hallam, but we have six kids.'

'Five and a half.' She smiled, but there were rooms for each of them, with studies for both Peter and Mel to use whenever they worked at home, there was a handsome garden, an enormous pool, and a little pool house for the kids to use with their friends. It had absolutely everything

372

they wanted and it was still in Bel-Air, which Peter preferred.

'Well, Mrs Hallam?'

'I don't know, Doctor. What do you think? Can we afford it?'

'Probably not. But once we sell my house we can.' It was the first time he had admitted it was his, not theirs, and Mel grinned. She loved the new house. 'Why don't we make a down payment on it?' But it was a project in which they would both have to invest, otherwise they couldn't manage it, and that suited Mel just fine. She wanted something that was equally theirs, hers as well as his, and she still had her money from the house in New York to invest. They put their house on the market the following week, and it didn't sell until Labor Day, but the other one was still available.

'Let's see.' Peter glanced at the calendar as they closed on the new house. 'The baby's due November twenty-eight . . . today is September third . . . you go on leave from the network in four weeks. That gives you exactly two months to get this place in shape for us, and with any luck at all we'll be in by Thanksgiving.' He looked totally matter-of-fact and Mel laughed at him.

'Are you kidding? It'll take months.' Even though the place was in perfect shape, they wanted to paint and change the wallpapers, alter the garden here and there, they had to pick out fabrics and order drapes . . . new carpeting . . . 'Dream on.'

Peter looked surprised. 'Don't you want your baby born in the new house?' In truth, she did, the nesting instinct was strong, but she still had three major interviews to do before she left on her four-month leave.

'It's your baby too, by the way.'

'Our baby.' And with that, his beeper went off, and the estate agent stared at them.

'Don't you two ever stop?'

'Not much.' Mel smiled. They were almost used to it after being married for eight months, during which time he had done nineteen heart transplants, countless by-passes, and she had done twenty-one major interviews and the news five nights a week. And predictably, the show's ratings had gone up. Peter had gone to call his office in another room just then, and he came rushing back and kissed Mel goodbye.

'I've got to go. We have a heart.' It was a donor they had desperately been waiting for, and he had almost given up hope. 'Will you finish here?' She nodded and he vanished, and they heard his car speed away, as the estate agent shook his head again and Mel only smiled.

CHAPTER 33

'. . . and thank you, God, for my Grandma' – he looked around sheepishly and grinned as he lowered his voice – 'and my new bike. Amen.' The entire Thanksgiving table laughed. Matthew had turned seven that week, and his grandmother had given him a brand-new bike. Suddenly he clasped his hands again and squeezed his eyes shut. 'And thank you for Mel too.' He looked apologetically at Val and Jess after that, but it was too late to start again. Everyone was dying to attack their food. Peter had already carved the turkey, and Pam had cooked her favourite recipe for candied yams. The twins had helped with the rest, and everyone was in a festive mood, including Mel, who claimed she had no room for anything. The baby felt huge now. Peter had teased her for the past two months that it was twins again, but the doctor swore that it was not. He could only hear one heart this time, and despite her age, she had opted not to have the amniotic-fluid test, so they had no idea what the baby was. But whatever it was, it was large. It was due in another two days, and most of all, Mel was grateful to have Thanksgiving with them. She had been worried that she would be in the hospital by then. And although they had a new housekeeper, she had wanted the day off, so Mel had cooked the dinner herself.

'Seconds anyone?' Peter looked around with a contented smile. His latest transplant patient was doing well. They had moved into the new house three weeks before and could still smell fresh paint all around them, but they didn't seem to mind. Everything looked beautiful and fresh, and each of them had their own rooms, even the new baby whose room was already filled with toys they all had bought. Matthew had contributed a teddy bear and an old set of cowboy guns, and without saying a word to Mel,

Pam had knitted a little dress for the baby to wear home from the hospital. She had been desperately nervous about doing it right, and the entire family knew about the project except Mel, who cried when she opened the gift on her last day at work, when she came home, feeling the letdown of her last Friday-night news for a while.

It had taken them all almost a year to settle down, and in some ways they never would. She would always be dashing off to cover the news, and Peter would be gone at two a.m. to try to repair another damaged heart. But there was something different between them all now. It was a stronger bond than had been there before. They had survived a lot in a year, the threats on Mel, the disastrous romance between Val and Mark . . . the new baby . . . the threat the new marriage presented to them all . . . even the ghost of Anne. Mel had brought the portrait with them; it hung in Pam's room now and it looked well there, and her furniture from New York was unpacked and out of storage at long last.

'Happy, love?' Peter smiled down at her as they sat by the fire in their room. The children were all downstairs in the huge playroom near the pool, playing games and having fun. And Mel looked up at Peter and took his hand.

'Yes, except I ate too much.'

'It doesn't even show.' They both laughed at the enormous bulge which seemed to shift slightly from side to side as Mel watched the baby kick. It seemed to do that constantly these days, and she was ready to be rid of it. Especially after tonight. With Thanksgiving done, she felt free to have the child, she told Peter as they went to bed that night. 'Don't say that tonight, or he'll hear you and come out.' They both laughed and went to bed, and two hours later, Mel got up and felt a familiar pain in her lower back. She got up and sat down in a chair, but all she wanted to do was walk around. She wandered downstairs and looked out into the garden that would be pretty the following spring, but already looked nice now, and sat down in their living room, feeling it was their home, and not just his or hers, but something they had built together and started fresh, like a whole new life.

She went back to their bedroom then, and tried to lie down again, but the baby was kicking too hard and suddenly she felt a short searing pain in her lower abdomen and she gave a small gasp. She sat up and waited to see what would come next, and suddenly there was another pain, and with a feeling of exultation, she touched Peter's hand.

'Hmm?' He barely stirred, and it was only four o'clock.

'Peter.' She whispered his name after the third pain came. She knew it would be hours, but she didn't want to be alone. She wanted to share the excitement of it all with him. This was the moment they had waited for, Peter most of all.

'What?' He suddenly lifted up his head and looked at her more seriously. 'Maybe it's just a false alarm.' She looked down at her enormous stomach and laughed, but the laughter was brief as another pain came, this time joined with a searing arc that shot across her back. She gasped and grabbed his hand, and he supported her as she breathed. And when the pain was over he looked at the clock. 'How often are you getting them?'

She laughed again and looked at him with love in her eyes. 'I don't know. I forgot to look.'

'Oh my God.' He sat up in bed. Hearts he knew, but babies were something else to him, and he had been secretly nervous about her for nine months. 'How long have you been up then?'

'I don't know. Most of the night.' It was five o'clock by then.

'How long were you in labour with the twins?'

'Hell, I don't know. That was seventeen and a half years ago. A while, I guess.'

'You're a big help.' He sat up, still keeping an eye on her. 'I'll call the doctor. You get dressed.' She had another pain this time, and it seemed longer than the ones before.

377

He was panicking but he didn't want to show it. He did not want to deliver his own child at home. He wanted her at the hospital in case anything went wrong. 'Go on.' He helped her up, and she came back a minute later with a vague look.

'What'll I wear?'

'For chrissake, Mel! Anything . . . jeans . . . a dress . . .' She was smiling to herself as she padded off again, and then the waters broke, and she called out to him from the bathroom where she stood wrapped in towels. The obstetrician told Peter to bring her in right away, and they left a note for the kids on the kitchen table where they'd all see it when they got up. 'Gone to pick baby up at hospital, Love, Mom' she wrote with a smile, as Peter urged her out the door. 'Will you hurry up?'

'Why?' She looked supremely calm and Peter envied her.

'Because I don't want to deliver our child in our new car.' He had finally sold Anne's Mercedes and bought a new one for Mel.

'Why not?'

'Never mind, love, never mind.' But he had never felt closer to her as he drove the familiar route he drove so often late at night and as he walked her into the hospital and wheeled her into the maternity ward, he was unbearably proud.

'I can walk, you know.'

'Why walk if you can ride?' But the banter barely covered up all that he felt for her. A thousand thoughts were rushing through his head and he was praying that everything was all right. The baby looked awfully large to him, and he had been wondering about a Caesarean. He asked the obstetrician about it again just outside the labour room, and his old friend patted his arm.

'She's fine, you know. She's doing just fine.' By then it was almost eight o'clock, and she had been in labour for five or six hours.

'How much longer do you think it'll take?' He spoke sotto voce so Mel wouldn't hear and the doctor smiled.

'A while.'

'You sound like Mel.' Peter glared at him and they went back inside. Mel said she wanted to push and the obstetrician said it was too soon, but when he looked again, he saw that things had progressed by leaps and bounds in the last half hour, and he had her wheeled into the delivery room, where she turned red-faced and pushed ferociously as Peter and the nurses urged her on.

'I can see the baby's head, Mel.' The doctor crowed and she beamed.

'You can?' Her face was dripping wet and her hair looked more than ever like flame against the white drapes, and Peter had never loved her more, as she pushed again, and suddenly they heard a cry. Peter took one long step to see the baby born, and the tears poured down his face as he smiled.

'Oh, Mel . . . it's so beautiful . . .'

'What is it?' But she had to push again.

'We don't know yet.' Everybody laughed and then suddenly the shoulders came out, the body, hips, and legs . . . 'A girl!'

'Oh, Mel.' Peter returned to her head and kissed her full on the mouth and she laughed and cried with him, and they handed the baby to her. He knew how much she had wanted a boy, but she no longer seemed to remember that as she held her daughter in her arms, and then suddenly she made an awful face and grabbed Peter's arm, as someone gently took the baby from her.

'Oh . . . God . . . that hurts . . .'

'It's just the placenta now.' The doctor looked unconcerned, and then Peter saw him frown, and a ripple of panic ran down his limbs. Something was happening to her, and she was in hideous pain again, even more so than before.

'Oh . . . Peter . . . I can't . . .'

'Yes, you can.' The doctor spoke softly to her as Peter held her hand, and he wondered why the hell they didn't put her out and see what was wrong, and suddenly as she pushed with all her might there was another wail and

Peter's eyes grew wide, and Mel stared at him, already knowing what had happened.

'Not again . . .' Peter still didn't understand and the doctor was laughing now, and he began to laugh too. She had had twins again, and no one knew, just as they hadn't with Jess and Val. She looked up at him half rueful, half amused. 'Doubles again.'

'Yes, ma'am.' The doctor handed the baby to Peter this time who held him with a look of awe and then presented him to Mel to hold. 'Madam' – the love spilled from his eyes as they met hers – 'your son.'

WANDERLUST
Danielle Steel

At 21 Annabelle Driscoll was the acknowledged beauty, but it was her sister Audrey – four years older – who had the spine and spirit. She had talent as a photographer; she had the restless urge of a born wanderer.

Inevitably it was Annabelle who was the first to marry, leaving Audrey to wonder if life were passing her by. The men she met in California were dull, worldly. Even in New York, they failed to spark her. Only when she boarded the *Orient Express* did she realise she was beginning a journey that would take her farther than she had ever dreamed possible . . .

FINE THINGS
Danielle Steel

Living on the crest of a highly successful career, he was
moving too fast to realise that he had everything – except
what he wanted most . . .

Sent to San Francisco to open the smartest department
store in California, Bernie Fine becomes aware of the
hollowness of his personal life. Despite his success he
grows increasingly disenchanted with his existence – until
five-year-old Jane O'Reilly gets lost in the store.

Through Jane, Bernie meets her mother Liz, who finally
offers him the possibility of love. But the rare happiness
they find together is disrupted by tragedy and Bernie
must face the terrible price we sometimes have to pay for
loving . . .

FAMILY ALBUM
Danielle Steel

Shipping heir Ward Thayer and screen star Faye Price fell hopelessly in love. Within weeks they were married. But how was Faye to choose between her Hollywood career and motherhood? How could she decide between fame and family? Faye's choice would not only change her life: it would shape the lives of generations to come.

From the uncertain post-war days, through Hollywood in the storm-torn political years and the turmoil of the Vietnam era right up to the present . . . FAMILY ALBUM follows the Thayer dynasty through generations of love and hope, of strife and reconciliation.

'A big lush saga in the Dallas mould . . . compulsive.'
Sunday Telegraph

sphere

To buy any of our books and to find out
more about Sphere and Little, Brown Book Group,
our authors and titles, as well as events and
book clubs, visit our website

www.littlebrown.co.uk

and follow us on Twitter

@LittleBrownUK

To order any Sphere titles p & p free in the UK,
please contact our mail order supplier on:

+ 44 (0)1832 737525

Customers not based in the UK should contact
the same number for appropriate postage
and packing costs.